KNIGHTS
OF
THE CROSS

Tom Harper is twenty-seven and is also the
author of *The Mosaic of Shadows*. He studied
medieval history at Oxford University and
now lives in London.

Visit Tom Harper at www.tom-harper.co.uk

KNIGHTS OF THE CROSS

A Novel of the Crusades

✝ ✝ ✝

TOM HARPER

Thomas Dunne Books / St. Martin's Minotaur

New York

THOMAS DUNNE BOOKS.
An imprint of St. Martin's Press.

KNIGHTS OF THE CROSS. Copyright © 2005 by Tom Harper. All rights reserved.
Printed in the United States of America. No part of this book may be used or repro-
duced in any manner whatsoever without written permission except in the case of
brief quotations embodied in critical articles or reviews. For information, address St.
Martin's Press, 175 Fifth Avenue, New York, N.Y. 10010.

www.thomasdunnebooks.com
www.minotaurbooks.com

Library of Congress Cataloging-in-Publication Data

Harper, Tom, 1977–
    Knights of the cross : a novel of the Crusades / Tom Harper.
        p. cm.
    Sequel to: Mosaic of shadows
    ISBN-13: 978-0-312-33870-1
    ISBN-10: 0-312-33870-8
    1. Crusades—First, 1096–1099—Fiction. 2. Byzantine Empire—History—
Alexius I Comnenus, 1081–1118—Fiction. 3. Turkey—Fiction. I. Title.

PR6120.H644 K58 2006
823'.92—dc22   2006046325

First published in United Kingdom by Century Books
an imprint of The Random House Group Limited

First U.S. Edition: September 2006

10 9 8 7 6 5 4 3 2 1

For my parents
who gave me afterward every day

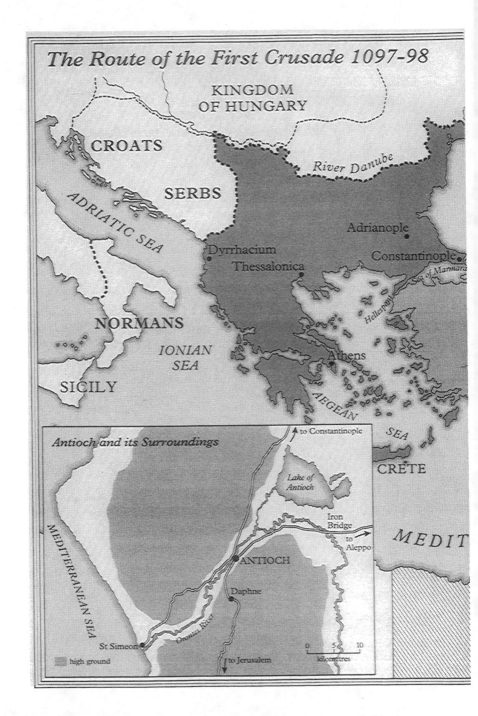

The Route of the First Crusade 1097-98

KINGDOM
OF HUNGARY

CROATS

River Danube

SERBS

ADRIATIC SEA

Dyrrhacium
Thessalonica

Adrianople

Constantinople
of Marmara

Hellespont

NORMANS

IONIAN
SEA

Athens

SICILY

AEGEAN

SEA

CRETE

Antioch and its Surroundings

to Constantinople

Lake of
Antioch

Iron
Bridge

to
Aleppo

MEDITERRANEAN SEA

ANTIOCH

Daphne

Orontes River

St Simeon

to Jerusalem

high ground

0   5   10
kilometres

MEDIT

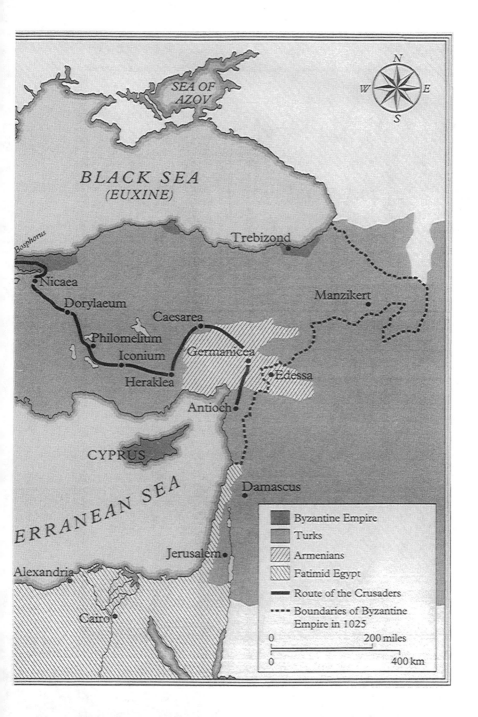

SEA OF
AZOV

BLACK SEA
(EUXINE)

Bosphorus

Trebizond

Nicaea

Dorylaeum

Manzikert

Caesarea

Philomelium

Iconium   Germanicea

Heraklea   Edessa

Antioch

CYPRUS

Damascus

ERRANEAN SEA

Jerusalem

Alexandria

Cairo

	Byzantine Empire
	Turks
	Armenians
	Fatimid Egypt
	Route of the Crusaders
	Boundaries of Byzantine Empire in 1025

0   200 miles

0   400 km

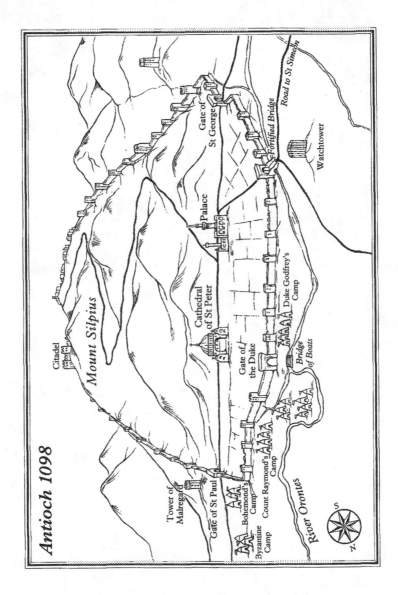

Antioch 1098

Mount Silpius

Citadel

Tower of Malregard

Gate of St Paul

Bohemond's Camp

Byzantine Camp

Count Raymond's Camp

River Orontes

Cathedral of St Peter

Gate of the Duke

Bridge of Boats

Palace

Duke Godfrey's Camp

Gate of St George

Fortified Bridge

Road to St Simeon

Watchtower

For lo I raise up that bitter and hasty nation,
Which march through the breadth of the earth
To possess the dwelling places that are not theirs.
They are terrible and dreadful,
Their judgement and their dignity proceed from
    themselves.
Their horses are swifter than leopards,
And are more fierce than the evening wolves.
Their horsemen spread themselves, yea,
Their horsemen come from afar.
They fly as an eagle that hasteth to devour,
They come all of them for violence;
Their faces are set as the east wind,
And they gather captives as the sand.

– Habakkuk
(adapted C. V. Stanford)

Having sworn allegiance to Byzantium, the army of the First Crusade crossed into Asia Minor in May 1097. At Nicaea and Dorylaeum they won two resounding victories against the Turks, capturing their capital and opening the road south towards Jerusalem. Through July and August, in the face of burning heat and hunger, the crusaders swept aside all resistance as they marched almost a thousand miles across the steppes of Anatolia. Outside the ancient city of Antioch, however, their progress halted: the Turkish garrison was all but impregnable, and as winter drew on the army was devastated by rain, disease, starvation and battle. By February 1098 they had suffered five months of attrition to no discernible gain. Rivalries festered between the different nations of the crusade – Provencales from southern France, Germans from Lorraine, Normans from Sicily and Normandy, and Byzantine Greeks. Fractious princes grew jealous of each others' ambitions, while the miserable mass of foot-soldiers and camp-followers seethed at the failure of their leaders to deliver them. And in the east, the Turks began to assemble an army that would crush the crusade once and for all against the walls of Antioch.

I

Besiegers

7 March – 3 June 1098

α

It was a restless day for the dead. I stood in a grave before Antioch, and watched the Army of God dig the corpses of their enemies from the fresh earth where they had been buried. Men half-naked and smeared with grime worked with passionate intensity to dispossess the dead, plundering the goods they had taken to the afterlife: unstrung bows curled up like snails, short knives, round shields caked with clay – all were dug out and hurled onto the spoil pile. A little further away a company of Normans counted and arranged more gruesome trophies: the severed heads of the corpses we had recalled from death. The day before, an army of Turks had sallied from the city and ambushed our foraging expedition; we had driven them back, but only with a great effort that we could ill afford. Now we opened their graves, not from wanton greed or cruelty – though there was that also – but to build a tower, to watch the gate and keep the city's defenders penned within their walls. We made a quarry of their cemetery, and the foundations of our fortress from their tombs.

The giant who stood with me in the grave shook his head. 'This is no way to wage a war.'

I looked up from the tombstone that I was trying to dislodge and stared at my companion. An unrelenting season of cold and rain had returned his stout features to the sallow colour of his ancestors, while his unkempt hair and beard were almost of a colour with the rusting links

3

of his armour. Like all who had survived the winter horrors, his skin hung loose from his bones, his shoulders seemed too narrow for his mail coat, and the tail of his belt flapped from being drawn so tight. Yet still there was strength in the arms which had once seemed like the columns of a church, and a gleaming edge on the axe which leaned against the wall of the trench.

'You've served twenty years in the Emperor's army, Sigurd,' I reminded him. 'Would you have me believe that you never plundered your enemies, nor took booty from the battlefield?'

'This is different. Worse.' He wormed his fingers into the earth and began tugging on the stone, rocking it back and forth to loose it from the mud that held it. 'Looting the fallen is a warrior's right. Looting the buried . . .'

His arm tensed and the flat stone toppled out, splashing into the puddles on the floor of the pit. We crouched, and lifted it like a bier between us.

'The Turks should have buried their dead within their walls,' I argued, as though that could forgive such savagery. Why they had buried their losses from the previous day's battle here, beyond the city and near our camp, I could not guess: perhaps, even after five months of siege, there were yet some barbarities they thought beyond us.

We slid the stone over the lip of the hole and hauled ourselves out, scrambling for purchase on the clammy earth. Standing, I tried to brush the dirt from my tunic – unlike Sigurd, I could not wear armour for such work – and looked at the labour going on around us.

They styled themselves the Army of God, but even He in His omniscience might not have recognised them. This was not the Divine Saint John's vision of St Michael and all the angels, clothed in white linen and with eyes like flames of fire: these men were the wasted survivors of untold ordeals, little more than a rabble, their eyes filled only with suffering. Their skins were as stained and torn as their clothes; they staggered rather than marched – yet fearsome purpose still consumed their souls as they dug and tore at the bones, stones and plunder of the Ishmaelite cemetery. Only the crosses betold their holy allegiance: crosses of wood and iron strung from their necks; wool and sackcloth crosses sewn into smocks; crosses in blood and brutalised flesh painted or burned or carved into their shoulders. They seemed not the army of the Lord but rather His herd, branded with His mark and loosed to roam the Earth.

As Sigurd and I crossed the graveyard with our stone held between us I tried not to see the impieties around us. A small and lonely corner of my thoughts marvelled that I could still feel shame at this, after the myriad horrors that I had seen in the months since we arrived at Antioch. I turned my gaze away, to the impenetrable city barely two hundred yards distant and the broad green river which flowed before it. At this end of the city the river was almost against the foot of the walls; further north it meandered away, leaving a wedge of open ground between the ramparts and the water. It was there, on marshy land and barely beyond bowshot of our enemies, that our army was camped. From the hillock I could see the jumble of unnumbered tents strung out like washing on a line. Opposite, the many-turreted walls of Antioch stood as serene and inviolate as they had for centuries past, while behind them the three peaks of Mount Silpius towered above the city like the knuckles of a giant fist. For five months we had stared at those walls, waiting for them to crack open with hunger or despair, and for five months we had starved only ourselves.

Crossing a ditch, we climbed towards the low summit of the mound that the Franks had thrown up after the rudimentary fashion of their castles. A Norman sergeant wearing a faded tabard over his armour indicated where we should place our burden, while around us sailors from the port of Saint Simeon laid out planks of timber. At the bottom of the slope, towards the river, a screen of Provençal cavalry sat on their horses and watched for a Turkish sortie.

'I've suffered wounds for the Emperor in a dozen battles.' Sigurd's voice was brittle. 'I've struck down men within an arm's length of ending his life. But if I had known he would have me robbing graves to please a Norman thief I would have cast aside my shield and hammered my blade into a ploughshare long ago.'

He leaned on the long haft of his axe, like an old man on his stick, and stared angrily at the land before us. 'That city is cursed. The city of the cursed, besieged by the army of the damned. Christ help us.'

I murmured my agreement. It was only as my gaze swept back down to the river that I realised what his last words had signified, what he had seen.

'Christ preserve us.' Where the river met the walls, a stone bridge spanned its course – the sally port that our new tower was intended to guard against. Now, I saw, the gates had opened and the drum of hoofbeats echoed from under the arches. Even before our sentries could move, a thin column of Turkish horsemen emerged and galloped forward. Their bows were slung over their shoulders, yet they did not hesitate in charging straight up the slope towards us.

'Bowmen!' shouted the Norman sergeant. 'Bowmen! A bezant for any rider you can unhorse.'

Between what we carried and what we had dug out, there was no shortage of arms among us, but the appearance of the Turks struck panic into our ranks. Some threw themselves into the excavated graves or upon the stones in the shallow foundation trench; others surrendered every defence and fled up the hill behind us. I saw Sigurd snatch one of the round shields from the spoil pile and run forward brandishing his axe. His shame forgotten, the war cry rose from his throat.

He would have little say in this fight, though. The Provençal cavalry had spurred to meet the Turks, desperate to close within spear-length. But rather than engage them the Ishmaelites loosed a rapid flight of arrows and turned back towards their walls. I saw one of the Franks grasping his stomach where a shaft had penetrated it, but otherwise the Turks looked to have done little damage. It was no more than a prick, a gnat's sting such as we had endured almost daily since investing the city. At least, it should have been.

But the swift retreat of the Turks had brought new courage to our cavalry and they charged down towards the river after their fleeing quarry. Behind them, I saw Sigurd lower his axe as he slowed to a halt and started screaming unheeded warnings.

The Provençals would never listen to advice from an English mercenary in Greek employ, certainly not when presented with a broken line of their enemy to ride down. There was little that Sigurd or I or any man could do save watch. As the Turkish horsemen reached the mouth of the bridge, they executed the drill for which they were famed and feared across Asia: at full gallop, they dropped their reins, twisted back in their saddles, nocked arrows to their bowstrings and loosed them at their pursuers. Throughout the manoeuvre they neither wavered in their course nor slowed their pace. In an instant their horses had carried them into the safety of the city.

I shook my head in awe and anger. All winter, men from every nation had sought to mimic the trick, galloping up and down the meadows outside Antioch until their hands were raw and their horses half-lame. None had mastered it. Nor was it merely vain display, for I saw now

7

that several of the shots had hit their mark, while the rest of our cavalry stood halted by the attack.

And, too late, they noticed how close they had come to the city. A hundred Turkish archers rose from the ramparts, and in an instant the air was thick with arrows. Horses screamed and reared while riders tried desperately to turn their heads to safety. I saw two animals go down, blood streaming from their sides: the rider of one managed to leap clear and run back but the other was trapped under the flanks of his steed and could not move. A fistful of arrows plunged into his body within seconds. His companion, on foot, was luckier: one arrow glanced off his coned helmet, another struck his calf but did not bite, while a third lodged in his shoulder but did not bring him down.

As he passed beyond their reach, the Turks on the walls put down their bows and took up a great shout, praising their God and mocking our impotence. If they hoped by their taunts to provoke us into another futile charge they were disappointed, for the survivors of our cavalry were limping back to our lines. There seemed to be more horses than riders among them, and a dozen beasts and men were lying motionless near the bridge. A small party of Turks emerged from the open gate to plunder them. A few of the men around me grabbed bows and loosed shots, but they fell short and did nothing to deter the looters. Sickened, I watched as two of the fallen were dragged back into the city. There would be no mercy or ransom for them.

'Fools!' the Norman sergeant raged as the Provençals reached our position. 'Knaves and cowards! You lost good horses there – and for what? To hearten the Turks at the sight of your witless sacrifice? When my lord Bohemond hears of this, you will wish yourselves in the infidels' houses of torture with the men you left behind.'

8

The Provençal leader's eyes stared down from either side of the strip of iron covering his nose. His ragged beard sprang wild beneath his helmet. 'If the men of Sicily could build this cursed tower and not waste time pillaging the dead, then the men of Provence would not have to waste their forces protecting them. *That* is what your lord Bohemond has commanded.'

I turned my attention away from them, for Sigurd had returned. He strode past the bickering officers, ignoring them, threw down the plundered shield and stamped on it. Even his strength could not crack it.

'Five months,' he growled. 'Five months and we've learned nothing more than how to kill ourselves.'

The clanking tread of men-at-arms silenced the recriminations. A company of Lotharingians were approaching along the muddy track, their long spears clattering against each other over their heads. I was grateful for the relief, for it had been a hateful day. By my feet the rubble of broken tombs was at last beginning to fill the foundation trench, but it would be a week or more before the tower was completed – if the Turks did not first find a way to destroy it. Even then it would take us no closer to the inside of those unyielding walls.

As the Lotharingians took up their watch Sigurd mustered his troop. They were Varangian guards, pale-skinned northmen from the isle of Thule – England, in their tongue – and most fearsome among the Emperor's mercenaries. Yet today their bellicose posture was tamed and the usual clamour of their conversation silenced. Battle was their living; months of labouring, guarding, digging and burying had drained it from them.

The Provençal cavalry trotted away, and we followed them towards the boat bridge back to the camp. With only scant food and guilty dreams awaiting us we marched in silence, without haste. Around us, though, the road thronged with life. The peasants and pilgrims who followed the armies hurried about with whatever they had foraged that day: firewood, berries, roots or grains. One lucky man had trapped a quail, which he dangled from a stick as he proceeded with a phalanx of triumphant companions around him. No less protected were the merchants who bartered with our army, Syrians and Armenians and Saracens alike: they drove their mules amid trains of turbaned guards, stopping only to force harsh bargains with the desperate and hungry. Grey clouds began massing over the mountain to our right, and I quickened my pace lest the rains come again.

We had reached the place where a steep embankment rose above one side of the path when I heard the cry. It was a place that had always made me nervous, for the ground rose higher than my head and any enemy from the west could approach entirely unseen; at the howl that now rose above the earthen parapet I froze, cursing myself for abandoning my armour. The slap of stumbling foot-steps came nearer. Sigurd crouched well back from the embankment, his axe held ready. The rest of the company were likewise poised, their eyes searching the edge of the little cliff for danger.

With a stuttering shout, a boy reached the slope and plunged over it, flailing his arms like wings as his feet fell away beneath him. He was lucky we were not archers or he would have died in mid-air; instead, he collapsed onto the road and lay there sobbing, a heap of cloth and flesh and dirt. Sigurd's axe-head darted forward, but he checked it mid-swing as he saw there was no threat in our new arrival. His clothes were torn and his limbs daubed with mud; his beardless face seemed pale, though we could see little enough of it under the arms which cradled it.

He pressed himself up on his hands and knelt there, his

head darting around to look at the fearsome Varangians surrounding him.

'My master,' he gulped, pulling a scrawny lock of hair from over his face. Recognising perhaps that I alone held no ferocious axe, he fixed his eyes on mine. 'My master has been killed.'

β

I pulled the boy up by the neck of his tunic, though he still had to tilt his head back to look me in the eye. 'Where? Killed by the Turks? Who is your master?'

He wiped a sleeve across his face, smearing it with more grime than he removed. I kept my grip on his shoulder, for there was no strength in his shivering legs. 'Drogo of Melfi,' he stammered. 'In the lord Bohemond's army. I found him . . .' His words gave out and he pulled from my grasp, sinking to his knees. 'I found him over there.' He pointed back to the top of the embankment whence he had come. 'Dead.'

I glanced at Sigurd, then at the darkening sky. Part of my mind scolded that too many men had died already that day without taxing my conscience; that a sobbing servant and a dead Norman knight were no concern of mine, especially when Turkish patrols might yet skulk in the countryside. Perhaps, though, it was the accumulation of so many deaths which weighed most on me: confronted by a snivelling boy grieving for his master, I was defenceless.

'It would be best if your men accompanied us,' I told Sigurd.

'Best for whom?' he retorted. 'The best course for my men is to return to our camp, before night brings out the Turks and Tafurs and wolves.'

'Any wolves near here will have been eaten long since. As for the others—' I turned to the boy. 'Is it far?'

He shook his head. 'Not far, Lord.'

'Then take us quickly.'

We found a path up around the embankment and followed the boy over the broken ground that rose towards the hills on the far side of the plain of Antioch. The red earth was sticky underfoot, and all the grasses sprouted spikes and prickles which tore my legs. We came over a low ridge and looked down into a small hollow in the hillside. It was perhaps fifty feet across and formed like a natural amphitheatre in the rising ground. Perhaps it had once been a quarry, for the surrounding walls were pitted and bitten, but the ground underfoot was soft. In its centre, unmoving in the grey dusk, lay the body of a man.

I crossed quickly and crouched beside him while the Varangians fanned out, sniffing for danger. Behind me I heard Sigurd hiss with disapproval.

'You found him here?' I asked the boy, who had knelt opposite me. Tears were running down his face, bright in the gloom, but he seemed to me more frightened than sorrowful.

'Here,' he mumbled. 'I found him here.'

'How did you know he would be here?'

He looked up, the terror now plain on his face. 'He was gone from the camp for many hours. The lord William, lord Bohemond's brother, he told me to find him. I looked everywhere in the camp, and then here. And I found him.'

'And what made you think he would be here?' I repeated. We must have come half a mile from the road at least, and none of our army would have been so foolish as to wander here alone.

The boy closed his eyes and squirmed his fingers together. 'He came here often. Many times I had seen him.'

'Why? What brought him here?'

My questions were reflexive, the natural consequence of seeing too many men unnaturally dead, but their brusqueness must have alarmed the boy. He trembled in silence, unable to answer.

'Was this how you found him?'

He nodded.

I stared down at the body before me. Drogo, the boy had called him – and a Norman of Sicily, I guessed, if he had served the lord Bohemond. He lay on his belly in the grass, still and silent as the twilight around us, and for a moment I wondered if he had not been stricken by some ailment, for there were no marks of violence evident. He had not even worn his armour, only a quilted under-coat stained with many weeks' wear.

But the sour smell of blood in the evening air belied innocent hopes. I put my hand to his shoulder and lifted, pushing him over onto his back. The heavy body fell flat against the ground, and an involuntary whimper breathed through my lips. The Norman Drogo had not died a natural death: he had died because a heavy blade had cut open his throat, pouring out his blood into a puddle on the grass below. It must have been a savage blow, for it had sliced more than halfway through his neck, so that as I moved him his head lolled back to let fresh rivulets of blood trickle down to his collar. It had stained everything: matted the dark hair of his beard, dyed the wool of his quilted tunic, and dashed across the cheekbones that framed the gaping eyes. Some had even splashed onto his forehead.

I saw all this, and doubtless a hundred other aspects of the horror, but one thought drove me above all others.

'The blood is still wet – still flowing. This happened only a few minutes since.' I jumped to my feet. 'If this was the work of a party of Turks, they cannot be far away.'

The boy, still on his knees, stared around in terror. 'We

must find them,' he mumbled, biting a knuckle until the finger turned white. 'We must avenge my master.'

'We must get back to the camp,' I snapped. I had seen scores of men die similar deaths – many worse – since we left Constantinople; I would not join their number in this lonely place. Night was drawing in from the east, and the rocky walls of the hollow grew evil with shadow.

'But we will take his body,' I added. Soon the night's carrion-eaters would emerge, and the body would become more terrible still if we left it behind.

Sigurd must have shared my thoughts, for he made no complaint as the Varangians formed a rough stretcher from their axe-hafts under the corpse and bore it back to the city. The darkness was complete by the time we reached our lines, and nervous sentries challenged us at every step. Our Byzantine camp was at the north-eastern walls, just behind the Normans of Sicily, and we must have passed through more than a mile of tents and pavilions, of makeshift paddocks, blacksmiths, farriers, fletchers, and armourers, all lit in the irregular glimmer of innumerable campfires. Gaunt faces on swollen bodies begged for food, money or compassion; haggard women asked after lost lovers, or sought new ones; children clawed each other in vicious sport, as the Army of God prepared for the night.

I chose a path which skirted the edge of the Norman encampment, for I did not wish to walk through their midst with one of their dead. Among them were too many veterans of their wars against us, and a Greek carrying a Norman body might be too obvious a provocation.

The boy, who had lagged behind us, now tugged on my arm. 'Where shall I go?'

I looked into his forlorn eyes. 'To your master's tent. Were there any family who accompanied him?'

The boy shook his head, sniffling. 'A brother, but he died on the march.'

'Any other companions? Others of Melfi?'

'Three knights who shared his tent.'

'Then tell them that we have his body for safe keeping. They may come and claim it from us for burial.'

If we could find space in this land for yet another tomb.

After a meagre supper, I picked my way through the maze of cloth and ropes to a clearing in the heart of our camp where a single tent stood in dignified isolation. Its size, and the richness of its fabric, bespoke a noble occupant, yet it was the solitude and space around which were the true extravagance in that place. Two guards, squat Patzinaks from Thrace, stood by the torches which illuminated the door. They did not challenge me as I stepped inside.

Within the tent the luxury was greater still. Silk curtains of red and gold, woven through with images of eagles and saints, hung from the ceiling to form discreet partitions; thick carpets hid the mud under the floor, while oil lamps on silver tripods gave a steady light to the scene. In the centre of the room stood a broad chair of gilded ebony; behind it, on a stand, three candles burned before a triptych icon of Saints Mercurios, George and Demetrios, each on horseback and wielding his lance. I touched the silver cross that I wore on a chain about my neck and offered a silent prayer to my namesake.

The whisper of parting silks broke the stillness.

'You are late, Demetrios Askiates,' said a petulant voice.

I bowed my head. 'There was a skirmish at the bridge, Lord. And afterwards I had to recover a Norman corpse.'

The general Tatikios stepped into the room and seated himself on the ebony chair. Though none would deny his knowledge of the lands of Asia, I doubted whether the Emperor could have chosen a commander more certain to rile the Frankish allies whom he had been sent to support. Against a race which wished death on any dark-skinned foreigner, Tatikios was a Turkopole, a half-breed whose Turkish blood was evident in his smooth, olive-shaded cheeks and dark eyes; where the Franks deemed headlong charge the only honourable form of war, Tatikios was a subtle tactician who judged any battle a failure of strategy. Worst, in the eyes of men who worshipped brute manhood, Tatikios was a eunuch. And deformed elsewhere, too, for he had lost his nose in combat and now wore a sharp-edged golden prosthesis, giving him something of the aspect of a haughty bird of prey. The barbarians thought him a freak, an effeminate clown, and treated him accordingly. As his nominal servant, I owed more deference.

'Take a pen,' he commanded. 'I must write to the Emperor.'

I did not argue that it would be easier to wait until daylight, for Tatikios, like so many in power, thought only of his own convenience. Nor did I argue that I was not in truth his scribe, for it served both our interests that he should treat me so. I sat down on a stool, hunched by its low height, and took the ivory writing desk from under it. The reed pen was slight between my callused fingers, and I feared that I might snap it merely by touching the paper.

'To his most serene holy majesty, the *Basileus* and *Autokrator*, the Emperor of the Romans Alexios Komnenos: greetings from his servant Tatikios.'

The eunuch frowned to see that my pen could not keep pace with his tongue.

'The situation at Antioch worsens daily, and is almost intolerable. In the past month, since the Franks defeated the emir of Damascus in battle, their arrogance and insolence has surpassed all bounds. Your noble army and her general are reviled by these barbarians; they speak openly of foreswearing their oaths to you and seizing the land which is owed you for themselves. Now that the winter is past, I urge your holy majesty to hasten to our aid, to take up the leadership of this quest which is rightfully your own and to force the barbarians to obey your commands.'

The air in the tent, heated by its oil lamps and its brazier, was warm about me. As Tatikios continued to speak the sinews between my ear and my hand seemed to dissolve, so that I wrote his words unthinkingly. Released from the moment, my mind turned back eleven months and countless miles, back to spring in the great palace of the city.

'The Emperor will not go.'

I was standing in one of the lesser courtyards, its pillars wreathed in green ivy. A shallow pool in its centre reflected the clouds of the uncertain sky above, while a bronze Herakles looked down in silence. My companion had just joined me from the hall within and still wore the ceremonial *camisia* with its gold lion's-head clasp, and a robe set with many jewels. It might have seemed cumbersome on his young frame, but with the confidence of his stature, and the untroubled certainty in his eyes, he wore it easily. His name was Michael, and the rumour in the palace was that few knew the Emperor's mind as well as he.

'The Emperor will not accompany the barbarian army to Asia,' he elaborated. 'The council has decided it. He will send gold, and food and men – but not his person.'

I nodded slowly. I had not expected to be summoned to the palace that afternoon, certainty not to hear the outcome of the Emperor's deliberations. I had not thought that they would concern me.

'The empire would not benefit. It would be imprudent for him to abandon his capital when his duties demand so much attention. Especially after the tragic loss of his chamberlain.'

I met Michael's guarded smile, acknowledging the deeper truths behind his words. We both knew why the Emperor could not leave the queen of cities, and it had nothing to do with gathering taxes or attending the business of government. If he absented himself from the throne of power there would be many swift to claim it for themselves, and he would not be the first Emperor returning to the city to find it barred against him.

'The wise emperor holds the rudder of righteousness against waves of injustice and lawlessness,' I quoted.

Michael laughed. 'The wise emperor holds tight to the arms of his throne lest he be swept away.'

'And will he allow a hundred thousand Franks to march across our lands in Asia, trusting in their oath to restore their conquests to him?' I had seen the Franks swear it in the great cathedral of Ayia Sophia; rarely had I witnessed an oath that its professors would more readily abjure.

'He will allow the Franks to march across the *Turkish* lands of Asia,' Michael corrected me. 'If they are successful, and honest, he will gain. If they are unsuccessful, he will have no part of it – he will not become another Diogenes Romanus, tempted into battle too far from home and made captive.'

'While the loss of a hundred thousand Franks and Normans will not sorrow him too greatly,' I suggested.

'When you make allies of your enemies, every battle is a victory.'

I picked a pebble off the ground and tossed it into the pool, sending waves rippling across the reflected sky. 'And what if the Franks are both successful and dishonest?'

Michael smiled, and eased himself down on the marble parapet surrounding the pool. 'An Emperor's mind has many eyes and is ever-vigilant. As a token of his faith with the Franks, the Emperor will send an army of his own to aid them. A small force, but enough to report it if the Franks forget their oaths. The council has appointed Tatikios to command it.'

I sighed, sensing this was more than gossip. 'Then the Emperor will not need to drag me across Cappadocia and the Anatolics protecting him. I shall say a dozen prayers of gratitude tonight.'

'Save your prayers: you will soon have greater need of them.' The humour was gone from Michael's young face. 'The Emperor desires you to accompany Tatikios, to serve as his scribe and to report back all you see. They are wild dogs, these barbarians, and the Emperor hunts with them at his peril. He will need swift warning if they turn on him.'

'And if they turn on me?'

Michael grimaced. 'While they are hungry, they will obey the hand that feeds them. But if they meet with success, and can feed their appetites themselves — then, Demetrios, be on your guard.'

'I fear, my lord, that under the present circumstances success remains as impossible as ever. If you are unable at this time to join us, then I beg you give me leave to return to the queen of cities immediately. I can accomplish nothing while these barbarians quarrel and thwart—'

Save for the rasping of my pen and the drone of Tatikios' voice, the tent had been quiet; now he broke off as urgent voices sounded at the door. I heard the Patzinak outside issue a challenge, and a loud reply which was too fast and foreign to understand. In a moment, the flap was pulled open and the guard's face appeared with the draught of cold air.

'Your pardon, General,' he said gruffly.
Tatikios' gold nose seemed to twitch in irritation. 'Yes?'
'The lord Bohemond demands to see you.'

γ

I had seen the lord Bohemond many times since we had
left Constantinople – debating at councils, leading
raiding parties, walking the lines to rally his men – but
every time it was as if I saw him anew. Partly it was the
effect of his physique, for he stood a foot taller than most
men, outstripping even Sigurd, with immense breadth in
his shoulders and arms like a mangonel. His hair was
cropped very short, and though like all the Franks he had
abandoned the habit of shaving, his beard was trimmed
close to the cheek. Yet it seemed that the elements of his
body were not at one with each other, for his skin was
mottled red and white, his hair brown but his beard russet.
Only the pale blue eyes remained identical in their
unyielding stare.

But it was not merely Bohemond's physical aspect that
drew men's eyes. Whether by his strength or by some
infernal blessing, he was possessed of an energy which no
man could ignore. In a busy room, the loudest conversation clustered about him; in war, the fiercest fighting was
at his standard. Though he dressed every inch the sober
prince, his simple armour now worn over a wine-red tunic,
he conveyed somehow a reckless, unpredictable air which
seduced the affections of men and women alike. He had
neither lands nor title, yet he had gathered an army which
was the sinew of the campaign. After every battle his was
the first name spoken, and in ever louder tones.

Tatikios was one of the few wholly immune to his charm. 'I did not expect you, Lord Bohemond. Have the Turks surrendered the city?'

Bohemond gave an easy smile. Perhaps it was the way the rings of his mail caught the light, but the tent seemed brighter where he stood. 'They will, General. Once we have our towers at their gates, the city will starve.'

'No army has ever forced the city walls from without?'

'No army has ever fought with the hand of God guiding them.'

'You would be wise to offer the Lord the humility which is His due.' The reflected lamp-light flickered on the eunuch's nose, making it almost impossible to heed his words seriously. 'So far He has visited only famine and pestilence on us.'

Bohemond shrugged. 'I would not have it otherwise. What glory would we win marching with full bellies against armies of women? What glory would the *Greek* way win us?'

'The glory of life preserved rather than wasted.'

'The glory of an empire lost? When the Greeks have the strength to reclaim their own lands, when their King dares to lead his army without fear of falling into captivity, then you may extol the Greek way to me.'

The discipline of a lifetime in the palace kept Tatikios' smooth face impassive. Indeed, I thought I glimpsed a smile on his lips. 'As you say, we Byzantines are a feeble nation, scarce able to master an army of children. Doubtless your father said the same twenty years ago as he defe-cated out his life on Kephalonia, once we had destroyed his fleet and driven his army into the sea.'

Bohemond went very still, all the more striking for his usual unceasing momentum. The contrasts of his skin seemed to heighten, like an alloy heated in the fire, and his fingers scratched at his sword hilt. 'There are some matters that you would do well to forget, eunuch, far from home as you are and surrounded by warriors ten times your strength. My father was worth a legion of your Greeks – and had you challenged him on the battlefield, rather than corrupting his allies with gold and lies, he would have walked across the Adriatic on your corpses.'

'Of course,' said Tatikios. 'But history should not stand between allies.' He clapped his hands, and a slave appeared from behind one of the folds of the tent. 'Wine for the lord Bohemond?'

'No.'

'As you wish. What brings you unsummoned to my tent tonight? What do you want of me?'

The vigour was returning to Bohemond's body. He stared down on Tatikios through narrowed eyes. 'You presume too much. I did not come to discuss anything with you, eunuch, but with your servant.'

Visibly confused, Tatikios looked to the slave who still waited in the corner. He seemed about to speak, but a soft laugh from Bohemond checked him.

'Not your slave; your scribe. Demetrios Askiates. Alone.'

The air outside was cold, sharp after the warmth of the tent, but the pace I needed to keep up with Bohemond drew heat into my limbs. He seemed impervious to all discomfort and danger: few Franks would have ventured into our camp without a troop of guards at their backs, thinking us little better than craven traitors, but he walked alone, his arms bared beyond the short sleeves of his tunic. My breath emerged in clouds as we strode between the lines of tents, heading gradually up the slope towards the northern arm of the mountain, and somewhere to my left I heard the melancholy notes of a lyre plucking at the night.

Gradually the tents thinned and the soft ground grew harder. We passed through the pickets and climbed to a stony outcrop on the side of the hill. Looking down, I could see the campfires of our army strung out in an enormous arc, and the torches on the watchtowers mirroring it. The moon shone through a tear in the clouds and illuminated the city cupped between the mountain and the flames. I seated myself on a cold rock beside Bohemond, and for a moment we gazed at the scene in silence.

'From here, you could almost forget the suffering among those fires,' Bohemond said at last.

'Indeed, Lord.'

He looked at me. 'I will be honest with you, Demetrios. The army is close to collapse. Perhaps your general was right – perhaps we have tempted God's patience too long in this place.'

'God's purpose is inscrutable, Lord.'

He did not seem to notice my words. 'Nor is it even the Turks who will be our downfall. We weaken ourselves too much with unnecessary strife. Provençal against Norman, Lotharingian against Fleming – even, I confess, Norman against Greek, when our past quarrels are resurrected.'

Puzzling that he should bring me to this remote place to mourn the failings of his allies, I murmured something vague about our fellowship in the body of Christ. Again, I was ignored.

'How can we fight as one while we divide ourselves with a host of petty allegiances? You cannot conduct a war by council. When my father went to war, he did not barter its course with his vassals: he commanded them.' He rested his chin on his hand, and stared down again. 'They tell me that you found the body of my liegeman, Drogo of Melfi.'

I felt a fresh pang of discomfort, and he must have sensed it for he touched my arm in reassurance. 'No doubt there are some who would work mischief with that fact, but I am certain that you discovered him in innocence. Happenstance.'

'His servant sought help. By chance, I was nearest.'

Bohemond straightened. 'Even chance may have her purposes. That it should be you whom the boy found, and none other . . . How did Drogo's death strike you?'

Unsettled by the sudden change of conversation, I fumbled for words. 'A tragic loss, Lord – no doubt his comrades will mourn him deeply.'

'No doubt – but you misunderstand me. How do you think he came to die?'

'His throat was cut open. Probably by a sword, to judge by the depth of the wound.'

'So they told me. A Turkish blade, you think?'

I hesitated. 'I cannot say.'

'But others will. If a man dies in battle, his friends honour him. If he dies unarmed and alone, far from his enemies, then they will suspect treachery – and will seek to avenge it. Already I can hear the whispers in my camp: that it was a Provençal, or a jealous rival, or a creditor – or even a Greek.'

I took the news in silence.

'If these rumours are sustained, some in my army may strike precipitately against those they blame.'

'I will pray for temperance.'

'Pray rather for deliverance.' Bohemond slid down from the rocky seat and turned to face me, blocking the moonlit city from my sight. 'Now is the moment when we must unite under the banner of God, or fall divided by our folly. The fate of Drogo cannot be a wound which festers among us.' He slapped his fist into the palm of his hand, startling a nearby owl into flight. 'If we allow feuds to rise among us, we will become mere pickings for the Turkish scavengers.'

'You could announce—'

'There is nothing I can announce that will calm my men – nothing save the truth. That is our only salvation. That is why I spoke earlier of providence. I have seen you often, Demetrios Askiates, lurking behind Tatikios, scribbling with your pen while your eyes and ears recorded all. I know there is more to your service than most – perhaps even that fool of a eunuch – suspect. I know that in your city you had a reputation for unveiling the truths to which other men were blind.' He smiled crookedly. 'The Duke of Lorraine and his brother positively swear to it.'

'I only serve—'

'Demetrios, you would see the siege ended, the famished fed and the city restored to your Emperor?'

'Of course.'

'Then help me.' I heard the jangle of his armour as he tapped a fist against his heart. 'Help me root out the canker of Drogo's death before it poisons us all. Discover who murdered him, so that rumours and speculation and recriminations do not cleave our army apart.'

His eyes, grey in the moonlight, fixed on mine. 'Please?'

δ

A chill dew still lay on the ground when I reached the Norman camp next morning. It soaked my boots and shrivelled my feet, yet it was the stares of those we passed which truly discomfited me. Their drawn faces looked up from steaming pots of boiling bones, examining the Greek interloper with his giant companion, and I saw only hatred. A few even summoned the strength to spit as we passed.

'You should have worn armour,' said Sigurd, unhelpfully.

'I don't want to appear a threat.'

'Better a threat than a target.'

'Trust has to begin somewhere.'

'Far from here.' Sigurd took a rag from his belt and ostentatiously wiped some imagined moisture from his axe-head. 'Have you forgotten that these are the same Normans who spent four years trying to defeat the Emperor whose gold they now take? Or that leading their kinsmen at the coast is the son of William the Bastard who stole my country? These men are the thieves of kingdoms, and I would want three hauberks and a stout wall at my back before I trusted myself to their company.'

Thankfully he spoke in Greek, which none of the Franks had troubled to learn.

'And now you've pimped yourself to Bohemond, the thief of thieves,' he continued.

'Surely you agree that a suspicious death should be

laid to rest. Distrust and dissension among us will be fatal.'

'It was a Norman death; we should be thanking God and praying for more.'

Sigurd's foul temper at last ran silent, and I was able to enquire after Drogo without risking offence. Even so, I was frequently answered with scowls. Often I had trouble making myself understood with those I asked, for none of us spoke a common language. Rather, over the course of months we had learned to barter words, trading and hoarding them. As with all commerce, ill will made it infinitely harder.

After half an hour, I found the tent I sought. There was little to distinguish it, a patchwork cone of mismatched cloths which had been sewn and re-sewn until the neat stripes of its inception became a labyrinth of criss-crossed lines. The flaps were still down against the cold, and I rapped on the stiff fabric to announce myself. A small voice grudgingly called me in.

There were four straw mattresses on the earth floor inside, though only one occupant. It was the boy who had brought us to the body, the dead man's servant, squatting on the straw and rubbing an oily tuft of wool along a sword blade. In the dusk and confusion of the night before, I had barely had time to look at him: now I noticed how deep-sunken his cheeks were, how the dark eyes seemed held in a perpetual terror. The brown hair which fell well past his shoulders gave him an unsettlingly girlish quality.

Despite the circumstances in which we had met the previous day, he gave no sign of remembering me. 'What do you want?'

'My name is Demetrios. This is Sigurd. You brought us to your master's body last night. Now the lord Bohemond has charged us to discover who killed him.'

He inclined his head close to the blade, as if checking for some imperceptible flaw. 'I did not kill him.'

So clumsy was the response that for a moment I did not know how to answer it. I crouched before him, trying to look into the downcast eyes, and softened my voice.

'What is your name?'

'Simon.'

'From where?'

'Cagnano.'

It might have been in Persia for all I knew. 'How long did you serve Drogo, your master?'

Misery filled the boy's face as he stumbled to answer my question, tapping his fingers hopelessly. Sigurd coughed impatiently, but I did not press the boy. His soul was brittle, and I sensed that even a little rough usage might snap it. As I waited, I watched the sallow light seeping under the edge of the tent. Every so often a passing shadow would interrupt it, but there was one shadow I noticed which did not move.

'Since Heraklea. I do not know how long it has been since then.'

'About six months,' I guessed. 'Who did you travel with to Heraklea?'

'With my master's brother. He died in the battle there. Afterwards, my master took me into his household.'

I remembered the battle at Heraklea – though in truth it had been barely a skirmish. On a dusty morning, the Turks in the garrison had made one charge at our vanguard, then fled away before us. We lost three men, probably fewer than those who died of thirst that day. I had thought little of them.

'What kind of master was he?'

The boy sniffed, and wiped his nose with the wool. It smeared black oil over his cheek. 'Fair. He rarely punished

me when I did not deserve it. Sometimes he gave me
food, when he could spare it.'

'Did he have enemies?'

'No.'

'Who else sleeps in this tent?'

Did I imagine it, or did the shadow under the hem
of the tent move? The boy, who had his back to it,
shifted on the mattress and twisted the sword's hilt in
his hands.

'Three companions of my master.'

'Servants?'

'Knights.'

'Their names?'

'Quino, Odard and—'

The snapping of canvas broke off the boy's words, and
we all three turned to look at the figure standing in the
open door. I could see little more than his silhouette, a
black form against the grey light outside. He stank of
horse sweat.

'Whelp!' he barked, affecting not to notice Sigurd or
me. 'My mount has waited for your grooming for half an
hour. If she has grown sores, or gone lame, I will visit her
afflictions on you tenfold.' He stepped into the room, and
let his stare sweep across us. 'Who are these?'

'Demetrios Askiates,' I told him. 'I—'

'Hah. A Greek. Tell me, Demetrios Askiates, what should
I think when I find two Greeks alone in a tent with a
boy?'

'One Greek,' growled Sigurd, unhelpfully. 'And a
Varangian from England.'

'A Varangian from England,' mimicked the knight. 'A
race named for a tribe of catamite slaves. You and the
Greeks have the same black soul, and your vices are
legendary.' He turned back to the boy. 'Get out and see
to my horse, or I will whip you into the Orontes.'

31

'I have not finished with Simon,' I said. 'Nor have you told me your name.'

'Nor do you deserve to hear it.' The knight had come further into the tent now, and as my eyes adjusted to the gloom I could make out more of his appearance. He was neither tall nor broad, but there was a lean strength in his body that a larger man would have done well to beware. His movements were quick and unpredictable, his limbs twitching all the while, and his face was lined well beyond his apparent youth. I did not think he smiled often.

'You serve the lord Bohemond?' I asked.

'I do.'

'Bohemond has charged me to discover how the knight Drogo came to die.'

I barely saw him move, but suddenly his eyes were very close to mine. His sour breath fanned my face.

'Even my lord Bohemond can err in his judgement. Or perhaps he believes that the Greek who found my brother Drogo, alone and isolated, may indeed have *personal* knowledge of how he was murdered.'

'Drogo was your brother?' I asked, astonished.

'*As* a brother. We shared a tent, our hardships, our food and our prayers. When his natural brother died he turned to us as his family.' He stepped back, his spurs dragging scars into the mud floor. 'But that is no matter for you. Leave my tent, you and your pederast friend, before I avenge Drogo's death on you both.'

Thus far, Sigurd had kept calm under the knight's provocation, but he controlled himself no longer. Grasping his axe by its head, he swept the haft like a scythe at the Norman's knees, meaning to knock them from under him. But the knight was faster: his sword swung before him and parried the blow, biting deep into the wood of the axe-haft. Both their arms must have stung from the impact, yet for a moment they held their weapons clasped together, unbending, each staring into the other's eyes. Then they pulled free.

'Next time it will be your neck that tastes this sword,' the knight hissed. He was breathing hard.

'Next time, I will break your blade in two and force it down your throat.'

I pulled at Sigurd's arm. Behind us, I could see the boy hunched over with terror on the bed. It tore at my conscience to leave him with the knight, but I feared worse would befall all of us if we stayed.

'We should leave.'

Outside the tent the air was hard, and I narrowed my eyes against the sudden light. I had no wish to linger any longer in the Norman camp, for the knight's anger at us was no more than most of his countrymen felt, but the sight of an old man sitting cross-legged in the doorway of the tent opposite spurred me to one last effort. Sigurd and I crossed to greet him, and I pulled a bloodied bundle wrapped in cloth from the pouch at my belt. I had intended it to encourage the boy, but perhaps I could make it tell elsewhere.

'The knight who just entered that tent, who was he?' I let the bundle dangle from my hand.

The man leaned closer and sniffed at the package. 'Quino.'

I remembered the name, for the boy had spoken it. 'He was a companion of Drogo?'

'Alas, yes.'

'As was . . .' I searched for the foreign name. 'Odard?'

'Yes.'

'And there was another, also?'

'Rainauld. A Provençal.' The old man did not hide his scorn of the foreigner, nor his hunger for what I held.

I did not ask why a Provençal had lived in the Norman

camp. Poverty and death had severed many bonds of allegiance, as those who survived flocked to whichever banner offered most hope of reward.

'Were there other servants, besides the boy Simon?'

'None who outlived the winter.'

I unknotted the bundle and showed its contents. It was the liver from a hare which one of Sigurd's men had snared in the night, its fresh blood soaking through the wrapping. Though it was no larger than a nut, the man gazed on it as if it were a full roasted boar.

'What else can you tell me of Drogo? What company did he keep?'

'Little.' The man shuffled back a little as though the smell of the meat was too great a temptation. 'He was always with one or other of the men from his tent – and rarely with any others. Sometimes one of the captains would visit; sometimes Drogo bought goods from the Ishmaelite traders. Few others.'

'Did he have any enemies?'

'Neither friends nor enemies.'

'And women?'

The man sucked in his cheeks and swallowed, as if there were too much spit in his mouth. 'One woman, yes. A Provençal. I did not know her. She dressed always in white – a white robe and a white shawl about her head. Her name was Sarah.'

'How do you know?'

'Because she announced herself at his tent. I heard her. Though whatever business she had inside, she kept quiet about that,' he added, wiggling the end of his tongue between his lips.

'When did you see her last?'

'Yesterday afternoon.'

The answer stopped me short. Long years of habit had already trained my thoughts in certain directions, and the possibility of a woman's involvement was prominent among them. That one should have called at Drogo's tent scant hours before he died . . .

I let the liver drop into the old man's hand. 'Did they leave together?'

'No.' All his attention was clearly fixed on the meat in his palm, his eyes moonlike in wonder, but the answer was confident enough. As he noticed me staring at him, he added: 'I saw her go before him, perhaps half an hour.'

'And when he left, was he armed?'

'No. No armour at all. Nor his sword.'

I remembered the blade that the boy Simon had been polishing, and wondered whether it had been his dead master's. 'Were his companions in the tent when he went?'

The man shrugged. 'I do not think so. I saw Quino and Odard return later, near dusk. I heard they had been working near the bridge. The Provençal, Rainauld, I have not seen.'

'Thank you,' I said. 'If you remember any other facts which seem important, any other men or women who visited Drogo, you may find me in the Byzantine camp.'

The old man did not respond to my words – I guessed he would sooner seek me at the Caliph's palace in Baghdad than in a camp full of Greeks. Instead, he gazed at the cloth I held in my hand, still stained with the rabbit's blood. 'Will you keep that?'

I looked at it in surprise. 'If you want it . . .'

Before I could finish my sentence, his clawing fingers had snatched it from my hand. With a glance of gratitude, he pressed it into his mouth and began sucking the blood from the fabric. We left him to his feast.

I did not want to delay any longer in the Norman camp; we hurried away, back towards our own lines. I still had Drogo's body in my possession, and I suspected it might

benefit me to examine it in daylight before his companions buried it. We walked quickly, ignoring the angry glares
that followed us.

'You think the woman has something to do with this,'
said Sigurd.

'I think the woman *may* have something to do with
this.' I tried to sound less certain than I felt, lest my confidence rebound on me later. 'The knight left his tent
without even his sword: it follows he must have planned
to meet someone he knew and trusted.'

'Someone with whom armour might have got in the
way,' Sigurd suggested.

'Perhaps.'

'I guarantee you it was no woman who swung the stroke
that killed him. His neck was almost cut clean through.
Even a man the size of Bohemond would need a sound
arm to manage it.'

'A man aroused by passion might find the strength,' I
said.

Sigurd tipped back his head and laughed, prompting yet
deeper scowls on the faces that we passed. Doubtless they
thought we mocked them. 'I see. Demetrios Askiates, the
famed unveiler of mysteries, needs only an hour speaking
with two men and a boy to discover all. Drogo and the
woman were lovers; she came to his tent and arranged to
meet him in that dell; he went there unarmed, but was
ambushed by a rival, perhaps with the woman's
connivance. Find the woman, find the rival, and Normans
and Provençals and Greeks will all be friends again. Is that
your answer?'

'It seems as plausible as any,' I said testily. 'I would have
thought you of all men might favour a simple solution.'

'Indeed I do. And I do not think you need invent a
jealous lover to explain why an unarmed man was killed
in a place surrounded by thousands who are impoverished,

starving, and desperate. Would you ever walk out of the camp alone and unprotected?'

'Of course not.'

'He would not be the first from this army to be murdered for whatever gold he carried – he would probably not even be the hundredth. Franks or Turks, Christians or Ishmaelites: there is not one of them within fifty miles who would not kill for food.'

I sighed. 'Nonetheless, for the good of the army, Bohemond demands that the murderer be found.'

Which in Sigurd's eyes, I thought, was probably an overwhelming reason not to find him.

We crossed through our camp, to the lower slopes of the mountain which reached into the plain of Antioch. To my left, I could see the vast expanse of farmland stretching flat as marble to the horizon; on my right, on an outcrop above, the tower they called Malregard looked down on the St Paul gate. The Normans had built it soon after we arrived, and though it had been stout enough then, the winter storms had beaten it until its stones were black and skewed. It leaned off the mountain like a falcon on its perch, poised for the hunt, and even four months on I shivered every time I passed under it.

A little way north-east of the tower, beside the stump of a myrtle bush long since turned to firewood, we reached the cave. We had discovered it by chance when a troop of Turks had used it to ambush us; after we had defeated them, Sigurd had put it to use as our armoury. It had only been intended as a temporary expedient, to keep off the rain until the city fell, but as the months passed it had gained lamps, benches, and even a ramshackle wooden door hinged into the cliff. As we approached I saw a Varangian in armour sitting on a boulder before it, spinning his knife in the dirt.

'Sweyn! Has anyone tried to disturb our Norman?'

The Varangian jumped to his feet at the sound of his captain's voice. 'Only one. She said you sent her.' His words faded as he saw Sigurd's withering stare. 'She's inside.'

Sigurd pulled his helmet from his head, but he still needed to crouch low to pass through the opening of the cave. Even I had to stoop a little. I followed him past the blushing guard, into the damp, stony air within. It was more a tunnel than a cave, extending some thirty feet back into the mountain, and I stepped carefully to avoid tumbling on the shields and quivers of arrows stacked across the floor.

The passage darkened near the middle, where the daylight receded, but it was quickly illuminated again by the lamp which had been lit at the far end. By its light, I could see the body of the Norman still laid out on the bench where we had left him, though the blanket which had covered him now lay in a heap on the floor. Before him, a slender figure with bare arms dabbed at his neck with a cloth.

She turned as we approached. 'Demetrios. I feared it might be the Normans come to bury him.'

She spoke lightly, despite the debased corpse on the bench – but then, she was a physician, and must have seen equal horror many times in her calling. She was dressed simply, as ever, in a honey-yellow dress tied about her waist with a silk belt, and an ochre *palla* which had slipped to her shoulder to reveal her long black hair. Like all of us, her face had tightened in the past months, yet to me it did nothing to diminish her robust beauty. Though even after a year of intimacy, I still found her brisk manner disconcerting.

'Doubtless the Normans will come soon, once they discover where we have hidden him,' I said. 'What are you doing here, Anna?'

'Seeing what the dead may tell us. Look.'

I stepped forward, pinching my nose against the odour of the decay which had already started despite the chill surroundings. I had not expected to find the man thus. Anna had stripped him of all his clothes, leaving only a round leather pouch on a string around his neck: the rest of him lay naked, entirely exposed in death. It would have been hard enough to stomach on my own, but to see it with a woman, and with Anna of all women, seemed deep sacrilege. Clearly the fire which had warmed his soul was long extinguished, so that his skin turned blue with cold – could the dead feel cold? – while the drying-out of his flesh had curled his limbs back like the edges of paper before a flame. I could hardly bear to look at the shrivelled, yellow-stained organs of his loins, nor at the blood-crusted rent in his neck, nor yet at the twisted pull of his face. I stared at his feet, and leaned on the cave wall for strength.

'And what do the dead tell you?' Sigurd at least could find a voice, though it was far distant from his usual thunder.

'That he was killed by a mighty blow to the neck.' Neither of us had the humour to mock the evidence of that statement. 'What do you think, Sigurd? Was it an axe or a sword which struck that blow?'

Sigurd shrugged, reluctant to look too closely. 'It seems too clean for an axe wound,' he said eventually. 'More like the slice of a sword. It was not a Varangian, though,' he added more confidently. 'We would have cut the head clean through.'

'Only a knight would carry a sword,' I said.

'Or someone who had stolen one.'

'Then there is the purse.' Anna lifted the leather pouch over the corpse's mutilated neck and pulled the string open, tipping a handful of silver Frankish denarii into her palm. The broad outstretched wings of angels were stamped on the coins' faces.

I turned to Sigurd. 'So much for your thief.'

'He might have been interrupted by the boy.'

'The man who inflicted this death on a knight would not have been troubled by a servant.'

'More curious still are the marks,' Anna interrupted. 'Look at his brow.'

I held my hand before me to block the sight of the man's eyes, which still stared upward at the rocky ceiling, and peered at his forehead. Anna had pulled the hair back, splaying it out on the bench like a radiate crown, and the curve of the brow was plain to see. In its centre, a swirl of dried blood in the form of a writhing eel meandered from the parted hair to the bridge of his nose. At first glance it seemed as though the two halves of his skull had been forced apart, but in truth the skin was unbroken under the mark.

'What of it?' I asked. 'With the force of the blow, some blood splashed onto his face and dribbled down. It left that stain.'

Anna looked at me in scorn. 'You think that while the man lay on the ground, a single drop of blood curled itself prettily into that shape? Look how broad and smooth the line is.'

'What are you saying?'

'And look here.' She pointed to a spot high on the man's left cheek, just behind his eye. 'What is that?'

I cracked open my fingers and gazed between them. 'It looks like – the imprint of a finger. In blood.'

'Exactly. The same finger, I suspect, as marked his forehead.'

Now Sigurd sounded incredulous. 'You think it was drawn as he lay dying?'

'Or after he died.' Anna was unperturbed by our doubt.

'Either by him or by his killer. The latter, I would guess. A man choking out his life might not manage so neat a design upon himself.'

'But why would anyone mark him so?' I wondered. 'Was it some secret sign?'

'Hah!'

Anna and I stared at Sigurd. 'It's not a secret sign. It's a sigma. In Greek, you'd write it thus' – he swiped his finger through the air in the form of a Σ – 'but in the Latin alphabet we write it so.' He pointed victoriously at the mark on the dead Norman's forehead.

'Why—' Anna began, but my thoughts were faster.

'S for Sarah.' Now it was I who sounded triumphant. 'Drogo's mistress was called Sarah. If a rival killed him, he might have marked him with the initial of the woman they quarrelled over.'

'Or S for Simon,' Sigurd countered. 'It would not be the first time a servant killed his master. Maybe the boy marked him in boast.'

'And then ran to tell us of it?'

'There is more.' Anna had kept silent while we argued our theories, but now she gestured back to the corpse. 'Help me turn him over.'

Our joy at the discovery drained away as Sigurd and I rolled the body onto its stomach. This time we needed no guidance from Anna, for the mark was plain to see, and familiar as our own faces. It had been carved, not painted, and though there must once have been blood it was now long gone, leaving only glossy pink scars. Two cuts had been made, lines of awful precision, one from the nape of his neck to the small of his back, the other straight across his shoulder blades: a giant cross of flesh.

'That would have hurt,' said Sigurd quietly. 'I hope his God appreciates it now.'

I breathed deeply, and wished I had not. I had occasionally seen pilgrims cut such marks into their cheeks or shoulders, once even into an Abbot's forehead, but never so large, nor so deep.

'He was lucky the wound did not fester,' Anna said. 'More than one man has died from similar pieties.'

Suddenly, I was overwhelmed by an onslaught of sensations: the stench, the blueing skin, the grim signs on the corpse that seemed to proclaim horrible warnings. Anna had said that the dead would speak to us, but never had I expected so many confused, clamouring voices. I choked for air and staggered towards the light at the end of the cave, but the edge of a shield caught my leg and brought me to the floor. There was shouting behind me, and ahead of me also, but it took several moments before I could open my eyes to see who spoke.

A face lined with hatred stared down at me, scrawny hair hanging lank about it. He still stank of his horse, still wore his pointed spurs, and still spoke with contempt.

'Does your Greek stomach fail at the sight of death?'

'Why are you here?' Sigurd asked above me.

'To bury our brother in the name of Christ, not leave him rotting in a Greek hole.'

Behind him I could see another Norman, indistinct in the gloom, and a small company of men bearing a litter beyond. I stumbled to my feet.

'Take him, if you want.'

The knight, Quino, reached down and pulled an arrow from one of the quivers by the wall. He snapped it in his fists, and threw the pieces at me. 'I will leave you to your toys, Greek. You will need them when I come to claim my vengeance.' He looked past me, to where Anna stood beside Sigurd, and laughed. 'On you, and on your whore.'

They took the body and left, their taunts and jibes

echoing back to us from down the path. If this was the company that Drogo had kept, I for one would find it hard to lament his death.

ε
———

It seemed that I would never escape the Normans that
day: in the evening Tatikios summoned me to attend
him at a council of the princes. They were never comfort-
able occasions, for most of the Frankish leaders distrusted
the Byzantines, and none of them approved of having
scribes present. But Tatikios insisted on it, believing men
would measure more carefully words which they knew
were recorded. As a tactic, it was never particularly
successful.

We met in the house of the Provençal leader Raymond,
the Count of Saint-Gilles. His camp was some distance
from ours, and by the time we arrived all the other princes
had taken seats on the square of benches in the centre of
the room. Tatikios had to perch on one end, in a corner,
his left leg trembling as he tried to balance himself.

There must have been a score of men in that square,
and twice as many watching with me from the surrounding
shadows, but only a handful who signified. All save one
were unshaven, as was the fashion of necessity, and all
wore mail hauberks in protestation of their prowess. Some
I had encountered elsewhere – the wan-faced Hugh the
Great, whose beard never grew thicker than goosedown;
the ruddy-cheeked Duke Godfrey with his eternal expression of disapproval; and of course Bohemond – others I
had seen only in council. Chief among them, at least in
his own mind, was Count Raymond. By his age, his rank,

44

his wealth and his vast army he ought perhaps to have been general of all the Franks, but none of the other captains would admit to his authority. He sat in the centre of his bench, his grey hair framing the sour, one-eyed face, and if there was no single seat of honour in the equal-sided square then the broad candelabra placed discreetly behind him certainly drew men's attention first.

'We meet in the name of the Father, and of the Son, and of the Holy Ghost.' The man beside Raymond spoke the blessing in Latin, to a muttered chorus of 'Amen'. Instead of a cloak he wore a crimson cope over his ringed armour, with scenes from the scriptures embroidered into it in gold. The domed cap on his head had the shape of a helmet, but was cut from the same rich cloth as the cope. Beneath it his expression was stern, though I had sometimes seen it soften to a half-smile when, as was common, one of the princes embarked on a long or fatuous digression. His name was Adhemar, the bishop of Le Puy, and though he commanded no army save his own household, his voice was always the first and also often the last at these councils, for he was the legate of the Patriarch of Rome, the Pope.

'What progress at the western walls, Count Raymond?' he asked. He always allowed the Provençal leader to speak second, perhaps in deference to his vanity, perhaps because they were of the same country.

'The tower at the mosque, by the bridge, will be completed in days. After that, we need fear no more attacks on the supply road. Nor will the Turks then manage to bring provisions into the city, or pasture their flocks.'

'Towers alone achieve nothing,' said Bishop Adhemar. 'Who will take on the task of garrisoning it?'

He had spoken to the room at large, yet the question hung unanswered. All around the square men looked to the floor or fidgeted with their belts – none would meet

Adhemar's eye. With good reason, I thought, for after five months of siege who would willingly incur the extra cost in gold and men of manning a fort on our front line?

At length, Count Raymond lifted his chin defiantly. 'The tower was my idea, and in its wisdom the council agreed it. If none other has the stomach for it, I claim the honour of captaining its defence.'

His words stirred new enthusiasm into the gathering. 'If you had thought of it sooner, we would not have lost so many lives earlier this week,' Duke Godfrey complained. 'We might even now be in the city.'

'And if we had waited for you to conceive it, our grand-sons would still be besieging Antioch fifty years hence.' Count Hugh jerked his head emphatically, so that his fine hair tumbled over his face. He pushed it back, but it would not stay. 'I propose we should reimburse Count Raymond from the common fund, as a signal of our gratitude.'

Raymond raised his hands in deference, while his single eye fixed Duke Godfrey with malice. 'Keep the common fund for the poor and feeble. I have money enough for the task.'

'So be it,' said Adhemar. He turned to Bohemond. 'What are the reports from your camp?'

Though the only man at the council with neither lands nor titles, it was Bohemond alone among them who looked a prince. He stood, letting the blood-red folds of his cloak hang free so that the swirling weave of the silk shimmered in the candlelight. It must have been a gift from the Emperor, for there was not a craftsman in the west who could have wrought it with such subtlety.

'The report from my camp, your Grace, is that only the Turks could rejoice at our progress. What of it that my men routed a thousand of them three days ago on the road to Saint Simeon? They have more. Their walls stand as tall today as yesterday. And we bicker in our tents because we cannot scruple to let one man shine above the rest.'

He had advanced into the centre of the square now, pacing and turning as he addressed his audience. Of those faces I could see, none looked sympathetic. 'You know, Bishop Adhemar, that there can only be one head of the church. Why do we suffer many heads in our army, pulling in so many different directions that we tear apart?'

'We acknowledge one captain over our armies, and His name is Jesus Christ,' said Adhemar. 'Before the Lord, every one of us is equal. It would be the sin of Lucifer to over-reach God's order.'

'We acknowledge one Lord over our church. But we also acknowledge His ordination of a single man to govern that church, your master the Pope, the better to accomplish His divine purpose.'

That provoked mutterings among the council, particularly in Duke Godfrey's corner. Bohemond ignored them.

'Why, then, should one of us not have primacy, even for a short time, in directing our affairs? Let one who has distinguished himself in battle, whose army has proved itself time and again against the Turks, be appointed to break this city open before we are slaughtered.'

'And I suppose,' Count Raymond interrupted, 'that such a man might then claim the city as the fair spoils of his victory.'

'Why not? He would have earned it.'

That brought Tatikios to his feet, though it was Raymond again who spoke first. 'Have you forgotten your oath to the Emperor, Lord Bohemond? To restore all the lands of Asia that are rightfully his? Would you so happily perjure yourself to your greed?'

'When the Greek King comes in person to share our sufferings and our war, then perhaps he will earn the honouring of my promise. But for now, he sits in his palace surrounded by the eunuchs while we – all of us – fester and perish in misery.'

His words drew many nods of agreement, though not from Raymond or Bishop Adhemar. But at last Tatikios was able to speak.

'Perhaps, in the folly of youth, Lord Bohemond still believes that it is only the point of the sword, where blood is spilled, that matters. The wiser among you, my lords, will know that no sword will cut true without a strong hand on the hilt. If the Emperor Alexios does not share your burdens here it is because he campaigns in our rear, guarding our supply lines and preventing the Turks from surrounding us.'

'Where else would you find a Greek but in the rear?' Bohemond asked, to widespread laughter.

'Where else would you find a Norman but banging his head against impenetrable walls, too dull to notice he had tipped out his brains? If you had heeded my plan, to hold back from the city and choke it from afar, then you would not now waste your forces in fruitless attrition.'

'If the Emperor had sent the men he promised, we would have had the strength to take the city. His treachery consigns us to failure.'

'His generosity keeps you from dying of famine.'

Bishop Adhemar clapped his hands. 'Enough. Be seated – both of you,' he added, with a pointed glance at Bohemond. 'Quarrelling among allies will profit us nothing. You are right, Lord Bohemond, that the Turks rejoice at our lack of progress. But how much more would they rejoice if they could hear your quarrelling now.'

With an unrepentant sneer, curiously satisfied for one so rebuked, Bohemond seated himself in silence.

It had not been unforeseen. On the day we left Constantinople, the Emperor had gathered the princes together on the shores of the Bosphorus. It had reminded me of a fair or a market, for the air was sweet with the sounds of harps and lyres and laughter, the smells of blossom and roasting meat. At the top of the slope, beneath the high bluffs, the Emperor had caused pavilions to be erected, each sewn with the standards of the princes. I still remembered the stupefied grins on their faces as they emerged, each from his own tent, marvelling at the treasure that they had found within. Bishop Adhemar and our own Patriarch had celebrated the Eucharist on the beach, handing the cup to each of the princes in turn, and they had sworn that the blood of Christ would be as the blood of brothers among them. Ladies from the palace had woven their hair with garlands of gold which gleamed in the May sun, and the sea had sparkled with promise. Afterwards, after the feast, the Emperor had summoned them to a council.

'You have come far,' he announced. The purple walls of his tent glowed like embers, rippling in the fresh breeze. Inside, the air was close and warm. 'But the holy road to Jerusalem is longer still – and harder. You will need clean hearts and pure souls if your pilgrimage is to succeed, if the lands of Asia are to be reclaimed for Christendom. Remember that you walk in the footsteps of Christ: be strong as he was strong, but also merciful as he was merciful.'

He paused, sipping from a great golden chalice. I fancied that there was more grey in his beard now than there had been six months earlier, and a slight shrinking of the stout shoulders beneath the gems on his robe. Even the act of breathing seemed to spur a dull pain: for all the attention of Anna and the palace doctors, it was still only weeks since he had suffered an almost fatal spear wound.

'The cares of my people prevent me from leading you, and I would not steal the least portion of the glory that you will undoubtedly earn. But I send you off with as much food and gold as you require, with my strongest general' – Tatikios, seated to the Emperor's left, inclined his head – 'and also with some advice. Twenty miles inland from that far shore, my domains cease. Beyond, you will find only Ishmaelites. But do not make the mistake of thinking that all who wear turbans and pray to Mahomet are as one: between Nicaea and Jerusalem there are more tribes and factions than there are birds in the air. Every one of their emirs and atabegs eyes his neighbours with jealousy, and plots the increase of his own realm. Every city is a province, and every province a kingdom. There are not two brothers who do not conspire against each other. Learn their ways, their allegiances and their feuds, and exploit them. If they unite, they will sweep you from their shores like grains of sand; while they are divided, they can be conquered. Send embassies to the Fatimids of Egypt, if you can, for though they are Ishmaelites they are of a different race and creed, and will fight the Turks with more ferocity even than you.'

The Emperor paused again, surveying the barbarian faces. Standing at the back, I could not tell what he saw – the salvation of his empire, an army ordained by God, a troop of barbarian mercenaries – but it seemed to sadden him. His voice was slower when he spoke again.

'You are tens of thousands marching against hundreds of thousands. You will pass through trials and battles too terrible to imagine. Many of you will doubtless die, others will wish themselves dead. Whatever your suffering, remain constant to each other, and to our God. The Devil will seek to work division and hatred among you, and if he succeeds you will die in the dust of Anatolia. You are entering a desert, a wilderness of dangers and temptations. You must not succumb.'

Somewhere near the back of the tent, someone sniggered.

★   ★   ★

'Another fleet will come from Cyprus next week with grain,' Tatikios was saying.

'We will see that it feeds the hungriest first.' Bishop Adhemar turned to his right. Despite the crowding on the benches, there was one place where the princes had pushed apart, leaving a few inches of clear space flanking the figure in their midst. Even by the debased standards of the siege he was exceptionally filthy; his clothes were rags seemingly sewn together with grime. His bare feet were hairy and callused, the horny nails yellow, while his long, twisted face resembled a mule's more than a man's. He sat in his isolation hunched over, his eyes closed, muttering words which none could understand.

'You will distribute food to the pilgrims, Little Peter?' Adhemar asked.

The man's eyes flicked open, their blue pupils fixing on something invisible to the rest of the council. I felt unease course through the assembled princes.

'Blessed are those who hunger and thirst for right-eousness, for they will be filled.'

To look at him, you would have expected a braying voice, or perhaps a haggard croak, but when he opened his lips the words were gentle, sweet, as though he had been waiting all his life to say them. It was the sort of voice that made men want to listen, even if they did not understand what it said. Among the pilgrims he was worshipped as a saint, though when he had led his own army his innocent followers had been slaughtered in their thousands, convinced to the last that his spirit would ward off Turkish arrows. All the Franks paid him respect, even those who distrusted his power. For my part, I hated him.

He had shut his eyes again, but still held the gaze of the room. 'When the people are diminished and brought low, the Lord pours contempt on princes and makes them

51

wander in trackless wastes. But the needy he raises from their distress; he blesses them with a fruitful house.'

It seemed that he spoke to himself, almost in a whisper, yet his words were clear across the tent. Anger and fear flitted over the watching faces, but none dared speak. None save Adhemar.

'The day is tired, and the hour late.' He stood, and the rest of the assembly followed in grateful release. 'Sound rest and fresh hearts will profit us more than words tomorrow. My Lords, goodnight.'

A handful of priests and knights followed him out of the tent, while the other princes drifted into small groups of urgent conversation. Only Little Peter, the mystic, did not join them: he stayed seated on his bench, staring at Heaven and mumbling incoherently.

A broad shoulder interrupted my view as Bohemond appeared beside me. He gestured at my ivory writing tablet. 'Did you find much worthy of recording, Demetrios?'

'A scribe must listen and write; he does not have to judge.'

'Then have you found anything else worth recording since last we spoke? Anything to explain the death of my liegeman Drogo?'

I detailed what I had learned that day.

'So he was killed by a knightly blade, and not for gain if his purse was untouched. You do not think it was a Turk?'

'A Turk would have robbed him.'

Bohemond scratched his beard and affected to think, though there seemed little doubt behind those pale eyes. As I waited, my gaze drifting over the room, I thought I saw Count Raymond's single-eyed stare fixed suspiciously upon us, though he turned away as he saw me.

'You think this Provençal woman, this Sarah, might have been the cause of the feud?' Bohemond asked at last.

'It is possible.'

'A Norman knight and a Provençal woman. A dangerous union.' He swept his arm in a circle around us. 'You have seen tonight how fragile our allegiances are. The death of Drogo cannot be another wedge between us.'

Having witnessed the distrust, intrigue and venom in the tent, I doubted it would make much difference.

5

It was the next afternoon before my duties allowed me to seek the woman Sarah. As the path to the Provençal camp took me through the Norman lines, I risked a second visit to Drogo's tent. Sigurd and his men were working at the tower that day, but the need to know more of the dead man's companions drove me to attempt it alone.

The skeletal man still sat cross-legged opposite, the mud pressed smooth under his legs. He might never have moved since the previous morning, though he waved a ragged arm in greeting as I passed.

'Is Quino there?' I asked.

The old man shook his head.

I tried to resurrect the other names in my mind. 'Rainauld?'

He was not, but I must have spoken more loudly than I intended, for suddenly a voice behind me demanded: 'Who asks for Rainauld?'

'Demetrios Askiates, on behalf of the Lord Bohemond.'

The man who stood in the doorway of the tent seemed vaguely familiar – he had been with Quino at the cave, I thought, when they had reclaimed Drogo's body. Lying dazed on the floor I had not marked his appearance; even now there was something about him which seemed to shrink from observation. His legs were thin as a crow's, his arms little better, but it seemed to be the form of nature rather than starvation, for the rest of his body was as slight, bony and frail. Only the ebony black of his hair showed any evidence of health.

'You are the man who stole Drogo's body.' His voice was shrill, accusing.

'I am the man who would find Drogo's killer. Who are you?'

'Odard. A friend of Drogo.'

It seemed that I had not wasted my time coming here. I chose to be direct. 'Is there any man whom you suspect of his murder?'

He recoiled a little and glanced over his shoulder. His movements were as quick and graceless as Quino's, but while the larger man insinuated unpredictable strength this Odard showed only anxiety.

'Drogo was a strong knight, and pious. It would have taken a mighty enemy to overcome him.'

'He had neither sword nor armour. Who were his enemies?'

Odard wove his fingers together and pressed them into his stomach. 'Drogo was much loved. Only a Turk would have done such a thing.'

'But I believe he knew his killer. Was it a rival? An envious neighbour? A friend?'

Odard shook his head despairingly. 'None. None of them.' He sounded close to weeping, though my questions were mild enough.

'Do you know who killed him?' I persisted.

'No! Quino and I were building the tower by the bridge all that day. Only when we returned to the camp did I hear the rumours, that a company of Greeks had been seen with his body. I did not believe it until the lord Bohemond confirmed it – and when I saw the corpse in the cave.'

I knelt down and drew the 'S', the barbarian sigma, in the mud. 'Does this sign mean anything to you?'

'Nothing.'

'What of a cross carved in Drogo's back? Did you make the cut?'

'No.' Odard had wrapped his arms around himself in a feeble embrace, and rocked back and forth on his heels. 'No.'

'But you had seen it. You cannot have shared his tent so long without noticing it.'

'I had seen it.'

'Why did he disfigure himself so?'

'Drogo was a man of exceptional piety. He sought to know God in all His works, and to prove his devotion to the Lord. It is written:"Peace He brings through the blood of His cross."'

'Then perhaps he has found peace now. Did a woman named Sarah ever visit your tent?'

The question prompted fresh turmoil in Odard's expression. As if he had suffered a blow, he staggered back a few steps, then almost fell on the ground as he collided with a figure emerging from the door of his tent. It was the boy, Simon, looking almost as wretched as his master. The sight of me did nothing to cheer him.

'Get back in the tent,' Odard squeaked. 'Your clumsiness would shame a leper. And you, Master Greek: leave me to my peace. I do not know the men you seek. I do not know who killed my friend, nor why the Lord God chose to take so devoted a servant. Go.'

'I would value words with Rainauld, your other companion, before I go.'

Odard stamped his foot, squelching it in the damp earth. I feared the shock might break his stick of a leg. 'Rainauld is not here. He has not come back these two nights.'

'Two nights?' Suddenly, my mind was awash with suspicion. 'Not since Drogo's death.'

'Perhaps he wanders witless with grief. Perhaps he has gone to Saint Simeon for food. Perhaps he has returned to his kinsmen in the Provençal camp. Seek him there, if you must.'

In council, Count Raymond had been one of the few princes to speak in defence of Tatikios and the Emperor, but the enthusiasm did not extend to his Provençal army. Everywhere I turned among the endless rows of tents, his followers seemed to delight in refusing me. Some pretended not to understand my efforts at their language, for even among the Franks their dialect was considered outlandish, but I could see in their eyes that they understood me. Others directed me falsely, often to the mute or blind, while most just looked away when I spoke of Sarah or Rainauld.

Throughout the fruitless afternoon, my mood worsened. Rain started to fall again and I cursed myself for having attempted the errand with neither guide nor cloak. I tried to believe that sufficient time would eventually yield something, but as the hours wore on and the mud climbed up my legs I made no headway.

Eventually, in a forlorn corner of the camp near the river, something found me. I had been sent there by my last informant, who swore that a woman named Sarah lived there, but it was merely another ruse to mock me. There were few tents, none occupied, and by the smell in the air I guessed it was where the Provençals made their latrine. The river bank had been gouged out with the tracks of men and beasts going down to drink or defecate, and the ground was soggy with the rising melt water. I almost lost a boot in the mire. Glad at least of the solitude, I spent a couple of minutes watching the traffic on the road on the far bank. The men and horses were barely two hundred yards away, yet the green waters of the Orontes between us could have been an ocean.

I turned to go back, and stopped. The soft earth had

hushed their footsteps, and they had approached to within a stone's throw: five knights, swords hanging at their sides, unsmiling. They had spread out into a loose line before me, so that I could run nowhere save into the fast-flowing torrent of the river. I dropped my hand to my belt and fumbled for the knife that Sigurd had given me, but it would avail nothing against armed knights.

They halted a little distance away and eyed me grimly. 'Demetrios Askiates?' their leader challenged.

I tried to meet his gaze, though his eyes were in shadow under his helmet. 'I am Demetrios.'

'My lord the Count of Saint-Gilles will speak with you.'

As befitted the richest man in the army, Count Raymond had not spent the winter shivering in a leaky tent. He had made his billet in an abandoned farm in the midst of his camp, where the council had been held the night before. It was a crude building, its rubble walls bound with timber, but its roof tiles must have been sound enough. A thick plume of woodsmoke rose from the chimney, sharpening the air.

We crossed the courtyard formed by the house and the barn, threading our way between the grooms, heralds, horses and soldiers who thronged it. Two guards with long spears flanked the door, but they did not delay me. I ducked under the lintel, grateful to have relief from the rain outside, and found a stool in the dim room within. Tables and benches were pushed back against the walls, and the floor was covered with mouldering reeds. In the corner a fire hissed and crackled, though there were so many servants and petitioners gathered in the room that we could probably have warmed it ourselves.

After some minutes a scribe emerged from behind an oak door. All in the room fell silent and tensed themselves in hope as his gaze skimmed the assembled faces. I wondered whether he could distinguish one dirty, dark-haired, bearded face from another but his look settled on me and an arm reached out. 'You. Come.'

The inner room was much the same size as the first, though it seemed at least twice as spacious simply by its emptiness. On a wooden bed in one corner sat Bishop Adhemar in his red cap and cope; behind a table, staring at him with his single, unyielding eye was Count Raymond. He neither stood nor offered me a seat, but contented himself with a grunt.

'My men found you.'

'Yes, Lord.'

'Hah! More than they manage with the Turks. One of their spies broke into our camp and drove away seven horses last night. Many more and we will have to *walk* to Jerusalem.'

'Your garrison in the new tower will deter them,' suggested the Bishop. He made me uneasy, for I did not know what to expect from a prelate of the Latin church, yet his manner was calm, almost gentle.

'Little will deter the Turks while they see how feeble we are.' Raymond stood, and walked to a small window in the wall. Through it I could see the sheer slopes of Mount Silpius rising to the clouds. 'Doubtless the thieves will be back tomorrow dressed as merchants, to sell our own beasts back to us and observe our strength. Wine?'

I was slow to realise that he was offering the drink to me, and fumbled my words trying to accept too hastily. His face twitched with impatience, unbalancing my thoughts still further, and it was only once a servant had brought two cups that I began to settle. The wine was warm, and I gulped it like a camel. It had been many months since I had enjoyed such luxury.

'Sit,' said Raymond. There were no other seats, so I had to perch on an unsteady leather saddle beside the door.

'You are working for Bohemond. He wishes you to discover who killed the Norman Drogo.'

I could not tell if these were questions or accusations. I answered with an indistinct murmur.

'Do you know why he would have you do this?' The count stroked a finger over his cheek. Almost uniquely among the Franks, he had continued to shave throughout the siege, but he often allowed his beard to grow as far as a silvered stubble, as though iron sprouted from his very skin. 'Do you guess his purpose?'

The eye fixed me with a hostile stare.

'I . . . He is keen that there should be no unanswered crimes to fester among the army,' I stammered, clenching my hand about the cup.

'Of course. Bohemond's care for the unity of the army is well known. Doubtless you noticed it at the council last night.'

'I . . .'

'He would see the armies united under a single general. Whom do you suppose he intends?'

I struggled for an answer that would not draw contempt, but the count sneered at my delay and continued unchecked. 'The mightiest?' Raymond thumped a fist against his chest. 'The holiest?' He pointed to the Bishop 'No. That Norman upstart, whose own father deemed him unworthy of the least inheritance, would subordinate the armies of the greatest lords in Christendom to his ambition. And why?'

'The better to prosecute our war against the Turks?' I hazarded, sinking under the onslaught of his bile.

He pushed himself out of his chair and leaned forward across the table. 'If you believe that, Master Greek, then Drogo's killer can indeed sleep peacefully. Bohemond is a brigand, a pirate like his bastard ancestors. He has already tried to seize your country; when that failed, he rebelled against his own brother.' He gestured to the window. 'Look out there. An impregnable city, a fertile valley, a port at the mouth of the river and command of the spice roads east. Who would not want this for his kingdom?'

'Would you?' I asked. It was an unthought response, and I regretted it the moment I said it, yet its temerity seemed to provoke some spark of respect in Raymond. He seated himself, and waved the servant to splash more wine into my cup. When he spoke again, it was with more restraint.

'I am master of thirteen counties, Duke of Narbonne and Marquis of Provence. In my own country I am Caesar, and I have earned my due: now I am willing to render the Lord God His. Of course I would covet Antioch for myself, but I do not forget the oath I swore to your Emperor to return the lands that are rightfully his. I will not dishonour my oath while I wear the Lord's cross.'

The bishop, who had attended our conversation in silence, now stirred. 'Bohemond swore the same oath.'

Raymond snorted. 'And you trust him? To Bohemond, oaths are mere vessels for his ambition.'

'There is still Tatikios to watch him,' I said.

Whatever regard I had earned from Raymond vanished. 'How many men does your eunuch have? A thousand? Half that?'

'Three hundred,' I admitted.

'Bohemond has ten times that number. And there would be more than just his army to oppose you. The men of Flanders, Normandy, and Lorraine would stand beside him – even among my own Provençals, your Emperor is not well-loved.'

I thought back on my afternoon of scorn and misery in Raymond's camp, and nodded.

'Could you defy Bohemond if he claimed the city?' Raymond taunted me.

Adhemar stirred again. 'You are lucky, Demetrios, that

61

the Count of Saint-Gilles honours his duty to the Emperor so.' His bearded face was solemn, yet even with the foreign words I thought I sensed a current of humour, as though he teased Raymond.

The count scowled. 'I *do* honour my duty, Bishop. To the Emperor, to Pope Urban, and to God. But I need not answer for it to a Greek hireling. I summoned you to speak of Drogo. You have discovered – or perhaps Bohemond has graciously told you – that one of his companions was a Provençal, Rainauld of Albigeois?'

'Yes.'

'And doubtless by the same effort you have discovered that the man has not been seen since Drogo's death.'

I had, though I was more intrigued by how Raymond came to know it.

'What do you infer by it, you whom Bohemond hired for your secret wisdom?'

I paused, feeling the full force of Raymond's eye on me. Even Adhemar watched with interest.

'He would seem a likely culprit,' I conceded.

'He would even now have undergone the ordeal of fire, if only he could be found. Did you know he was one of my men?'

'I thought he served Lord Bohemond.'

'He does now. He lost his horse at Albara, and afterwards had to fight on foot. I would have found him a new mount eventually, but Bohemond offered one sooner, so he sold his allegiance to the Normans.' Raymond swirled the wine in his cup. 'Bohemond delights in stealing my men, and the winter has sent many opportunities.'

There was silence as I considered this news. 'What would it profit Bohemond if Rainauld had killed Drogo?'

'Are you such a fool? I may have a single eye, Askiates, but it seems that I see more clearly than you. If a Provençal, even one who has left my service, has murdered a Norman, then Bohemond will use it to diminish me. My army will not mutiny, and my priests will not excommunicate me, but when I speak in the council my voice will weigh less with other men. Whatever lessens my authority benefits him – that is his purpose.' Raymond stabbed a finger heavy with rings at me. 'And you, Greek, you are his willing pawn.'

I looked to Adhemar, but his head was bowed in prayer.

$$\zeta$$

Tatikios was in a peevish humour that evening, and spent an hour dictating another petition for relief to the Emperor. Christ help us, I thought, if the Franks ever saw the correspondence. It was well after dark before I was able to return to my tent, damp and famished, to see what humble supper awaited me. Anna and Sigurd were there, with a few Varangians clustered around a single candle. The shadows were deep in the canopy above.

'Welcome to my mead hall,' said Sigurd mirthlessly. 'Have you found out who killed the Norman?'

I lowered myself onto the ground and took the wooden bowl that Anna passed to me. The broth in it was long cold, and the only trace of meat seemed to be the scum of fat on its surface.

'One of the companions who shared his tent has been missing for two days. Even you, Sigurd, might guess something was suspicious from that.'

Sigurd waved his crooked knife at me, but before he could retort Anna was speaking.

'If one Norman killed another then there is hardly reason for you to involve yourself. Bohemond must be satisfied – has he paid you?'

After my conversation with Count Raymond, I was no longer so certain what would satisfy Bohemond. 'The man was not a Norman – he was a Provençal who had taken service with Bohemond.'

'Hah.' Sigurd's knife flashed in the candlelight as he held it up and licked the crumbs off it. I looked for the bread it had cut, but in vain. 'Bohemond did not hire you to prove that his Normans were ill-disciplined barbarians intent on murdering each other. That we knew. There is an answer he wants you to find, Demetrios, and my guess is that he already knows it far better than you.'

'And what of it?' Anna interrupted. Though there were men present, she had unwrapped the *palla* from her head so that her black hair hung loose behind her neck. It shimmered in the candlelight, but her face was firm with anger. 'What does it matter if it was a Norman or a Provençal or a Turk or even a Nubian who killed that man? Bohemond and Raymond and the other princes have killed far more men by their impatience and ambition.'

'This is a war, and men die in it,' said Sigurd.

'Of course men die in war. But it should not be because we gorged ourselves when there was plenty, and now suffer famine. Where were the princes five months ago, when our gravest danger was gluttony? Before the orchards were reduced to firewood?'

She looked around, challenging us to argue, but there were none in that group who would defend the Franks. Besides, it was the truth. When we had arrived at Antioch, the land had been fat with fruit: trees bowed with apples and pears, vines dripping grapes, pits and granaries bursting with the newly gathered harvest in every village. Within two months, the fertile plain had become a wasteland. No animals grazed the fields or sat in their barns for they had all been slaughtered, and our horses had devoured the winter hay. The granaries had been ransacked until not one seed remained, and the withered vines had been gathered and burned. We had plagued the land without thought for the future, and the greasy soup now in my hands was our reward.

'It was not even that their strategy was frustrated,' Anna

continued. 'There was no plan then for getting into Antioch, any more than there is now.'

'Enough.' I raised my arms in barely exaggerated horror. 'I have just spent an hour hearing Tatikios make the same complaints.'

'Perhaps they expected God to deliver them,' Sigurd suggested. 'They seem to know His mind uncommonly well.'

I thought of Drogo's naked body in the cave, the long cross scarred into his back. I thought of all the others whom I had seen make similar professions on their bodies, knights and pilgrims alike. 'You cannot deny their piety.'

Sparks spat into the gloom as Sigurd rasped his knife against a stone. 'When the Norman bastard came to conquer England he carried a banner of the cross – a personal gift from the Pope in Rome – and the relics of two saints. If you had seen what the Normans did to my country in the name of their church, you would not acclaim their piety.'

'And the most pious of them all is that dwarfish hermit,' Anna added. 'The man who led ten thousand pilgrims to their death, all the while promising them they were invulnerable. That is the sort of piety they practise. They forget that reason and will are divine gifts no less than faith.'

There were times when I thought that Anna had spent so long peering at the blood and flesh of men that she neglected the spiritual realms, yet I never came away the winner when I challenged her.

Sigurd must have seen the darkness that crossed my face. 'Better not to mention the dwarf priest who orphaned Thomas.'

It was a kind thought, though too late. Thomas was my son-in-law, a Frankish boy whose parents had followed Little Peter to their doom in his expedition against the Turks. After the massacre, a series of misadventures had at last led Thomas to my house. Gratitude for my hospitality – not least for my daughter, though I had not known it then – had driven him to betray his countrymen in the Frankish army, after which I could deny him neither my daughter nor a place in the Varangian guards. He had married Helena three days before I crossed into Asia, at a small church in the city. I had ached to give her up, even to a man who had saved my life, and ached doubly to leave them so soon afterwards. But Thomas was safest where the Franks were furthest away and by staying he had at least saved himself the horrors of march and siege. The Army of God had left too many young widows already: I did not need Helena added to their number.

Sigurd was watching me. 'Has Thomas sent word recently? Have you become a grandfather yet?'

I shrugged, though the question weighed keenly on me. 'There has been nothing from Constantinople in weeks. Winter has closed the passes, and who knows what storms have wracked the coasts?'

A frown of concern was on Anna's face. 'The child will come any day now. I should be there.'

'Helena will be perfectly safe.' Though Sigurd's voice never lacked force, this time I thought he seemed a little too insistent. 'You will worry Demetrios needlessly if you think otherwise. Helena will have her sister present, and her aunt, and probably a legion of other women to assist the birthing.'

Anna nodded, though to my mind it was without conviction. I knew she fretted about my daughter's child, so much so that she could not hide it from me. It did nothing to soothe the tension every man feels when faced with the mysteries of birth. Nor could I forget the sight of Maria, my late wife, lying white in a lake of her own blood as she tried to bear me a third child. She was often in my dreams now.

Anna stroked my cheek, her expression now recomposed. 'Helena will be well protected,' she said. 'Thomas will see to it.'

'If he hasn't beheaded himself trying to wield his axe,' said Sigurd, trying – in his own fashion – to lighten the mood.

With a glance at how low the candle had burned, Anna rose. 'I should return to my tent. No doubt the sick and the hungry will be there before dawn, seeking succour.'

A glance passed between us: mine half pleading, hers half regret. Perhaps in a different year we would have been married by now, but I had not wanted to diminish Helena's wedding with another ceremony so soon afterwards. Then we had left for war, where marriage seemed inappropriate, and so we lived more like brother and sister than husband and wife. Though not entirely without error.

'I will see you tomorrow.'

The next day I went again to look for the missing Rainauld, and the following day as well, but each time there was nothing. On the third day I did discover something of him, though not from his friends. Instead, I found an Ishmaelite waiting at his tent. I saw him from some distance as I approached, and was instantly confused, for he neither skulked like a spy nor guarded himself like a merchant. He stood alone outside Drogo's tent, his turbaned head proclaiming his faith to all yet apparently careless of his safety.

'Demetrios Askiates?' he asked as I drew near. It took me a moment to realise that he had spoken in Greek.

'Who are you?'

'I am Mushid, the swordsmith.'

'A Turk?'

'An Arab.' In addition to the white turban knotted over his head, he was dressed humbly in a brown robe with a red belt. His dark-skinned face was unlined by age and framed by a beard whose hair was black as tar. It was a little longer than mine, and split in the middle where it had grown unevenly, but otherwise he might have passed for a Greek. His brown eyes were clear and round, with neither malice nor fear disfiguring them.

'You're brave. Not many Saracens would walk unarmed into this camp.'

He smiled, his teeth very white. 'A swordsmith is never unarmed.' He tapped his hip, and I heard the rap of something solid under the robe. 'I do not provoke battle, but I defend myself if it comes.'

His voice was light, and his smile constant, yet something in his words made me wonder how much more steel was hidden under the plain cloth. 'How did you know my name?'

'They say you come here every day. They say you are looking for the man who killed Drogo of Melfi.'

He did not explain who 'they' might be, and I did not ask. There was no shortage of 'them' in the camp. 'What do you know of Drogo?'

'When he was penniless, he sold his sword to eat. Then, when his fortunes improved, he needed another blade. I made it for him. Later we became friends. He had lost a brother – and mine too died last year. When they told me he was dead, I . . .' For the first time, he seemed to hesitate over his words. 'I was sad.'

'When did you see him last?'

'A week ago. On the day he died, I think.'

'Where? What time?' Suddenly I was alive with hope. Bohemond had promised to ask through his army whether anyone had seen Drogo in the hours before he died, but thus far none had admitted it. Doubtless they feared blame. If this swordsmith had met him, he must have been among the last to see him living.

'On the road, at about the ninth hour – three hours past noon. He was happy with me; his new sword had slain three Turks in the battle the previous day.'

'Did he say where he was going? Whom he purposed to meet?'

'He had been at the mosque, building your tower. He felt guilty that you had desecrated the dead.' The swordsmith fixed me with an earnest stare. 'Even in war, the dead should be honoured.'

'He did not say where he was going?'

'I did not ask. I thought he went back to the camp – where else?'

'Indeed.' I paused, feeling certain that I should put more questions to this Saracen who had fallen across my path, who might remember something significant of that afternoon. To fill the silence, I asked: 'What do your fellow Ishmaelites think of you, that you sell the blades by which they die?'

The swordsmith shrugged. 'What they say in their thoughts, they keep there. What they speak with their tongues is that trade affords no enemies. Many, after all, supply the food which sustains you, the horses you ride to battle. Why not your weapons?' He laughed. 'Besides, we are not all as one in Islam because we all wear turbans and beards.' He jerked his head towards the triple peak of Mount Silpius, and the walls that ringed it. 'The Turks in the city, they are *Ahl al-Sunna*. I am of the *Shi'at 'Ali*, like the Fatimids of Egypt. We believe differently – as *Rum* and *Franj* do.'

'The Byzantines and Franks are united in Christ,' I protested, though I knew it to be scarcely true.

Mushid frowned. 'But you believe it is ordained to eat leavened bread, not unleavened. And that your priests should marry. And that . . .'

I held up my hand. 'Enough. I am neither monk nor

theologian. Indeed, I wonder if you know more of my religion than I do.'

'Only two kinds of the Nazarenes pass through my country: merchants and pilgrims. I speak with both, and learn their ways.'

'And you are of a different faith to the Turks? A different party of Ishmaelites?' I could not quite comprehend how I had come to debate religion with a Saracen swordsmith outside Drogo's tent, but I remembered the Emperor's exhortation to learn their divisions.

'Our differences would seem as obscure to you as yours do to me. Yet they can bring us to war against each other. The Fatimids of Egypt have fought the Turks for decades.'

'And you are one of them?'

'No. I—'

He broke off as a figure in mail came striding up between the rows of tents. With a coif about his neck and a helmet on his head, he was almost unrecognisable, but there was something familiar in the sharp, snapping move-ment of his limbs. Behind him, I could see the boy Simon leading a grey palfrey.

'You,' he barked, raising a gloved fist. The voice was Quino's. 'I ordered you never to come here again.'

For a moment both Mushid and I hesitated, neither sure whom he addressed. As he drew too near to ignore I said at last, 'I was seeking Rainauld.'

'Rainauld is gone. Do not use him as your excuse for spying. I have been out on the plain harrying Turkish foragers; what have you done, Greek? Nothing but prying and lying, I would say.'

'Prying where the lord Bohemond sends me.'

'And you,' he continued, turning to Mushid. 'Do not come here.' Twisting awkwardly in his armour, he pulled the helmet from his head and fixed the Arab with a look of pure venom. As he disappeared through the flaps of the tent, I heard him shouting for the boy to attend him or feel the flat of his sword.

I glanced at Mushid. His eyes registered neither anger nor fear, but only sadness. 'Quino seems as fond of you as he is of me,' I said.

Mushid gave a small laugh. 'He and Drogo suffered many adventures together. I think Quino was jealous of our friendship – and I am, of course, infidel. He did not like me. I thought—'

For the second time that afternoon, our words were interrupted by a sudden arrival. We did not see him coming, for he burst around the edge of the tent and ran almost straight into Mushid. It was a Norman, a thin man whom I did not recognise. His tunic was dark with sweat, and he could barely gasp out: 'Quino. Is Quino here? Or Odard?'

I nodded my head at the tent. 'In there.'

'Why?' asked Mushid.

If the Norman was surprised to be questioned by an Arab in the heart of the Christian camp, the urgency of his errand drowned it. 'It is Rainauld. They have found him.'

I knew the moment he spoke that it was not good news. From the land of the missing, the living 'reappear' or 'return'. Only the dead are 'found'.

'Where?' I demanded, snatching the Norman's arm before he could enter the tent. 'Where is he?'

'In an orchard, near the Alexandretta road.'

I did not wait for Quino to emerge, but started running. It was a full two miles to the road, through the Lotharingian and Fleming lines, across the shifting timbers of the boat bridge, and up the far slope of the valley to the first ridge. My lungs burned with the effort, and my enfeebled limbs could barely keep me upright after so many months of hunger. I had to stop at the road and bend double to try and restore some order to my body.

As soon as I looked up, though, it was plain where I should go. There were as many wayfarers and draught animals on the road as ever, but a little way along a great number seemed to be drifting from the path, drawn up the hill by some invisible power.

'That must be the way,' said a voice beside me.

I looked to my left, to see Mushid staring up the road. I had not noticed him following me, but the run did not seem to have troubled him much.

'I think I see the orchard.'

He ran on, and I forced myself after him. My bones felt empty, my sinews tight as bowstrings, but I managed to keep sight of him as we sprinted along the road and then up the scrubby slope. The broken ground was treacherous, not least because I could not summon sufficient care to look where my feet fell, but at length it flattened into a terrace cut out of the hillside. Once it had perhaps supported a grove of apple trees, but now there were only stumps and wild grasses. At the far end, where a low wall of broken stone embanked the hill, a crowd several score strong had gathered.

I pushed my way through the gaunt faces, feeling the cruel hope abound in them. Like our pagan ancestors in the amphitheatres of old, they had come for death. They would not be disappointed.

When I had first seen Drogo's body I had seen no marks of violence: here, the violence was everywhere, splashed across the tawny grass and the weathered stones of the wall. I stepped forward, past the anonymous safety of the ringed crowd and into the human arena they had created. Before me, a solitary man knelt on the ground, blood covering his arms as far as his elbows. I did not recognise him, though his ragged tunic made him look more a pilgrim than a knight. With one hand, he jerked a knife at the surrounding throng.

'I killed him,' he shouted defiantly. 'I claim him.'

I stopped, overwhelmed by the confession and the dizzied pounding in my head. The air about me seemed suddenly dark.

'Why did you kill him?' I asked.

'I have not eaten in nine days,' he shrieked. 'I hunted him, and I slew him.'

'What?' I could not comprehend this.

With a grim cackle, never taking his gaze from his audience, the man reached into the grass and raised the corpse to view. The breath that had clung in my throat at last escaped. Hanging from his hand, its mangy fur matted black with blood, was the lifeless body of a wild dog.

'With this knife I killed him,' the man shouted. He plunged his knife into the dog's belly, and a fresh trickle of fluid oozed out. 'See? See?'

A wave of jealous hunger seethed through the crowd, and they began to press forward. No wonder the pilgrim was so desperate; they would never let him keep the meat for himself.

But I had no interest in battling for a dog's carcass – or at least, my will to find Rainauld was stronger. 'Where is the Norman?' I called, keeping clear of the pilgrim so as not to provoke him. 'Did you find him too?'

'Over here.'

I looked around. A little distance away, unnoticed by the famished crowd, Mushid was standing by the stone wall. As the man and his dog disappeared in the mob, I squeezed through to see what he had found. A low brick archway was set in the wall to allow drainage, its mouth almost entirely obscured by weeds and flowers. The Arab was squatting before it, pulling back the foliage to allow in more light. As I joined him, I wished he had preserved it in darkness.

There was no blood, but that was no mercy. The corpse that lay under the crumbling vault must have been there for days. Wild animals had ripped the clothes from it, chewing and tearing terrible rents from the body. What flesh remained was black and swollen; his limbs lay splayed out at unnatural angles, while the smell in the untouched air of the culvert was unbearable. I could not number the dead or dying I had seen in the past months, but they were nothing compared with this horror. I staggered away, and gasped out what little was in my stomach onto a patch of poppies.

When I turned back, a small crowd had gathered by the arch. I recognised Quino's compact shape and half a dozen other Normans in armour. Two of them held the hapless pilgrim who had killed the dog, while the rest watched a trio of men-at-arms drag Rainauld's body into the open. Mushid, prudently, had vanished.

Quino had his back to me, his face hidden, but I could see clearly as he slammed a fist into the pilgrim's cheek. 'What did you do?' he hissed. 'Why did you kill him?'

The man groaned, and spat blood onto the ground. 'Please,' he mumbled. 'Please. I found him. The dog led me to him. I did not touch him. Please, my Lord, have mercy. I have not eaten in nine days. I have not—'

I stepped forward. 'He did nothing, Quino. Look at the body. It has been there for days – weeks, even.'

Such was the anger on Quino's face as he spun around that I was driven backwards a pace. His voice, though, was almost imperceptibly soft. 'You would do well to go far from this place, Greek. Two of my closest companions, my brothers, lie dead, and each time it is you who finds them. Next time it will be you who feeds the crows and carrion-eaters. I, Quino of Melfi, swear it.'

75

'Demetrios is charged by me to find who killed your companion. You will not hinder him.'

I looked up to the voice which had spoken above us. He sat atop a warhorse so white that it was almost blasphemous in this place of death, so tall that even its saddle was above the height of my eyes. It was Bohemond. At his side an attendant carried the red banner emblazoned with the silver serpent, while behind him a company of mounted knights pushed back the crowd of onlookers.

'You,' said Bohemond, pointing to the pilgrim still held by Quino's men. 'You found the body?'

'Yes, Lord.' The man was weeping openly, though whether from gratitude or fear or horror none could tell. 'I was hunting a dog. Please, my Lord, I have not eaten in nine days.'

'Then you will eat tonight.' Bohemond reached into the velvet bag on his belt, and tossed something glittering at the man's feet. The guards let him go as he fell to snatch it.

'Is the corpse Rainauld of Albigeois?'

Quino, his face contorted with anger, nodded. 'So far as any man can tell.'

'Turn him over.'

One of Bohemond's knights rode forward and slid the end of his lance under the corpse until it toppled onto its back. Narrowing my eyes, as if by doing so I might diminish the sight, I peered at it. Thankfully, I did not have to look long for the cause of his death. Plunged into his chest at the centre of a bloom of dried blood, I could see the leather-bound stump of a knife handle.

Bohemond saw it too. 'What do you say, Demetrios? Did he do this himself?'

The final, guilt-ridden act of a murderer? 'I cannot say,' I answered truthfully.

For a moment, Bohemond said nothing. His face was

76

tied in concentration; he did not seem to notice as his horse skittered beneath him. At last: 'Bury him. I will think on this in the night, and pray for God's wisdom. Attend me in the morning, Demetrios.'

He rode away, and I followed him towards the road, keeping among the knots of men and women drifting back to the camp. If Quino discovered me alone, I doubted Bohemond's name would be any shield.

As I walked, I chiselled at my thoughts, trying to shape them into some more familiar form. Rainauld had not been seen since Drogo's death, and though that was now six days previous my every sense insisted that his death was linked to Drogo's. Whether it had happened before or after Drogo's, and by his own hand or another's, I could not know. Whether Rainauld had lain in that vault for two days or six was an equal mystery, though the decay of his body seemed to bespeak an earlier death. The sight was something I would yearn to forget, but amid the rot and scavenging and torn clothes, I was certain that I had seen something significant. A mark on his back as the Norman turned him. The shiny, puckered skin of a cross-shaped scar.

η
_____

My dreams left me little rest that night and each time I awoke I longed for Anna's embrace to warm my shivering fears. In the morning I rose early and made for Bohemond's tent. The chill in the air spurred my steps, but I had no enthusiasm: I feared he would demand many more answers than I could supply. Nor was I even sure what answers he desired, for his shock at the discovery of Rainauld's body had appeared entirely genuine. If Sigurd and Count Raymond were right, if my role had merely been to name Rainauld as Drogo's murderer, what then? Would he have me declare that Rainauld slew his friend and then killed himself in a frenzy of guilt? I was not sure that I could say so – but neither was I certain that I could insist on perpetuating doubt so damaging to the army.

As so often, my worries were wasted. Bohemond's banner was gone from outside his tent, and the lone guard was brusque in his dismissal.

'There were reports of Turkish raiders in the mountains: Bohemond has gone to seek them. He will not return before nightfall.'

Relief and disappointment mingled in my heart. I had not wanted to confront Bohemond, with his persuasive ways and hidden purposes, but without him I was left adrift. I could not speak to Quino without fear for my life, and I could not seek Odard without risk of seeing Quino. Inspecting tents for leakage with Tatikios attracted me little better. Unthinkingly, I left the Norman camp and walked down to the river.

The Orontes was largely deserted at that hour, save for a few women sitting on rocks upstream, rinsing their laundry where the water was not yet fouled with the effluence of our camp. A few blackened twigs poked out from the surface where they had been twisted into a fish trap, while on the far bank a pair of children tried their luck with lengths of twine. They must have baited their hooks with leaves, for food was too scarce to risk in the river. Otherwise the water flowed on implacably, black as the clouds hanging overhead. I sat on a rock and watched it pass, keeping my back to the looming mountain which overshadowed all behind me.

The minutes passed. Damp began to seep into my cloak; the figures on the opposite shore cast and recast their lines without success. A flock of birds wheeled overhead and a bough from an olive tree drifted down the river, spinning lazily in midstream. Suddenly, I heard a scrabbling sound from beneath the bank. As I watched, a grimy pair of hands reached over the rim and grasped a tree root which the flood waters had exposed. A shock of black hair followed, then a face so dirty that it was unrecognisable, and finally the whole dripping body. He was naked, yet his modesty was preserved by the extraordinary quantity of mud that clung to him. Was this how Adam had looked when the Lord first breathed life into him? For a moment he was oblivious to my presence, reaching under the root to pull out a folded tunic, but as he turned he yelped and almost tumbled back into the river. My own surprise was hardly less.

'Simon,' I said, conjuring the name as I at last recognised the face beneath the dirt.

'What?' He was bent forward as though he had been kicked in the groin, one hand protecting his privacy. He edged backwards, trying to work his way behind a low boulder. As a servant, in a camp with few partitions, he surely could not be so squeamish. Perhaps he had believed the endless Norman jibes about the vices of the Greeks.

'Dress yourself,' I told him. I made great show of prising a few pebbles from the earth and watching them skip across the water while he pulled on his tunic. Lines of mud were streaked across it.

'What were you doing?' I asked. 'The current is strong – you could have been swept all the way to the sea at Saint Simeon. Can you swim?'

He shook his head. Water sprayed from his ragged locks as off a dog. In his hand, I noticed, he clasped a wilted bunch of green plants.

'What are those?'

'Mine!' The fear as he recoiled at the question was evident. 'They grow in the river bank, in places few can see.'

'I do not want your herbs,' I assured him, though it was hard to hide my hunger. I could smell onion grass, and wild sage; the aromas were like hot coals in my stomach. 'I want to speak with you.'

His gaze darted over my shoulder, back towards the Norman camp. 'If I speak with you, Quino will beat me. He swore it.'

'Did he?' If there were secrets that Quino wanted hidden then I especially wanted to hear them. 'What will he do if he learns you gather food in his ignorance? That you keep it from him?'

'He . . .'

'I am charged by Bohemond, your master's lord, to discover all I can concerning Drogo's death. Two men from that tent are now dead, and the longer that rumours persist the worse it will be for all of us. Tell me what you know, and Bohemond will see that no harm befalls you.'

'What do I know?' A tear cut a pale scar through the mud on his cheek. 'If I knew who killed my master, would I hide it?'

'A man may unwittingly know more than he believes. And a servant hears much. Tell me the truth.'

Simon sniffed, and wiped his arm across his face. 'You sound like Drogo. He often spoke of truth.'

'Yes? He was devout? There is no shame speaking of your master's virtues,' I encouraged him.

'He prayed often. Especially after his brother died. He — he was different after that.'

'How so?

'There was a burden on his soul. We all suffered on the march, and here at Antioch, but always it seemed that he suffered more.'

'He was not an easy man to serve,' I suggested.

'He was fair.' Simon looked down at his feet, so that his hair curtained his face. 'I think . . . I think perhaps a demon assailed him.'

'A demon?' I echoed, astonished. 'Did you see it?'

Simon's voice was now a whisper, yet it beat with the urgency of confession. 'Often in the night I heard him wrestle with it. He called out to the Lord God, begging him to see truthfully, but the demon blinded him to light.'

'The cross!' I exclaimed, my mind fusing together two thoughts. 'The cross on his back. Was that part of his penance? His struggle with the demon?'

Simon lifted his head and stared at me. A few solitary hairs hung forlorn from his chin: he must have been trying to grow his beard in mimicry of his elders, yet the effect was only to make him seem younger. 'How do you know of the cross on his back?'

'I saw his corpse. And I know that Rainauld bore the same mark. Did Quino and Odard carry it too?'

The boy did not move, yet still he seemed to shrink. 'I

do not know how the mark came to be there. It was in December, near the feast of Saint Nicholas. All four returned to the tent one night with their backs bound in bandages. Next morning, when they dressed, I saw the sign of the cross seeping through. I thought it was a miracle, that God had favoured them.'

'Did you find out how it happened?'

'They never spoke of it. Once I asked my master. I thought he would want to celebrate such a sign of divine grace, but he beat me with a stirrup. I did not ask again.'

Behind him the river flowed its course. The two boys opposite had given up their fishing, and were now throwing rocks at some piece of debris floating on the water. A crow flew down and perched on the fish trap.

'Had they suffered any arguments in the past weeks? Had one taken against the others? Did they quarrel – over food, perhaps, or spoils? Or a woman?'

Simon's gaze dropped again. 'There was no quarrel.'

'A disagreement?' As he spoke, I had heard the sharp edges of words carefully chosen.

'No.'

'But there was some discord among them.'

'There was . . . anger.' Still refusing to meet my gaze, Simon reached up and pulled a piece of dried mud from his skin. It came away smooth as a scab.

'Why?'

'I do not know!'

I had grown so used to Simon's mumbling and whispering that his sudden shout stunned me. The crow on the fish trap fluttered squawking into the air.

'Five weeks ago they went to Daphne. They were gone all day. When they came back, they were different. They would not speak to each other, but cursed me for every straw that was out of place in their beds. I have never seen Quino so angry.' Simon trembled as the torrent of words poured out of him. 'After that day, they did not often come in the tent together. They ate apart, and chose different watches. I rarely saw Quino and Odard – that was good. Drogo found other friends.'

'A swordsmith?' I hazarded.

Simon looked at me curiously. 'A swordsmith, yes. He was a Saracen, an Ishmaelite. It was another thing to make Quino angry.'

'And they never spoke of what had passed at Daphne?'

'Never. One or two times, I heard Rainauld mention a house of the sun. I think it was a place they had been that day, for always it drew the same silence from the others.'

'"The house of the sun." It meant nothing to you?'

'Nothing.'

He paused, looking at the wilting herbs in his fist. 'I should go back. Quino is not as good a master as Drogo.'

'Come with me.' I spoke on impulse: I did not know how I could pay the boy, and I could not even feed myself, but the pain in his face was more than I could ignore. I took his arm. 'Come and serve me, and I will see you are kept safe from Quino's rages.'

He shook free of my grasp. 'I am bound to Quino. If I left him, he would think it a betrayal. His vengeance would be unforgiving. I must go.'

At that I wanted to snatch him by the shoulder and drag him away from the Normans. But I resisted the impulse. However miserable the fate he chose, I could not compel him. 'A final question. Did you ever see a woman named Sarah visit Drogo?'

Simon's head jerked up like a rabbit's; his stare fixed on my face, then swiftly switched to my boots. 'Never.'

He was lying, I was sure of it, but I could not in conscience risk causing more delay and provoking Quino's wrath. I watched him run across the field, back towards the grey ranks of canvas, and wondered what malevolent power swayed the occupants of that cursed tent.

That evening I went to see Tatikios. The lamplight was bright on the gilded fabric of the room, but he was in a dark mood. He paced before his ebony chair, muttering to himself and constantly darting glances towards the door. In every corner a Patzinak stood holding a spear.

'Demetrios,' the eunuch snapped. 'Did you see anyone outside the door?'

'None worth remarking. Why?'

'Bohemond came here. He warned that sentiment in the armies turns against us.'

Irreverently, I thought that Tatikios ought to find a goldsmith to recast his golden nose in a more imposing form. At present it only served to make him seem petulant.

'The Franks have ever been jealous of our civilisation,' I answered. 'When the war goes amiss, it is natural that they blame us.'

'My position is impossible.' Tatikios had not paid me the least attention. 'The barbarians blame me because the Emperor does not join their siege, but I can achieve nothing. With less than half a legion at my disposal I am forced to follow a strategy I did not recommend. And the Emperor is deaf to my pleas for aid.'

I thought back to the courtyard in the palace. *When you make allies of your enemies, every battle is a victory.* Whom did the Emperor truly wish to see broken by the siege, I wondered?

'I am between Scylla and Charybdis,' the eunuch continued. 'And now Bohemond warns that the barbarians may purpose violence against us.'

'Did he name any conspirators?'

'No.'

'Then it is nothing more than gossip. I walk daily

through the Norman camps and I see the hatred they bear us. That does not mean they will slit our throats in our beds.'

Tatikios slumped into his chair. 'This is no place for a general of Byzantium. I should be at the Emperor's side in the queen of cities, or commanding great armies on the frontiers. Belisarios did not conquer Africa with three hundred mercenaries and a horde of murderous barbarians. Will my exploits here ever be carved on the great gate of the palace, or lofted high on a column? I do not think so.'

He fell into silence. After a minute to allow his self-pity free rein, I said: 'I would like to take a troop of Varangians to Daphne tomorrow. There may be food there as yet untouched.'

Tatikios waved an arm dismissively. 'As you wish, Demetrios. We will not need the men here. The city will not fall tomorrow, nor any other day if this course persists. Go to Daphne, if you will. I doubt that you will find anything.'

θ
―――

We had to walk to Daphne, Sigurd and I and a dozen
Varangians, for our horses were too few and feeble
to waste. We passed the new mound opposite the bridge,
where two wooden towers had now risen on the rubble
of the cemetery, and followed the Saint Simeon road
south-west until we had left the city well behind us. By
a plane tree a path forked down to the ford, and we
splashed our way through the waist-deep water. The river
was cold and urgent, harrying our steps and always threatening to dislodge our feet from the weed-green rocks, yet
there was something pleasing in its eagerness. Though I
was not thirsty, I stopped midstream where a boulder gave
me purchase and scooped a palmful of water into my
mouth. The chill trickling down my throat was exhil-
arating, though it stirred my stomach to fresh pangs of
hunger.

As we climbed the slopes of the far shore, my mood
sobered. None of the lands south of Antioch were safe, but
the eastern bank of the Orontes especially was the preserve
of the Turks. I had chosen a minimal company to escort
me, for I had little confidence in my errand, but I regretted
it ever more as we advanced down the empty road. The
rising sun crossed our path so that we could see barely
more than the stony ground at our feet, while the flashing
bows of light from the Varangians' axes would have acted
as a clear beacon – or target – to any spies in the hills.

86

Sigurd, whose own axe twitched in his hands, gestured down the long valley to where the river now turned towards the sea. 'It could be worse,' he grunted. 'The march from Dorylaeum – that was bad.'

It had been. For six weeks in high summer we had limped across the Anatolian highlands, chasing a beaten army which spoiled or destroyed every living thing in its path. Without food or water, men and beasts had died in unnumbered thousands, their bones left by the wayside because we were too weak to dig graves. We could not travel by night for fear of ambush so the July sun shrivelled our bodies as hard as olives, the sweat wrung from us until we could sweat no more. The jaws of cisterns gaped empty where the Turks had cracked them open; we lacerated our cheeks trying to chew the spiny bushes for moisture. My tongue had become like a splinter in my mouth, so dry that I had imagined I might snap it in two between my teeth. In the evenings we did not pitch camp but fell where we stopped. Not all of us rose in the mornings. Oxen became the steeds of lords, and dogs were our pack animals. And every day the land around remained unchanged: a waste of dust and thorns, broken only by mountains on a horizon which never approached. None of us who emerged from that desert would ever entirely wash away the dust on our souls.

'There.'

Thankfully Sigurd's voice recalled me from bitter memories. Shielding his eyes, he pointed ahead to where a gaggle of low houses had come into view at the top of the ridge. We walked on towards them, crossing a wooden bridge over a stream and climbing to the village between terraced fields overrun with weeds. It was a humble place, a dozen stone cottages built together in pairs and a score of timber shacks surrounding them. Even at mid-morning there was an unnatural quiet about it: no women drew water from the well, no goats bleated in the enclosures, and nothing pulled the ploughs which lay rotting by the barns. Sigurd slung his shield on his arm and lifted his axe in caution.

'We need to find the house of the sun,' I said, uneasy at the sound of my voice in the silence.

'What does that mean?'

I shrugged. 'Perhaps a house which faces east. Or one with no roof.'

A sudden squawk tore away the stillness. With a ruffling of wings, a brown hen ran around the corner of the nearest house, stopped abruptly, and began pecking at the muddy ground.

'Get her,' Sigurd shouted. One of his men was already moving forward, his blade poised to chop away the bird's head, but at that moment a new voice began screaming abuse. The door to the house had opened and a wizened woman stood on the doorstep, waving her fist and shouting every manner of curse. She ran forward under the Varangian's axe, scooped up the hen in the folds of her skirt, and stared defiance at us.

'Why do you do this?' she spat. Though much corrupted, her language seemed to be Greek. 'Why do you try to starve us? You have torn up our fields and slaughtered our animals – are you now taking my last hen? In the name of the Christ and his blessed mother, are you not ashamed?'

'We do not want to steal from you,' I assured her, though fourteen hungry faces belied my words. I had to repeat myself thrice before she could understand me. 'We are looking for a house – the house of the sun. *Helios,*' I emphasised, pointing to the sky.

'In the valley.' She threw out an arm, pointing further down the road. Her skin was almost black, and wrinkled beyond every vestige of youth, yet the strength of her voice made her seem little older than me – younger, even.

'You will find it in the valley of the sinners. By the water. The road will take you.'

I wanted to ask for further description, to learn how I might know the house that I sought, but she would give us nothing more. Lifting her skirts, she turned and stamped back into the house, never loosing her grip on the hen.

'That should have been our lunch,' Sigurd complained.

'We cannot steal from these people,' I snapped. 'They are Christians – Greeks. These are the people we fight to save.'

Sigurd looked at the desolate village, and laughed.

On the far side of the hilltop, the road descended into a steep ravine. It was as though the lips of the earth had been prised apart, opening a glimpse onto a world utterly removed from its terrestrial surrounds. The slopes were thick with pines, bay trees in blossom and fig trees budding with fruit. In a gully beside the path a multitude of streams tumbled down through moss-covered rocks, touching and parting until they at last united on the valley floor. Wood-birds sang, and the smell of laurel blossom was heavy in the air. It was a garden, as near to paradise as anything I had seen in my life.

'It doesn't look like the valley of sin,' said Sigurd. He had snapped off a sprig of laurel and stuck it into his unruly hair, like a victorious charioteer at the hippodrome.

'Does that disappoint you?'

Sigurd kicked a pebble from our path and watched it tumble down the slope into one of the brooks. 'If there's sin to be had, it's best to know what I forsake.'

The road levelled out as we reached the bottom of the valley. The vegetation was as thick as ever: broad oaks over-hung the stream, and vines trailed in the water. Every few hundred paces, though, there were gaps in the foliage where once the villas of our ancestors had stood. Their ruins were still there, gradually receding beneath the green tide. Some were now little more than rubble under the ferns and ivy; others had walls still standing, or columns poking out of the bushes. There were about ten in total, all shaken down over the centuries by war and time and the tremors of the earth.

I remembered the words of the woman in the village. 'One of these must be the house of the sun.'

'None of them has a roof,' Sigurd observed.

We walked on, scanning the remains for anything that might suggest a sun. Above us the true sun arced in its course, slowly pushing back the shadows cast by the steep walls of the ravine. Different features drew our attentions – a yellow flower with radiate petals, a star carved into a fallen lintel, a fragment of golden mosaic tiles – and we began to drift apart. It was hard to feel danger in the sweetness of that place.

I had just scrambled back to the path, having been drawn away by a stone covered in pine blossom, when I saw her. She was standing on the far bank of the stream: a dark-haired woman, her head uncovered, in a dress which seemed much stained with mud and berries. There were leaves tangled in her hair, and had it not been for the hardness of her face I might have believed her a nymph or dryad.

'What do you want?' she called. Her dialect was Frankish, and her voice strangely harsh against the surroundings. 'Do you want for pleasure, far from home? I can help you forget your suffering, for a little while.'

I closed my eyes. I knew why the villagers called this the valley of sin. Three months earlier, fearing that the impieties of the Army of God might be the reason why its campaign had faltered, Bishop Adhemar had expelled all women from the camp. As an attempt to stamp out sin, it had failed utterly; if anything, it had only spawned worse vices. After a few days the women had begun to drift back into the camp, their presence thenceforth ignored by Adhemar, but there was talk that some had made a new home in the glades of this valley, where the tempted of the army could indulge their lusts more privately.

'I am looking for a house called the house of the sun,' I said. 'Do you know of it?'

She shook her head, her long hair swinging freely behind. 'I need no houses for my affairs.'

'May I ask – did four Norman knights come here once, perhaps a month ago?'

'Many men come here: Normans, Provençals, Franks, Lotharingians. Even Greeks.'

'These men did not come for such pleasures, I think. There were four of them,' I said again.

As brazenly as if she were alone, the woman reached into the folds of her skirt and scratched herself between her legs. 'I saw them.'

My hopes quickened. 'Where did they go?'

'They had a bullock with them. It screamed horribly.' Deliberately ignoring me, she seated herself on a rock and dipped her naked toes into the stream. The water rippled around them. 'None of us dared go near.'

'Near where?'

She looked up, coiling a lock of hair about her finger. 'How much would you value it?'

'Half a bezant.' It was the only coin in my purse, and I was loath to spend it on this harlot. But in the pursuit of secrets, even worthless ones, I have ever been spendthrift.

She smiled, though there was no joy in it. 'For half a bezant, I could give you more than knowledge.'

As she spoke, there must have been a touch of a breeze,

for the scents of pine and laurel were suddenly thick on my senses. They cloyed about me, sickly smells bespeaking all manner of sweet damnation. For a moment, even the harlot's face seemed kinder.

I shook my head, as much to myself as to her, and held up the coin so that she could see it. 'Where did they go?'

'There.' She pointed to a low-lying patch of ruins, further down the valley where the slopes became cliffs. 'They went in there.'

I threw the coin across the stream. She caught it one-handed, the arm of her dress sliding back as she reached out. 'They would not lie with me either.'

I called Sigurd and the others to join me, and walked slowly towards the ancient villa. High trees had grown around it, shading it with the canopy of their leaves, while shrubs and flowers flourished among the masonry. Two walls were all that remained standing: the rest, the detritus of atria, baths, colonnades and fountains were piled in broken heaps around me. A fluted column lay between the two posts of a door that had long since rotted to oblivion. I stepped over it, and looked for any sign that the whore had spoken truthfully.

'Here.' Moving more impatiently than I, Sigurd had already reached the back of the ruin. Its rear wall must have been built sheer against the cliff, though it had mostly collapsed now, for I could see square crevices cut in the rock where stones had once been fixed. Where Sigurd stood, a few blocks remained as the ancient masons had laid them, the surrounds of a long-disused fireplace. As I approached, I saw what he had seen: two suns, their rays like spikes, engraved into the wall on either side of the hearthstone.

'Those carvings,' I exclaimed. 'Are there any other markings?'

To my surprise, Sigurd bellowed with laughter. It echoed off the high cliffs above and startled a flock of birds into flight. 'Truly, Demetrios Askiates does discover what other men do not. Who else would see those scratchings, and miss what lay at his feet?'

I looked down. It had been hidden by the high weeds as I approached, and my stare had then been fixed on the wall, but now I could see what Sigurd meant. On a patch of ground before the hearth, curiously free of any growth or dirt, a broad mosaic of a burning sun gazed up at the sky. Its beams wriggled and twisted like snakes in yellow and orange, trimmed with gold, and from its centre the untamed face of Phoebus Apollo gazed on us. His wild hair branched and forked from his head, spraying out into the surrounding beams, while his plump nose and swollen eyes looked more like a satyr's than a god's.

'This is miraculously preserved.' I glanced involuntarily at the sky, fearful that I might blaspheme to speak of miracles in the works of the pagans.

'More than miraculous.' Sigurd swung an arm in a rough arc about us. A low rampart of earth and dying weeds circumscribed the border of the mosaic, as if it had recently been dug clear. Peering closer, I could see white scuffs and scratches in the tiles where a hoe or spade might have scraped them. And, ringing Apollo's head, the dark nimbus of a circular crack.

I dropped to my knees and tried to prise my fingers into the gap. My nails were quickly as chipped and torn as the mosaic, but the fit was too snug: I could not work anything loose. Even the blade of my knife was too thick.

'Look at the eye,' said Sigurd, staring down from above me. 'The pupil.'

I twisted about and looked in the god's eye. It was formed from a dozen or so tiles in whites and blues, but the black circle at its centre was not so solid. In fact, it was a hole, just wide enough for a man's finger. I poked my forefinger in, and pulled away a round fragment containing the eye and its socket. In the recess beneath, a heavily rusted iron ring lay set in mortar.

'Help me,' I called, tugging on it. The broader slab that held the now one-eyed god's face was too heavy. Sigurd crouched beside me and pulled the ring, lifting the disc free of the ground. Eager Varangian hands slid it away, as a wide black void opened in front of us.

'We're not going in there without light.' Sigurd pulled a dry branch from the undergrowth and wrapped its end in dry grass and leaves. Taking the steel from the pouch on his belt, he struck streams of sparks from the flinty rock until the makeshift torch flared alight.

'I've rescued you from dark holes before,' he warned me. 'This time, I go first.'

Even with the added bulk of his armour, he fitted easily through the opening. It was not deep, for as his feet reached the bottom the crown of his head was still level with the ground and he had to crouch to press forward into the tunnel beyond. An isolated arm reached back into the well of sunlight to claim first his axe and then the torch. After a brief interval, and a muffled shout that all was safe, I followed him down.

It must have been a millennium or more since the passage was cut, yet its brick-vaulted roof still held up the weight of the ages. I could see little, for Sigurd had already advanced some way ahead, but I felt the floor sloping gradually down as it led me deeper into the rock, under the cliff. I moved hesitantly, keeping my hands pressed against the mossy walls and wondering what devilment might lurk in the darkness ahead of me. Once, during my childhood at the monastery in Isauria, one of the monks had taken the novices into the hills, to the ruins of a temple where our ancestors had worshipped their false gods and idols. The building had been a wreck, its roof staved in and its marble long since plundered to adorn churches, yet still I had felt the ageless evil lingering in the crumbling stones. As the moon rose, the monk had told us of the blood sacrifices our forebears had made to their gods of violence and vengeance, had spoken such vivid warnings against the long arm of the devil that eventually I became convinced that Satan's dark fingers were poised behind me, waiting to snatch me away. Although I had since seen more of the works of Lucifer than I dared to remember, in the black confines of that tunnel I once again felt the pricking evil of his hand stretching towards me.

'Look at this.'

I had at last caught up with Sigurd, some thirty paces down from the entrance, where the tunnel opened out into a square chamber. The bricks which had lined the walls before now gave way to solid rock, except on the far side where a doorway led on to a second chamber briefly visible in the light of Sigurd's torch. The smoke stung my throat and eyes, but I could see where he pointed. In the middle of the floor at our feet, a heap of ash and half-burned branches.

'This is recent,' I murmured. 'What is beyond?'

'Come and see.'

I followed Sigurd through the far opening and into the room beyond. It was longer than the antechamber, some fifty feet in all, with a gently curving roof and a floor laid with mosaics. On either side, the rock had been carved into benches worn smooth with use, while the plastered walls were covered in faded paintings. At the back, a stone altar stood raised on a dais.

It was as well that Sigurd held the torch, for I might have dropped it in shock. As it was, even his stout arm wavered. The images on the wall were grotesque, fantastical:

processions of men with the heads of beasts and fowl; insects crawling out of the earth; a hand reaching from a tomb. The fiendish iconography continued on the ground, where a simple progression of mosaic tiles showed the silhouettes of more creatures, and dark symbols that I did not recognise. Halfway along the cave they vanished under a dark wave which had evidently been spilled across the floor.

'It's as well the bishop can't see us now,' Sigurd whispered. His voice was faltering, and it was only with the reluctance of a chained prisoner that he moved forward.

'What is this place?' The black veneer cracked and crumbled underfoot, and I could see pale imprints where boots other than mine had trod before it dried. I had a sickening feeling that I could guess its substance; its origin I did not care to guess. I touched my chest, where the silver cross hung under my armour, and prayed for a shield against the evils of this cave.

'This is a place where we should not be.' Sigurd held his torch before the altar, illuminating the frieze in its face. A man in a conical cap was wrestling with a bull, one arm grasping its neck while the other plunged a sword into its side. Blood gushed from the wound, while carrion-hungry animals looked on.

'It must be some temple of the ancients.' I did not recognise the gods from the poems and stories of the past, but I knew how profligate and varied their pagan deities had been. 'But what did four knights from the Army of God purpose here?'

Sigurd gave no answer. Resting his axe against the altar, he stepped away into the corner of the cave where he crouched down, reaching for something. As he turned back I almost shrieked, for in his hand he now brandished a cloven hoof.

'If the devil's about, he'll be limping,' he said, with more

96

cheer than I could summon. 'Although I never heard that he had the feet of an ox.'

Trembling, I took the hoof from him. It gleamed in the torchlight, shadow deepening the furrow between the two toes. As he had said, it looked as though it had come from a cow or an ox, though in that heathen place I trusted nothing. I passed it back to Sigurd, remembered the harlot's words by the riverside: *They had a bullock with them. It screamed horribly.*

'What do you think . . . ?'

I could not bring myself to finish the question, but Sigurd was less oppressed by our surroundings. He tossed the hoof in his hand and looked again at the images on the walls. 'What do I think they did here? I think they did what we all would do with a bullock and a hidden cave. I think they ate.'

1

We left the valley, so full of fruit and sin, and hurried back towards the city. For a time, the mysteries of the cave had numbed me to the danger of the Turks, but now I was forever glancing behind me, starting at every brushed leaf or snapping twig in the undergrowth by the roadside. I could not shake the fear that I had entered where I should not have gone, and that I might yet pay a divine price.

'You saw the image on the altar,' I pressed Sigurd. 'A man killing a bull, doubtless in some pagan rite. If Drogo and his companions went down there with a bullock, it can only have been to one purpose.'

Sigurd shook his head, though his eyes never left the road ahead. 'At least two of them loved Christ so much that they had themselves carved head to toe with crosses. Do you think they would be the kind of men to make sacrifices to gods who have been forgotten for a thousand years?'

'Do you rather think that they travelled miles into a dangerous land, happened upon a secret temple that had been buried for centuries, and used it to cook lunch?'

'I can think of other pursuits they might have enjoyed down there – and better reasons for going to a valley full of eager women.'

'Even for men who had carved themselves with pious crosses?'

Sigurd snorted. 'Perhaps . . .' He paused. 'What's that?'
I stopped, my hand dropping to my sword. 'What?'

Even as I asked the question, I heard it myself: a rumble
in the air, as of distant thunder or tumbling rocks. But it
did not cease or fade; instead, it grew ever louder, more
ominous, the rushing approach of pounding hooves. I
looked at the shallow valley around me, but the scrubby
vegetation was too sparse to hide us and we would never
reach the ridge in safety.

'Form line!' Sigurd wheeled about so that we faced back
towards Daphne and dropped to one knee, setting his huge
shield before him. His men fanned out beside him, locking
their own shields into a wall, though it was barely enough
to span the road. I squeezed in beside Sigurd, drawing my
sword and thinking feverishly of Anna, of my daughters
Zoe and Helena, and of the malignant curse which had
attached to me in the cave.

'We should have spears,' the Varangian on my left
muttered. 'With spears, we might have a chance against
them.'

'Not against their arrows.' Sigurd dug the butt of his
axe into the ground and seemed ready to say something
more. But at that moment the debate was cut short as
horsemen cantered into view. Peering over the rim of
Sigurd's shield, I could see their horses' gaunt necks
thrusting forward, the spray of mud they kicked behind
them, and the long spears their riders held erect. My low
vantage kept me from seeing any but the leading riders
and the churning mêlée of legs beneath, but the raised
spears seemed to stretch too far back for hope.

'Tancred!'

Sigurd spoke as the cavalry slowed their advance, and
the momentum which had pulled their standard out
behind them gave way to a breeze which whipped it into
our sight. All of us recognised it, the blue and crimson

stripes surmounted with a rearing bear. It was the banner of Tancred, Bohemond's nephew and lieutenant. Not one of the Varangians relaxed his guard.

The Normans stopped a few paces away, grim figures in their coned helmets and mail. After a discomforting pause, their leader trotted forward.

I had heard it rumoured, once, that he was the half-bred son of a Saracen, and there was certainly nothing in his features to deny it. Unlike most of his kinsmen, his hair and eyes were dark, the former spilling out in curls over his coif, the latter still immature, lacking confidence. Even after all the privations of the siege he still filled his armour, though he was smaller than Bohemond or Sigurd. At the age of twenty, his face had taken on the set of command but had not yet left behind the scars and pimples of youth. On the battlefield, I knew, his recklessness made men fear to serve him.

'Greeks,' he said, staring down on us. Despite the bear on his banner, his voice was more a chirrup than a growl. 'You are far from home.'

'Nearer than you,' I answered.

'What brought you here? I did not expect to find a Greek risking his skin where the Turks prowl.'

'Foraging.'

Tancred's horse, a dappled stallion, skittered uneasily. 'Did you find food?'

'Only this.' Sigurd picked up the bullock's hoof from where he had dropped it and tossed it up to Tancred. With a spear in one hand and a heavy shield on the other, Tancred could do nothing but watch it fall to the ground. He laughed.

'Is that all? We have been foraging too – but to greater avail.' He gestured forward with his spear arm. One of the men behind him loosed something from his saddle pommel and threw it forward, sniggering as it landed in front of us. I closed my eyes, trying to stop up my throat as the lifeless eyes of a Turk's head gazed at me from the mud.

'We have a score more, if you wish to see them,' Tancred bragged. 'Tribute to my uncle.'

'Doubtless he is worthy of the gift.'

'Worthier than a eunuch and his army of catamites and traitors.' Tancred kicked his horse forward and reined it in just above us. 'What are so few Greeks doing so far from the city, so feebly armed?'

'Get off your horse and I will show you how feeble we are,' Sigurd challenged him.

'Perhaps you have an understanding with the Turks? Perhaps you have the safe passage of ambassadors?' The bite in Tancred's taunts seemed yet more dangerous because of the childish voice in which he spoke them. 'What business does the King of the Greeks have with the Sultan? Would you make an alliance with him against us, divide up our lands as the wages of treachery?'

'We came only to forage,' I repeated. I could see the Normans growing restless, the spears inclining towards us.

'I will leave my uncle to judge the truth of that. Unless I choose to bring him a dozen more trophies.'

'He would prefer me alive.' I needed all the strength of Sigurd's shield to keep from shaking as I tried to deflect the murderous Norman. 'Indeed, I am in your uncle Bohemond's employ.'

'Why would my uncle waste one bezant on a Greek?' The disbelief was plain on Tancred's young face. 'What is your name?'

'Demetrios Askiates.'

'I have never heard him speak of you.'

'He asked me to find the killer of Drogo of Melfi.'

'Drogo?' The name was clearly known to Tancred, but I never discovered whether it would have provoked aid or anger, for at that moment – for the second time in the afternoon – we were interrupted by the noise of galloping hoofbeats. They came from the direction of the city, and in an instant Tancred's lieutenants were shouting at their men to form a rough line across the valley. Sigurd and I and the rest of the Varangians loosed our ranks, so as not to block the way, and turned to face the new danger.

'There should be no other Christians in these hills.' Tancred stared down the road. 'It must be Turks.'

'If we're lucky, it may be a grain caravan,' said one of the Normans nearby.

Tancred looked at him in scorn. 'Do you think that is the sound of laden mules?'

It was not. Hardly had the words been spoken when the horsemen came around the bend at the bottom of the valley, a squadron of twenty or so Turkish cavalry. The brass inlay on their helmets, poking out from the turbans wound about them, gleamed in the sun; some carried spears, while others had bows slung across their shoulders. They could not have expected to meet us, for they rode unprotected in a loose column.

'Charge!' shouted Tancred, tucking his spear under his arm. He spurred his horse, and the Norman line swept into motion, gathering pace as it advanced down the slope. There must have been fifty of them, and if they could close swiftly enough they might yet trap the Turks in their column. Sigurd and our company stayed where we were.

The Turkish horses were smaller than the Normans', but they had an agility and an affinity with the uneven land which their adversaries could not match. The moment they had come within sight of the Normans, the Turks had wheeled about and begun their retreat. Already they were almost at the steep bluffs around which the road disappeared, though the curve seemed to slow them, allowing the Normans to close.

'If Tancred gets any nearer, he'll have to duck,' Sigurd observed.

Sure enough, a second later three of the Turks swivelled in their saddles and loosed a volley of arrows at the leading Normans. The horses swerved and shied, almost throwing their riders, and the distance between the two forces widened. Once they were past the cliff the Turks would have an almost straight road back to the city, and the Normans would be hard pressed to catch them.

Looking down the valley after the fleeing horsemen, I let my gaze wander. In the gap where the road rounded the cliff I could see the green valley descending towards the river beyond; up on my right, the ridge of the valley followed the line of the road until it ended in the bluffs.

I paused, keeping my gaze fixed on the cliff. The main body of the Normans were under it now yet it seemed I could see something glinting above. It could not be the Turkish riders, for they would have needed winged steeds to climb it. Perhaps it was a spring, or a puddle.

'Christ's shit.' Sigurd spoke it so mildly that at first I thought he must have dropped his shield on his toe, or pricked himself on a briar. Then I saw where he looked, and the obscenity was on my lips also. As if smitten by an unseen hand, two of the Normans had fallen from their horses at the foot of the cliff. Even as I watched, one of the other animals collapsed onto its knees. The heights above, where I had imagined I saw a puddle, now bristled with archers who were pouring arrows over the precipice.

'Come on.' Shouldering his shield, Sigurd grabbed my arm and dragged me after him, running across the slope of the valley towards the cliff. His men followed as we stumbled through the gorse and rocks, the sound of our bouncing armour jangling in my ears. My thighs burned with the effort; with every step my legs had to be kept from sliding away down the hillside. With the footing so treacherous I could risk only the briefest glances forward, and I prayed that the Turks on the cliff ahead were too preoccupied with their attack to look back.

Following Sigurd, we came around the crook of the valley and crested the ridge on its northern arm. From where we stood, it ran down gently to the head of the cliffs where the Turkish archers still loosed their arrows on the unseen Normans below. We crouched in the shadow of a boulder as Sigurd swiftly counted them.

'Twenty-three,' he announced.

'Two to one,' I said.

'Not if you count a Varangian worth three of them. We'll advance in line, quietly. If they see us, close ranks and make the shield wall. They're isolated on that promontory, and without their horses. Get close enough, and we'll deny them their favourite tactic.'

'What's that?'

Sigurd grinned. 'Running away.'

It was a tactic I would happily have embraced myself, but I had no choice. Already we were moving on, spilling out from the shelter of the rock and advancing slowly down the loose scree towards the enemy. Mimicking the Varangians around me, I dropped into a low crouch with my shield held before me. Sweat trickled from under my helmet, running down behind the nose-guard, while I fervently wished I had painted my shield some colour other than red. Still the distance between us closed, and still they did not see us: I could hear their bowstrings snapping now, and the screams of men and horses echoing up from the road below.

'Now,' said Sigurd from my right. 'We'll sweep them off that cliff. Just be sure you don't get between them and the edge. We—'

Whether the Turks heard him, or whether one of them

turned back, I did not see, but no sooner had Sigurd spoken than a great infidel shout rang out from the cliff. Some already had arrows nocked, and they turned in an instant to loose them at us. From either side of me came the ringing crack of iron embedding itself in leather.

'Come on,' bellowed Sigurd. He was on his feet, drawn up to his full size like a bear facing its hunter. The axe seemed to dance in his hands. He ran down the last few yards of the slope while the arrows swarmed towards him, and slowed not an inch as he punched his shield into the face of his first adversary. The arrows which stuck from it snapped with the impact, and I saw their splinters tear great rents into the Turk's skin as he collapsed backwards.

The rest of our company met the enemy, a crimson line of swinging axes and barbarian cries, and I realised too late that the drama of the spectacle had stilled me in my place. In every battle I had ever fought, from the mountains of Lydia against imperial usurpers to the alleys of Constantinople against mercenaries and thieves, I had begun with the same alloy of dread and anger molten in my heart; in every battle, I had forced the fury to vanquish the fear. It seemed to grow ever harder as I grew older, but still I could not fail before God and my friends. I charged forward.

No arrows flew now, for the Turks had abandoned their bows for spears and knives, but the air was still clouded with blades swooping, stabbing, hacking and biting. I threw up my shield as a spear lunged out of the fray, and managed to deflect it past my shoulder. The man who held it stumbled on, too committed to break off his attack, and in a second an almost forgotten instinct had swung my sword into his jaw. Blood gushed out of his mouth as he sank to the ground, and our stares met in shared disbelief. Then his head slumped forward, and mine jerked up to seek the next threat.

But already the battle had passed me. On horseback, or with the bow, few could equal the Turks, but on foot and face to face they were no match for the raging Northmen. A slew of their dead lay scattered on the rocky ground before me, while their last remnants made a desperate stand on the brink of the cliff. Even as I watched, Sigurd kicked one in the ribs so that he staggered back, lost his footing and flailed over the edge. Seeing the cause was lost, that they could retreat no further and fight no longer, his companions threw down their weapons and dropped to their knees.

I joined Sigurd at the cliff edge. Both of us were breathing hard, both dashed with blood and the grime that fixes itself to men in battle, both still too much in thrall to the frenzy of war to speak. Below us, I could see Tancred's Normans huddled into a grove of pine trees just off the road. Several of them, men and horses, lay sprawled out, pierced with arrows. A little further down the road the company of Turkish archers they had originally pursued sat mounted in a line, looking up at our cliff uncertainly.

'Get those bows,' Sigurd barked. 'Let them see they're defeated.'

The Varangians, who had already begun stripping the dead of their armour, were quick to obey. Kneeling by the cliff, they loosed a desultory volley of arrows towards the mounted Turks. They did not fly with any great accuracy or range – only one struck within twenty paces of its target – but it was enough to convince our enemy. Before the last arrow had dropped, they had turned their backs to us and cantered away towards Antioch.

Suddenly I felt my limbs go as weak as straws. I sat down on a rock and surveyed our bloodstained promontory. One of the Varangians was down, his shoulder gouged by a Turkish spear, but his companions were giving him water from a flask and I guessed he would live at least long enough to see whether the rot set in. Otherwise, we had suffered few injuries. Of the Turks, meanwhile, I counted eleven dead or dying among us; some had been forced over the cliff, while others must have managed to squeeze around our line and run for safety. We would not pursue them.

Sigurd caught my gaze. Even his arm did not seem so steady as it had before. 'Another bloody skirmish,' he said, kicking at a loose helmet on the ground. It clattered like a cymbal as it bounced over the cliff and down to the road. 'More scars to no purpose.'

'We saved Tancred and his men,' I reminded him. 'Their gratitude may yet serve us in its turn.'

'Their gratitude. They will feel no gratitude – only envious shame that they owe their lives to a rabble of womanly Greeks.' Sigurd turned away. 'And when we get back, Demetrios, we will find that this bloodshed has not loosed one pebble from the walls of Antioch.'

Sigurd's glum prophecy proved all too accurate. No sooner had we regained the road, leaving the Turks unburied on the cliff top, than we were facing the sneers of Normans whose sudden rescue only sharpened the barbs they threw at us. Their temper was improved somewhat by the discovery of a herd of horses tethered in the next valley, doubtless left there by the archers on the cliff, but we almost started a fresh battle quarrelling over whose spoils they were. Tancred, invoking the precedence of nobility, claimed them for himself, while Sigurd bluntly reminded him what we had achieved while the Normans had been cowering in the trees. In the end, as voices rose and swords edged from their scabbards, I forced them to agree that we would take only as many mounts as we needed for ourselves, and let Bohemond adjudge the final division.

Though I was never a natural horseman, it was a blessing at last to have a beast to carry me. The long day in hostile lands, the trials of the pagan cave, and finally the murderous terror of battle had drained the strength from me, so I was content to slump in the saddle, my legs hanging loose, and let the horse walk me home. The Turkish prisoners we had taken, five of them, straggled behind us under the gaze of the Varangians.

At the ford we encountered more horsemen. Tancred spurred to meet them, churning a foamy path through the water, and greeted them as friends. Drawing near, letting the river ride up over my boots, I heard them exchange greetings in the Norman tongue.

'You have returned safely, praise God,' said one. 'Three hours ago, we saw a company of Turks ride out from the St George gate. We feared you might meet them. An hour since, they returned, fewer in number.'

'We met them,' Tancred said. 'And by the grace of God, we taught them that there is not one inch of this land where they can walk in safety. But how did they know to seek us? We left last night, and travelled in the dark.'

'The enemy has many spies,' the Norman offered.

It seemed more likely that they had seen our company of Varangians leaving in the morning, but I did not say so.

'Too many spies,' Tancred agreed. 'And even now they may be watching.' His stare seemed to settle on me. 'We had best hurry on to the camp. Doubtless my uncle will want to know of my victory.'

We rode on, dismounting to lead our horses across the boat bridge and continuing along the well-worn path around the walls. As the crowds thickened near the camps, Sigurd had to order his men to close ranks around the Turkish prisoners, in an effort to ward off the jeers and mud and stones that the Franks hurled at them. Several times I felt my shield shiver with the impact of pebbles, and I had to stroke my horse's neck to calm her skittish nerves. The laughter of the Normans ahead did nothing to dim the taunts.

We halted in the forlorn square of mud which served as the Norman exercise ground. Bohemond was waiting there atop his white warhorse, surrounded by a clutch of his household knights.

'You have been in battle,' he said coolly, his gaze darting over Tancred's depleted company.

'We encountered a troop of Turks,' Tancred answered. There was still that wheedling petulance in his voice which, despite his broad frame and high charger, made him sound like a child. 'When we gave chase, they led us into a trap. It was only by ferocious effort that we escaped it. We captured two dozen of their horses,' he added, sensing that his story had inspired little avuncular pride.

'How many did you lose?'

'Eight,' Tancred admitted.

'Horses?'

'Men.' He paused, blushing. 'Eleven horses. But I have made good the deficit, uncle. And I cannot be blamed for our losses when spies and traitors infest our camp. They knew to expect us there – and they laid their trap accordingly.'

'Fool.' Bohemond trotted forward until his mount was beside Tancred's, then reached out of his saddle and slapped his nephew across the cheek. 'A hunter may set a snare, but he cannot force his quarry to spring it. For that, he relies on the animal's own brute stupidity.' He kicked his horse away and stared at the Varangians. 'And if you fought so valiantly to rout your enemy, why is it Greeks who carry the spoils and guard the prisoners?'

Tancred chose to ignore the question. 'Why, after five months in this cursed place, are the Turks still free to ride in and out of their city as they please, and to swamp our camp with their spies?'

Bohemond looked in scorn on his nephew. 'First learn to fight a skirmish, and leave wiser heads to govern the war. As to the spies, we will see what your prisoners can tell us of that.'

'*My* prisoners,' I corrected him. 'We took them in the battle.'

'While your nephew cowered behind a pine tree,' Sigurd added, unhelpfully.

Tancred spat at him. 'Because you were too cowardly to charge the Turks with us.'

Sigurd tapped a fist against the side of his helmet so that it rang like a bell. 'Not cowardly – clever. Perhaps when you reach your manhood you will understand.'

'Enough!' Bohemond raised a fist to still us, his eyes pale with anger. 'These prisoners will avail you nothing, Demetrios. Look at them – do you think they will command a penny's ransom from the Turks? All they will bring you is five more mouths that you can ill afford to feed. Leave them with me, and I will see they are treated according to the laws of Christ.'

He spoke truthfully, at least as regarded their value, yet I was uneasy at consigning any man, even an Ishmaelite, to the care of the Normans. Sigurd growled a warning under his breath, while the five Turks looked on hopelessly, unable to understand the men who haggled over their fate. I caught one of them staring at me, his dark eyes wide with uncomprehending fear, and felt fresh qualms assail me.

But Bohemond would not be denied. Before I could forestall him, he had ordered his men to surround the prisoners and lead them away. A crowd of soldiers and pilgrims had gathered around the exercise ground, drawn to a quarrel like flies to a wound, and I dared not provoke any further fight. As the Turks disappeared between the tents, staring helplessly back at us, the most I could do was touch my chest where my cross hung – for the dozenth time that day, it seemed – and pray that they would be treated mercifully.

Sigurd watched them go. 'It dishonours a man to be robbed of his prisoners,' he said sourly.

'It dishonours him worse to disobey his betters,' Bohemond snapped.

'When I meet a better man, I shall be sure to obey him.'

⋆　⋆　⋆

There was no profit in arguing further with the Normans. As ever, they gave the sense of men poised on a knife-edge, waiting for the least excuse to fall into a quarrel. Sigurd sent his company back to the camp with the horses, while he and I went in search of Quino and Odard. It seemed an age since we had stood in that pagan cave, with its blood-soaked floor and terrible altar, yet it had been only a few hours ago. Four Normans had entered that cave and only two still lived: I was eager to question the survivors before any further misfortune befell them.

The boy, Simon, was sitting outside the tent cradling a shield in his lap as he worked fat into the hide covering. For the briefest second, his eyes flickered up to greet us, then fixed back on his work.

'Is your master present?' I asked.

Without answering, he laid the shield on the grass and hurried through the canvas door. He did not reappear; when the flap opened again, it was Odard who emerged. Unlike most men, who had shrunk within their clothes in previous months, he seemed still too large for his tunic. It rode high above his knees and elbows, showing off limbs that were little more than bones.

'Greek,' he said, in his high, pecking voice. 'You are not wanted here.'

'Nor were the prophets in Israel – but they spoke words worth hearing.' It was a response I had honed in many years of knocking on unwelcoming doors. It had yet to persuade anyone.

Odard's head snapped twice to the left, as if something had surprised him, though I could see nothing. 'The prophets of old spoke salvation. I have heard salvation. You, I think, bring only lies and spite.'

'The prophets say: "You have forgotten the Lord your God, and made adoration of graven idols,"' I said. 'Does that not seem worthwhile to you?'

The tic of Odard's head grew more pronounced, and I

saw him flexing his fingers like claws. 'I have not forgotten the Lord God,' he protested. He pointed to his chest, where a cross of black cloth was sewn onto his tunic. 'I live and walk in the name of Christ.'

'And was it in the name of Christ that you uncovered a pagan temple, an evil place in the valley of Daphne?'

'I have never—'

'You were seen, Odard. You journeyed into the valley of sin, and your sin betrayed you. The harlots among whom you walked saw you. They saw you and your companions go down that hole with a bullock – what did you do then? Did you sacrifice it on the altar? Did you make a burnt offering to Baal, or Amun, or Zeus?' Though I had chafed to escape my childhood in the monastery, it had at least left me a priest's intimacy with scripture.

Odard recoiled, bunching his tunic in his hand where the cross was sewn. He would not meet my gaze, but sank his chin on his collar and gibbered nonsense to himself. At last, still not looking up: 'They saw us go down to that hole, yes, and take the bullock too. But they did not see the truth of what we did there, did they?' I could not tell if he spoke to me, or himself, or some invisible companion. 'You have found me out, Greek; you have discovered my sin and I will confess it, wretch that I am. Yes, we went down that hole, with a bullock, and before God I confess we sinned. We slaughtered the animal, and burnt him and devoured him, but we did not do it for Baal or Amun, no. We did it for our own appetites, our own gluttonous greed.'

'You dug out that forgotten cave just to eat in peace?' I asked in disbelief.

'Rainauld found the entrance – Rainauld. Other hands had cleared it, not ours, perhaps the whores' or brigands'. Rainauld saw the opening and went down. We were foraging,' he said, blinking rapidly. Dark skin ringed his eyes, so they seemed more the hollow sockets of a skull than part of a living man's face. 'Foraging in hostile lands we found a bullock. A bullock. In our greed, and weakness, we sinned: we did not bring it back to the camp to share with the Army of God. No. We slaughtered it and devoured it in secret, hidden in the cave where the smoke of our fire would not draw the Turks. We were sinners and we were frail and we succumbed to the urgings of our flesh. Would you do different?'

'It's as I told you,' Sigurd said, never a man to shirk from triumph. 'They went there to eat.'

We were walking slowly back to our camp through the lines of Norman tents. Dusk was approaching, but though I was left exhausted by the day I could not look forward to the night, for I feared the dreams that would visit me.

'You believed his story?'

'It makes sense. They had a bullock; they could not bear to surrender the least portion of it; and so they ate it in secret, hidden from Turks and Franks alike. We saw the blood where they slaughtered it and the ashes where they roasted it. What more do you need?'

'You do not find it curious that the place they stumbled on to slaughter the animal, a hidden place we only found by great effort, chanced to be a pagan shrine with an altar showing a sacrificial bull?'

Sigurd shrugged. 'I once knew a man they nicknamed The Boar, on account of his strength. He died on a hunt when he was gored by a boar. Was that significant? A sign of some mysterious, deeper truth? Or simply chance? There were scorpions and ravens painted on the walls of the temple as well – if a scorpion had scuttled out from the stones, would you have thought it a message from the gods?' He clapped me on the back. 'I believe in Jesus, the

Lord God and all His Saints – and when they fail me, I sometimes turn to older gods as well. But I also believe that men eat when they are hungry, steal when they have nothing, and die when they are stabbed. I do not need ancient demons and pagan forces to explain every co-incidence of this world. Speaking of eating,' he added, 'I smell meat cooking even now.'

I sniffed the damp air and nodded. We were almost back at the Norman exercise ground now, and though I had intended to avoid it, the aroma was too much for my famished stomach to ignore. Perhaps Sigurd was right about the bullock.

The light was receding, but as we came into sight of the muddy square I saw Sigurd's nose had played us true. On the far side, dozens of Normans milled about the orange embers of a fire over which a carcass turned on a spit. There was a festive mood, with much laughter and shouting: for most, it would have been weeks since they had eaten a solid piece of meat.

A Norman pilgrim, bent and lined with age, hurried past me towards the fire, a knife and a bowl in his hand. I took him by the arm, flinching to see his anger at being slowed even a second from eating.

'Has a foraging party come back?' I asked. 'Are there fresh flocks to provision the army at last?'

'Fresh flocks indeed,' he mumbled. His words were indistinct, for he had lost most of his teeth. 'Flocks of wolves guised as sheep. They'll come no more to this camp.'

He shook free of me and hastened on. Now I could see firelight glowing on the black limbs of the animal bound onto the spit. A man brandishing a knife stepped into the glow, his features like rusted iron. It was Tancred, free of his armour and dressed instead in a rich cloak. Bending across the coals, he carved a thick slice from the roasting carcass and gobbled it off the point of his knife.

There was a strangely bitter smell coming from the meat, as if it had not been hung properly.

Tancred must have seen us coming for he turned to face me. The skin around his lips shone with a sheen of hot fat, which dribbled unchecked onto the noble cloth of his cloak.

'Demetrios Askiates,' he greeted me, merrily waving his knife. 'Come and join our feast – it is your spoils, after all. There is plenty for all, though it will soon become scarce if these animals learn what fate awaits them in our camp.'

He took another great bite and wiped his mouth with his sleeve. I could see Quino behind him, laughing in the shadows; further back I thought I glimpsed a figure who could have been Bohemond. But I did not look at any of these, for my stare was fixed on the fire, unwilling to believe the sight I beheld. My stomach rose, choking to be free of me, and if Sigurd had not gripped my shoulder I would have collapsed weeping in the mud.

It was no animal they roasted. It was a man. Through a prism of tears, I watched Tancred and the Norman throng revelling in the firelight as Sigurd dragged me away.

Three weeks passed after that abomination. I did nothing to delve into the deaths of Drogo and Rainauld; I avoided any errand which took me near Quino, Odard or Bohemond, and they for their part did not seek me out. They would have found scant welcome if they had, for every day the memory of the prisoners whom I had betrayed into their care visited torments upon me. Anna and Sigurd tried to plead my innocence, but I did not heed them. I was sullen, ashamed, and withdrew from their company too often. I must have been more irritable even than Tatikios, whose soul seemed daily to shrink within him at the Frankish sneers and threats he endured. Nor could any of us find solace in the affairs of the siege: the walls of Antioch remained as unyielding as the mountain behind, and its garrison safe within. Each morning we woke to the Ishmaelite chants resounding from their church towers, and each night the same sound mocked us to sleep. One day I met Mushid, the Syrian swordsmith, walking by the Orontes, and I asked him what the words said.

'Our God, Allah, is greatest, and none other is to be praised,' Mushid told me, translating easily into Greek. 'It is the second pillar of our faith.'

After that the song rang more bitterly still in my ears, an inescapable, unceasing rebuke proclaiming the triumph of our enemies.

One day, a week after the feast of Easter, Tatikios summoned me to take a message to Bishop Adhemar in the Provençal camp. The past months had told terribly on him: his hair had thinned, his skin had paled, even the golden nose seemed tarnished. He no longer dared set foot outside the Byzantine encampment; indeed, he could spend days on end never leaving his tent. Once, visiting a nobleman's house, I had seen a menagerie filled with every manner of exotic beast: it had struck me then that while many of the smaller and humbler creatures met their captivity with philosophy, those who were greatest in the wild became most wretched in the cage. Such an animal was Tatikios: without armies to command and princes to flatter, with no campaigns to direct or enemies to out-manoeuvre, the life was strangled from him.

'Pay the bishop my respects, and ask him why eighty bushels of grain sent to me by the Emperor from Cyprus have not arrived.' Tatikios paced before the golden saints and eagles on the wall. 'Tell him – no, demand of him – that if he and Count Raymond abuse their command of the road from Saint Simeon, I will see to it that the Emperor's bounty dries up.'

'Yes, Lord.' I bowed. The longer Tatikios spent in his tent the more punctilious he became, as if by walls of protocol alone he could protect himself. It did not seem to soothe his worries.

Although Bishop Adhemar travelled and fought as the legate of the Patriarch of Rome, he made his camp with the Provençals of Count Raymond. He was the most exalted man in the army, inasmuch as the bickering princes could acknowledge any one master, yet he did not set his tent away from the masses or take shelter in the comfort of a farmhouse. Nonetheless, there was no mistaking his tent among the muddied and frayed surrounds: the white cloth gleamed as if woven from alabaster, and the pole which held it up stood at least a head taller than the others around. Outside the door two banners proclaimed his faith: one a simple design of a blood-red cross on white cloth; the other his own standard, the Holy Virgin cradling her child. A few beggars and paupers – though who in that army was not a pauper? – knelt hopefully nearby, their bowls poised for any charity that might emerge, but otherwise there was only a single guard in a blue cloak. On hearing my errand, he was swift to let me pass.

'Greetings, Demetrios Askiates.' The bishop rose from behind a wooden table and lifted a hand so that the palm faced me. He pronounced a blessing, in Latin words that I did not understand, then waved me to be seated. 'Have you come to speak of Drogo?'

Even the name of Drogo dredged up thoughts of death and anger. 'Your Grace, I have a message from my master Tatikios.'

'He desires to know what I have done with his grain?' the bishop guessed. He leaned forward, watching for my reaction, and I met his gaze. Though his eyes were kindly, and warm like polished oak, there was a sharpness in them which I fancied might cut through to the soul. Despite his white cassock and crimson cap, he did not have the look of a holy man: his face was taut and cracked, like hide stretched over a shield, and his shoulders seemed more suited to bearing a sword than a staff. He must have been twenty years my senior, the years etched into him, yet there was unbending strength there which I would not want to meet in battle.

'Tatikios desires to know why eighty bushels of the Emperor's grain have not reached him,' I said.

'Then your errand is futile.' He smiled at me. 'If the grain had been in my hands, it would already have passed to his. I can only suppose that some of Count Raymond's

119

men must have misnumbered the shipment, and taken it by mistake.'

'Their mistake means we go hungry.' I was unwilling to accept excuses that we both knew to be false.

'Every man in this camp goes hungry. But if Tatikios can control his appetite and forgive the injustice, I will see that the deficit is made good in the next shipment.'

I nodded. We both knew that the Franks delighted in denying the Byzantines our rations, and that we could do nothing about it save protest. When the Franks had passed through Constantinople, the Emperor had used his command of their provisions to force obedience; now the trick was revisited on us.

'And what news of Drogo?' the bishop asked. He spoke lightly, but did not try to mask his interest.

'There is no news of Drogo,' I said harshly. 'Nor of Rainauld. Bohemond seems to have lost his interest in the question, and even if he had not, I am no longer minded to serve him.'

'It was an evil thing that his nephew did with the prisoners. If I could have stopped him . . .' He parted his clasped hands before him, like a man releasing a bird.

'There seems to be much evil in this army that you cannot stop.' The memory of Tancred swept aside all caution and respect for rank. 'Prisoners are killed, food is stolen, and you – you who wield the authority of God Himself – claim impotence. How is it that God's legate has so little power in the Army of God?'

Adhemar did not flinch. 'The brighter the light, the darker the shadow. Sometimes evils, great evils, must be borne in a higher cause.'

'The cause of letting thousands die besieging an unbreakable city?'

'The cause of salvation – and of peace also.' He leaned forward, his brow creased by intent or sadness. 'Do not scoff when I say peace. For all my life – and yours also – the peace of God, to which all Christians should adhere, has been nothing more than a dream in Christendom. Norman against Greek, Frank against German, father against son and emperor against king – ambition and greed have stirred every lord against his neighbour. Dukes become kings and earls become counts, but at what profit? A lord may add another county to his estate, but it is a wasted land, its fruits and its people pillaged by war. In such circumstances, famine and pestilence and hate and despair and all other works of the Devil flourish, while faith and justice are obliterated.' He closed his eyes in pain, and I wondered what images he saw behind them. 'You have seen the princes, Demetrios, their pride and their jealousies. Only a single power could impose peace on them: God's power, as vested in the Pope. All my life I have worked to advance that power. Now we are at its crisis.'

His words were heartfelt, supple and strong as steel, but all his preacher's art could not mask the contradiction at their core. 'You would make peace by waging war?' I asked. 'Truly, it is said: "I bring no peace but the sword."'

Adhemar shook his head. 'You do not understand our purpose. Since the time of Pope Gregory, the church has fought with words and swords to bend the princes of the Earth to its rule, so that under one authority there need be no struggle. Now, at last, my lord Pope Urban has united all the tribes of Christendom under the banner of the cross. Their feet tread the road to Jerusalem, and their souls walk the still thornier path to the peace and fellowship of Christ. For the first time in history, the lords of the Earth have willingly submitted themselves to the direction of the church.'

'Would they have followed you without the prospect

of war and plunder?' Afterwards I might wonder that I had spoken so freely, so intemperately, to a man of Adhemar's station, but for now his proselytising energy provoked equal response.

'The church must work in the world God made. And human flesh is weak. But if we can keep hold of their ambitions, and govern their wills, then eventually we may guide them to a higher path. This great project is the crucible in which the power of the church, and the peace of Christendom, will be forged. Do you wonder, then, at the fires that burn us?'

'I wonder that you claim to govern their wills, yet cannot command eighty bushels of wheat to reach my camp safely. Nor even keep Tancred from committing the foulest abomination. I see no power – only vain words.'

'There are many powers in this world, visible and invisible,' said Adhemar patiently. 'When Christ came, he did not bring an army of angels to smite his enemies. His was the power to teach and to endure suffering; the power of compassion over anger. If I had ten thousand knights at my command I would be a rival to the princes, and they would sift my words through suspicion and distrust. It is only by forsaking the means to their form of power that I gain the spiritual power to engage their souls. Moral strength comes from weakness in arms – but it is a transient strength, easily spent, and thus much must be sacrificed to the greater end.'

He sat back, apparently drained by the sermon, while I at last let deference reassert itself. It seemed to me that he spoke in paradox, theological riddles to cloud his impotence, but I did not say so. Instead, his last words had spurred a new thought in me.

'On the subject of Drogo, your Grace, there is an aspect of his death which goes beyond my understanding.'

Adhemar gestured to me to continue.

'A month before he died, he and his companions journeyed to the valley of Daphne. I have followed their path and seen where they went. Beneath one of the ancient villas, they discovered a hidden chamber.' As best I could remember, I described the form and the decoration of the cave. 'It was as nothing I have ever seen.' Nor had I discovered anything from the priests in our camp, who had shied away from any report of such pagan evil, enjoining me only to confess and forget it. 'I wonder whether in learning to combat idolatry, you have heard of anything similar?'

Adhemar scratched his white beard, his eyes apparently fixed on some knot in the wood of the table. 'A bull,' he murmured, repeating what I had told him. 'It was an animal, I believe, much worshipped by the ancients. Stephen!'

He called, and a young dark-haired priest appeared from behind the inner curtain of the tent. I felt a stab of wounded confidence that words I had spoken so intemperately to the bishop had been heard by another. The priest ignored me, however, and inclined his head to his master.

'Fetch the writings of the fathers from my library,' Adhemar said.

The priest disappeared and Adhemar looked back to me. 'We shall see what ancient authorities can tell us of ancient idolatry.'

In a few minutes the priest returned, bearing two enormous volumes. They were artfully made, stitched with crimson thread and bound with stout iron locks, while the leaves within seemed tinged with a great age. Unlocking one with a key that he took from his robe, Adhemar cracked it open and turned slowly through the pages. They whispered and crackled like fire. I could not read the script but I could admire its beauty: row upon row of words in perfect alignment, broken every so often by oversized letters swirling across the page. So even was the text that it might have been hammered out from a mould, like coins in a mint.

'His Holiness, my master, foresaw that I might need the direction of wisdom in the wilderness.' Adhemar licked his finger and turned another page. 'These are from his own library in Rome. Ah.' He took a candle from the priest, who had fetched it unprompted, and held it close to the parchment. 'Here is what Eubulus says of the ways of the pagans. "I have heard that the Persians falsely worship a hero who – they say – sacrificed the Bull of Heaven, by whose blood they believe the world and life were created. They name this hero Mithra; they celebrate his rites in secret caves, so that veiled in darkness they may shun the true and glorious light of Christ. They say—"'

He broke off, snatching the candle away so that the page fell into shadow. 'There are some lies which a Christian should not hear repeated, lest entering by his ear the Devil poison his heart.'

Being deemed unworthy of secret knowledge was ever a spark to my temper, but I managed to restrain it. The words which the bishop had already confided were portion enough for my mind: what could Drogo and his companions have purposed in a Persian temple?

'Of course we need not range so far from Truth,' Adhemar said. He seemed distracted, still leafing through the book in search of something. 'It is written that when the Israelites were at Sinai, the Lord said to Moses: "You shall slaughter a bull before the Lord; some of its blood you shall smear on the horns of the altar with your finger, and all the rest you shall pour out at the base of the altar."'

'It is also written: "I delight not in the blood of bulls or lambs or goats."'

Adhemar's face lifted swiftly from his reading and he glared at me. 'You have no cause to remind *me* what is written in scripture. But among the credulous and wicked, much that is written can be twisted to the purposes of evil. As is warned of here, indeed.' His finger came to rest on a fresh page of text. 'From the writings of Tertullian: "The Devil, by his wiles, perverts the truth. The mystic rites of his idols vie even with the sacraments of God. He . . ."' Adhemar's aged brow creased as he concentrated on his text, muttering under his breath in unintelligible Latin. When he looked up, the sharp edge of his eyes seemed dulled by confusion.

'This is remarkable,' he said, his voice deliberately controlled.

'What?'

'In this same passage, Tertullian writes: "The Devil too baptises his own believers; he promises the indulgence of their sins by a rite of his own."' The bishop's fists clenched white around the book, so tight that I feared he might rip the pages from it. '"*There in the kingdom of Satan, Mithra sets his mark on the foreheads of his soldiers.*"'

All resentment and irritation flooded from me. 'When we found Drogo, there was a mark on his forehead in blood. A mark in the shape of a Latin sigma.'

'So I have heard.' Adhemar closed the book and snapped the iron clasp shut.

'I thought it might be the initial of his killer – or of a lover whose affections they rivalled. Could it instead stand for Satan?'

'Do Greeks believe that the Devil writes in Latin?' Despite his evident shock, the bishop managed a thin smile. 'The mark may be the shape of an S, but there is another form it resembles. A form much associated with Satan and his works.'

Adhemar's eyes searched my own. 'Do you not see it? It is the form of a serpent.'

That night, after supper, I left our camp and climbed a little way up the mountain, to a small hollow in the lee of the tower of Malregard. We had long since driven the Turks from these slopes, and Tancred's cannibalism had deterred any spies, but there were still enough footpaths and posterns unguarded that I could not be easy in my mind. Yet I needed to escape the confines of the camp, the clamour of men and beasts and arms, to find an expanse in which my mind could wander. Perhaps I had chosen unwisely, for the fear of marauding Turks pressed my thoughts far harder than any distraction in the camp, but I squeezed myself in the shadow between two rocks and let curiosity gradually tease away my fears.

The questions which exercised me offered scarce comfort: it was a lonely place to contend with the ways of the Devil. Several times I tried to reason a path of thought, and each time I found my way barred by some insuperable image: the cave, the bloody mark on Drogo's face, the flies crawling on Rainauld's rotted corpse. Rainauld and Drogo had entered the temple of some Persian demon; Quino and Odard too. Had their deaths then been some form of divine punishment for their impiety – or the hand of the Devil reclaiming his own? Suddenly I was assailed by the vision of a diabolical claw, wreathed in smoke, scratching out its evil sign on Drogo's body. I trembled, and fastened my hand around my silver cross. Such fancy would serve me nothing.

A noise from the slope below broke my thoughts in panic. I leaned forward, bowing my head as I tried to discern the least whisper around me, but it needed little effort. The beat of footsteps crunching into the stony soil was unmissable, coming ever closer, and I cowered back with my cloak thrown over me. 'Deliver me from evil, Lord,' I prayed silently, closing my eyes lest they betray me. 'Have mercy upon me, sinner that I am.'

The footsteps halted, terrifyingly close, though there seemed to be only a single man. I had my knife with me, but stuck in the cleft I could hardly hope to spring on him in surprise. And what if he were a Frankish sentry, one of the tower guards come to relieve himself? I might easily provoke a massacre if I knifed him in the dark.

'Are you trying to become a hermit, Demetrios, to emulate Saint Antony?'

My eyes sprang open. In the hollow before me stood Anna, her silk belt luminous under the folds of her *palla*. She was turned towards me, and though I could not see her face I could tell there was a smile on it. Abashed, I scrambled out.

'You should take more care,' I scolded her. 'Wandering the mountain at night, you may find yourself emulating any number of saints more gruesome than Saint Antony.

'Saint Demetrios, for example, stabbed with a pagan spear. Why have you come here?' The levity in Anna's voice vanished with the last question, unable to overcome her worry. For weeks now she had fretted at my ill mood, sometimes remonstrating with me, more often just watching me with concern. Far from soothing me, her anxiety only added shame to my misery.

'I came to find the peace to think. Why have *you* come?'

'I followed you. I feared you might find too much peace on this mountain in the dark.'

'No peace at all with you about.' I stepped forward and wrapped my arms around her to show that I meant no anger. She pressed forward, her cheek cool in the spring air, and for a moment we embraced in silence.

'What thoughts did you come to think?' she asked, drawing me over to a rocky shelf where we could sit in shadow.

'Evil thoughts.' At supper I had avoided recounting my conversation with the bishop, but now I found I could summon the words with ease. At first I spoke to the night, not meeting Anna's gaze, but as my story continued I leaned ever closer towards her. My eyes began to sift her face from the surrounding darkness, and I slipped my hand into hers so that our fingers wove together.

'You cannot think Satan himself killed Drogo?' she said when I had finished.

'No.' It was true – I did not think so, though I could not entirely disbelieve it either.

'Even if the murder was the Devil's work, he need not have troubled to stir himself. There are many acolytes too ready to hear his bidding.' Anna paused. 'What did Bohemond say?'

'I have not told him. I have not spoken with him since I saw the cave.'

'He has lost his enthusiasm for finding Drogo's killer?'

'Yes.' I remembered the Count of Saint-Gilles's cynicism. 'When it seemed a Provençal might have been the murderer, Bohemond was eager to prove the man's guilt. Now that Rainauld is beyond suspicion, his interest wanes.'

'It will wane still further if he discovers that his men worshipped at the shrine of a Persian demon. That will not enhance his standing in the Army of God.'

'His standing matters nothing while the army wastes itself against this city.' Again, my anger welled within me. 'For what he and his nephew have done, I would happily see their heads impaled on Turkish spears. If his men have communion with the Devil, if Satan has come to claim them for his own or if God has wreaked his vengeance, so be it. I no longer care what befalls them, nor even whether Antioch falls or stands. I would like to see Jerusalem, but not in the train of this army of thieves and murderers. That is no pilgrimage.' I lowered my voice, aware that my words might carry too far in the quiet of the night. 'Let them all kill each other, the sooner that I can return to my family.'

My face had grown hot with anger. Then, suddenly, there were cool lips against my own, drawing the fever from me. I started, then pressed forward in haste to meet her kiss. For long moments we said nothing.

'Whatever befalls the Normans, you won't stop seeking Drogo and Rainauld's killer,' Anna said, pulling her hood back over her hair.

'Because Bohemond has bought me?' I challenged her.

'Not at all.' She set her finger against my mouth to hush me, then stroked it over my cheek and into my beard. 'In part, because Bohemond may find the truth unwelcome. But mostly, I think, because you cannot let a mystery be until you have torn off its veil and revealed it to the world.'

Anna spoke truthfully, and I opened my arms to acknowledge it. Somewhere in the night an owl was hunting, while insects chittered and water dripped from a mossy ledge nearby. Down on the plain the Army of God would be dousing its fires and settling onto muddy straw and reeds. But up on the mountain, under a starless sky, Anna and I sinned in silence on the rocky bed we had made.

ι δ

Anna's embrace comforted me that night, but stark guilt gnawed at me next day. The memory of the cave had weighed heavy on me for weeks: my soul could hardly bear further sins. I was in a black humour as Sigurd and I walked the road on the west bank of the Orontes, checking all who passed for hoarded food or treachery. The worst straits of our famine had abated in the month gone by, as spring had opened the mountains and the seas to the Emperor's convoys, but a little food had proved almost worse than none. Our grain became the seed of a thousand quarrels, envy and greed flourishing on its stalk, and it took frequent patrols to keep peace in the camp.

'We would do better,' said Sigurd, 'turning our efforts against the city.'

We would indeed. With sun and food, the army's strength had begun to recover, but the spring had produced no thaw in the Turkish defences. Across the sparkling river, beyond the tents, Antioch's long walls faced us as stoutly as ever. From the heights where we stood I could see the red-tiled roofs of the houses within, and the terraced orchards climbing up the slope behind. In the fields to the north tiny figures steered ploughs and oxen, tilling the ground for the new season's crop. They could be confid-ent, I feared, of still being there to reap the harvest.

'If I were the princes, I would grow more nervous every day,' said Sigurd. 'Once their armies find their health, they'll turn to greater mischief if they cannot spend their vigour in battle.'

'There's little danger of mischief, then.' A stone had worked its way into my boot, and we paused while I extracted it. 'It's been two months since Bohemond defeated the last relief army. There are more Turks left in Asia, and the news of our siege will have travelled far. If they come again in strength, we will be hard pressed to defeat them.'

'Then perhaps they'll allow us to go home.'

Sigurd might joke, but we both knew the danger. Rumours of impending Turkish armies swept around the camp every day, but recently they had become more consistent, more specific. Only that morning an imperial courier had brought Tatikios a message. He would not divulge its contents, but it had left him pale. As long as we had none save the city's defenders to oppose us, the priests could preach that time was of no import in the service of the Lord. But that delusion was folly. Sooner or later, it would be exposed on the spears of an approaching army.

'Demetrios!' A Varangian, his fair hair blowing out behind him, came running up the road. 'The doctor has sent me – she says you must come. She has discovered something about the dead Norman.'

'Drogo? What is it?'

'She would not say.'

'Where is she?'

'In her tent, treating a Frankish pilgrim.'

I left Sigurd and ran back. Anna had caused her tent to be set on the southern edge of our camp, facing the open ground that separated us from the Normans. A narrow stream ran off the mountain nearby to give fresh water, and nourished a plentiful supply of reeds for the patients' rest. As was her custom when the sun shone, Anna had rolled up the walls of her tent. Underneath the canopy were four crude beds, planks raised on stones and covered with rushes; three were empty, but a half-naked figure was lying face down on the fourth, apparently asleep. A poultice bound in cloth oozed green fluid onto his back. On a stool beside him Anna kept patient vigil, her dress covered by a much-stained apron.

'What have you found?' I asked, panting with the effort of running.

She looked up from her patient. 'I wondered whether Drogo's name would bring you.'

'When you call, of course I come immediately.'

She wrinkled her nose in mock disbelief, then gestured back to the bed. 'Look at this.'

As soon as I looked, I saw why Anna had summoned me. From the poultice, I guessed there must have been some cut or boil on the man's neck, but that was not the first wound he had suffered – nor what drew my gaze. Among the warts and freckles and pimples, a long scar ran up his spine, disappearing under his dishevelled hair; another intersected it just below the shoulder. The skin was puckered tight, with none of the glossy sheen of a freshly healed cut, but the lines were straight and clear as the day they were carved, unmistakable in the cross they made.

'I see why you thought of Drogo.'

'He came to me to lance a boil. He was reluctant to remove his tunic, but the pain was so great that at last he surrendered.'

'This was cut some time ago. He—'

Something of my voice must have penetrated the man's dreams, for he shuddered, and turned his head abruptly towards us. 'Who are you?'

'Who are *you*?'

'Peter Bartholomew.' He winced as his movement strained the burst boil. 'A pilgrim of the Lord.'

133

I could have guessed from his ragged clothes that he was no knight. Nor was there any nobility in his face: his nose was crooked, as if it had been broken in a fight, his teeth were cracked, and the skin was pocked with sores. 'Do you follow Christ faithfully?'

'As faithfully as I may.'

'Really?' Anna pointed to the base of his spine, just above the folds of his tunic. The skin around it was covered with blisters, some bubbling up, others long since burst and crusted with pus. I grimaced; I had been in the army long enough to know the symptoms of an immoral disease.

Bartholomew's ratlike eyes blinked at us. 'Even Job, who was perfect in the Lord's sight, was smitten with sore boils from head to toe. I endure my trials as best I can.'

'Doubtless the Lord will judge you as you deserve. Was it He, pilgrim, who carved His sign in your flesh?'

Bartholomew yelped and tried to leap up from the bed. The poultice tumbled from his back, spilling pulpy leaves over the soil, but I had expected his move and clamped my hand on his shoulder to hold him down. He writhed and twisted like an eel in my grip until Beric, the Varangian who had summoned me, stepped forward and pinned down his arms.

'Who put that mark on your back?'

'I did it, as a mark of my piety before the Lord.'

'You did not carve it by reaching your hands over your shoulder. Who helped you?'

'A . . . a friend.'

'His name?'

'He is dead now.'

'Is he?' Trying to ignore his stink, which was very great, I leaned close to Bartholomew's ear. 'You are not the only man to bear that cross, Bartholomew. I have seen it on two others, though their piety earned them no favour from the Lord. They were dead.'

'Dead?' Spit drooled out of the side of his mouth.

'You have heard of Drogo of Melfi? Or Rainauld of Albigeois?'

'I know of the knight Rainauld. He was a Provençal, as I am.'

'Then you know what befell him, how his broken body was found ravaged in a culvert.' I pulled out my knife and laid the flat of the blade against his neck. He shivered at the touch of the cold iron. 'You would not wish to suffer the same fate.'

The pilgrim's ugly face creased into sobs. 'Have mercy,' he wailed. 'I came here for healing, and now I will be murdered. Have mercy on Your servant, Lord. Deliver me from my enemies, from the workers of bloody iniquity who set snares for my soul. O Lord my shield, God of mercy, You alone are my defence and my refuge, have mercy—'

'Silence,' I snapped. 'Do not pretend to invoke His name, lest hearing you He visits still more afflictions upon you. Why did you have the cross carved?'

'To show my piety.'

'To whom?'

'To the Lord God.'

I slapped my knife against the raw skin of the boil that Anna had lanced, and he screamed. 'When two or three men bear exactly the same mark, I think it is more than personal piety that moves them. You were part of some secret order or brotherhood, were you not, and this was your sign?'

'Yes,' shrieked Bartholomew. 'It is true – there was a brother-hood. You could not understand it for it was a fellowship of purity, of sanctity.'

'A fellowship of purity?' I repeated. 'Why should that have been kept a secret?'

'Because the Devil has many spies lurking to snatch

us. Because the Army of God has become corrupted. Our leaders have forgotten Christ and are fallen prey to selfish greed; our camp festers with vice and blasphemy. Why else has God deserted us before this city? Voices cry out to them to straighten their ways, but they suppress us. That is why we meet in secret and hide the marks of our faith, lest the ravening wolves of Satan consume us.'

'And Drogo and Rainauld were adepts of this group?' I did not know whether to trust him, but there was a terrified force in his words that betold their truth.

'I cannot say.'

'You *will* say.' I tapped him with my knife again, though this time on unbroken skin.

'I cannot. We are sworn to secrecy – and even if I have betrayed that, I cannot betray my companions. I do not know their names.'

'You must have seen some whom you recognised.'

'My eyes were only focused on God.' Having revealed his secret and survived, Bartholomew seemed to be finding new strength.

'How did you discover the group, if you knew no one in it?'

'My friend – who is dead – brought the priest to speak with me. She spoke with me for many hours, opening my eyes to truth and repentance. Afterwards—'

So confused were my thoughts that it took a full sentence for me to hear the meaning of his words. '*She?*' I exploded, spinning him round so that he stared up at me. 'The priest was a *woman*? What sort of heresy was this?'

'No heresy but the truth of Christ. Consider the Holy Virgin Mary, the mother of Jesus – she was a woman made a vessel of God's purpose. Why not another? Sarah lived—'

'Sarah? Her name was Sarah?' I felt like a man flailing on the edge of a cliff, snatching at branches not knowing if they would snap or hold. 'She was a Provençal?'

Bartholomew shook his head, plainly terrified by my frenzy. 'She was not a Provençal. I thought she was a Greek, though she did not speak of it. Her name was Sarah.'

'Demetrios!'

The sound of my name spun me around in redoubled confusion. Stooped under the tent flaps, a Patzinak behind him, Sigurd was watching me. His face was grim.

'What is it?' I asked.

'Tatikios has summoned us.'

'Tatikios can wait,' I insisted. 'My business is urgent.'

'You must come. He has decided to leave Antioch.'

Sigurd led me at a run to Tatikios' tent, saying nothing. My fears redoubled when I saw a band of Norman knights gathered in front of it, but they did not hinder us. Tatikios' guards were nowhere to be seen.

I had always thought the interior to be spacious, but it seemed crowded as we entered now. Four more Normans were standing near the door, three of them in armour and one in chains between them. They formed an immovable mass of iron, about which Tatikios' slaves scurried in haste, bearing bundles of cloth and arms. The rich partitioning curtain had been ripped from its hangings, and the icon of the three warrior saints had vanished from its stand. In the centre, standing by his silvered chair, stood a highly agitated Tatikios.

'Demetrios. You have come at last.' He twisted his hands together, made as if to step forward, then slumped into the chair instead.

'You are leaving, Lord?' I asked in confusion.

'Yes.'

'Why?'

'The better to bring this siege to a close. And for my own safety.'

'Your safety is assured while the Varangians serve you.' Sigurd stepped forward, his axe prominent in his hands. 'A brutish gang of Normans will not trouble you.'

'On the contrary.' Tatikios' voice had jumped high as a girl's. 'It is they—'

'It is we who have saved him.' The moment the leading Norman spoke, all attention switched to him, to the strength of command in his voice. With his head hidden under a helmet and his back to me, I had not recognised him, though size alone should have warned me. As he turned to face me, he revealed the red-and-white mottled skin, the russet beard and dark hair squeezed beneath the dome of his helmet, the eyes as pale as a winter sky.

'I owe my life to the Lord Bohemond,' Tatikios protested. Absent-mindedly, he scratched the side of his golden nose as if it itched.

'How?'

'We have discovered a plot,' said Bohemond. 'A base conspiracy among those who hate the Emperor.'

'They planned to murder me,' Tatikios squeaked. 'Me – the Grand Primikerios, plenipotentiary of the Emperor himself. Can you conceive it?'

'Wickedness indeed,' said Sigurd inscrutably.

'Why should they do that?' I asked. 'What would they gain?'

Bohemond turned to the man in chains behind him, secured between the two knights. 'Well, worm? What did you hope to gain by your treachery?'

'Mercy, Lord.' Long hair covered the prisoner's sagging face so I could not see him; he moaned as Bohemond aimed a kick at his knee. 'Have mercy on me.'

'Confess yourself.'

'I planned to steal into the eunuch's tent late at night

and stab him in the heart. I despise the Greeks. Their presence in our army draws the Lord's wrath. They promised to feed us, and we are hungry. They promised gold, and we are poor. They promised to fight, but they sit comfortably in their palaces. Now, at their Emperor's command, they pay the Turks to assail us in secret, that we might be destroyed.' His voice, which had been curiously unpassioned, now began to rise. 'Only when their filth is driven from our camp will the Lord favour us with victory. Only—'

'Enough.' Bohemond slapped his hand across the man's cheek. The prisoner subsided into silence. 'You see, my Lord Tatikios, the ignorance of some of my followers. I crave your forgiveness, but too many in my army do not love the Greeks. Their charges are lies and slanders, but however often I deny them they are believed.'

'How did you discover this plot?' I asked.

Bohemond did not even look at me to answer. 'One of his companions betrayed him.'

'Luckily so,' declared Tatikios fervently. 'You, Demetrios, are charged with ensuring my safety. You are supposed to guard against rumours and betrayals. *You* have failed me – and it is only by the good offices of Lord Bohemond that I am saved.'

I bowed my head, and said nothing. I could guess why I might have failed.

'But if the conspiracy has been discovered and the murderer captured, then why are you leaving?' Sigurd broke in. 'To abandon the siege now would be—'

Tatikios drew himself up in his chair, and fixed a haughty stare on Sigurd. 'I do not abandon the siege, Captain. If you suggest that I do, I will have you dragged across Anatolia in chains to learn humility.'

The axe seemed to tremble in Sigurd's hands, but he kept silent.

'This wretch, I fear, is only one gust in a storm.'

Bohemond gestured to the prisoner. 'There is a whirlwind brewing in my camp – and among all the Franks – and I cannot pledge to halt every evil they may concoct.'

'If it were only my own safety, that would matter nothing,' said Tatikios stiffly. 'But there are other concerns, higher duties. If we are to prosecute this siege to its end, we shall need reinforcements. The Emperor is campaigning in Anatolia – I will undertake an embassy to persuade him to advance swiftly in all his power and might.'

Bohemond nodded. 'A wise plan. Although . . .'

'What?'

'If you leave now, while our prospects seem bleak, there will be many in the camp who misconstrue your motives. Some will talk of fear – others, perhaps, of cowardice. And if they think the Greeks have abandoned them, they may even believe themselves released from their oath to your Emperor, free to seize whatever lands they can.'

'They will soon find their error when the Emperor returns.'

'It would be easier if you left some token of your trust, evidence to persuade my companions to adhere to the Emperor. If you were to confirm one of our number in possession of lands, for example, none could deny the good faith of the Greeks. It need not even be lands that you already possess,' Bohemond added, seeing the doubt on Tatikios' face. 'If you assigned future conquests to our charge – under the Emperor's authority, of course – you would prove your good will at little cost.'

Bohemond could not hide the hunger in his voice, nor in his eyes, as he stared down on the eunuch. Tatikios, to his credit, did not look away, but gazed back as impassive as if he were in the Emperor's palace. I hoped he could see the doubt written bold across my face.

'You speak wisely, Lord Bohemond,' he said at last. 'I

would not desire my departure to become a pretext for any man breaking his oath. Any who did would surely be called to a reckoning before God and my Emperor. As a sign of my earnest desire for friendship and favour between our peoples, I will do as you suggest.'

I fancied that I saw Bohemond's tongue shoot out like an adder's, licking his lips in expectation.

'Your nephew Tancred currently claims the lands of Mamistra, Tarsus and Adana in Cilicia. I confirm them in his possession, as vassal to the Emperor.'

A spasm passed through Bohemond's back as if he had been struck by a lance. 'The lands of Cilicia were taken from Armenians,' he protested, unable to keep the wound from his voice. 'They are not the Emperor's to bestow.'

'The Armenians held them from the Emperor. Now Tancred does. I will have my scribe write out the charter. And as a further pledge of my honour,' he continued, before Bohemond could object, 'I will leave my tent and my supplies and a company of my men here at Antioch, until I return.'

'We will value them, Lord.' The calm had returned to Bohemond's voice, though the skin on his cheeks throbbed red. 'But you cannot forget your own safety. There are many brigands and Turks between here and Philomelium, and the road is dangerous. You will need an escort.'

'I will sail from Saint Simeon, and take the Patzinaks. Sigurd will remain here as captain, in command of the Varangians. Demetrios, you will see to the well-being of our camp followers and servants.'

'What will become of the Norman conspirator?' I asked.

'He will be judged and punished according to our laws,' said Bohemond harshly.

'Good.' Tatikios clapped his hands together, and rose.

There seemed a confidence in his bearing that I had not seen in weeks. 'I must make my preparations and go. My cause is urgent, and the road long.' He looked to Bohemond. 'I shall report to the Emperor all I have seen, and pray that he comes to rescue his noble allies.'

Bohemond bowed. 'I shall pray that he comes in time.'

Tatikios left two hours later, a stiff figure on a grey palfrey. Two hundred Patzinaks followed on foot, their spears straight and rigid as the bars of a cage, while two dozen horses carried his baggage. We could ill afford to lose the animals, and a detachment of Varangians was sent to escort them back when the men had embarked from the harbour. With a leaden heart, I watched the column ride towards the pale sun as it dipped behind the mountains into the sea.

'We won't see him again,' said Sigurd.

I laughed, though there was no joy in it. 'Because he won't return?' I asked. 'Or because we shall not be here when he does?'

A wispy feather of down, perhaps from some newly hatched bird, had drifted onto the blade of Sigurd's axe. He brushed it away, and gave no answer.

I had not believed a word of the plot that Bohemond claimed to have discovered, and my distrust proved well founded. I never heard of any punishment meted out to the Norman who had confessed; to the contrary, the next time I saw him, some days later, he was mounted on a fine colt and lavishly dressed. No doubt he had been well rewarded for serving Bohemond's purpose.

Two nights after Tatikios left I saw more of Bohemond's schemes. It was after dark, on a grim evening, when a Frankish priest called at my tent. I recognised him from my interview with Bishop Adhemar, a dark-haired man named Stephen.

'His Grace the Bishop of Le Puy sends greetings,' he announced to me and Sigurd. 'The princes hold a council tonight, and you would benefit by attending.'

'Benefit whom?' I asked, suspicious of any Frankish invitation.

'Come and learn.'

As captain, it was Sigurd's place to go, but he insisted that I accompany him. 'Someone may need to restrain my temper. And I would not trust Bohemond further than I could swing my axe.'

The council was held in Adhemar's tent, its furniture stripped away and four benches arranged in the customary square. As ever, Count Raymond had contrived to sit facing the door, where men looked first, with the bishop at his right. On the bench to their left, resplendent in a wine-red robe with a golden belt, was Bohemond. I avoided his gaze and tried to seat myself on the end of the bench opposite Adhemar. Almost immediately there was dissent.

'My Lords, who are these peasants who disturb our council, foreigners who creep in to spy our secrets? Call your knights, Bishop, and send them away to the dungheap they crawled from.'

It was the Duke of Normandy who spoke, his fat cheeks puffed up like a cow's. A well-fed belly pressed against the rich silk of his tunic, and he swayed slightly as he spoke. He had distinguished himself by spending almost the entire siege far from Antioch, safe on the coast, and I wondered what it signified that he had returned now. I knew that Sigurd hated him above all Normans, for he was the son of the bastard who had conquered Sigurd's English homeland.

'Peace, Duke Robert,' said Adhemar. 'These men speak for the Emperor himself, to whom you are all sworn. It is right that they should attend our council.'

'A dog may bark when his master is away, but you do not invite him to your table. These are not princes – they are vagabonds. They are not our equals.'

Adhemar frowned. 'All are equal in the eyes of the Lord – while they keep His peace. Soon we shall need every sinew of our strength if we are to survive.'

The threat in his words silenced them, and they retreated glowering to their benches. Adhemar offered a prayer, then turned to Duke Godfrey.

'The Duke of Lorraine brings news.'

'From my brother Baldwin,' said Godfrey. The jewelled cross he wore swung from his neck as he stood. 'He has sent a messenger from Edessa.'

When we were halfway across Anatolia, the Duke's land-less brother Baldwin had broken away from the army and ridden east, hoping to seize Armenian lands for himself. In a progression of violence, cunning and murder, he had – according to reports – first been adopted heir of the local ruler, then bloodily deposed him, and now ruled the far-flung lands of Edessa as tyrant. Having had some dealings with Baldwin at Constantinople, I could well believe the story.

'Baldwin sends word that, even now, Kerbogha the Terrible, Atabeg of Mosul, marches his army towards Antioch.' A babble of panicked chatter burst across the room. 'From every province of the Turkish empire, from Mesopotamia, Persia and distant Khorasan, he has assembled an army to drive us from Asia. Already when Baldwin wrote they neared Edessa – within a month, or even within weeks, they will be here.'

The tumult in the room stopped as Adhemar banged his staff on the ground. In an instant the sallow-skinned Count Hugh was on his feet.

'We must retreat immediately,' he announced, his tongue flapping to keep pace with his terror. 'There is no glory in a rout. We must fall back on Heraklea, or Iconium, and join with the Emperor's forces. Remember that we are but the vanguard of Christendom, and even as we speak fresh armies of the pious are pouring out of the west to aid us. After we have reinforced ourselves, then we can battle this Turk as he deserves.'

'Retreat?' Raymond bored his single-eyed glare into the hapless Hugh. 'Have you forgotten the torments that brought us here – the passes so steep that even crows could not get into them to feast on our dead, and the salt deserts where we withered? If we journey north, rocks and thorns will rip our ragged army apart long before the Turks come. Besides, Jerusalem is to the south – and I will not turn my course until I have fulfilled my vow to walk in the footsteps of Christ.'

His outburst drew approving nods and murmurs, though there was little conviction in them. I saw Adhemar whisper something in his ear, but before the bishop could speak to the council Bohemond had risen. As ever, there was something in his presence which commanded attention, and the company fell silent.

'Count Raymond speaks the truth. We cannot go back: the road will destroy us.'

He paused, allowing others to mutter their assent. Looking at the Count of Saint-Gilles, I saw his head crooked to one side, the eye half-closed, almost as if he were falling asleep.

Bohemond hooked his thumb on his belt. 'But the Count of Vermandois speaks the truth also. There is no glory in a rout.'

'Then what would you have us do?' snapped Godfrey. 'We cannot fight; we cannot flee: shall we sit in our tents until Kerbogha burns us alive in them?'

Bohemond showed no concern. 'The Duke of Lorraine asks what I would have us do. I will tell you. Kerbogha the Terrible rushes on us like a bull. If we fight, we are gored on one horn. If we run, we are gored on the other. If we do nothing, we are trampled under the hooves. What, then, do we do?'

'Exactly.'

'We strike it clean between the eyes.' As if from the air itself, a bone-handled knife appeared in Bohemond's hand. He rolled the hilt in his palm. 'In the scant time remaining, we take the city and make it a bulwark to withstand everything the Turks may throw at us. For six months we have sat out here like women, hoping that the Lord would send some miracle to break open the city. Now we have His sign. If we cannot force the city, we are unworthy of our quest. When I hear that Kerbogha is coming, I am not afraid.' His restless gaze dropped a moment on Hugh, and moved on. 'I rejoice that now, when the fire is hottest, we may prove ourselves true before God. Every alternative is death. What does the council say?'

'It says we meet in the peace of Christ, and all weapons are to be left outside,' observed Adhemar mildly.

'And I say that famine has starved Bohemond's mind,' said Hugh. '"Take the city", he says. Shall we knock on the gates? For six months we have tried to take the city, and—'

'No!' Bohemond thumped a fist into his palm. 'For six months we have tried *nothing*. Now that ruin is upon us we may at last begin to try. Our stratagems have failed. The Greek King has proved a false ally, and his manless minion has abandoned us in our greatest need. Only if we unleash our desperation can we hope to escape this trap. In peace we esteem humility the only grace, but in war the truest spur is glory. Let the council agree that whoever takes the city, he alone will rule it. With such a prize to be had, we will break down those gates like clay.'

'No.' Old though he was, Adhemar's voice rang above the clamour that Bohemond's words had sparked. 'The city belongs to no man.'

'Except the Pope?' Robert of Normandy did not bother to stand but stabbed a fat finger at the bishop. 'We know that Rome allows no kings but her vassals, that she would extend her domain over realms temporal as well as spiritual. Will your master not be satisfied, I wonder, until his fiefdoms stretch from Rome to Jerusalem?'

'Have a care,' Raymond warned. 'Do not rekindle long-forgotten feuds.'

'My master the Pope does not covet this city.' Adhemar's sharp-eyed gaze swept across the room. 'One city alone is in his heart, and we are still far from reaching it. As for Antioch, none shall have it outright, because none shall take it outright. We fight in the name and service of the

Lord: only through Him shall we find victory. We march as the Army of God, and as the Army of God we shall claim the spoils. If Kerbogha does not destroy us first.'

'You are also bound by oath to return it to the Emperor,' Sigurd muttered. No one seemed to hear him.

'I disagree with Bishop Adhemar.' Still Bohemond would not yield. 'We fight in the name of God, and with His aid, but we fight also as Normans and Lotharingians and Frisians — even, sometimes, Provençals. I demand to know the will of the council as to whether the worthiest of these should take the city.'

Adhemar thumped his staff three times on the ground. 'There is only one issue before the council: whether we fight or flee in the face of Kerbogha's advance. We will know the will of the council on that alone. Who favours flight?'

There was silence. Looking around, I could see the searching expressions on many men's faces each trying to guess his neighbour's intent. Some arms wavered in uncertainty, but none was raised.

'Who favours battle?'

Immediately, and in unison, Raymond and Bohemond showed their hands. With greater or lesser enthusiasm, every other man around the square followed their example.

Adhemar nodded. 'It is decided. We will face Kerbogha here.'

'Nothing is decided — nor will be until you acknowledge the truth. Unless one man is assured of the city, none will hazard the risks needed to take it.' Bohemond pushed through the corner between two benches and stormed out of the tent. Several of his lieutenants followed.

'Bohemond does not care to be frustrated,' said a voice. I turned and saw Count Raymond at my side. 'He has seen off your emperor's general, but still Adhemar checks his ambitions. For how long, I wonder?'

'For as long as the Franks stand by their oath to the Emperor, and their God.'

Raymond gave a rasping chuckle. 'Their God will tell them that they honour Him best by preserving the lives that He has gifted them. As for their oath, who is now here to hold them to it? A company of Englishmen and a scribe? Do you feel safe, Demetrios?'

'I put my trust in the Lord,' I said instinctively.

'I put my trust in stout armour and a sharp blade. You are isolated in your camp, I think – on the fringes of the siege and with none but Normans nearby. When Kerbogha comes, it will be from the north. Are you ready to stand in the first line of defence?'

'Would you rather have me flee like Tatikios?'

'I would rather have you surrounded by the Emperor and ten thousand of his legions, but that will not happen. Thus, I offer you my protection. Move your tents within my encampment and I will assure your safety.'

'Tatikios believed that we should not commit to any Frankish faction lest the Emperor lose the allegiance of the others.'

'He has already lost the allegiance of the others – they merely wait for one of their number to be the first to repudiate him. As for Tatikios, this is no longer his concern.'

'If we move now, men will see another instance of Byzantine cowardice. They will say we do it to escape the enemies approaching from the north.'

'You would do better to fear the enemies camped to your south.' Raymond stooped to pass through the door, and I followed him into the mild evening. 'When the Turks come and find us trapped between the river and the city, it will not matter if you are in your camp or my camp or even Duke Godfrey's camp.'

He looked to the north, where the sky was firming into darkness. 'There will be no escape when Kerbogha comes.'

We moved our camp next day, squeezing our tents into the spaces left by Provençals who had died or fled. Every day, it seemed, the weather grew warmer and the skies bluer; trees blossomed and the earth hardened, but nothing could shake off the mournful cloud building over the army like a thunderhead. At night our camp-fires hissed with whispered rumours of Kerbogha, and each morning fresh patches of bare earth revealed where more tents had vanished away. Yet still the princes could find no way of cracking the city – nor even seemed minded to try. They garrisoned their towers and shot arrows at defenders on the walls, but they moved not an inch closer.

One day, in the middle of May, I was sitting by the river alone, wondering how I might save Anna if Kerbogha overran our camp. Despite all my pleas she had refused to take ship to Cyprus, claiming that she would be most needed when the Turks attacked. I feared gravediggers would be more use. I buried my hand in the earth of the river bank and pulled out a fistful of pebbles, tossing them one by one into the green water. If only I could have cast my cares away so easily.

The clash of metal rang out and I stared round. A little way upstream I could see a loose knot of figures standing near the bank. They carried a rustic armoury of axes, hammers and billhooks, waving them viciously above their heads. In their midst I could see the flashing blade of a lone sword.

I scrambled to my feet and sprinted towards them. They were peasants, Franks, their ragged clothes scarce fit for rubbing down horses. By the turbaned head which bobbed between them, I guessed they had happened on a lone Turk far from his lines. They were baiting him like a dog, and if they did not disembowel him with their tools they would soon drive him into the river.

'What are you doing?' I shouted as I drew near.

'An infidel spy.' One of the Franks leaped back as the Turk's sword swung past his chest. 'The lord Bohemond will pay well for his corpse.'

'Demetrios Askiates?' With a ringing clang, the Ishmaelite parried a blow from a billhook and looked up. In shock, I saw that it was not a Turk but a Saracen, the swordsmith Mushid. 'In the name of your God and mine, get these hounds away from me.'

'Leave him alone.' I drew my own sword, for in those days it never left my side, and jabbed it at the nearest Frank.

The peasant, a gaunt and hairless man, spat at my feet. 'His life is ours. No Greek will keep us from him.'

'And no Frankish villein shall kill a man under my protection.' I rolled my wrists and swung the sword. The peasant had begun to raise his sickle; my blade caught on its curve and tore it from his hands. As the other Franks stared, Mushid brought the flat of his sword down on the knuckles that gripped a hammer. They sprang open and the tool dropped to the ground. Before it landed, a kick in the belly had sent another of the Franks sprawling back, while I reversed my blade and thumped the pommel into one more adversary's face. Blood dribbled from his lip.

'We will return here, traitor,' the gaunt man warned me. His gaze darted to the fallen sickle, but two hovering swords warned against rashness. 'I will come back with my brothers and I will rip out every inch of your entrails so that when I finally throw you in the river you will float all the way to Saint Simeon.' He stumbled away, drawing his bruised companions after him.

'You fight well, considering the poverty of your blade.' Mushid wiped his own blade on the hem of his white woollen robe, squinted down it to check for cracks, then replaced it in its sheath. The iron barely whispered as it slid into the scabbard.

'The Varangians have been teaching me. I fear I will have more than peasants and pruning hooks to fight before long.'

Mushid's dark eyebrows lifted. 'Kerbogha?' I must have shown some surprise, for he laughed. 'You forget, Demetrios, that I travel widely in my trade. These past weeks the talk has been of little else.'

'Do you know where he is?' In the back of my mind, I wondered what other rumours this smiling, itinerant craftsman might carry, and to whom he might report them.

'At Edessa. He thought to reduce the city first, but it has proved harder than he thought. I suspect he will soon abandon it and hasten on to greater battles.'

'And easier pickings.'

'Come, Demetrios: your swordplay is not so bad.' He looked at the sky. 'But I must hurry on, for the wars of this world need swords to fight them. Will you accompany me through the camp? I do not want to dirty my blade again on peasants.'

As we walked north, through the Norman lines, a thought occurred to me. 'You said you travel widely. Have you ever been to Persia?'

'Often. It is said that the Sultan in Isfahan himself carries one of my blades.'

'Tell me: on your journeys, did you ever encounter the worship of a Persian deity named Mithra?'

Mushid looked perplexed. 'There have been no gods save Allah in Persia for four hundred years – since the Prophet, praise him, converted its peoples to truth.'

'You have never heard of this Mithra?'

'Never. Why?'

I hesitated. 'You were friendly with Drogo. Did he ever speak to you of religion?'

'A little. Our friendship was easier without it. He was very devout, I think.' He paused, his smooth face furrowed in thought. 'You ask about ancient gods, and then about Drogo's faith. What are you truly asking, I wonder?'

'I seek any thread I can grasp. Drogo's murderer has still not been found.'

'That is bad. The Devil draws strength when his deeds go unchecked.'

'Then he must be strong indeed at the moment.'

We walked on a little in silence, our hands ever on the hilts of our swords to discourage the hate-filled looks we drew. Eventually, Mushid said: 'If a man in my village were killed, I would seek his murderer nearby, among his friends, his lovers, his servants and his master.'

'Drogo's friends were building the tower by the bridge, and it was his servant who brought us to the body. His lovers . . .' I thought of the woman, Sarah, whom many had seen but none could find. 'I do not know. As for his master, Bohemond—'

I broke off in surprise as I saw where we had arrived. Even as I spoke Bohemond's name, we had come into open ground, in the midst of which stood his huge, crimson-striped tent. A banner emblazoned with a silver serpent hung limp in front of it.

'I must leave you here,' said Mushid.

'For Bohemond?' Though I hated the memory, I thought of Tancred's abomination with the Turkish prisoners. 'You do not know what Normans will do to Ishmaelites like you.'

Mushid smiled. 'Even Normans can stem their hatred if there is gain to be had. Bohemond seeks a weapon to slice open the city. Perhaps I can supply the blade he needs. Thank you for guiding me here.'

He inclined his head, then strode confidently into the tent. Neither of the guards challenged him.

Two weeks later, at the end of May, Sigurd, Anna and I sat around our campfire, eating fish stew. Our provisions had improved immeasurably since we had moved to Raymond's camp, for he controlled the supply road to the sea, but there was no satisfaction in it. In those days every meal seemed a last supper before the Turkish onslaught, and the bread was ash in our mouths. Nor did the coming of summer lighten our mood, for our armour weighed doubly heavy in the heat, and the flies which swarmed about the marshes near the river plagued us every hour. We no longer starved, but instead watched disease and pestilence slide their fingers ever deeper into the body of the army. And above all hung the black threat of Kerbogha, now – it was said – less than a week away.

'To think that it has been a year since we left Constantinople,' said Sigurd. He speared a lump of meat out of the pot and chewed it off his knife. 'Your grand-child will have children of his own before you see him.'

'If I live to see him, the delay will be worth it.' If all had gone well, Helena should have given birth by now. Every night I prayed for their safety, imploring my late wife Maria to plead for them in the world beyond, but still there had been no word. It seemed there were none I loved who did not live in the shade of death.

'I will be satisfied to live until next month,' Anna declared. 'If Kerbogha comes while the Franks still bicker . . .'

'Do not say that,' I snapped. 'Too often, the fates hear our foolish hopes and honour them. Wish to live a month, and they may grant it too precisely.'

'Superstition,' scoffed Anna. 'I am surprised . . . What is that?'

She pointed through the fire, where some movement in the night had drawn her gaze. It came nearer, at last revealing itself as a child, barely taller than my waist. His hair and clothes were ragged, his face filthy, but his eyes were bright in the firelight and his voice was as clear as water.

'Which one is Demetrios Askiates?'

I rubbed my eyes. The surrounding smoke ringed him with a hazy nimbus, and his head seemed to burn out of the flames between us like some conjuror's trick. Against the darkness beyond he was almost ethereally bright.

'I am Demetrios.' I touched my hand to a stone in the earth, its rough strength anchoring me to the world. 'Why?'

The apparition frowned, as if trying to lift phrases from his memory. 'You have desired to speak with my lady.'

'Has he?' Sigurd's ribald tone broke the illusion, and at once there was only a shabby urchin beside our fire. 'You did not mention this, Demetrios.'

I ignored him, and Anna's angry glare as well. 'Who is your lady?'

'Her name is Sarah. She will see you alone,' he added, as he saw Anna and Sigurd making to rise.

The child did not take me far, but led me quickly through the camp to the river. Many who followed the army had abandoned us now, and the empty intervals between fires lengthened. Sometimes the boy disappeared completely, dissolving into the night like mist, but he always emerged to lure me onwards. At the river he seemed to stop, a smudge of white in the darkness, and I hurried to keep close.

'Demetrios Askiates. You have answered me. Or perhaps I have answered you.'

I halted. Where the boy had gone I did not know, but the shape I had thought was him now spoke with the assured, sweet cadence of a woman. My eyes strained against the veiling darkness, but apart from her white dress I could see nothing.

'Are you Sarah?'

She laughed – or perhaps it was a ripple in the river. 'I have many names. You know me as Sarah.'

'How did Drogo know you?' I stretched out my hand, hoping for some tree or boulder to lean on, but there was nothing.

'As a teacher.'

'What did you teach him – other than to carve scars into his back?'

'I did not teach him that.' Her voice was clouded with remorse, and suddenly I felt an irrational urge to hug her close to console her. 'There will always be men whose minds distort their learning.'

'Were Drogo and Rainauld such men?'

'It was not their fault. Drogo's heart had turned to thorns: whatever tried to reach him was torn to pieces. As for Rainauld, he followed Drogo, perhaps too much.'

'And what did you teach them?'

'Faith in Christ. A purer path.'

'There are enough priests and bishops in this army whose duty that is.'

Again I heard her rippling laugh. 'Priests and bishops. Their duty is to their masters, the princes of this Earth. They preach obedience, that by it they may have a share in the spoils of war. They care nothing for the souls they shepherd. Look about the camp, Demetrios – can you deny that the Lord has abandoned us?'

'The Lord passes by, and we do not see him.'

156

'If we are pure, he will restore us to happiness. For the moment, this camp is a wicked and dirty place, ruled by crows and beset by wolves. Only prayer and truth can free us. "God is with us," the princes say, but even as they speak their doom marches on. They and their clergy, they are all corrupted. Only the righteous will escape this place. The rest will perish.'

'To question the clergy is treason.' The warmth of the night was suddenly gone from my bones.

'You do not believe that. In your heart, you know that I speak the truth.'

'I know that your adepts broke into pagan shrines and died murderously. Is that the purity you taught?'

'No! I told you, they would not heed me. I thought Drogo sought salvation. In truth, he sought only revenge.'

Though I could not see Sarah's face, I sensed that at last I had cracked through her serenity. It left me feeling strangely soiled, as if I had broken something precious. 'Revenge on whom?'

'Revenge for the loss of his brother. Revenge for the torments he suffered on the plains of Anatolia, and here before the walls of Antioch.' The white dress fluttered like a moth in the darkness as she moved on the fringes of my sight.

'But revenge *on* whom? His brother died on the march, killed by Turks.'

Sarah's voice seemed to grow softer, as though she were trickling away. 'I thought that in Drogo's grief he might hear truth. That through his sadness the Lord might enter. But there are other powers which can enter through a broken heart, and Drogo succumbed.'

She had passed beyond seeing, and as she stopped speaking a wave of solitude enveloped me. 'Wait,' I pleaded, stumbling forward. 'You visited his tent in the hour before he died. He must have told you something.'

'I tried to reason with him, to draw him back to the light. But he had found a new teacher, and would not hear me.'

'Who did he go to meet in that dell?' I demanded. 'I must know what brought him there.'

Once more Sarah laughed, though now the sound held only sadness. 'Keep seeking, and perhaps you will find what Drogo sought and found.'

'What was that?'

'Truth.'

'What truth?'

'I cannot tell you that. Not until you tire of the self-serving lies that the priests tell. When you are willing to discard their deceptions and unveil their secrets, then I will show you truth.'

'Tell me!' I ran towards her voice. Whatever her secrets, I was desperate to know them.

But she was gone, moving soundlessly across the meadow, and my only answer was the gurgling of the river.

ιζ

I awoke next morning with a searing headache. It was the first day of June, and already the heat seemed harsher, parching all life from the air. The shallow streams that fed the Orontes had dried to dust, and I crouched in the river to splash the sweat of a sleepless night off my face. It did nothing to soothe the pain within, nor wipe away the confusion which governed my mind.

In the middle of the morning, Count Raymond summoned Sigurd to his farmhouse and asked for a company of Varangians to relieve his garrison at the tower by the bridge. Every hour, more scouts rode in from the east bringing fresh news of Kerbogha's advance. The breadth of his army covered the plain from mountain to mountain, they said, a hundred thousand strong. Even slowed by their numbers they would be at the Iron Bridge, where the road from the north crossed the Orontes, by the end of the week.

'The Varangians should be standing in the vanguard against Kerbogha, not guarding this place,' Sigurd complained. We were standing on the top of the tower, the city spread out before us little more than a bowshot away. A bowshot, a river, and walls four times the height of a man, I reminded myself, and still impregnable as ever.

'Your battle will come, and when it does a hundred Varangians will be little more than pebbles beneath the feet of a thousand Turks.'

'Pebbles sharp enough to make them bleed.'

'Is that enough?' There was more sharpness in my voice than I had intended, but I did not try to master it. 'Will you be satisfied to die in this desolate place, far from home and family, with none but pagans and barbarians to see you fall?'

'I have been far from home and family for thirty years. If I die here, or in Thrace, or drowned in the ocean it will be the same.'

'You have a wife in Constantinople.' He seldom spoke of her, but I knew she had borne him two sons and a gaggle of daughters.

'A warrior's wife knows that she will one day be a widow.'

Sigurd looked away, perhaps finding my argument tedious, and I leaned out on the rough-hewn wooden parapet. The tombs we had despoiled made a poor foundation, and I was forever fearful lest the entire edifice should collapse in a hail of splinters. Every time Sigurd moved, the rampart swayed, while the open shaft at the tower's centre yawned open behind us.

With a nervous sigh, I turned my attention outwards. The sun was high, heating my armour so that it became a forge around me, and although it was not yet midday an afternoon stillness seemed to grip the landscape. I lifted a nearby bucket with both hands and tipped water into my mouth, letting some splash through my beard and down my neck. At the foot of the tower a band of Normans was nailing animal hides to a crude frame, fashioning a shield under which they could approach the walls unscathed. It seemed a forlorn hope to indulge so late; perhaps they planned to use its shelter to destroy the bridge, and so deny the Turks in the city a route to our flank.

'Do you want an arrow in the eye? Join that seam tighter, or every Turk in Antioch will make it his target.'

There was something in that stinging voice I recognised. Craning my head out through the embrasure I looked closer at the construction. A dozen Normans were busy around the frame while a sergeant paced about, overseeing their labour. He had removed his helmet in the heat, though his hair was still lank with sweat, and he moved gracelessly, spasmodically, jabbing here and there where the work prompted his anger. From my high angle I could not see his face, but I was certain that I knew his name.

I slid down the ladder in the well of the tower and ducked out through its door. Just beyond the stockade, at the bottom of the mound, I found him.

'Quino,' I said to his back.

He spun around. In a second, his sword was in his hand. Though we were in open daylight, and surrounded by his allies, he was tensed like a cornered beast. 'You would have done better to avoid me.'

'I have nothing to hide from. Do you?'

'Only catamite Greeks who speak poison and lies.'

'Poison and lies?' Perhaps it was something in his temper which prodded me to retaliate; perhaps it was the shroud of mystery and ignorance which had stifled me so long; or perhaps it was my fear of the coming Turks: whatever the reason, I abandoned all caution and advanced towards him. 'Is it a lie that you and Drogo and the others were adepts of a mystic named Sarah, a false prophet who preaches treason and impiety to your rightful church? Is it a lie that you journeyed to a pagan temple in Daphne and slaughtered a bullock on the altar of a Persian demon? Is it a lie that two of your friends, your so-called brothers, are dead – and you live to see them silent in the grave?'

Though I should have expected it, I was unprepared for his answer. He hurled himself at me like a boar, lifted me by the collar of my mail shirt and threw me down on my back. The hard earth thumped all breath from my lungs, and I lay stunned as he advanced to stand over me. His sword shook in his hand.

'Worm! Snake! I will cut those lies from your tongue and feed them to you until you choke. Who told you those things? Who?'

'All who saw you,' I hissed, squirming backwards along the ground.

'I will kill him. Kill him! And I will kill you too, Greek. You will not live for the Turks to slaughter. Your prying and your lying—'

He was standing in front of me, little more than a yard away, when without warning the ground at his feet exploded in a puff of dust and stone. He leaped back, and I pushed myself up on my elbows to see what had happened. A small axe, no larger than a hammer, lay where it had gouged a rent in the earth.

We stared up. On the rampart of the tower Sigurd's broad shoulders squeezed out between the battlements.

'Forgive my carelessness,' he bellowed. 'But be warned – my next throw may be more careless still.'

During Quino's brief distraction I had the wit to scramble to my feet and retrieve my sword.

'I do not know if you killed Drogo,' I told him. 'But I know that he died with the mark of Mithra on his forehead, and that you were in that cave with him. If we live through Kerbogha's coming I will see that you are driven from this army as a traitor and a heretic.'

His head jerking like that of a man possessed, Quino rammed his blade back into his scabbard. 'Then I fear nothing, for you will not survive the battle. But I will grant you this one favour: when you run away from the Turks, shrieking like a woman, the blows that kill you will still strike you on your front.'

'As Rainauld's did?'

'Do not speak of what you do not know.' He kicked a stone towards me; I watched it bounce wide. 'For now, it will suffice me to snare the crows who feed you lies.'

Quino stormed away towards the camp, leaving me to wonder what his final threat had meant. And what evil I had stirred.

That night the princes met again in Adhemar's tent. It was a terse affair, every face grim, and the business was brief. Too brief, perhaps, for what later came of it.

'Kerbogha's army will reach the Iron Bridge in two days. I have reinforced the bridge with a company from the tower, and they will defend it, but against such numbers they cannot hold it.' Raymond's voice was hard and grey. 'After that, we must choose where to fight.'

'If Kerbogha reaches the city, our quest will be over.' Duke Godfrey tapped the brown cross sewn on his tabard, for like almost all the princes he had come in armour. 'We shall have shamed our God and our honour as men.'

'What numbers do we have?' asked Adhemar. 'Count Raymond?'

'Six hundred and forty knights, though fewer than five hundred horses. Some three thousand men-at-arms.'

'Duke Godfrey?'

'Two hundred and twelve who can ride. Of the rest, no more than a thousand. Every day they are less.'

'Lord Bohemond?'

Bohemond, who alone in the company had come un-armoured, looked up as if surprised. 'Three hundred horse. Nine hundred who will fight beside them.'

So Adhemar went on, until every lord had declared his strength. The dark-haired priest, Stephen, had hovered silent in the background and now whispered something in the bishop's ear.

163

'A little over three thousand knights, in total, and five times their number on foot. How many does Kerbogha have?'

'Has anyone ridden close enough to count?' Sigurd muttered.

Raymond glared at him. 'My marshal has seen the army. He guesses it to be three times our size. Perhaps more.'

'Christ preserve us,' whispered Hugh. Had his skin been any paler I might have seen the bone beneath.

'We will commit ourselves to the Lord's mercy.' Adhemar looked around the square, his face severe. 'As for where we commit ourselves to battle, I propose we tempt them over the Iron Bridge and meet them on the near bank. With the river on our left and the arm of the mountain to our right, we will keep them from using their numbers to encircle us. What do you say, Count Raymond?'

Raymond nodded. 'It will serve. What does the lord Bohemond think?'

He looked across the tent to Bohemond, who in his silken robe seemed dressed more for a banquet than a battle. Perhaps that was why he had spoken barely a word all evening.

'It is a wise plan. I can think of nothing to improve it.'

'Truly?' Raymond's face hardened with suspicion, while every other man in the room watched Bohemond intently.

'Truly. It is, after all, the same tactic by which I defeated the army of Aleppo.'

'The army of Aleppo was a quarter of the size of Kerbogha's. And you would have been crushed had I not remained at the city to guard your back. We will not be able to divide ourselves this time.'

'Are you trying to persuade me against your own plan?' Bohemond furrowed his brow in mock surprise.

'I am wondering that you do not try and unpick its defects.'

'You have just done so yourself. It is the same problem which stifles all our plans. The city.' Bohemond stood, a strangely confident smirk on his face. 'I look at the city and all I see is a millstone. A millstone about our necks, one that we cannot shake off. A millstone that will grind us to powder against Kerbogha's army if we do not break it.'

'You have said this before,' said Raymond, his contempt evident. 'It is not relevant.'

Bohemond laughed. 'Not relevant? My lord Count, it is more relevant than anything that you have said this evening. To my mind, indeed, it is *all* that is relevant. Take the city, and every question is answered, every strategy decided.'

'It is too late to consider such paths,' said Adhemar. 'In three days Kerbogha will be here.'

'Is your faith so weak? Three days is more than enough time for a miracle. As for my tardiness, I have urged this course on the council for months. In this wilderness I have been a lone voice crying out for reason. You have denied me, and the siege has faltered. Will you deny me now, when the only alternative is defeat?'

'What do you ask?' Adhemar's face made it plain that he knew.

'I ask the council to relinquish its claim to Antioch. To grant its possession to whoever takes it first, that by the triumph of one man we may be spared the destruction of all.'

Before Adhemar could answer, Sigurd was on his feet. 'It is not the council's to give. You – we – are all sworn to yield it to the Emperor Alexios. No man can dispose of it save he.'

It was a true claim, and one that might once have weighed with the princes, but it was a poor moment for Sigurd to raise it. Even as he seated himself, I saw the wolfish smile spreading across Bohemond's face.

'If your king comes to claim it, I will be the first to kneel before him and surrender it. Until then, I say it is the one prize that may spur us to salvation before Kerbogha comes. I ask the council to give its judgement.'

He took his seat, serene amid the consternation and doubt that he had stirred. All around me I could see counts and dukes testing his words in their minds, probing his devices. All looked troubled.

'If the city is to be surrendered to the Emperor, I will not object to one of our number holding it in steward-ship for his coming,' said Godfrey. Murmurs of approval sounded around the room. 'And if one man distinguishes himself in its capture, he will be the rightful steward.'

'And what if he does not surrender it when the Emperor comes?' growled Raymond.

'Then he will be judged a liar and a thief by the council, and punished accordingly.' Bohemond's voice rang with honest confidence, though I saw his fingers tapping fever-ishly on the bench beside him. 'Besides, who would content himself with Antioch while the holy city itself remained to be conquered? Will the council allow this, or are we to face Kerbogha without hope of victory?'

No one spoke. At last, Adhemar tapped his staff on the floor. There was little strength in the sound. 'What does the council say? Shall we grant Antioch to the wardship of its conqueror, until such time as the Emperor comes?'

'I say yes,' said the Duke of Normandy. 'If we gain the city, it is a small price to pay.'

'As long as it is understood that we still honour our oath to the Emperor,' said Godfrey.

Raymond blew air between his lips, making a noise like wind. 'I say Bohemond has wasted too much of our time on this matter. If he can conquer the city, by all means let him enjoy it for a short while. For my part, I will concentrate on defeating Kerbogha.'

166

Adhemar let his stare drift deliberately over the gathering. 'Does anyone oppose this?'

None did.

'Then it is decided.'

I struggled under a heavy burden of dreams that night. In one, I was back on the high tower of the palace in Constantinople, looking out over a blood-drenched field as flocks of eagles wheeled overhead. In another, I was in the culvert by the orchard, looking at Rainauld's body, except that when I touched him he was not dead. He spoke to me in words that I could not afterwards remember, warning me of some tremendous evil, and when I turned away it was only to see a black bull charging towards me. It chased me through fields and hills, over streams and across rivers, and every time I looked behind me it seemed that one more stride would bring its horns goring into my back. I ran on; suddenly I saw that I had climbed to a great height, and that the ridge ahead was in fact the brink of an enormous cliff. I slowed, but immediately the thunder of hooves overwhelmed me. Helpless, I ran faster, my whole being throbbing with my heart, until with a soundless scream I hurtled over the cliff, felt my body drop away beneath me, and awoke with a cry in my tent. It was still dark, and I recoiled as I realised that there were yet more hours of the night to endure. I reached out for Anna to comfort me, but propriety had led her to her own tent and I felt only earth.

Next morning, Sigurd and our company were ordered to begin dismantling the boat bridge. It was claimed that

Kerbogha might use it to attack our flank, though I guessed the princes feared equally that it might become the path of a rout if the army panicked. With the bridge removed, the east bank of the Orontes where we were camped became a closed sack, squeezed between the river and the walls. Whether that would firm our hearts or condemn us to slaughter, none could tell.

'Do they suppose that because Varangians wield axes, we must be foresters or woodcutters?'

Sigurd, who would have frozen to death before ever using his battleaxe on firewood, swung a carpenter's axe into a mouldering length of rope. The fibres sprang apart, unravelling where they had broken, and I gripped the side of the boat we stood in as its prow swung downstream. Its dank timber was spongy under my hand.

'We should leave this in place,' I grumbled, scrambling back onto the portion of the bridge which remained intact. It swayed under my weight, and from beneath the planks I heard a rumbling as the hulls shifted and knocked together. 'It's so rotten that Kerbogha's army would sink through before they were halfway across.'

Sigurd swung his axe again, and the rope that had held the stern of the boat in place parted. For a moment it stayed nestled against the bridge; then the current took it, and it began to drift away towards the sea. Long strands of weed trailed behind it.

A gap-toothed peasant, one of the labourers who had been assigned to carry away the planks we tore up, wandered over. With the morning sun already heavy on our backs, he was in little hurry. 'It will be well to break this,' he said, his words thick with foreign sounds. 'Already the Turks lurk on the far bank.'

'How can they?' I paid him little attention, for I was trying to prise up the next section of the decking. 'All their gates are guarded by our towers. They are stopped up like wine in a bottle.'

'They are enemies of God,' said the peasant seriously. 'Satan favours the Ishmaelites, and leads them on secret paths. Perhaps he sends demons to carry them over water.'

I glanced at Sigurd, but he was working loose a mooring post that we had driven into the river bed and offered no help. 'If they have demons to carry them across the river, why bother demolishing the bridge?'

Either he did not understand me or he did not care. 'Last night they killed a boy who went too close to the river. He was found this morning, stuck with their hateful arrows.' A rivulet of spit oozed down to his chin as he thought of it.

'Truly it is said, "Be watchful, for you know not at what hour they will come."'

My bored platitudes did nothing to deter him. To my irritation, he eased himself down onto the edge of the bridge and sat there, trailing his bare feet in the green water. I wondered if I could cut loose the section that held him.

'It was a cursed house,' he announced with relish, cleaning a grimy fingernail on his tooth. 'The boy, the unfortunate, had two masters and both died. Perhaps the priests speak rightly when they say, "A servant cannot serve two masters". He was picking herbs on the river bank when the Turks, curse them, found him. They say he was found with a sprig of thyme in his hands, stained with his blood.'

Though I had set my back to the peasant, ostensibly to work loose a nail, his final words began to nag at my interest. Against my better judgement, I looked around to prompt him further. But my question was never spoken, for as I turned towards the city and the camps I saw a great column of knights proceeding from among the tents. At their head rode Bohemond, his great stature raised still higher by the white stallion that carried him. His red cloak tumbled over the animal's flanks and his spear was held aloft so as to gleam in the sun. Behind him the crimson banner with its twisting serpent hung in the still air.

I put down my hammer as it became clear he was approaching the bridge. His steed grew large in my sight, until it was so close that it dwarfed the city and mountain behind. I had to crane my neck to look up, only to be blinded by the sun above.

'Demetrios Askiates,' said the shadow that shielded the sun. His voice seemed to draw the warmth from it. 'I had hoped to find you here.'

'The Count of Saint-Gilles ordered me to destroy the bridge, lest Kerbogha try to outflank us.' I felt the eyes of two hundred horsemen, and the foot soldiers beyond, gazing at me, doubtless wondering why a carpenter should delay their lord.

'Count Raymond did not know that I must cross this river one final time.' Bohemond let his spear slide through his hand so that the butt thumped onto the wooden deck, the noise echoing off the water below. He looked at my sweat-soaked tunic. 'Where is your armour?'

'On the shore.' I pointed to the near bank, where I had left my mail, sword and shield to be close in case of attack. 'Why, Lord?'

'You speak Greek, I presume?'

'I *am* Greek.'

'Then I have need of you. Arm yourself, and follow.'

He was not a man easily disobeyed, even by his adversaries, yet I hesitated. 'I am charged with dismantling the bridge,' I said again, knowing the folly of asking for explanation.

'Then burn it into the water when I have gone and swim after me.' The shaft of Bohemond's spear swung like a pendulum in front of me. 'Come.'

'Why – to run away from Kerbogha?' Sigurd's arms were folded across his broad chest, and he betrayed no fear of the lord before him.

'Is that what you would do? Flee in terror, as your fathers did before the Duke of Normandy? Suffice it for you to know that I undertake a final foraging expedition. What fruits we shall reap I cannot say, but I promise that they will be sweet. Now come with me, Demetrios, before I lose patience.'

'And Sigurd?'

Bohemond laughed. 'I need a man who speaks like the Greeks, not one who fights like them.'

Even without his taunts I would have been minded to refuse him, yet there was something in his manner which made men want to follow, which promised glory and adventure and fortune wherever he went. I was not immune. Nor could I forget my charge from the Emperor, to observe the barbarians and report any treachery. Only the previous night, Bohemond had won approval to hold the city if he took it: now he marched out in strength, and with a need for interpreters. If he had some secret design, it would profit me to witness it. And I was curious.

'If I am not back before Kerbogha's army arrives, see that Anna is protected,' I told Sigurd.

'They will have to break my axe in two before they harm her.'

'You will be back before Kerbogha.' Bohemond spurred his horse, and it began to trot forward over the remaining portion of the bridge. 'We will march through the night, and by dawn we will have returned. Look for my standard then.'

If Bohemond intended to march through the night, he first seemed intent on marching through the day. With no mount to be wasted on me, I joined the back of his column, lonely under the hostile glares of his men-at-arms, and followed in silence. The heat of the sun and the weight of my armour made common cause against me: the thin tunic I wore beneath my mail did nothing to cushion or smooth the jabbing iron, yet it gave no respite from the heat either. When once my head slumped, I scalded my chin on the metal, for I had no tabard. The men I marched with made loud, coarse jokes about Greeks; frequently they trod on my heels, or tried to trip me with their spears. With sweat stinging my eyes and my armour chafing, I was trapped in a boiling world of misery. And still we tramped onwards, fording the river out of sight of the city and following the road into the hills towards Daphne.

I had only half believed Bohemond when he claimed that he went to forage, and my doubts were well founded: he kept us far from any village or farm, and when we did pass fields or orchards that remained unscathed he allowed us no delay to plunder them. His knights rode up and down the line, hemming us in like sheep and showing the flats of their swords to any who deviated. Mercifully, I did not see Quino.

We must have marched two hours or more, for the sun was already declining when Bohemond at last called a halt. We were in a hollow, a broad natural bowl surrounded by hills and beyond all sight of habitation. A meagre stream ran through it, feeding a marshy pool, and we scooped the brackish water into our mouths as if it were sweet milk. Insects chattered in the bushes. We pulled off our boots and stretched out on the dry grass, too tired to wonder why Bohemond had brought us there. On the rim above, I saw the silhouettes of horsemen patrolling the heights.

'My friends.' The words echoed around the bowl, carrying to its furthest reaches. Bohemond had dismounted and was standing on a rock a little way up the slope, looking down on us like a statue in the Augusteion.

'You have marched hard and far today.' An afternoon breeze tugged at the red folds of his cloak. 'And still there are many miles to travel.'

A low, indistinct groan sounded around the hollow.

'Yet take heart. At the end of this night, a glorious prize awaits those who dare to snatch it. For months we have suffered and waited before the cursed city, borne only on the faith that the Lord God will rescue us. Now, at our darkest hour, as Kerbogha the Terrible approaches, the Lord stretches out his hand and offers us deliverance.'

Bohemond looked at the ridge above where his knights stood sentinel, then turned back to his audience and lowered his voice. 'Listen. From here we will travel by secret paths into the hills above Antioch. The watchman who holds one of the towers there looks kindly on our cause: I have struck a bargain with him, and he will admit us. Once inside, one party will make to secure the citadel, while another hastens to throw open the gates to our brothers on the plain.' A jubilant grin shone from his face; for the first time I noticed that he had shaved off his beard. 'Who is with me?'

'What if it is a trap? It has happened before.'

It was a courageous man who questioned Bohemond, even one of his own household, but he showed no anger. 'If it is a trap, then we will fight our way clear, or die in glory as martyrs of Christ. For my part, I have spoken with the watchman, and I trust to his promise. But if we take the walls, trap or no, I will not be dislodged unless I bring all the towers down in ruin about me.' His gloved hand pulled out his sword and held it up by the blade, so that it appeared as a perfect cross. 'Do you hear the rustling on the breeze? It is the sound of our grandsons' scribes, sharpening their pens to record our deeds. Some of you may see an impregnable city, but by God's grace I see only a new chapter of His greatness waiting to be written. Who will follow me to the walled city? Who will come with me into Antioch?' With a quick jerk of his wrist, the sword leaped from his grip and spun in the air, planting its hilt back in his hand. 'Through God, we will do great deeds and trample down our enemies. I ask again: who is with me?'

Many of the army had risen to their feet as he spoke, some in awe and some in doubt. Now, to a man, they brandished their arms and bellowed their war cries. Some beat their spears on the rocks, others thumped the pommels of their swords against their shields. The hollow rang with the clamour of five hundred men raised to a frenzy, resounding so loud that I feared it might dislodge the very slopes which cupped us. But above all else, over all the shouting and drumming, one phrase swelled imperious.

'*Deus vult!* God wills it!'

Bohemond held his arms aloft, his face enraptured like an angel's. 'Enough. We should not allow the Turks to hear us, even so far away. We will crawl up on them like snakes, and strike before they have seen we are there. By dawn, I promise you, this long siege will be over.'

ι θ

Though the agonising heat had passed, our journey
back through the night felt longer than the afternoon's march. Worst was the darkness, masking our way
and forcing endless knocks and collisions along the
column. Frequently men fell, tripping on rocks or slipping off the steep paths we followed. Some escaped with
little more than curses and bruises, while others were left
to hobble after us as best they could. Spears swayed and
bumped each other, rattling like bones over our heads;
one swung so low that it almost stabbed through my skull
when its owner stumbled ahead of me. Frogs croaked in
the underbrush and bats squeaked in the trees – once I
froze as I heard a bell off on my right, though I guessed
it was only a goat. I touched my chest, feeling the silver
cross through the layers of cloth and iron, and prayed to
Christ to keep me safe through the perils ahead. And thus
our jangling, clanking, toiling column wound its way over
the hills.

On the crest of a ridge we paused for breath. A few
half-empty water-skins were passed down the line, and I
drank gratefully. At last I knew where we had come: ahead,
the dark bulk of the mountain loomed black against the
silver sky; down to my left, far below, I could see the scattered glow of watchfires, and the meandering course of
the Orontes like white silk in the moonlight. We were on
the southern shoulder of Mount Silpius, and the string of

yellow lights glimmering on the next ridge must have been the high towers of Antioch.

Before that, though, a steep ravine cut through our way. There were no paths down – even goats did not venture here, it seemed – and our column fanned out into a straggling line, each seeking the safest route. The ground underfoot was loose and treacherous: many times I had to jerk my feet away from rocks which gave beneath me. Once I was too slow, and I found myself thrown onto my back and sliding down with my shield rattling after me. A cloud of dust rose, filling my nose and mouth, and when I threw out a hand to halt myself I grasped only spiky branches. All around me I could hear similar sounds of tumbling rocks and cursing men, and my heart pounded for fear that a volley of Turkish arrows might fly hissing out of the night. None came.

The stream that must have carved the gully had dried up, leaving only a rocky channel at the bottom. After a few minutes to catch our breath we were moving again, now climbing the far side of the ravine. We scrambled up the shifting scree, heedless of the pebbles cascading down behind us or the rattle of our scabbards striking the ground. Enveloped in darkness and surrounded by alien voices, I felt that I had relinquished my soul to some intangible power, driven on without will or reason. I wished Sigurd were there to calm me with his implacable strength, his unbending faith in the power of his arms, but he was far away.

At the top of the slope we stopped again. The Romans who had built the walls of Antioch had used its terrain to their full advantage, and the greater length of the southern walls rose seamlessly from the steep gully. Here, though, the wall turned away along the ridge of the mountain, and there was a short stretch of open ground in front of us. We waited, pressing ourselves into the earth just

177

below the lip of the ravine and praying that we were beneath the gaze of the guards. Half-whispered commands passed along our line. My face was buried in the grass, and somewhere nearby I smelled the scent of wild sage.

'*Greek.*'

A rough hand jostled my shoulder, and again the word was hissed in my ear. '*Greek!*'

I rolled over. A Norman whom I did not recognise was squatting beside me. 'What?'

'You must go to Lord Bohemond. That way.' He pointed east along the gully.

Too dazed to question him, I lifted my shield and edged across the slope, always keeping my head low. About a hundred yards along the line, I found Bohemond crouched in a small hollow with three of his lieutenants. Even in the dark his face gleamed with purpose.

'That is the tower.' He pointed ahead, where a slab of grey stood out against the night. A thin bar of yellow light shone from a narrow window. 'There should be a ladder hidden in the bushes at its base.'

I said nothing.

'The tower is kept by a man named Firouz. He is a Turk, but he speaks your tongue. You will accompany the first party up the ladder and tell him that I have come.'

I did not ask how he knew this, or how he could be certain that we would not meet a shower of spears and arrows when we reached the wall. 'Now?'

'As soon as the watch has passed.' Bohemond looked up at the sky. 'We must be swift. Dawn is not far off.'

We waited in silence, watching the walls. As the minutes passed the stones seemed to become brighter, more distinct, and the light in the window faded. A bird began to mewl its mournful song, and was swiftly answered by another. Bohemond fidgeted, while I kept still and felt my limbs grow stiff and damp with dew.

'There.'

I looked up. A light was advancing along the walls, dizzyingly high above us, blinking as it passed behind the teeth of the battlements. It disappeared into the tower. Bohemond's knuckles were now white around an exposed tree root.

'Do you have a cross?'

I fumbled about my neck and dragged my silver cross from under the mail.

'Wear it openly. It is not yet so light that we will be obvious to each other.'

The torch emerged on the far side of the tower, so close that I could see the shadows of the men who carried it. I heard laughter: no doubt the news of Kerbogha's approach had lifted their spirits. I prayed that it would equally have blinded them to danger.

The light reached the bend in the wall, turned, and vanished out of sight.

'Now.'

A dozen knights rose from the shadows and ran across the open ground. With a shove against my shoulders I was sent staggering after them. My shield and armour weighed on me like rocks; every stride seemed to fall short of where I stretched it. My legs throbbed with the effort, and with my head bowed I could see neither friend nor foe. To any archer on the rampart I would be an effortless target.

I came under the walls and dropped to my knees. On my right I could hear the urgent sounds of men searching through undergrowth; then a hiss of triumph. Wood creaked as the knights gathered round the ladder and raised it above them, shuddering as it swayed through the air. It knocked against the wall, rebounded, then settled on the stone.

'You.'

One of the knights who held the ladder beckoned me over. 'Climb up there and explain that the Lord Bohemond has come.'

Too drained to argue, I swung myself onto the ladder and began to climb. For months I had stared at these walls, willing them to open and wondering how it would feel ever to break through them: now, as I pulled myself hand over hand toward their summit, I could think of nothing save the frailty of the ladder. It might have been left by the original Roman architects, for the timber was brittle to the touch and every rung groaned beneath my tread. Higher and higher I went, my hands shaking so hard that I almost lost my grip. If I fell, or if the ladder broke now, the impact would snap my back in two.

The ladder held. Now I could see the edge of the parapet looming above me. Three more rungs. Two. I stretched out my arms, feeling the ladder wobble with the movement, gripped the battlements and hauled myself between them. My armour rasped in the night as I slithered through the embrasure on my belly; then I was through and standing, gasping, on the top of the wall.

I was inside the city.

I had no time to think about it. A man in scaled armour and a turban was striding towards me, his dark face twisted with dread. It seemed strange that after so much danger we should arrive to find ourselves feared, but somehow his anxiety quelled my own racking terror. At his feet, I noticed, two Turks lay in pools of blood.

'*Bohemond, pou?*' he asked, waving his hands furiously. So little did I expect it from this Ishmaelite, and so thick was his accent, that he had to repeat it twice more before I understood he spoke in Greek.

'*Bohemond, etho.* Bohemond is here.'

A Norman had come up behind me. 'What does he say?' he demanded.

'He asks where Bohemond is.'

'Tell him Bohemond awaits my sign that he has brought us here in good faith.'

I put this to the Turk.

'Too few Franj, too few. If I give my tower, it must be to Bohemond only. And his army – he promised he brings his army.'

I relayed his words in the Norman dialect. While we spoke, the knights had continued to crawl over the wall, but with only a single ladder for access they were still alarmingly few. No wonder the Turk trembled to betray the city to us.

'Mushid, he say Bohemond come with army. Where is Mushid?'

It was the last name that I had expected to hear in that place, while men lay dead at my feet and knights hurried past into the tower. Before I could question him, though, a new voice sounded from the foot of the ladder.

'Firouz!'

The Turk thrust his head out between the battlements and stared down; I looked out beside him. At the foot of the ladder stood Bohemond, his face ashen in the early dawn.

'What is happening up there?' he called. 'Is it safe?'

I lifted myself forward so that he could see me clearly. 'It is safe. There is no trap. But the Turk is anxious – he wants you to join him as proof of your intent. He fears you have brought too few knights.'

'Tell him I have many more men in the gully. If we had another ladder, they would be over sooner.'

I translated his words.

'There is a gate,' said the Turk, agitated. 'Not big, but faster. At the bottom of the tower, down the hill.'

I was about to relay this to Bohemond, but suddenly an enormous *crack* tore through the air. The ladder was gone: it no longer leaned against the battlements but lay in splintered pieces on the ground. Three or four bodies were strewn among the wreckage, unmoving.

An unearthly scream of rage howled forth from Bohemond, so loud that it must have been heard in the encampment on the plain. His sword was in his hand, and for a moment I thought he might smash it on the wall in his fury. But before he could move a new sound rose from further along the rampart, shouts of anger and alarm. A clutch of fiery torches appeared from one of the distant towers, and by their light I saw spears hastening towards us.

I grabbed Firouz and spun him about. 'Are they your men?'

He shook his head. 'They have heard us. We are trapped. Your men are outside; they will only see us cut in pieces. We are dead.'

As if to prove his words, an arrow slammed into the battlement in front of us. I dived to the ground, pulling Firouz with me as more arrows clattered off the stones above. Some of the Normans had managed to form a line across the parapet, kneeling behind their tall shields, but we were too few. Soon, I feared, every Turk in Antioch would be upon us.

Firouz began to crawl back towards his tower, dragging himself through puddles of blood. Following, I hauled on the hem of his armour and pulled him back.

'You spoke of a gate,' I shouted, trying to make myself heard over the rising roar of battle. 'There are five hundred men beyond the wall with Bohemond — if they can break in, they may yet save us.'

He stared at me witlessly. His beard and armour were smeared red with blood, and I feared for a second that an unseen missile might have struck him. Then he nodded.

'Through the tower.'

Ducking beneath the arrows that fell around us, we scrambled on our knees into the guardroom. A dead Turk lay sprawled over a wooden stool, stabbed through the eye, while three Normans struggled to barricade the far door. In one corner an opening in the floor led onto a twisting stairwell.

I lifted my silver cross and thrust it before the Normans, just in time to stay their swords. 'Come with me. There is a gate.'

I led the way down the curving steps, my shield held before me and my sword arm pressed uncomfortably close to the wall. No one opposed us. At the bottom another door led out onto the mountainside, inside the city. It was land we had dreamed of treading for months, yet now we did not even notice.

'Which way?'

Firouz pointed down the hill. Not far off, about halfway between two looming towers, I saw a small gate set in the wall, scarcely as high as a man. Thick timbers barred it, but it was not defended.

'Be swift,' said one of the Normans grimly. 'I hear more enemies approaching.'

We ran down to the gate. The knights circled us with their shields, while Firouz and I worked feverishly to loosen the bars which held the door. It could not have been opened in years, for the wood was thick with grime. I strained in vain to pull the bar free from its rusting brackets.

'Make haste.'

I looked back. A company of Turks were charging up the hill, spears raised before them. More arrows started to fall, several of them thudding into the Norman shields. One even stuck in the timbers of the gate.

I knelt, mumbling prayers under my breath, and thumped the pommel of my sword up against the bar.

The impact numbed my arm, but I repeated the blow again. Still it did not move. The din of battle sounded on the walls behind us and the Turks on the slope below drew ever closer.

'There.' The bar had moved. Another blow lifted it higher, before a third dislodged it completely. It fell forgotten to the ground. Still the gate would not open, for an iron bolt held it. I hammered frantically. Behind me one of the knights broke ranks and charged down the hill, tearing into the Turkish line like a ram. I heard the chilling ring of clashing metal, and he was swallowed beneath them.

With the ponderous grate of age, the bolt slid clear of its socket. In an instant Firouz and I had our shoulders against the door and were heaving it open. The sun was rising and grey light flooded the hillside beyond. Barely twenty yards away yawned the gully where the Normans waited.

I do not remember what I shouted, only that I had to repeat it for what seemed an eternity before the first of Bohemond's men began sprinting across the open ground, shields held aloft against the archers on the walls. The first one came through the gate, caught an arrow in the throat and died immediately; the second threw himself to the earth, rolled aside, then leaped into a crouch with his shield before him. Together with Firouz and the other knights we formed a thin line in front of the door. Spears stabbed at us; one grazed my cheek and another glanced off my shoulder. In another minute we would be slaughtered.

But our line did not shrink; instead, at last, it began to swell. Norman spears thrust over our heads, stabbing back the Turkish attackers. Behind me I could feel a press of bodies pushing me forward, and as our line bulged out men squeezed in among us. When I slipped on the bloody ground, the Turks did not charge through the gap; instead, a Norman was instantly in my place. In seconds I was left behind, while ever more Normans ran by to join the battle. Some found the steps in the tower and gained the walls, throwing down the Turks who defended them to be hacked apart by the men below.

Bohemond strode through the gate, his red cloak like fire behind him. His bloodless sword shone pale in the dawn. 'The city lies open before us,' he bellowed, and every man roared approval. 'But victory is not assured. William – bring your company with mine to the western gates, so that we may throw them open and complete the rout. Rainulf – take my standard to the highest point and plant it where all can see that the city is taken.'

In the rush that followed his words I was entirely forgotten. Most of the Normans hastened down the slope with their captain, their appetite for plunder and slaughter undimmed, though a few stayed behind to secure the towers and dispatch the Turks who survived. All ignored me. For a time I sat in silence on a mounting block, watching them, but soon the stink of blood and death overwhelmed me. I walked away, wandering dazed and alone across the scrubby mountainside. The first fingers of sunlight were reaching over the ridge above and a new day dawned over Antioch. It gave me little hope.

I reached a small promontory on the shoulder of the mountain and looked down. Thick smoke rose from the city below, and an occasional gust of wind brought the faint echoes of screams and clashing steel to my ears. I could see the great gates lying open, the hordes of tiny figures swarming through like ants come to ravish a carcass, but I had not the strength to care. I was empty, poured out like water, my heart melted like wax.

Antioch was ours.

II

Besieged

3 June – 1 August 1098

κ

The Franks exploded into the city like a vessel of flaming oil, splashing fire and death wherever they touched. On the walls, in streets and squares, in their homes and fields, men died and women were broken. Worthless possessions were dragged from houses merely because they could be stolen, then abandoned because they were cumbersome, then set alight because they would burn. Order was hateful, confusion master. By afternoon most of the killing was done.

I had waited seven months to enter Antioch; within hours, I could not bear to stay. All morning I sat high on the mountain, alone, watching the devastation in the shade of the cliff. Sometimes my conscience whispered that I should go down, try to save the innocent, but each time I quashed the thought. It would have effected nothing save my death. I still reviled myself for my cowardice.

As the sun came around onto the face of the mountain and the cries from the city lessened, I rose to descend the crumbling slope. I dared not risk the centre of the city, where the sack had raged fiercest, but kept to the fringes and made for a small gate in the south-west, near the bridge. Even here, the ruin was complete: in half a day, the Army of God had wrought a century's worth of destruction. Doors lay sprawled flat; charred houses yawned open to the sky; clothes and dishes and tools and carved toys were strewn about like the debris of a receded flood. Worst, though, were the bodies. Most bore hideous testament to their brutal deaths, and in places their blood had turned the dust to mud. I pulled a length of my tunic from under my mail and bunched it over my nose, using the other hand to keep my silver cross clearly visible. Gangs of Franks still roamed, seeking easy loot and violence. In one street I saw a knight wrapped in orange cloth running after a half-naked woman crawling on her knees. The fabric billowed from his shoulders like wings; he seemed so drunk on pillage that he could not move straight but weaved between the pillared arcades. I stuck out a leg and tripped him as he passed, hoping that he would be too crazed to rise. He fell among a pile of Turkish corpses and did not move. The woman he had pursued looked round. Her breasts were withered and shrunk in to her skin, her hair torn; with not a speck of gratitude, she plucked a stone from the rubble and hurled it at me. It bounced off my shield as I watched her vanish down an alley.

At last I reached the walls. The gates were pushed open and unguarded, and I passed through the shadow under the arch without incident. It was only when I had gone a few paces beyond that I thought to look back, to wonder that I had slipped so easily through the door that had defied us so long. I had not even looked to see how the walls appeared from inside. Much the same as from outside, I supposed.

Whether it was the world that had changed or me, nothing seemed as it had before that day. Without the throngs of people, the film of smoke and noise, the camp felt a different place. The patched and torn fabric of the tents was now more dismal, their yawing angles more precarious. On the hill in the distance, the tower that we had erected to guard the bridge stood abandoned. Men had died to build it, and a day earlier it had been our first defence against a sortie from the city. Now it was useless, impotent.

The camp was not completely deserted. Near the river, I found Anna with Sigurd and his company of Varangians. Crates and sacks were piled around them, while dismantled tents lay like discarded clothes on the ground. As Anna saw me she gave a little shriek and ran to embrace me. The day had left me so numbed that her arms around my waist were like hot irons, and it took an act of will to keep from thrusting her away. The evil I had witnessed and abetted defiled me. It would be many days before I could take comfort in kindness.

'You survived,' she said. I had rarely seen her drop her composure; now she was almost weeping.

Sigurd set down the bag he carried and gazed at me severely. 'I told her you would come back. If there were Turkish spears and arrows flying about, I thought you'd have sense enough to let the Normans stand in front of you.'

'I survived.' I lifted Anna's arm away and stepped free. 'You did not join the battle, Sigurd?'

'There's rarely honour to be won when the Franks take the field. And after the siege, little plunder either, I think. Besides, Count Raymond did not invite us.'

'Did he expect it?'

Sigurd nodded. 'The Provençals were roused not long before dawn. When the gates opened, they were ready. Was it Bohemond?'

'He found a traitor who kept one of the towers on the mountain.' Briefly, I described the night's business.

'And how is the city now?'

'A charnel house. It was well you did not go in.'

'Soon we shall have to.' Sigurd pointed to the north. 'Have you forgotten that Kerbogha and his army are only two days' march from here? Just because you have been busy, it does not signify that he has not. When he hears that the city has fallen he will redouble his speed.'

In the momentous confusion of the past day, Kerbogha had vanished from my mind entirely: his name now was a hammer on my thoughts. I craved rest, weeks of solitude to mend the fractures in my soul. Instead, it seemed, I had days – or hours – before the next onslaught. I was not sure that I could bear it.

'We cannot go into the city,' I said. 'The Franks are maddened, frenzied. If we go in, they will kill us.' Nor, I might have added, did I want the taint of their barbarity on me any more. 'I have suffered long enough on this quest. We will go back to Constantinople.' Perhaps there I could make myself clean again.

Sigurd looked at me cautiously, perhaps weighing my fragile state. When he spoke it was with unusual calm. 'We cannot go back to Constantinople, not now. You know that.'

I rounded on him. 'Why? Because it will be cowardice? Because your honour as a warrior does not allow it?'

'Because Kerbogha's army would catch us and kill us – or worse. Do you want Anna enslaved in an Emir's brothel?'

I wanted to hit him but did not have the strength. 'Do not test our friendship by playing on my fears for Anna. I can see the risks of our journey, but Antioch will be no safer. Kerbogha will come and besiege it, and all within will be trapped like sheep in a pen, to be slaughtered at his pleasure. If we travel by night, and with nothing more than we need, we can slip past his army unheeded.'

'And after his army? Mountains so steep that even goats cannot walk their paths, and then the desert. A wasteland without food or water, whose only inhabitants are Turks and brigands. Look at us – how far would we get?'

'We could take ship from Saint Simeon.'

'If the Franks who control the harbour allowed it. How likely do you think that is, when half the army is trying to flee? And even if they took you and Anna they would not take a hundred of my men.'

The conclusion was unspoken but inevitable. He would not leave his Varangians to face battle without him.

'Kerbogha may reach his fist around the city,' Sigurd continued, 'but he will find it harder than you think to squeeze it shut. We have spent seven months trying without avail — why should it be quicker for him? The walls still stand unbroken. We are outnumbered but I doubt that we are fewer than the Turks who defied us so long. And if the Emperor is in Anatolia, as Tatikios said, then he may arrive to relieve us within weeks.'

'No.' It was a sound argument, but I could not accept it. Others had devised the schemes and fought the battles by which we had taken the city, but it had been my hand that drew the bolt which unlocked the gate. To see the devastation inside again, even for a minute, would be unbearable.

In deference to my frailty, Sigurd had restrained his temper; now he loosed it. 'Very well. You, Demetrios, can beg the Franks for a ship that they will not give you, or make yourself a target for Kerbogha's archers, or throw yourself off a cliff in the mountains; I will not lead my company into certain death. To be trapped in the city may be a grim fate, but I would rather face a grim fate behind stout walls than outside them.' He turned to Anna. 'What do you say?'

She frowned, her fingers twisting in her belt. Her gaze would not meet mine. 'I am not a soldier. I think . . . I think Demetrios is right to fear that we shall not survive a siege.'

'Then you will come with me?' I said.

'But I also think that his thoughts are agitated. They

do not run clear. You are not a soldier either, Demetrios. Perhaps at this moment you would rather walk free and die than face the awful confines of Antioch. But we must stay alive, or try to. What was it you said two days ago? Even if you had become a great-grandfather before you saw your family again, the delay would be worth it.'

I shook my head, tears stinging my eyes, and turned away from them. A thousand thoughts warred in my mind, but they did not matter.

'We will stay in Antioch.'

We set our camp on the western ramparts, near the Duke's Gate. A few of the Frankish captains had roused themselves from debauch and placed sentinels near the gates, but we found a stretch of wall between two towers that none had claimed. It was not a place where I would have chosen to be, guarding the line between two armies, but it kept us from having to venture any further into the city. And whoever attacked, from whichever side, they would pay dearly to prise us out.

As quickly as possible, we set about strengthening our position. Each tower had one door opening onto the adjoining walls and one at its foot leading into the city. Using timbers and rubble, we filled in the lower portions of the stairwell in one of the towers so that it became impassable. In the guardroom above, we stacked broken beams with which we could bar the upper door if necessary. It was hot, weary work, but I did not resent it. The simple monotony of the task lifted heavier burdens from my mind; there was something pure in the effort which I snatched at. For the first time in what seemed an age I peeled off my armour and moved freely, rolling my tunic down to my waist. It was alarming to see how gaunt I had become.

'We had best forage what food we can.' I leaned against the stone wall of the guardroom, enjoying the feel of its coolness on my skin. 'When Kerbogha comes, the supply routes will be cut.'

'Agreed.' Sigurd stepped out into the sunlight on the wall. 'Beric, Sweyn. Take a dozen men and see what provisions you can find in the city. Sheep or goats would be good. And fodder for the horses.' He paused; through the arch of the doorway I could see him looking up at the top of the tower. 'We should mount our standard, let the Franks know we hold these walls.'

'They might take it amiss.' I followed him onto the broad walkway which joined our towers. Looking back across the city, I could see the three peaks of Mount Silpius looming over us. On the highest, in the centre, it was just possible to make out a red flag strung between a pair of pollarded pines. 'I do not think Bohemond will suffer any other banner to fly over Antioch.'

'Shit on Bohemond. When the Emperor Alexios comes it will be the eagle of Byzantium, not the Norman snake, which holds sway.'

'He will not thank you for reminding him.'

'Then I will teach him manners with the blade of my axe.'

'I would like to see it. But to flaunt our standard now would be foolhardy. We are already hated by the Franks; it would be better to keep from offering them a clear target.'

'Why not raise the banner of the cross?'

I turned, and saw Anna walking out of the tower. She had been arranging her medicines in the guardroom: her sleeves were rolled up and her uncovered hair was tied back with a ribbon. I hoped that none of the Franks caught sight of her.

'No.' I shuddered. If I was honest, the pillaging of

Antioch had been little worse than the violence that any victorious army would inflict – Frankish, Turkish, Saracen or even Byzantine. When the Emperor whose honour I now served had seized Constantinople, I had spent three days guarding my home and family from the depredations of his army. But the Franks fought not for a king or a lord but in the name of God. It should be different, I told myself.

'Why not? It is the symbol of Christ – not of any army. Will you forswear Him because of what the Franks have done by it?' She pointed to my own cross, which hung on its chain against my chest. 'Will you rip that away and melt it down?'

I did not answer.

'God will judge the Franks for what they have done in His name. It is not for you to judge Him.'

'It's still a betrayal to hide our own banner,' Sigurd objected.

I opened my arms in surrender to Anna. 'We will raise the banner of the cross.'

'We don't have one,' said Sigurd.

'Anna can make it.'

Anna glared at me. 'I sew wounds, Demetrios, not clothes or flags.'

'If Sigurd sews it, it will look more like a spider than a cross.'

The strain of the moment passed, though the ache of unease lingered between us. It was unnerving how easily we could come to quarrel. Anna at last consented to make the banner and withdrew to find cloth, while Sigurd turned his attention to our defences again. The city's houses were built close against the walls, with only a narrow alley between us and them. Immediately adjacent, we looked down on the red-tiled roofs of houses set in a square around a courtyard. A shady plane tree grew in its centre, masking the wreckage that the looters had left scattered about beneath.

'If enemies reached that roof, they could lay a ladder across the alley and attack us on the wall,' Sigurd said.

'If enemies get so far that they are on the roof, we shall probably be doomed anyway.' I tried to make it a joke, but neither of us smiled. 'The courtyard will pass as a stable for the horses, though.'

'Too well.' Disease and battle had reduced our mounts to a mere thirteen – and if that was an unlucky number I feared it would soon be unluckier still.

'Let us hope Beric and Sweyn find fodder. And food for the riders as well.'

The light was softening as the sun slid away, gilding us with a burnished light. Perhaps I should have read it as a sign of the Lord's benevolence, the glow of the victory he had bestowed, but I did not. The very presence of beauty on such a day of torments seemed itself blasphemous: I could not bask in the radiance but willed the sun ever lower, hoping that night would hasten on.

We had broken one siege; now there was another to endure. Did the golden sun presage triumph, I wondered, or would it prove the last glimmer before we fell into darkness?

κ α
_____

The Varangians returned late, empty-handed and bruised. The siege which had seemed so fruitless from outside the gates had bitten harder than we thought: the city was almost starved. What little food they discovered had been furiously contested, Beric reported, in running skirmishes with the Franks which lasted into the night. It was not an auspicious beginning.

If we were to be trapped together in Antioch, there would have to be an understanding. Next morning, Sigurd and I left the walls to seek out the princes, to learn what arrangement would be made for our common defence and welfare. I had not seen any of the leaders since Bohemond had entered the city, and though I shuddered to meet with the architects of this devastation again we could not ignore each other. Like slaves in a galley, we were chained together by fortune, and one could not founder but the others would follow.

Nonetheless, I would avoid Bohemond if I could. Instead, I sought Adhemar.

I had feared to walk in Antioch again, but the new day brought new life to the city. The world had turned, and if the marks of the sack were still scorched into every street and building there was still a sense that peace and order had begun to settle again. The sun had gone down on the rage of the Franks; when it dawned, they were restored to obedience. Armed knights guarded every corner, while pilgrims and peasants hauled the dead from the roadsides and loaded them onto handcarts. There would be much digging in the fields that day if the corpses were not to fester around us. The frenzy of destruction had passed, the outpouring of seven months of frustration: now the Frankish faces were solemn, some almost stricken, as if they themselves could hardly believe the fury that had owned them. A contrite stillness clasped the city, and few gazes were raised to meet ours.

Brief questions and Adhemar's name brought us at last to the cathedral, the great church of the apostle Peter, who had been Bishop of Antioch before journeying to Rome. It was a worthy monument, with mighty pillars outside and a great silver dome rising over the centre. The Turks, in their impiety, had desecrated it: next door they had erected a minaret, and within they had defaced all Christian ornament to make it acceptable to their own god of asceticism. Already masons and labourers were busy inside trying to unwork the sacrilege.

I left Sigurd in the square and stepped through the bronze doors, crossing myself as I passed the threshold. In silence, I offered a prayer to Saint Peter, though I doubt he could have heard it over the cacophony of hammers and chisels that rang around the hall. Dust clouded the air, muting my tread and swirling in the columns of sunlight that came through the windows. The Turks had certainly erased every trace of Christ – the icons had been removed, the statues plastered over, and the walls repainted with the twisted, bewitching designs the Ishmaelites favoured. The iconostasis had been torn down and I could see clear to the back of the church, where workmen on ladders prised away the mortar that encased the original carvings in the sanctuary. Keeping a wary eye lest some piece of masonry fall from the roof, I picked my way through the rubble towards them.

'Is Bishop Adhemar here?' I shouted up. A mouthful of dust parched my tongue.

'He left, not long ago.' The man on the ladder did not look down but continued to pick at the mortar with his chisel. Beneath his blows a solemn face was emerging from the masonry blanket that had buried it.

'Where did the Bishop go?'

Fragments of plaster trickled down the wall. A cheek had appeared. 'I did not hear.'

I turned away. Behind me, another labourer was carrying a pile of planks in his arms towards the middle of the hall, perhaps to build a scaffold. As he dropped them under the dome, I accosted him.

'Do you know where Bishop Adhemar has gone?'

The man looked up. His clothes were ragged, and he stooped even without his burden. Some unkind blow seemed to have broken his nose, though the sores and pimples which pocked his face were the worse disfigurement.

'He has gone to the palace. He said—' He broke off, staring at me. 'You! The Greek.'

I had recognised him a moment sooner and mastered my surprise. 'Peter Bartholomew. Do you still have that cross carved on your shoulders? Or has it vanished under the pox sores?'

'You should not speak of such things in a church,' he hissed. His jaw trembled.

'This will not be a church again until the bishop consecrates it. When he does, I think it will be you who should fear to enter it. Have you seen the priestess Sarah recently?'

'I do not know what you speak of.' With a great heave of his shoulders, Peter Bartholomew set his back to me and hurried out through a side door. For a large man, I thought, he scuttled very much like a beetle.

I did not follow him. It was only four nights since I had talked with the ethereal priestess on the banks of the Orontes, but already she was almost forgotten. Drogo, Quino, the temple at Daphne and the sect they had worshipped – all were like relics of a different lifetime. I would never know how or why Drogo had died, but if I escaped Antioch alive I would not care.

I remembered my confrontation with Quino the day before the assault, at the tower by the bridge. *You will not live for the Turks to slaughter,* he had promised. Where in the city was he now, I wondered? And what had become of his companion, Odard?

I rejoined Sigurd outside, and we walked down the road between the cathedral and the palace, a great thorough-fare built straight as a spear through the city. Once, when Antioch was at its mightiest, the colonnades must have run its entire length unbroken; now they only remained in places. Even there, grime and cracks now veined the marble, and several times the path was blocked where the lintels had collapsed under a heap of shattered tiles. For long stretches the ancient design had vanished completely, usurped by squat brick buildings whose wooden balconies pushed out over the street. Lattice screens covered their windows, but I sensed movements within where furtive eyes looked down on us unseen. It would be a long time, I feared, before those who had survived the horrors of the day before would trust us.

At the southern end of the city, where a second road branched away towards the fortified bridge, we found the palace. It barely deserved the name, being little more than a large villa whose grounds had been overlaid with outbuildings and courtyards, but that had not saved it from the looters. The train of its sack ran far down the street: shattered pottery, torn fabrics, broken artefacts and trinkets. There was even a lion's head carved from stone, which some ambitious thief had dragged almost a hundred yards before abandoning.

'I wonder what happened to the Turk who owned that?' Sigurd muttered.

I shook my head. There were things in the debris which looked sickeningly like severed limbs, ignored or forgotten by the burial crews. There might be peace in the city, but it bore little scrutiny.

We came to the palace. Horses stood tethered to the iron rings in its walls, while men-at-arms milled about in the dusty square. From the west, men and mules brought baggage in from the camp that they had dismantled; from the eastern slopes of the mountain there limped a steady flow of battered knights. Clearly not all the Turks had yet been driven from the city.

Unchallenged and unnoticed, we passed through a long, broad courtyard, under an arch and into a second courtyard. A cloister ran around its edges; in its centre a dry fountain stood flanked by cherry trees. There was no fruit on them. In the shade of their branches a handful of Franks stood or sat and argued. As we approached, a knight in the cloister saw us and ran to intercept us, but the bishop, standing by the fountain, had already noticed us. He lifted his hand, half in greeting, half to still the guard, and walked to meet us. His white beard spilled over a full coat of mail, girded with a thick sword belt, but instead of a helmet he wore a crimson skullcap. Despite the burning sun, his face seemed drained of colour and strength.

'I wondered what had become of you,' he greeted us. 'I heard that you accompanied Bohemond when he forced the walls.'

'I was there,' I agreed. 'Since when I have worked to establish a stronghold on the walls, lest the Turks come upon us. What have you done?'

There were many meanings to my question, and I saw in the bishop's eyes that he heard all of them. His answer was more simple. 'There is much to do before Kerbogha comes. You missed the fighting in the city, but they did not surrender it easily. The army is drained, and they will find little here to succour them in the short time given us.'

'Enough time, surely,' I said. 'If we have learned one thing in the past seven months, it is that the walls of Antioch are not quickly breached. They will shield us until the Emperor comes.'

Adhemar grimaced. 'If only that were so. We can shut the door to the city, but without the lock it will not hold long.'

'What?'

He pointed over my shoulder, up to the furthest of the mountain's three summits. It thrust out over Antioch like a buttress, and atop it I could see the imposing outlines of walls and turrets. It was the ancient citadel, built high above the city to command its protection.

'When Bohemond's men reached the citadel they found it barred against them. It is impregnable: a single road runs up from the city to meet it and on all sides the mountain drops sheer away. While the Turks hold it, there is a gaping hole at the heart of our defence. When Kerbogha comes, he will climb into the valley behind the mountain, reinforce the citadel through its outer gate, then pour men down into Antioch.'

'But its strength is also its weakness.' Sigurd spoke for the first time. 'If a single narrow path over steep cliffs is the only way up from the city, it is also the only way down. We can block that path and stop them up in the castle, isolate them.'

'Perhaps.' There was a hopelessness in Adhemar's voice. 'But Kerbogha's army is beyond numbering. He will throw in ever more men until our bulwark cannot contain them and we are swept down the mountain in a torrent.'

'Where is Bohemond now?' I asked.

'Besieging the citadel. He hopes to force it before Kerbogha comes.'

The beat of hooves interrupted us. Ducking to clear the arch, a horseman cantered into the courtyard. Four knights rode behind him, bearing spears; streaming behind one I saw the bear banner of Tancred. The leader, Tancred himself, reined his horse to a halt and swung himself from the saddle, throwing the reins and his helmet to the guard who came running. Like Bohemond, he had shaved off his beard, stripping years and authority from his face so that he seemed little more than a child. A petulant child, I thought.

He strode towards us, one fist clenched tight. As he reached the paving around the fountain he opened it and hurled its content down. A hundred tiny black pellets bounced and scattered over the stones.

'Peppercorns!' he shouted. He stamped his boot, and I heard several splintering to powder beneath it. 'I have searched every house and granary in this cursed city, and all I find are cloves and peppercorns. We cannot live on this.' He spat into the fountain.

Adhemar frowned. 'There must—'

For the second time, a new arrival interrupted him. Another knight, too humble to merit a horse, came running through the gate towards us. His scarlet face streamed with sweat and he collapsed onto his knees by the fountain, groaning as he saw that it would give nothing to quench his thirst.

Other men had hurried out from the cloister around the courtyard, among them Count Raymond and Duke Godfrey. They clustered around the messenger, drowning him in shade, though for the moment he seemed too drained to speak. At last he managed to gasp out a few short words.

'At the bridge. Kerbogha.'

Despite the midday sun, we ran all the way to the bridge. The walls by the gate were already crowded with Franks who had come to see the new threat, but Sigurd managed to drive a path up the stairs and forward to the rampart. It was like being in the hippodrome when the Emperor gave out bread or meat: those who had views through the embrasures defied all demands to surrender their places, while those who could not see jostled and shoved to dislodge their neighbours. It was a miracle that no one toppled off.

A head taller than most of the crowd, Sigurd saw an opening and prised his way in, angling his broad shoulders so that I could join him. One man trod on my foot, another thumped me in the spine, but I fended off their assault and leaned through the opening. If doom was upon us, I wanted to see it.

Such is the perversity of the soul that the actual sight merely kindled disappointment. I had expected a hundred thousand Turks in burnished armour, their spears like wheat and their host innumerable, with Kerbogha himself a giant in their midst, flanked by the banners of fourteen emirs. Instead, there seemed only to be about thirty horsemen, cantering along the river bank and loosing occasional arrows at us. I knew from futile experience that few of the missiles would reach the walls. From the top of the watchtower beyond the bridge our garrison shot back in desultory fashion.

'Kerbogha,' snorted Sigurd. 'This is not Kerbogha. These are the scouts of the outriders of his vanguard. If thirty of them can scare the Franks, they will run all the way to Nicaea when they see his full force.'

I agreed, and was about to abandon my tenuous vantage. But it seemed that not all the Franks dismissed the Turks so readily, for as I began to move I heard a great commotion by the gate below. There were shouts, the ring of armour and the pulse of hooves. Hemmed in by the crowd around me I could see nothing, but in an instant a column of Frankish riders burst into view through the battlements. At their head, on a white stallion, I saw a knight with red feathers in his helm.

'Roger Barneville,' said Sigurd. I knew him too, a Norman captain from Duke Robert's army. Though he was not as mighty as the princes, he had joined their councils on occasion to offer advice. He was renowned as a skilful soldier and a formidable warrior.

'What is he doing?'

Fifteen knights had followed him out through the open gates and formed a line driving towards the Turks. To the cheers of the garrison they swept past the tower and charged up the slope, following the Alexandretta road away from the river. Though the Turks had twice their numbers, and bows to fire against the Frankish spears, they offered not the least resistance. They turned their horses and galloped away, dust billowing behind them.

'Does Roger think they will tell Kerbogha to retreat to Khorassan because fifteen knights dared to oppose them?' Sigurd asked.

I made no reply. The dust still whirled where the Turks had vanished, but instead of dying away with their passing it seemed to build, creeping ever wider along the ridge. It was too far off for me to see clearly, yet I thought I glimpsed dark shadows moving under the eddying cloud. Still it grew, as though a storm wind whipped it to new heights.

'What . . . ?'

The swirling shadows resolved themselves as a line of

Turkish horsemen emerged from the dust. They crested the ridge and charged down the slope; a second later, I heard the thunder of their hooves rolling across the river. The Normans saw them and in an instant swerved their horses back towards the city. But they had been drawn perilously far away. There was no thought of battle, for the Turks were ten times their number and had fresh horses under them. Even as I watched, they began to outflank the Normans, driving them away from the refuge of the bridge and forcing them towards the river.

A shout rose from the gate below. 'Where are the reinforcements? Will we allow the Turks to chase us from before our own city?' It was Count Raymond's voice, honed to a cutting edge by a lifetime on the battlefield, but though I heard much clamour and jangling no one rode out to help.

Now the Normans had reached the river. The summer drought had shrunk it into a thin channel between cracked mudflats; even in its centre, rocks protruded from the water. The first of the Normans slid his horse down the embankment where animals came to drink and splashed across. Others followed, picking their way over the uneven course while the water foamed white with falling arrows. I counted fourteen men on the near bank now: only one remained on the far side, the red feathers still sticking defiantly from his helmet. It was Roger Barneville, who having led the charge up the ridge now found himself in the rear of the retreat. The Turks were close behind him, their arrows whipping past, but if he could ford the river he would quickly come under the protection of the walls.

His horse cantered down the muddy embankment and onto the naked river bed. The treacherous ground slowed his pace; the pursuing Turks drew nearer, but still he managed to duck their arrows.

Barneville was almost at the water's edge when suddenly

his horse stopped short. The jarring halt threw him forward but he managed to keep in the saddle; when he tried to spur the horse again, though, it would not move. Had an arrow struck it? I could not see any wound. The horse seemed to be straining forward, struggling to lift its hooves, yet rooted to the ground.

Roger glanced over his shoulder. The leading Turks were on the river bank, looking down on him. Panicking, he tried to kick free of his stirrups, but it was too late. An arrow buried itself in his back and he jerked up like a puppet. At such close range it would have driven clean through the armour.

The shouting around me died away to nothing. Every man looked on in horror.

'Who will help him?' bellowed Count Raymond, now up on the walls.

No one answered.

Roger Barneville was alive – I could see him still fumbling with his bridle, trying to dismount – but the Turks had not finished. One of them galloped forward, spear in hand, and as he came up to Barneville he drove it through him like a spit. I saw the point gleaming in the sun as it emerged from his chest. He must have cried out, but he was too weak to be heard: we could only watch as he toppled slowly from his saddle into the river. A second Turk rode past; his sword flashed, and blood welled into the water. As he wiped his blade, another horseman stabbed his spear into the river like a fisherman seeking octopus. When he lifted it out, a misshapen bulge was fixed to its tip. A red feather hung limp beneath it.

It took much to outrage the Franks, but they were silent with shock and shame now. I heard one voice mumbling that they had too few horses, another that there was little they could have done in any event, but none raised their voices to agree. The Turks crossed the river and rode impudently along the base of the walls, waving their bloody trophy at us. Few arrows flew to punish them. In the distance, Roger's horse tipped back its neck and screamed, mourning its master or bewailing its captivity, while the Turk who had struck the final blow drew up his own mount near the bridge and shouted violence at us. His words were alien, but the meaning was unmissable.

The crowd on the walls was ebbing away. Sigurd and I followed.

'Fool,' he hissed when we were out of hearing. 'Senseless, worthless, idiot fool. How many times have we seen ten Turks lure us to battle, only to become a hundred? Why do the Franks refuse to learn the ways of their enemy?'

I had no answer.

'Today we saw thirty become three hundred. What will we do tomorrow, when the three hundred become three thousand, then thirty thousand? Will we ride out to be slaughtered every time Kerbogha sends a company of scouts to goad us?'

I looked up at the mountain. Smoke was rising from the furthest peak, above the citadel, but I did not see Bohemond's banner flying there.

'It is a bad beginning.'

κ β

That evening we made a fire on top of the tower that we had occupied. Beric the Varangian had ridden to Saint Simeon that day and had fetched back fish and grain at exorbitant cost. I did not think that that path would be open to us much longer. As long as we held the tower by the bridge we could defend the road, but all afternoon the Turkish vanguard had harried the defences with fire and arrows. The Franks had withstood them, but they would not hold out for long when Kerbogha came in his full might.

'We would not be able to go to Saint Simeon often in any case,' Beric said. He pulled the pan from the fire and scraped charred fish into our bowls. 'I almost killed my horse getting back here before dark.'

'That will be tomorrow's supper, then,' said Sigurd.

'And what shall we do the day after?' I pulled apart the sticky flesh in my fingers, wincing at the heat. 'It took us four months to close off the city; I doubt Kerbogha will be so slow.'

Sigurd scowled as he tasted the bitter fish. 'If I am alive the day after tomorrow, then I will consider what to eat.'

'Do not say that.' It was a warm night, and the fire made it warmer still, but Anna pulled her shawl closer about her. 'We must survive. There is no gain in thinking of the alternative.'

I reached out an arm to comfort her, but she shrugged free of it. I wrapped my arms around my knees and stared intently at the flames.

'I wonder how Bohemond finds the city that he schemed so hard to win,' Sigurd mused. 'It is not the best beginning for his new empire.'

'A curse on him and his empire,' I said. 'I would like to see them both thrown down in ruin and picked over by crows, if I did not fear that we would fall beside him.'

Sigurd belched. 'He may be our brightest hope.'

'Then our plight is truly dire.'

'Bohemond is a snake, Demetrios, like all Normans. When the bastard William landed in England, his army was too small, his supplies too few, and winter fast approaching. Within a month he was master of the kingdom. Bohemond is hatched from the same egg. He is a snake in a corner, and therefore most dangerous. The Turks will need a long spear to force him out.'

'Or a single well-aimed arrow. How have we come to rely on allies like these?'

'When the Emperor comes, we will not have to.' Sigurd licked the last juice off the fish's skeleton and cast it into the fire.

'If we are still here when he comes.'

'Halt!'

The challenge from the foot of the tower echoed up to us. I jumped to my feet and leaned out through the embrasure. In the orb of a burning torch below, I could see a tall man in a long white robe standing at the door. A Varangian faced him, axe in hand.

'Who is it?' I called down.

The visitor tipped back his head. The torchlight flickered on a dark face fringed by a black beard. 'Demetrios? It is Mushid. The swordsmith.'

I relaxed my grip on the battlements. 'Come up.'

We shuffled closer in our circle and made an opening for Mushid. As he seated himself by the parapet, I heard a muffled thud from under his robe. He would be wise to keep his wares close at hand in the city, I thought, though foolish to venture here at all. At least he had taken some precaution – I saw now why I had not recognised him immediately.

'You've removed your turban.'

He nodded. 'I do not want my head raised on a Franj's spear.'

'If you are so cautious for your neck, why enter Antioch?' asked Sigurd. He had not met Mushid before, and watched him across the fire with narrow eyes.

'For many reasons. I came to see if it was true, the rumour of the ruin which the Franj had worked.'

'It is.'

'So I saw. All through the city I have seen not one Turk today, save those being thrown into pits to be buried.'

'The Franks boast that not a single Turk survived the sack. I am sorry.'

'It was not your fault.'

It was, though. Again I remembered hammering back the bolt, the shouting of the Normans and the clatter of arrows about me. I remembered climbing that frail ladder, mounting the walls that had defied me for so long and being too terrified to care. I remembered—

'Mushid.'

'Yes?'

'Two nights ago I was with Bohemond's men on the walls, translating for the Turk who betrayed the city. He was agitated – he thought we had too few men and that Bohemond had not come. He said . . .' I commanded my mind back. 'He said *Mushid promised that Bohemond would come.*'

Mushid folded his hands together and stared into the

fire. It hissed and crackled; the reflected flames danced on the battlements around us. No one spoke.

'There are many men called Mushid in my country, as there are many called Demetrios in yours.'

'There are not many who visited Bohemond alone in his tent three weeks ago.'

Again there was a long pause. At last: 'It was my name you heard.'

'You plotted with Bohemond to let him seize the city?'

'I brought messages to him. Firouz, the captain on the tower, he is an armourer. I am a swordsmith. We have friends through the guilds. I travel freely wherever men need arms. Sometimes I carry more than swords.'

'But why?' demanded Anna. 'Why betray the city – and your own people? Did you revel in the destruction you saw today?'

Mushid shrugged. 'They are not my people. They are Turks; I am an Arab, a Saracen.'

'But you worship the same god—'

'We all say we worship the same god – Jews, Franj, Byzantines, Turks and Arabs. But we do not agree *how* He is to be worshipped. Why do you think you have endured so long in such hostile country? Because of the power of your arms? You survive because every lord from Cairo to Constantinople wishes to make you his tool. The Byzantines and Fatimids seek to destroy the Turks; the Armenians would become their own masters; the emirs of Damascus and Aleppo and Antioch each hope you will destroy their rivals. You have marched into an ancient game played out in the dust of Asia. You see in straight lines, but all about you others move obliquely. That is why you live now: because each of your enemies hates his neighbour more.'

He fell silent, and leaned back against the wall. The empty spaces between the battlements were like black teeth above him.

'If that is so, then whom do *you* serve?' Sigurd asked.

'I am a swordsmith. I serve myself, and those who buy my blades. Others make schemes; I carry their messages.'

I shifted on the hard stone beneath me. 'Why are you here now?'

'I heard that you had occupied this tower. It is prudent to know where your friends are in these times.'

'That was not what I meant.'

Mushid lifted an eyebrow. 'Then what? Do I carry more secrets of hidden plans? Having worked the city's betrayal once, will I do it again? Is that what you ask?'

'If a man sits at my fire I like to know why he is there.'

'Then you are wise.' He smiled. 'I did not weep to see the Turks lose Antioch, because they were *Ahl al-Sunna*. Having helped the Franj, I will not turn away so quickly from them. And if Kerbogha takes the city, there will be more killing. You will have killed all the Muslims, he will kill all the Christians, and Antioch will become a wasteland. Nobody will win.'

'How can you bear it?' Anna spoke so quietly that her words seemed to entwine with the hissing fire. 'Whichever doctrines divided you from the Antiochenes, they were your brothers. By your hand, many thousands of them now lie in an open grave. How can you sit by our fire and discuss this calamity as if it were nothing more than the forging of a sword?'

'First, because they did not die by my hand. They died by the hands of a thousand Franj, not one more or less guilty. Do not try and blame me for what your allies have done.'

'They are not my allies. And hateful though they are, their evil would have remained undone if you had not arranged for the gate to be open.'

It was as if hot lead had been poured into my belly. I squirmed where I sat, praying that Anna's fixed stare did not move onto me. In my account of the battle at the walls, I had not told her the truth of my role: the fear that she would blame me for all that had happened since was unanswerable. How could it be otherwise, when I could not defend it myself?

'Firouz the armourer opened the gate,' said Mushid. 'If I had not carried his messages to Bohemond, he would have found another. Even if he had not, even if I alone were responsible for unlocking the gate, I would not bear the blame for what happened afterwards. Many doors open: it is for men to choose which they enter – and what they do inside.'

I had rarely seen Anna bested in argument, but now she had no reply. None, at least, that she could voice, though her face evinced an inconsolable anger.

'Would you rather that I had done nothing?' Mushid continued. 'Would you rather now be cowering in your tent before the walls, watching Demetrios pull on his armour? Would you rather see three thousand Franj, with barely a sound horse between them, marching to fight the mightiest Turkish army in a generation? Would you rather be in the camp when Kerbogha's victorious janissaries overran it, massacring every man and boy and dragging you away by your hair to the slave-brothels of Mosul where—'

'Enough,' I snapped. 'That is not necessary.'

Mushid looked at me almost curiously, then bowed his head. 'I am sorry. I meant no insult. It is bad to offend one's host at his own fire. All I wished to say is that there would have been a terrible killing in any event. Perhaps you do not like what I have done, but I have been on many battlefields, both as victor and vanquished. I assure you of this: it is always better to be among the living than the dead.'

I could see from the faces around the fire that his

argument satisfied no one, me least of all. It did not lift one straw from the burden of guilt I bore. Yet unless the dead came to lend their voices to the debate, it was irrefutable.

I was uneasy with the turn that the conversation had taken, and with the enmity that seemed to have flared up between Anna and Mushid. Still, there were questions I wanted to ask.

'Your friendship with Drogo – was that part of this plot?'

Mushid studied his knuckles, his face impassive. 'No. As I told you once before, I met Drogo when I sold him a sword. It was much later that Firouz confided in me his plan, after Drogo had died. He was simply a friend, a good man to sit with by a fire. It is sad that he lived under so unfortunate a roof.'

'Unfortunate indeed, but not uncommon.'

'And still the misfortune continues. His servant was found dead by the river three days ago.'

'Simon?' A torrent of images flooded my mind: the boy shivering under Quino's brutality, picking herbs from the river bank covered in mud, rubbing an oily cloth over Drogo's sword. Was it possible that he had suffered the same fate as his master?

'Simon, yes. I was in the Norman camp when they discovered him.'

'How did it happen?' So many men had died in the past days – and weeks and months – that it was astonishing I could feel anything from one more death. In truth, I felt nothing, for the news had a numbing effect that I could not resist. Yet somehow, if it were possible, in the recesses of my soul I felt a cold hand squeeze tighter about me, felt a more profound absence of feeling itself.

'He was pierced with arrows. He had been hunting for herbs on the bank – a party of Turks must have seen him from the far side and chanced their aim.'

Perhaps, I thought, I had known it already. I remembered dismantling the boat bridge two days earlier, and a peasant telling me of a boy killed picking herbs. I had felt a sickening premonition, but then Bohemond had arrived and dragged me away, and all else had been forgotten. Not that remembering would have helped by then.

Mushid was still speaking. 'It was a tragic end. Had he lived another day, he would have entered the city in safety.'

Through the welter of thought and memory that flurried about me, I found myself thinking that if this city, besieged and starving, had been Simon's best hope of safety, how wretched must he have been? Hardly less, I supposed, than we who had survived.

Much later I lay on the stone of the rampart under the dark sky. Anna lay against me, my chest against her back and my knees crooked inside hers, like two bowls stacked together. My arms were wrapped around her chest, which swelled and sank gently under her cotton shift. We had no mattress save our cloaks, for every stick of straw in the city had gone to feed the horses. The hot night meant there was no need for blankets.

'I don't trust the Saracen,' said Anna. 'Neither should you.'

'I don't.'

'He has already betrayed the city once. Who can tell what other secrets he hides? Thousands of innocents have died because of him.'

Again, the frantic memory of the gate on the mountain rasped through my mind. I could not discuss this with Anna. 'He saved us from certain death. How can I hate him, if because of him Helena's child has a grandfather?'

'I do not say you should hate him. But you should not draw him near you either.'

As the night had come on, I had insisted that Mushid

should stay in our tower until dawn. There were too many Franks on the streets, knights and pilgrims alike, who might recognise him as an Ishmaelite and tear him apart. He had resisted my urging but I had sensed gratitude when finally he allowed me to prevail. Now he slept with the Varangians in the guardroom along the wall.

'As much as you do unto the least of my people, you do unto me,' I quoted. 'He will be gone in the morning.'

'Good.'

Anna nestled back into me. Her long hair prickled against my nose and I shook my head to breathe freely again, unwilling to push her away even an inch. Warmth flowed between us – and with it, I fancied, some small measure of my cares.

'What was it that struck you when you heard that the Norman's servant had died?' Anna asked at last. 'I saw your eyes. You looked – guilty.'

I paused, trying to order my thoughts. 'I saw the knight, Quino, the day before Simon died. At the tower. I accused him of worshipping a pagan idol. I suggested that it might have been he who killed Drogo.'

'Did you think so?'

'I don't know. I have not considered it in many weeks; there has been too much else to distract me. But now three of Quino's companions are dead. Even when Bohemond wanted their murderer found, Quino gave no help. And when I challenged him he threatened to kill me.'

'The Saracen said the boy was killed by Turks.'

'He said the boy was found on the river bank, pierced with arrows. Three nights ago the Turks were pent up in Antioch. Any raiding party on the far bank would have had to pass the watchtower by the fortified bridge, the guards by the boat bridge and the rest of our picket line.

And even the Turks might struggle to hit a boy in the dark from across the river.'

'But why would the knight . . . ?'

I remembered the snarl of Quino's voice as we wrestled at the foot of the tower, the frenzy in his eyes. 'It was the boy who told me that the knights had gone to Daphne, to the pagan cave. If Quino guessed that, what would he not have done to protect himself? The western princes do not bring heretics into their palaces to dispute theology with them, as the Emperor does. They burn them alive. And I – I revealed to Quino that I knew his secret. I gave him cause to suspect that the boy, Simon, had betrayed him. A day later Simon was dead.'

I rolled away, setting my back to Anna's. Almost immediately, she turned over so that our positions were reversed, and her arms squeezed around me.

'You must not think of it,' she said. 'Perhaps Quino killed the boy, perhaps he did not. There are too many other concerns, more pressing, to trouble you now.'

'No.' I struggled free of her embrace as the images of a thousand slaughtered Turks clamoured in my mind. Whatever Mushid said, whatever blame the Franks held, it was my hand which had opened the gates of death to them. Against their deaths, Simon's was nothing – a tear in a torrent. But their lives were beyond salvation now, while Simon's I might still redeem.

The few inches between me and Anna yawned like a chasm, and the silence lasted so long that I thought she must have fallen asleep. At length, though, I felt the touch of her hand on my shoulder as she pulled me back towards her. I did not resist.

'The baby will be three months old by now,' said Anna. 'I hope Helena has kept him healthy.'

I simply hoped that there was a baby to be healthy. We did not speak of the other possibility.

'If you are worried, perhaps you should go back. It would be good for Helena to have a doctor and a mother to help.' I spoke carefully, for any implication of weakness or cowardice would enrage Anna. 'A starving, doomed city is no place for a woman.'

To my relief, she did not pull away from me. Nor was there any anger in her voice, only weary sadness. 'It is too late for that. It would be suicide, trying to evade Kerbogha's army. Sigurd says that in two days we shall not even be able to leave the walls.'

'There are still ships at Saint Simeon,' I urged her. 'You could take passage to Cyprus, and thence to Constantinople. With the summer seas, it would be as safe a journey as any.'

For a long time she was still. From down in the city I could hear occasional shouted challenges from the Frankish patrols, sometimes the braying of animals. Otherwise Antioch seemed asleep. I doubted whether dreams would be any relief for its inhabitants.

'No.'

'It would be better—' I began.

'No. While I am here, I worry for Thomas and Helena, for Zoe and your grandchild, and for all who are dear to me. I fear for myself, and for what will become of me when Kerbogha comes. But if I left now, I would live every minute in fear for you. And that would be worse.'

I closed my eyes. A wave of warm confusion swept through me, threatening to spill out in tears. I kissed Anna on the nape of her neck.

'You are a fool.' My voice was shaking. 'You should never have come, and then you should not have stayed.'

'Neither should you. But we are both here now.'

κ γ

Mushid had gone when I woke; he had slipped away just before dawn, the guard told me. He was probably wise to have done so, for the Frankish watchmen would have been most drowsy then – and we had nothing to offer him for breakfast. I longed for activity, for distraction from the cares that ravaged me like carrion-birds: I oiled my armour, polished my sword until I could have shaved in its reflection, worked the leather of my shield and even cut a new hole in my belt to fit my shrunken waist. After that, there was nothing to do save pace the walls and watch.

During the night, more Turks had come up on the far bank of the Orontes. It seemed that the Franks had at last learned patience, for they did not ride out to attack. Nor, though, could they avoid battle, for at first light the Turks renewed their assault on the tower by the fortified bridge. I could see it from where I watched, the wooden palisade raised on its mound and the banner of the Duke of Normandy hanging limp from a spear above it. The Normans had packed it with defenders, and for now seemed able to withstand the constant Turkish siege, but still it was merely the advance parties of Kerbogha's vanguard whom they faced.

At noon Adhemar summoned us to another council. It was a relief to know that we were not forgotten, though I feared it was only the bishop – and perhaps Count

Raymond – who cared anything for us. They brought us together in the great church of Saint Peter, where the customary four benches had been set in a square under the silver dome. After so many meetings in the confines of Adhemar's tent or Raymond's farmhouse it was strange to be placed in so cavernous a hall, where broad spaces stretched behind us and every word rebounded from the roof. The labourers had been cleared out for the council, but their work was far from finished: half-exposed icons stared out from splintered holes in the plaster; fragments of stone and rubble lay in heaps on the floor; and all was shrouded in dust.

Adhemar began by invoking the Lord. 'The city is ours, praise God. By His right hand, and to His glory, we have conquered.'

All save the citadel, I thought grimly.

'By His grace, may we still hold its walls in a month,' Bohemond added. He sat beside Adhemar, with the east end of the church and the high altar at his back. Count Raymond, whose place it was by custom, had been pushed further down the bench almost into the corner.

'We have earned a mighty victory, for which we must be duly grateful. But it will be for nothing if we do not now hold Antioch against the new threat which rushes to overthrow us. We are the army of light, but a storm rages, and a single breath may extinguish us for ever. Only the hands of the Lord will cup us in safety,' said Adhemar.

'And sharp swords, and swift arrows.' I had not seen Bohemond since the assault on the walls, but he did not seem to have enjoyed the fruits of his conquest in the intervening days. His dark hair was matted with dirt and sweat; the beard he had so carefully shaved before the battle was already sprouting back, unchecked; his eyes were sunk deep in dark pits. I guessed he had not slept since entering the city. The tunic he wore under his armour was stained yellow, while a grimy bandage bound his right forearm.

'Already, my lords, you have seen Kerbogha's vanguard attacking the outer forts. Now he looks to bring the greater part of his army to bear on us. A rider came this morning from the Iron Bridge, to say that the garrison there is under heavy siege. Even with all Christ's favour, they will not stand more than a day. That is all the time we have to organise our defences.'

Count Raymond lifted his head. 'The time *you* have to organise *your* defences, you mean. Antioch is your city, until the Emperor comes. Or had you forgotten it?'

'Do you think that when Kerbogha comes he will confine his war to the Normans?'

Adhemar thumped his staff on the stone floor, lifting a cloud of dust. 'Enough! We will fight as the Army of God – as one people. There will be no Normans or Provençals on the walls to face Kerbogha – only Christians.'

'If we fight as the Army of God, then under what title does Bohemond hold the city?'

'Under the title of survival,' said Bohemond angrily. 'If not for me, we would all have met the same fate as Roger Barneville, hacked apart under the walls. Would you prefer that, Count Raymond?'

'You would have allowed it, if we had not yielded to your ambition.'

'The ambition of men is all that will aid us now.'

'No!' Adhemar lifted himself on his staff and stared first at Bohemond, then at Raymond. Looking at him, I saw with shock how the recent days had emptied him. His skin was pale, and shiny like a potter's glaze; there was no longer any humour in his face. His hand trembled as he gripped the staff, and he seemed suddenly twenty years older.

'The grace of God is all that will aid us now, and He

is only ever served in unity. Put aside your quarrels. Every division between us opens the door to Satan's works.'

He sagged back onto his seat. The effort those few words had taken was plain. For a few moments there was silence.

'We must divide the keeping of the walls among ourselves,' said Bohemond at last. 'Duke Godfrey will watch the northern flank, by the gate of Saint Paul. Count Hugh will take the north-western portion, Count Raymond the length south of the Duke Gate, and the Count of Flanders the area by the fortified bridge. I will fight on the mountain, for Kerbogha is sure to attack first at the citadel. The Duke of Normandy will aid me there.'

'That is strange.' All eyes turned to Count Raymond, though he himself seemed to be staring at a statue of Saint Justin half-excavated from an alcove. 'I have just heard the lord Bohemond ordering the dispositions of the army, yet I believed we were the Army of God. Is the disinherited whelp of a Norman pirate not content with the throne of Antioch? Does he now presume to raise himself to the throne of Heaven? Because if he does, he may find he has very far to fall.'

In an instant, Bohemond was on his feet. 'If the Count of Saint-Gilles accuses me of blasphemy, I will answer his lie. He may be lord of thirteen counties, but in single combat I will strip him of them one by one.'

Adhemar made to interrupt, but Raymond's voice was stronger. 'You will not do that – unless you would defend this city with none but a few hundred horseless Normans.' He turned to the rest of the council. 'For months, the lord Bohemond has begged us to make him warden of Antioch. At times, his grovelling has been almost an embarrassment. And now that he has had it for three days, he makes himself overlord of us all; he tells us where to place our armies, and how to fight.'

'Enough. Will you still bicker here when the Lord comes in glory and judgement?'

All turned to see Little Peter, the stunted, mulish man who rose from the bench to my left. He had the strange capacity to shrink from notice if he chose, but when he spoke it was as if his every word was life itself. He hobbled into the centre of the square, dragging his bare feet through the dust, and stared around. The short hermit's cape twitched from his shoulders.

'Why do the nations rage, and the peoples plot in vain? The kings of the Earth take counsel together, they conspire against the Lord's anointed. But He who sits in Heaven laughs; He scorns them. He will break them with a rod of iron, and dash them into pieces like clay. Be wise, O kings, be warned. Serve the Lord with fear; tremble even as you kiss His feet, or He will be angry – and you will perish.'

His words were like ice on the princes, freezing their tempers and chilling their thoughts. Several, I saw, made the sign of the cross. Even Adhemar looked discomfited.

'You do well to rebuke us, Little Peter,' the bishop said. 'No man's pride should blind him to the Lord's will.'

'Turn your eyes to the heavens – but turn them also to the ground on which you walk, lest among the grass you stir a serpent. When beasts contend among themselves, their shadows block the light from the humble creatures below, and their hooves trample them. But the pure are not deceived: they look up, and they see through you like water. We are small, meagre creatures, far beneath your power and might. But a thousand ants, if stirred to war, may strip a horse of all its flesh. With no thought but for your own desire, you have led your people into calamity, into torment, into death. How long will they suffer you to command them to ruin?'

Bohemond rose in anger. 'Who are these worms you

speak of? For the past two days, it has been my knights who have defended the walls and besieged the citadel, while your pilgrims burrow themselves deep into the city. When they are brave enough to cease from cowering in their holes, and come out to fight, then perhaps I will hear their complaint.'

For long moments the hermit's jittering frame stopped moving. His head swivelled up, and his cold-eyed stare fixed on Bohemond's. 'Be warned, Norman. You sit on your pyre and speak words of fire: your doom will come. The Lord pulls down the mighty and shatters the proud, but He shall exalt the meek and raise the humble to His throne. The fires approach, and only the truest alloy will survive their purifying flames. For the rest, you will burn away to ash.'

κ δ

The watchtower by the fortified bridge fell the following day. The Turks had brought up siege engines, and at first light they began a bombardment of fire and stone that the dry timbers could not withstand. Even then, the Franks defended it to the last. From my vantage point on the walls, I saw a thin knot of them straggling down the slope, shields locked together as the tower burned behind them. They were a tiny number against the thousands of Turks who assailed them – though still not the tenth part of Kerbogha's army. A few Franks managed to reach the safety of the city; many more did not. The Turks hacked their corpses apart and mounted their heads on a line of wooden palings before the gate. Of the tower, nothing survived: I watched as the beams reeled on their foundations, then crashed down in flames. Many of our men were crushed beneath it. A cloud of burning splinters rose in the air above, and smoke from the embers poured over the south-west quarter of the city, souring the light of the sun.

The same day, a band of Provençals came from the north. The Iron Bridge, our last redoubt on the Orontes, had fallen to Kerbogha; the garrison was dead, captive or routed. There were others fleeing after them, they said: a sally by Duke Godfrey's cavalry might yet bring them home before Kerbogha overtook them. The plea was refused, for we had no horses to spare. After that, no more Franks returned from the bridge.

It was an unnatural time. Every waking minute we were assailed by the sounds and sights of war, reminders of our desperate plight, yet long hours passed sitting on the walls until our limbs grew stiff from disuse. I could see Turks flooding the plain before Antioch, planting their tents and standards in the fields that we had so recently occupied, but we did not fire so much as a single arrow towards them. We could not fight; we could not flee; we could not even forage, for there was not a crumb to be found in the city. We diced without stakes, lest jealousies fester, and told stories we all knew by heart. Every sword and axe was honed fine as a feather, but so long as the Turks kept us hemmed within our ramparts our weapons were mere ornaments. And still the tide of our enemies flowed in.

On the Monday, the fifth day since we had taken the city, I resolved to seek out Odard. I needed some distraction to drive away the guilt which besieged me in the empty hours, and finding him would serve as well as anything. That much, at least, I owed to Simon. Whether or not he cared, in whichever corner of the afterlife he haunted, was of little importance.

I began my search by seeking out a Norman sergeant. It was harder than I had expected, for most of Bohemond's army was camped up on the mountain besieging the citadel, but at length I found a wounded knight standing guard by one of the western gates. He watched me with suspicion and though he seemed to recognise Odard's name it provoked only a mocking leer.

'Odard is no longer in our company,' he told me. Perhaps he hoped the news would distress me. 'He lost his horse, his sword, his armour, and finally his wits.'

'And his life? Did he lose that too?'

'Why should I care if he had? He was no use to our army.'

'Where can I find him?' I pressed.

The Norman shrugged. 'Perhaps among the peasants and pilgrims. Try the hermit, Little Peter: the lunatic and the feeble are his congregation.'

I did not like to have dealings with the mule-faced mystic who had orphaned Thomas, but my desire to speak with Odard was stronger. I found Little Peter at the cathedral, standing on the steps with a great crowd of Franks in front of him. They looked to be pilgrims rather than knights, though the lines between the two were dissolving: their clothes were torn and their bodies gaunt, and in their hands they carried a brutish armoury of slings and farm tools. Their faces were little friendlier. One of their number, a tall man with a cloth tied over his head to ward off the sun, seemed to be shouting at the hermit.

'If Christ is with us, why do we cower in this city? Is it the princes? If they are too timid, if their greed blinds them to their duty, then let them surrender their power to the faithful, the humble beloved of God. Our place is on the road to Jerusalem, not in this place of the heathen.'

Little Peter clambered onto the base of a column, raising himself above the throng, and looked down. His voice was shrill and anxious, far removed from the mystic certainty with which he had chided the princes.

'You are ignorant,' he snapped. 'Or blind. Have you not seen the ten thousand Turks who bar the way to Jerusalem?'

'Has the devil stolen your balls, Little Peter? Is that why you have grown no taller?' Cruel laughter rang in the square. 'When I first heard you preach, you promised we would be borne to the Holy Land on the wings of angels.'

'I told you that the path of the pilgrim is a thorny road that only the pure may tread.'

'Then why do *we* not tread it? Why does God curse and afflict us? Why do the Turks starve us and smite us?'

'I will tell you.' Another voice spoke up, that of a woman I could not see. 'Because our leaders are corrupted by sin – by pride and greed. Their sin draws down God's wrath from the heavens.'

'I have told them this,' said Peter. His feet were slipping from the pedestal, and he had to fling his short arms around the pillar to stay upright. 'I prophesy, but they do not hear.'

'There is only one true king, and the princes of the Earth are nothing before Him. Prophesy them that.'

'It is better to die a martyr than a slave,' someone else shouted. 'If the princes are too fearful to trust in the hand of God, let them open the gates and we will be His army.'

'No!'

Surprise murmured through the crowd as the stooped figure of the bishop appeared at the top of the steps. With the great door behind him he seemed little taller than Peter, and his crimson robes were pale in the glare. Only his staff kept him upright.

'A martyr's death is a gift of God, not to be snatched cravenly from Him. The true Christian does not fear death, but nor does he embrace it.'

'Do you say we should not trust in Christ?' one of the pilgrims challenged him.

'I say you should trust in Him to work His purpose. You should not presume to anticipate that purpose. You could fling open the gates of Antioch and rush out, so that the Orontes flowed red with your blood, but then you would die as suicides, not martyrs or Christians. Look at yourselves. Each one of you wears the cross. You have undertaken this journey, at great cost and peril, for the salvation of your souls. But the path of the cross, the road to Calvary, is neither short nor easy.'

A fit of coughing convulsed him, and he broke off. His words were faint, barely audible even halfway across the square, but no one took advantage of his silence. 'The greatness of our object does not lift stones from our path. It is the torments in our way that make the object great. All the terrors that assail us, all the sufferings we endure – it is these things you will think on when you reach Jerusalem and bend your knee at the holiest shrine, these things that will sanctify your journey. Do not think that by seeking certain death in battle you will cheat suffering, or win the martyr's crown. The way of oblivion is the way of the Devil. The way of Christ is patience, humility, and obedience. Now go.'

With these final words, he lifted his staff as if to part the sea of faces before him. But he was too weak: before he had raised it a foot in the air his strength was gone, and he let it swing back onto the ground. The crowd muttered, but none approached. Instead, in twos and threes, they began to drift away.

I pushed against them, hastening to the bishop. By the time I reached him, one of his priests had taken his arm and guided him to a stone bench. Sweat beaded his forehead below the rim of his mitre, and his hands trembled.

'You are losing control of your pilgrims, Little Peter.' Close to, his voice still bore some of its former strength.

The hermit had clambered down from the plinth, and now stood bolt upright in front of the pillar. 'What can a shepherd do when his flock deserts him, even in the midst of ravening wolves?'

'Get a dog,' I suggested.

Adhemar smiled, his dry lips cracking with the effort. 'Ever a practical answer, Demetrios Askiates.'

'It seemed to me that your sheep were a greater threat than the wolves just now,' I said to the hermit.

'And rightly so. When they are led into disaster by the lords of folly, when the precepts of the Lord are everywhere forgotten, it is right and lawful that they should rebel against wickedness.' He stabbed a filthy finger towards Adhemar. 'Be warned, Bishop: you and your princes cannot afford to neglect the care of those who follow you.'

'Be warned yourself!' Adhemar still had the power to summon anger when it was needed. His staff inclined towards Little Peter so that the silver tip hung over him, and his face was black with fury. 'Why do you think that you, a peasant, are invited to our councils? You come because you command the allegiance of the pilgrims, the poor and the weak who follow this army. If you cannot keep them obedient, your power is broken. The good shepherd does not abandon his flock, but when his flock abandon him he is no longer a shepherd.'

'I am commissioned by God for this task,' the hermit squealed.

'I am ordained by the church. I do not threaten you: I speak plainly. Outside these walls are countless hosts of Turks. We are beset by enemies, and the only path of salvation is unity. If you cannot deliver it, I will find others who can.'

He rose, pain creasing his body. The priest who had lingered nearby ran to aid him, but the bishop shrugged off his hand and hobbled away. He disappeared into the church.

'The Lord sends plagues on those who displease Him,' said Little Peter to the air. He turned to go.

'Little Peter,' I said. 'A question.'

'What?' His round blue eyes, at once clear and utterly fathomless, peered into mine. Involuntarily, I felt myself edging back.

'There is a knight named Odard. Odard of Bari. He served Bohemond, but now he has left that army. He lost his horse and his arms; he must have joined the ranks of the pilgrims. Do you know him?'

Little Peter's long nose twitched. 'There are many pilgrims. Though each may love me as a father, I cannot know them all as sons. His name was Odo?'

'Odard.'

232

'He lost everything?'

'I believe so.'

'And he was a Norman?'

'Yes.'

'Then perhaps he has joined the Tafurs.' Little Peter gave a leering smile as he saw the horror spreading across my face. 'You have heard of them?'

'Who has not?'

'Few dare venture into the realm of the Tafur king. Fewer, perhaps, emerge. Who can tell? But I tread there. Christ is with me, and I fear no evil.'

'Will you take me?'

The hermit cackled. Spit ran down his chin, but he affected not to notice it. 'I will take you there, Greek. Whether they let you leave – that is in God's hands.'

A ccompanying Little Peter was an uncomfortable experience. We met near the palace, and within minutes we
had plunged away from the main roads into a labyrinth of
alleys and passages below the slopes of Mount Silpius.
Wooden balconies hung crooked from the mud-brick walls;
rubble and filth littered our path. Not so long ago it must
have been a Turkish quarter; now their only relic was their
absence. Their homes and streets had been filled with Franks,
in such poverty as I had never seen even in the worst slums
of Constantinople. Children ran naked around us, throwing
mud and excrement at each other, while their mothers sat
with breasts shamelessly bared in the doorways. I blushed,
my eyes seeking in vain for a safe refuge, but Little Peter
seemed immune to sinful thoughts and moved serenely on
with his lolling, limping gait. We struggled to make progress.
The alleys were barely wide enough for a dray cart, and
wherever Peter went the Franks clustered so close that the
narrow paths became impassable. Some were satisfied to feel
the hem of his short cloak, but others fell on their knees
before him and implored favours or benediction. With eyes
shut and palms outstretched, his face turned in bliss towards
the sun, he touched their wounds and murmured comforting
words. He was like some shrunken, shrivelled effigy of the
Christ, and his congregation of the desperate seemed to
adore him for it. No wonder so many had followed him so
far – and at such cost.

At a pinched crossroads, deep in shadow, we found a sign. It hung from the web of criss-crossed ropes that stretched overhead: a splintered plank daubed with the words *Regnum Tafurorum*. Two long shields bearing white crosses hung at either side of it, while on a nail above the plank was mounted a grinning skull.

'The realm of the Tafurs.' Even Little Peter seemed cowed by the name as he spoke it.

'Is there really such a man as the Tafur King?'

Peter shrugged his misshapen shoulders. 'His name is often spoken.'

That much I knew. Early in the siege, around December, rumours had sprung up of a new leader among the poor, an impoverished knight who had made himself master of the dispossessed. It was said that their desperation knew no restraint: that they sliced open the bellies of corpses in search of swallowed gold, and pulled the dead from their graves to eat in times of famine. That they existed was beyond doubt: I had seen them, barefooted and shirtless, labouring on the siege works and fighting in battle, where their reputation for savagery was well earned. Most had vowed silence and would not talk to outsiders, but still the whispered stories of their king seeped through the army, and at night every howl and scream was believed to rise from their camp.

'Have you seen him, this king?' I asked. It was said that Little Peter was the only man allowed to pass their borders.

'He sits on a throne of bones as high as a man and wears a crown forged from spears. He drinks from a cup made from the head of a Turk, and his tent is sewn from their skins.' Peter's voice wavered between horror and awe, and his eyes were wide.

I felt a kick of disbelief. 'Surely those stories cannot be true?'

He frowned. 'Why not?'

'You have seen it?'

'Perhaps. If I had, I would be sworn to secrecy. No one tells the Tafur king's secrets.'

Unwilling to be questioned further – or perhaps reluctant to incur the Tafur king's revenge – Peter hurried on. I kept close, for I did not want to be lost in that place.

I do not know how long we walked in the heat and the stink. Sometimes Tafurs passed us, staring at me with hostile eyes as they answered Peter's brief questions. All were dressed alike in white loincloths and wooden crosses, which they hung around their necks on thick ropes like yokes. At last, after many turns, Peter stopped at a door. Waving me to be still, he rapped on the carved panel. It cracked open and I heard a short challenge, which Peter answered in the Provençal tongue. The door swung in and led us through a short passage into a central courtyard.

For all the tales of skeletal thrones and human cups, the reality of the Tafurs was at once far more ordinary and yet more terrible than I had imagined. The square was strewn with wood and stone where the surrounding windows had been hammered out, and half a dozen Tafurs, barely clothed, lounged on the rubble. One was sucking on a bone that might have been a cow's. All were watching another of their number, who knelt in the centre of the yard, and the woman on all fours in front of him. The only sound was the regular slap of his cross as it swung against his chest: the man showed no more emotion than if he had been digging a patch of weeds, while the woman stared ahead, unblinking. From the blood crusted on the inside of her thighs and the bruises on her ribs and breasts, I guessed that every trace of feeling had long since been raped out of her.

I cannot say exactly what happened next. A hundred fractured pictures exploded in my skull: my wife Maria lying on her bed, her skirts soaked red; my baby daughter cradled in my arms as victorious legionaries sacked Constantinople; the silver cross that hung around my own neck, a symbol which had comforted me so often. Unthinkingly, I reached for the knife at my belt. All the Tafurs were watching me, and even before the blade was out of its sheath one had risen and thrown himself towards me. A fist swung at my face, struck my chin and knocked me on my back. As I lifted myself on my elbows, I tasted blood on my lip.

'Demetrios!' Little Peter whimpered with terror, darting about like a wasp. 'Has the Devil possessed you?'

'Perhaps he was jealous,' said a voice above me. Would you like to take your turn with the Turkish bitch, Greek? Or is it only boys that rouse you?' A bare foot planted itself in my groin and squeezed down; I tried not to moan. 'Are you a eunuch? If not, I have a knife. I could make you so.'

'Let him be,' squeaked Little Peter. I had not expected him to have the courage to speak out. 'He is a friend of the bishop, and I have sworn him my peace.'

'But I have not – and I am no friend of the bishop.' With a last, agonishing jab of his foot, the man stepped away. My eyes were clenched shut with pain, but above me I heard the voice asking Little Peter: 'Why have you come?'

'We . . . He seeks a man named Odard, a Norman. I have heard he joined your band.'

'He did – though much use he has been. His senses have been torn away, and he jabbers nothing but riddles and nonsense. What does the Greek want with him?'

I opened my eyes. The man who had struck me now stood over me, watching with malicious interest. Behind him the Turkish woman had crawled into a corner and now lay curled up like a corpse while her assailant wiped himself with a cloth.

'Two of Odard's companions were murdered,' I said,

speaking slowly as the blood slid over my tongue. 'I seek to know who killed them.'

'Who?'

'Drogo of Melfi, and Rainauld of Albigeois.'

The Frank disappeared through a broken door into the house. I staggered to my feet and seated myself on a lump of stone, clutching my groin where it still ached. A dozen dull eyes watched me. The hermit perched in the corner and made himself still, fixing his gaze on heaven and muttering unintelligible incantations. I hoped that he was praying for me.

The Frank emerged back into the courtyard. Behind him, shuffling reluctantly, came Odard. He too was naked to the waist, and though he could not have eaten any better than I had in the past months he seemed larger than I remembered. Perhaps it was merely that I had shrunk more. He still looked like a walking skeleton, his skin barely binding the bones within: I could have counted each one of his ribs, while his fingers had become talons.

'What will you ask him?' said the Tafur.

'Why the boy who served him, Simon, died by the river six days ago.'

'And why should I let you, Greek?'

I stared hard at the crude cross around the Tafur's neck. 'Because Odard has committed deeds that are abominations in the sight of God. He has worshipped on pagan altars and sacrificed to ancient idols. If we are abandoned now by Christ, it is because of Odard's evil.'

Odard, who had hovered in the Tafur's shadow, now darted forward. 'Lies! Lies!' he shrieked. 'You are the crow, Greek, trilling lies and death. Curse you! Curse you!'

'You did not go down to that temple to eat, did you? You prostrated yourself before the Antichrist, and gave yourself into his power.'

Behind Odard the Tafur band had begun to rise.

Suddenly their leader stepped forward and hooked his arm around Odard's neck. It seemed so thin, and the grip so firm, that I thought it might snap off his shoulders.

'Truly?' hissed the Tafur in his ear. 'Has the Devil broken your mind and brought curses upon us?' He turned to me. 'Or is it you who speaks for the prince of lies and darkness?'

All my attention was on Odard; I did not notice the Tafurs sidling up to me until it was too late. I jerked back with a cry as one of them stepped behind me and locked my head in the same vicelike grip as held Odard. A second man pinned my arms at my sides. Little Peter had vanished.

'I speak the truth.' My throat burned, and the arms clamped around my stomach made me want to retch, but it was nothing against the fear of what I would suffer if they disbelieved me. I directed my words to Odard again. 'Was it Quino? Did Quino come to you, tell you I guessed your secret? Did you fear that Simon had betrayed you – that his testimony would see you burned on a pyre? Was it you who drew the bowstring while the boy picked herbs on the river bank? Tell me. Confess it, and win mercy.'

The hand on my neck choked short my words, so that I feared Odard had not even heard them. Certainly he did not heed me: without regard for his safety he twisted and fought against the Tafur's grip. It availed him nothing.

'Those are solemn charges,' said the Tafur. A callous smile belied his concern. 'You swear its truth; he denies it. Who can decide?'

'It would be easier to judge if he answered me.'

Odard stamped his foot on the Tafur's, and was rewarded with a blow to his belly. His head jerked about like a puppet's.

'He will not answer you. His wits are broken.'

'Then let me take him away, to see what I may coax from him.'

The Tafur shook his head, chuckling. 'No. You say he has profaned his holy faith. If he has not, then you yourself are an enemy of Christ. The Lord is just in all His works – He will decide.'

Fear began to warm my veins. 'How?'

'You will suffer the ordeal of combat. God's favour will decide it.'

Before I could argue, the hands that held me dropped away. My knife, which lay on the ground where it had been struck, was picked up and placed in my fist. The Tafur pulled a similar knife from his own belt and passed it to Odard, keeping his arm gripped tight so that he did not turn the blade on his captor.

The rest of the Tafurs stepped away and leaned against the walls, watching with undisguised anticipation. Two of them blocked the gate by which I had entered, while another barred the inner door. Even the brutalised Turkish woman had sat up, staring at us through a curtain of torn hair.

'This is not justice.' The words seemed to fall from my mouth unnaturally fast now the pressure on my throat had been released. 'This is sport.'

'It is the will of God,' said the Tafur solemnly. 'Only the man who doubts His cause fears Him.'

I set my hands by my side. 'I will not fight.'

'Then pray that God defends you.'

The Tafur let Odard go and stepped back. Even before I could lift an arm to defend myself Odard had flown forward, his knife poised to rip me open. I ducked, spinning away from his flailing blade, and as he stumbled past me I kicked out at his knee. He fell with a howl onto a pile of rubble.

I glanced at the Tafur. 'Is it enough?'

He did not need to answer. The tension coiled into Odard's frame made him quick as a whip: he leaped to his feet and moved towards me again, more carefully this time. Grime and blood were smeared on his face where he had fallen.

'I have no quarrel with you,' I said loudly. 'Tell me the truth of Simon's death, why he died, and we will set our blades aside.'

Odard screamed something indistinct and charged. He feinted to his right, then swung left, but I had read it in his eyes and avoided him.

'Fight honestly,' called one of the watching Tafurs. 'Fight to kill.'

'Whom did you worship in the cave?' I persisted. 'Was it Mithra?'

Odard lifted his drooping face and fixed his stare on mine. 'What was he to you?'

He ran at me, moving right again, and this time it was no feint. His blade sliced across my arm, but I did not feel the welling blood. His momentum had brought him crashing into me and we both collapsed to the ground. Sharp stones bit into my back. I tried to roll him over, tried to escape his pressing weight – who would have thought so scrawny a man could be so heavy? His right hand, his sword hand, was trapped under my shoulder, and as it wriggled free I saw that his fist was empty. That was brief respite. Fingers and nails scratched my wrist as he sought to prise away my own knife.

Odard's bare torso pressed close against my face. The smell of his sweat and of my own blood mingled in the air about me as my right hand jerked against the attack. If he seized my knife now I would die.

'Drogo. It is time to finish this, Drogo.' His black eyes seemed to spin in their sockets. 'You led me into the path of sin, the way of death. Now it is yours.'

He swooped down, leaning across me and sinking his teeth into my arm. I cried out, and before I could master the pain my fingers sprang open. The knife dropped from my grasp and in an instant Odard snatched it away.

'What have you done to me?' he whispered. Strange contortions wracked his face, as if a demon struggled to escape, but now his eyes were still. I wondered if it was me he saw, or Drogo or Quino or none of us. 'What have you done?'

'Nothing. Odard, I have done nothing to you, I swear it.'

'He is innocent, Quino. What has he done to us?'

'Nothing.'

I saw Odard's gaze sidle over to his right, to the hand which held my knife. Surprise creased his brow.

'This is not mine.'

His thoughts were shattered, so much so that I could not guess whether he would throw the knife away or plunge it into my heart. I doubt whether he knew himself. I would not wait to discover it. Drawing on his distraction, on the fact that he had released my arm, I drove a fist into his jaw. As he reeled backwards I pushed myself off the ground, trying to shake him off me. I unbalanced him, but did not dislodge him: instead we rolled over and over, locked together in each other's arms like lovers. Dust rose around us and filled my eyes; splinters dug into me, while Odard's hands snatched at my tunic. The knife seemed to be lost.

And suddenly there was no more struggle. I had come to rest on top of him, and my first thought was that my arm had bled more than I realised, for the sweat ran red on his chest. Then panic struck me, as I saw the blood spreading between us. That did not come from my arm: had I been stabbed without knowing?

At last I saw the truth: the knife was buried to the hilt in Odard's chest. Whether it had been my hand or his that had guided the weapon I would never know, but somewhere in our frenzied grappling it had pierced his heart. He was still breathing, just, but his head was still and his eyes were closed. His left arm flapped limply, like a broken wing.

I bent my mouth close to his ear. 'Why did Simon die?'

Odard did not answer. He had joined Drogo, Rainauld, Simon and the other denizens of that cursed tent. I wondered what he would say to them in the world beyond.

I hauled myself to my feet and glanced around.

The Tafur leader watched me, smirking. 'The Lord has spoken. Truly, this man was a heretic. Now, Greek, you may ask your questions.'

His ringing laughter chased me from the courtyard. None of the Tafurs tried to stop me.

My arm still bled a little, but there were deeper cuts to my soul which I could not bind. Nonetheless, I tried. As if my pain was not a part of me, as if I could escape my very self, I ran. Through Antioch's alleys and passageways, past houses, mansions, churches and empty markets, I ran until my lungs faltered and my legs burned. Even then I could not free myself from my torment, though at least the ache in my body dulled it.

I might have run for miles, or merely in circles; at last I stopped to see where I had gone. I was on the eastern outskirts of the city, against the foot of the mountain. At the end of the road I could see orchards and olive groves rising in stepped terraces over the lower slopes, the sheer cliffs looming above them. A golden light washed over the landscape and the air was still, yet the beauty only sharpened my feeling of desolation. I had killed men before, of course – for war, for money, for pride and for hate – but never had I slain a witless innocent in such vicious entertainment.

I could not dwell on it now. I was far from our camp

on the walls, and soon the light would dissolve into shadow. I did not know whether I had left the realm of the Tafurs or not, but it had been terrible enough in daylight. By night, it must have been beyond imagining. I would go back to Anna, though I dared not think what I would say.

It should have been an easy journey, for the sinking sun pointed straight to the walls, but in the maze of streets I soon lost sight of it. I tried to remember the bearing and tread a straight path, but that was impossible: this quarter of the city was so tangled that I could barely walk fifty paces before I was spun around a corner, or found the road blocked. Within ten minutes my sense of direction was uncertain; after twenty, I had lost it completely. The hazy shadows deepened, the houses melted together, and my pace grew ever more hesitant. A rising panic drove the guilt and pain from my heart, which now beat only with the urgency of escape. Though I had seen no Tafurs, I feared there might be other Franks keen to take advantage of a solitary Greek.

At a crossroads I found a man squatting by a wall. He was wrapped in rags; his teeth were gone and the skin on his bare head was mottled purple with disease. Had it been any darker, I might have thought him a pile of discarded refuse.

'Which way to the church of Saint Peter?' I asked.

He said nothing, but after a few moments a single arm extended to his right.

'Thank you.'

I hurried on the way he had indicated. Either I was more badly lost than I had feared or this was a little-travelled short cut, for the way quickly narrowed until barely two men could have walked abreast. High walls towered on either side, unbroken by windows or doors, and though I could see a ribbon of blue sky stretched above none of its light reached into those depths.

The road ended abruptly in a brick wall. I cursed. I had been played false by the derelict at the crossroads, and doubtless he would think it a fine joke when I returned. I turned to go back.

Two men were standing in my path, pressed shoulder to shoulder against the confining walls, their faces hidden in the gloom. I had not heard them arrive.

I opened my palms to show that I was harmless. Perhaps that was a mistake.

'It's a dead end,' I said. 'I have come the wrong way.'

They did not answer. The man on the right stepped forward, cocked his head, and drove a fist into my stomach. As I doubled over, I sensed his companion moving closer.

A hard blow struck me on the back of my skull, and I fell into darkness.

'**D**rink.'
I had slept without dreams. When the voice came, I did not know if I heard it or imagined it. I could not even tell if I had opened my eyes, for whatever I did the darkness remained complete.

'Drink.'

The rough grain of a carved cup pressed against my lip. An unseen force tipped back my head, and I felt cool water pouring in. My mouth was dry as stone, and I held the water on my tongue to let it seep into the flesh.

'Where am I?'

'Alive.'

The voice was soft, feminine. Was it Anna's? I leaned forward, knocking my teeth on the cup, but still the night rebuffed me.

'Who are you?'

The cup eased away without answer.

When I next awoke, it was to the feel of fresh air on my cheek. I was sitting beside a lake surrounded by high mountains, grey and blue in the distance. Low clouds scudded over the peaks, and birdsong blew in on the breeze that furrowed the water. I could smell charred smoke, as if a candle had recently been extinguished nearby.

A woman in a white shift walked towards me along the shore. A hood covered her hair, and her face was strangely indistinct. Even when she drew near it seemed as though I looked at her through smeared glass, though I could see nothing between us.

'Where am I?'

'You are lost in the wilderness. You must find the path that will take you away, to Jerusalem.'

I looked around. There was no break in the mountains. 'I see nowhere to go.'

She laughed – a soft, half-mocking laugh whose meaning I could not fathom. 'You do not see because you walk in darkness. You must kindle a flame, a light to see by.'

'How?'

She did not answer; instead, she vanished, and in her place I saw Rainauld and Odard standing a little way off. Their heads lifted in recognition and they began to approach. Panic flared down my spine; I began running across the shingle beach, my feet sliding and jarring on the rounded stones. Behind, I could hear them striding effortlessly after me.

I was dreaming.

I opened my eyes, and was back in darkness.

The cup was at my lips again, but this time when I drank the water was bitter. I spat it out, but immediately a soft hand was pressing against my forehead, tipping it back so that my mouth hung open. The liquid splashed down my throat, and I held my breath so that I would not taste it.

'You must drink this. It will release you from your pain.'

'I have no pain.'

'Then it is working.'

I was laid out on a bed or a table, I realised. I could feel hard boards under my back, softened a little by a thin cloth. I tried to lift myself, but my arms were powerless.

'Let me go.'

'You are free to go, if you wish. It is only the bonds of sin which hold you.'

Something in the darkness rippled like woven silk, though it might have been my mind imagining it. My thoughts seemed to be ebbing away from me, and when I tried to grasp them they merely flowed through my hands like water.

Three candles had been lit in an alcove at the far end of a low room. They cast a feeble light, but after the hours of darkness I had endured they were bright as the sun to my aching eyes. Their orange glow shone on coarse walls, humped and gouged where chisels had carved the stone, and on ranks of bowed heads facing away from me, row upon row stretching back into the shadows. Before them, her face towards me, stood a woman in a white woollen robe. Her eyes were closed, her head tipped back in a rapture that was at once sublime and wholly sensual. She was chanting something, a liturgy perhaps, though it was in no language that I could comprehend.

Two men came forward from the congregation and knelt. One was older, and looked to be some sort of acolyte, for he wore the same kind of white robe as the priestess. The other was a youth, dressed as a peasant. I could see his shoulders trembling beneath his tunic. The woman took a jug and poured water over his hands, then over the acolyte's, and then her own. The acolyte knelt and rose three times in front of her. Turning aside, he repeated the obeisance at a stone altar covered in a white cloth. There was a book sitting on the altar; the man lifted it, and with more bows passed it to the woman. She raised it above her, then held it flat over the youth's head, declaiming her strange rite. The words were still foreign to me, but as I listened more closely patterns of repetition began to emerge. Despite the

248

unknown sounds, there was something familiar in the voice as well. It sounded like the woman in my dreams – and somewhere else. I could not think where.

She passed the book back to the man, and laid her hands on the youth's forehead. More phrases were repeated. Then she took him by the arm and lifted him to his feet, turning him to face her congregation.

'Resolve in your heart that you will keep this holy baptism throughout your life, according to the usage of the Church of Purity, in chastity, in truth, and in all other virtues which the Lord ordains.'

I sank back on my harsh bed. For a few moments, my thoughts had run almost clear: now they were agitated beyond reason. A baptism? How could it be a baptism? There had been no chrism – nor any priest that I had seen. And the language had been neither Greek nor Latin, for I had heard the latter tongue often enough in the past months to know its sound.

Whatever unnatural service it had been, it was now finished. The worshippers who had knelt on the floor rose. The woman stepped away from the candles and steered the youth, the initiate, into the midst of the congregation. The older man who had assisted her turned to follow, and as he did so the candlelight illuminated his face. It was hard to see through the throng and by the unsteady light, but I had seen him recently enough, and the crooked nose and blistered face were quite distinctive. It was Peter Bartholomew.

I surrendered to confusion and lay back.

Later, after the cave had emptied, I heard the voice from my dream again. This time I was not at the lake in the mountains; I was in darkness. It had the same earthy smell as the cave, and I wondered if for once I was not asleep. There was little way of knowing.

'How is your pain, Demetrios?'

'Endurable.' The ache at the back of my head was the least of my discomforts. For the rest of me, my arm throbbed where it had been cut by Odard's knife and my back was stiff from lying still so long, but I could survive that. My stomach, I noticed, was pulled tight as a drumhead. How long had it been since I ate?

'How long have I been here?'

'A night and a day.'

No wonder I felt hungry. 'Where am I?'

'In the church of the pure.'

'In Antioch?'

She hesitated. 'Beneath it.'

'How did I come here?'

'We found you at the roadside. You had been robbed and beaten and left for dead. We saved you.'

'Thank you.'

I thought back to the two men looming over me in the alley, and flinched.

'I must go,' I said. 'My companions will fear for my life, if I have not returned in almost two days.'

Warm breath played over my cheek – she must have been mere inches away.

'You have witnessed our service, Demetrios. You have seen our secrets. We cannot release you now to betray us.'

I jerked up, ignoring the agony racking my skull. I tried to leap off the bed, but though my arms and legs were free there was some cord around my waist binding me down. I fumbled at it, but I felt no knot, and in the darkness I could see nothing.

'Do not struggle. You will suffer no harm here. In truth, you are probably safer. Kerbogha arrived yesterday. His army is on the mountain, trying to force the walls. They say the fighting is very terrible.'

'All the more reason that I must find my companions.'

If Anna were left defenceless when the Turks broke in . . .

'Let me go.'

'It is for your own good. Once, you asked me to help you. I told you then that I could do nothing until you were willing to discard the deceptions worked on you by the priests. I can help you now, but again, only if you will receive it.'

At last I knew the voice. Sarah, the priestess who had ministered to Drogo and his friends. Had they been baptised in the same rite that I had just seen?

'What deceptions? I am a Christian.'

She laughed. 'Have you ever spoken of God to an Ishmaelite? They say that we worship the same god, but that they alone know the true way to venerate Him.'

I slumped back. 'Are you an Ishmaelite?' How could she be, when her followers carved their backs with crosses?

'No.' Her voice was sharp, insulted. 'But they are right that one may name God truthfully and worship him in error. That is what you have done.'

'How?'

'Are you thirsty?'

I rolled my tongue around my mouth. 'A little,' I admitted.

'Drink.'

Again the wooden cup tipped against my lips, spreading the bitter liquid within me. I gulped it eagerly, then suddenly stopped my throat in panic. 'What is this – some foul communion of your heresy?'

'It is water, and a little artemisia to ease your pain. You need have no fear.'

She paused. From somewhere on my left I heard the grate of a cup being placed on a table. I strained my ears, but there were no sounds beyond, no evidence of the congregation who had been there earlier. Were we alone?

'You said I worshipped God falsely. How do you say it is right to worship Him?'

'That is hidden knowledge.'

Frustration rose within me, rolling back the pain and confusion: the childish anger at being barred from secrets. Again I tried to rise from my bed, and again the bonds restrained me. 'Why hidden? So you can lord it over your followers, tempt them in with curiosity?'

'Hidden, because it is dangerous. It is not pride or selfish delight which hides these mysteries. They are open to all, but only if those who desire to know them have a pure and seeking heart. I can tell you these things, but you must wish to know them. Not for advantage, nor malice nor greed, but from the sincere yearning for salvation.'

'Who does not desire salvation?'

'Many. And even of those who do, the greater part lack the pure soul and true heart to persevere. They desire truth, but from ignorance. They do not understand what they seek. When they find it, it is beyond them. Their faith suffers; sometimes it is ruined altogether. Sometimes they themselves do not survive.'

Her words filled me with dread. A part of me – the part which had sought unpleasant truths from every pimp, thief, mercenary and noble in Constantinople – bridled at her overblown warnings. But in another, more profound part, I shivered at the awesome promise and threat entwined in her words.

'The knowledge I have to give is not some scroll or book, to be filed away on a shelf once you have read it. My knowledge is the knowledge of life, of light. Once learned, it cannot be forgotten. It will consume you like a furnace, and if your soul is flawed you will be broken. It is not enough to know it – you must also believe it.'

I raised myself on my elbows, feeling the cord press against my waist. 'I will hear it.'

All that followed, I heard as if in a dream. Afterwards, indeed, I wondered if I *had* dreamed it. Scenes and images passed through my head as she spoke – glowing angels with fiery wings, lush gardens of fruit, rearing serpents – but more as if I were walking through a church, peering at the icons each in turn. My soul seemed to swell in my head, pressing against my skull as it grappled with her story. One voice screamed that it was falsehood, a deception wrought of evil to damn all who heard it. But another voice counselled caution, testing her words and wondering in terror if they were true.

'Much of what I have to tell will seem familiar. That is because the liars and demons who possess the church have twisted it, by the merest fraction, into error. The prince of darkness knows that the best lies sit closest to truth. Only when I have finished will you see how far from truth the church has turned.'

I nodded.

'I will tell you from the beginning. Many ages ago, after Satan fell from Heaven, he divided the waters of his prison firmament, and raised up earth from beneath the waters to become land. He made himself a throne, and caused his rebel angels to bring forth life: plants and trees and herbs, animals, the birds of the air and the fish of the sea. But still it was not enough. He took clay from the earth and moulded man, and from that man he took more clay and made woman. Then he snared two angels from heaven and made them prisoners in the clay, so that their spirits were clothed in mortal form. In his depravity, he bade them sin, but they were pure and did not know how.

'So Satan placed them in a garden. From a stream of his spittle he made a serpent; he took its form, and

253

entered the garden. He slithered into the woman's body and filled her with a longing for sin until her desire was like a glowing oven. He filled the man with a like desire for sin, so that both captive angels were consumed with lust. Together, they spawned the children of the Devil. The spark of the angels is divided and scattered among the people of the Earth, but it is not lost. A fragment of their being remains within us: that is why we must forswear the dark substance of this world, and seek to kindle a flame from the angelic fire within. Only thus will we free ourselves from the vessels which bind our souls, and escape this wicked Earth for the realms of light.'

Sweat had begun to pool on my skin in the close air of the cave, but I barely noticed it. Far hotter was the fire that raged within me, scalding and blistering my soul even to think on what she had said. Her warning had been honest: her words were pure fire. Even if I disbelieved them, even if I longed to tear them from my memory, I would not forget them. They would undermine the walls of my faith with doubt, perhaps to destruction. Even repeating them might be mortal sin. And I feared there was a part of me, an insistent part, which clamoured that she might speak truth.

'You have opened the first door of our mysteries, Demetrios Askiates. What do you say? Are you afraid to cross the threshold?'

I did not have the strength to lie. 'Yes.'

'Good. Only the proud rush in where they do not see clearly. The humble tread fearfully, but journey farther. Yet, in your soul, the truth begins to stir. Have you never felt the empty weight of your sinful clay? Has it never seemed to you that your spirit is snared in a vessel from which it cannot escape? Surely – in the clarity of grief, perhaps –

you have ached to shake off the trappings of the flesh and liberate the divine spark within?'

Caution and reason implored me to resist her, but I could not deny the simple accuracy of her words. I remembered running through the labyrinth of streets and alleys after Odard's death, desperate to lose my guilt. I remembered lying next to Anna on the walls, our bodies touching but our souls sundered by the secret of what I had done. Was it all as Sarah said?

Her soft voice was like balm on my thoughts. 'You begin to see clearly, Demetrios. All your life you have lived in sin and error – now at last the light of God begins to glow in your heart. Take it. Cup it in your hands and breathe on it, so that the flame grows and the fire takes hold. For now it is the merest ember, but in time it will burn away your sin like sun on a dawn mist.'

'But how—'

She pressed a sweet finger to my lips. 'Sleep now.'

I did not sleep. I lay on my bed while questions and arguments roared through my head like storms in the desert. Some whipped up into towering columns of confusion; others eddied and flowed in thick clouds of chaos. At times I thought they were gone, that the grains of thought had settled, but they always returned with renewed ferocity. Pain thumped against the back of my skull and hunger cramped my stomach: my body was failing. I no longer knew if that was a curse or a blessed relief.

Yet even as my senses collapsed, my perception of the cave improved. Light began to filter in through long cracks in the ceiling, and gradually the darkness resolved itself into a palimpsest of grey shadows. Rough-hewn walls emerged around me; dark figures moved in the recesses of the cave. My bed seemed to be in a corner, while at

255

the far end I could make out the vertical lines of a stair or ladder rising through the ceiling. It was often in use, though even when a man came down it no additional light was admitted. How deep was this place, I wondered? Were we in a cave below a cave?

Later, I did not know how long, Sarah returned. Her robe was like a shaft of moonlight before me, though her voice was much troubled.

'Have you thought on what I told you, Demetrios?'

'I have.'

'How does it seem to you?'

'Difficult.'

'Truth does not strike us all as it did the holy Saint Paul. For many, it is a long and arduous road.'

'The ways of the flesh are hard to shake off. Is that why your followers carve themselves with crosses, to mortify their sinful bodies?'

'As the cuts are made, as the sign of the Lord enters their flesh, they say they hear Satan himself screaming in fury.'

'Drogo and Rainauld had heard your truth. They marked their bodies. Their faith must have been prodigious.'

'Do not talk of them,' said Sarah sharply. 'The pure novice bows his head and fastens his eyes on his own path. If he looks at his fellow pilgrims, he distracts his thoughts from righteousness.'

'Drogo and Rainauld are dead. Their companion Odard too. If that is the ultimate end of our road, then I wish to know it.'

'To know where you travel is not a journey of faith. It is the way itself which matters; you will know the destination when you reach it. But if it will soothe your thoughts, I will tell you that their fate owed nothing to their faith. As I told you once before, they had abandoned my teaching. Another teacher – a false prophet – seduced them.'

Her words cut through my tangled thoughts. 'Who?'

'It does not matter.' Exasperation and suspicion swelled in her voice. 'I think you do not—'

A shout from the ladder silenced us both. Whatever door or panel covered its mouth had been thrown back, and a column of sunlight poured into the room. All around me white-robed acolytes were staring as if at an angel – and, indeed, the figure who descended the ladder might well have been a messenger of Heaven, for the light ringed him with a shining nimbus, and thick tendrils of smoke curled above him in its beam.

As my eyes adjusted, I saw that it was not an angel of the Lord but a scrawny man with a crooked nose. Nor was there anything ethereal about the screeching panic in his voice.

'The city,' he shouted. 'They are burning the city.'

κ ζ

The spell of Heaven was broken. Men and women rushed to the ladder, tearing at each other in their frenzy to get out. The messenger himself was pulled down and subsumed in the fray. Cascades of smoke rolled through the trapdoor, darkening the cave once more, while a devouring roar began to sound in the distance.

I was forgotten, but I was not free. I strained at my bonds, but my desperate efforts only seemed to pull them tighter. I reached under the bed and felt for a knot or clasp. My hands scrabbled on the wood; a splinter pierced under my fingernail. Wrenching my arm, I found the loop of cloth that bound me and followed it along, until at last I touched a bulge. It was almost beyond my grasp, and I would never loose it where it was. I tugged on the cloth, sliding it around until the knot rested on my belly.

I did not have the time to look about, but I sensed that I was now alone save for the swelling clouds of smoke. It crept into my eyes and mouth, rasping my throat raw and pricking tears down my cheek. If I did not escape it soon, it would choke the life out of me as surely as any noose. Yet I could not afford to pull the knot tighter in my haste to undo it.

Near panic, I poked my fingers into the knot, prying and teasing at the twisted fabric. My brittle reserve was bent almost to destruction by the effort of keeping my panic in check, but though my mind was in uproar my hands remained calm. The light from above was completely masked by the smoke; I could not see where I worked but tried to trace the loose ends back through the whorl of the knot.

It is only the bonds of sin which hold you, I heard the priestess say, though she had long since fled. Her voice was cool and unforgiving.

At last my finger slid through the knot and emerged the other side. I groped for the loop of cloth beside it, tugged, and felt it slither free. The tension relaxed; with one binding released, the others began to uncoil themselves. I pulled on them again, and they came apart. Perhaps it had been a feeble bond, but it had been strong enough for a feeble prisoner.

I swung myself off the bed and staggered forward. After two days lying supine my legs were weak and unsteady, but the joy of my freedom and the desperation of my predicament impelled me forward. I staggered through the smoke, trying not to breathe, kicking over unseen relics left by the fleeing pilgrims. My hands were on the ladder. I stepped onto the lowest rung, felt firm wood beneath my feet, and climbed. It seemed to me that the air should have been clearing as I rose, yet the clouds around me remained as thick as ever. My head came through the trapdoor opening; I was in a wooden hut or shed, and through its open door I could see daylight and a dusty courtyard. I hauled myself onto the ground, picked myself up, and ran outside. I was free.

It was scant relief. Enough of the artemisia lingered in my veins that for a moment I wondered if I had climbed into Hell itself. The air was as stifling as it had been in the confines of the cave, and an enormous pall of smoke hung over the city as far as I could see, so that the sun's light turned to rust and bathed us in an eerie, infernal twilight.

A small gate led out into a street, where dark figures scurried past. I was about to make for it when a grating, rumbling noise erupted behind me. I turned. The timbers of the hut that I had come from must have been burning over me; now they gave way, and the roof crashed down into the shell of the walls. The trapdoor and the cave were buried beneath, while a plume of dust and ash rose over it.

In the street I met a new world of confusion. Frantic pilgrims fled by in every direction, wailing prayers and screams. Many had had the clothes burned from their bodies, their skin shrivelled and blackened by the fire; others, whose legs had been crushed in falling buildings, dragged themselves through the dust by their hands. I saw one frenzied woman running past with her baby still sucking her breast, heedless of the consuming calamity.

I looked to my right. Through the smoke I could see shreds of flame burning in the air, so high that it seemed they must have descended from the heavens. A hot wind stroked my cheek, and I felt my skin tightening as the blood seethed under it. The thunder of the fire was everywhere: the crackle of the flames, the roar of buildings tumbling over on each other, the howl of the wind gathering itself in to feed the blaze to yet greater heights. Against that the beat of hooves was nothing; I did not hear it until it was almost upon me.

A horse charged out of the red smoke, a sword in its rider's hand. Too late, I thought to wonder how the fire had started, whether Kerbogha was laying waste the city. I was unarmed, though in that inferno even the strongest shield would have burned free of my arm. Yet the horseman did not look Turkish: the coned helmet silhouetted against the red smoke was Norman. Was he part of a rout, the remnant of a broken army?

Whether he did not recognise me as an ally, or whether

he did not care, he had no mercy for me. He saw me standing transfixed in the road, swerved towards me and drew back his sword arm. A fresh gust of wind fanned my face as the beast rushed past, inches away; I did not even have the wit to duck. The sword swung forward and struck against my shoulders. I fell to the ground.

Though I was almost too numb to care, I did not die. The Norman had not hit me with the edge of his blade but with the flat, using it as a cudgel or a drover's stick. My back smarted, and there would be a livid weal rising under my tunic even now, but if that was to be the worst injury I suffered that day I would count myself blessed.

As I rose to my feet, the knight wheeled his horse and trotted back towards me. Reflected flames danced on his helmet as though it still sat in the armourer's furnace.

'Worm! Provençal coward! How dare you cower in dark holes when the defence of the city commands every man to the walls?'

'Kerbogha?' I mumbled. 'Has Kerbogha taken the city?'

'He will if you delay. Seek out your lord, and offer yourself up to his service.'

The Norman turned his horse away, spurred its side and galloped down the street. Through the swirling haze, I saw other fleeing pilgrims suffer the brutal touch of his sword and tongue as he passed.

His words had only increased my confusion, but I ignored it. The fires were raging hotter and closer, and if I did not fly before them my bones would be burned to embers. I turned after the Norman, away from the heat, and ran.

I knew little of Antioch, and had lost myself so many times already that I had no idea where the cave had been. I had to trust to the instincts of the crowd and follow them blindly through the smoke. I felt as though I had almost ceased to be human, but ran like a brute animal, my only instincts escape and survival. Norman knights on horse and on foot snapped at our heels and flanks, wraiths in the choking fog driving us on. I did not try to withstand them. They could have herded us towards the abyss and I would not have resisted.

Gradually, from the corners of my eyes, I began to recognise landmarks. A tavern sign, a crooked house, an empty fountain befouled by birds – they seemed familiar. I had passed them with Little Peter on my way to the Tafur kingdom, whenever that had been. Two days ago? It did not matter. I must be in the south-eastern quarter of the city, near the palace; from there I could find my way to the walls, to Anna and Sigurd and sanctuary.

The crowds around me were thicker now, but the air was clearer and cooler. Like a host of rats people poured from the corners and crannies which had hidden them, scurrying to safety. And suddenly, sooner than I had expected, I was out of the narrow alleys and into the wide expanse of the square by the palace. The throng was no less, for the tide of the dispossessed stretched clear across its boundaries, but for the first time in three days I knew where I was. On the edges of the square I could see knights with spears trying to push the fleeing pilgrims onwards towards the walls, while at the centre, like steadfast trees in a river in flood, two men sat on horseback, arguing. In silhouette, the knight's helmet and the bishop's mitre were almost identical but I could see just enough to recognise the men beneath. I pushed towards them.

An invisible circle of deference seemed to surround the two nobles, an island of space, so that the crowds flowed around them at a respectful distance. Even in the chaos of the moment, I needed a fresh draught of courage to break through and approach.

'I had no choice.' Soot had stained Bohemond's skin dark as a Saracen's, but the unyielding bite of his words was as clear as ever. 'All Kerbogha's strength is concentrated on the citadel – our line is almost broken. We cannot suffer cowards to cringe in hiding, when every arm that can carry a spear is needed.'

Opposite him, Adhemar's horse moved nervously from side to side. 'Burning down the city to keep Kerbogha from taking it is no answer.'

'The vermin had to be smoked from their holes. I am not to blame if the wind fanned the flames too high.'

'You are to blame for everything – you have brought ruin upon us.' I had never seen the bishop so wild. Streams of sweat and tears flowed down his grimy face; he hunched over in his saddle, and abused Bohemond like a prophet of old.

'Do not provoke me, priest. I am the only man who may yet save us.'

'Look around you!' Adhemar stretched out his hands, waving them at the fleeing hordes. 'Look in their faces. They are broken, defeated; they are fleeing the city. Stone walls and locked gates will not hold them. Our army will be routed, and you will be to blame.'

'For three days I have contended with Kerbogha. I have not slept, I have not eaten, I have not even got down from my horse to piss. These worms are your flock, Adhemar: if you and your dwarf hermit cannot rouse them to battle, I will. If you cannot deliver them, let them flee or burn. I need men – not noble men or skilled men or even strong men, but men with the spirit to fight, to battle against our destruction. If you cannot summon these men, then come to my mountain yourself and put your spear in Kerbogha's path. If you dare.'

He kicked his horse, and rode into the mêlée. From the edge of the circle, I saw another knight spur after him.

Adhemar looked down. 'Demetrios.'

'Your Grace . . .' After so long in the cave, and now

caught up in the consuming panic, even familiar faces looked strange to me. 'Has . . . has Bohemond done this?'

Adhemar gave a grim nod. 'He believed that too many pilgrims were hiding themselves from battle. He set the fire to smoke them out, but I fear he has merely opened the city to Kerbogha.'

'Has Kerbogha broken through?'

'I do not know. The last I heard was that we still withstood him.'

Amid all the turmoil I did not hear the sound of feet approaching. Suddenly a dark figure had thrown himself between me and the bishop, was clutching the horse's bridle and staring imploringly at Adhemar. He swayed from side to side, his free arm swinging wildly, and as his face turned towards the firelight I saw its features clearly. A crooked nose, and a host of pox scars. Peter Bartholomew.

'Your Grace,' he shrieked. 'What has this liar told you?'

Without wasting a word, Adhemar swivelled his sword and slapped the blade hard against the wretch's shoulders. Bartholomew screamed and fell back, but did not let go his grasp of the bridle.

'Blessed are you when men persecute and revile you,' he gasped. 'Your Grace, the Lord has granted me a vision. You must hear it – by Christ you must hear it, before this Greek poisons you against me.'

The earth shuddered under our feet as a colonnade on the far side of the square crashed down on itself. Thick pillars toppled over and shattered on the ground; a cloud of ash and sparks erupted. Through it, set in an alcove on the rear wall, I saw the scorched face of an ancient statue staring down impassively on the destruction. A few men whose courage and order remained ran towards the blaze, carrying buckets and hurling water on the flames. The statue vanished in a steaming mist.

I looked back at the bishop. Peter Bartholomew was still at his side, still clinging to the bridle and ranting. Perhaps he feared that I was about to betray his heresy and wanted to denounce me first, but my only concern was to find my friends in all the fire and riot. I did not say farewell to Adhemar, did not even look at him, but threw myself back into the crowd and plunged on. There was little merit in trying to strike my own path, for no man could have imposed himself on the mob's surging course. Instead, like a drowned man, I let it draw me effortlessly along, away from the mountain, down towards the walls and the river.

It did not take long to reach the walls: the road was wide, and the crowd inexorable. At the bridge a troop of Norman knights stood with brandished spears, stabbing back any who approached the barred gates, but they were little use. Peasants and knights swarmed up the steps to the walls above. Where the crowds were too thick, makeshift ladders had been leaned against the rampart, sagging under the weight pressed onto them. I remembered the scaling ladder that had snapped on the night we took the city, and chose the stairs. Looking up at the hordes clustered on the walls, it seemed impossible that there could be room for any others, yet still we pressed on up the steps. The city dropped away beneath me; when I turned my head at a bend in the stairwell I could see the roofs and domes stretching back to the mountain. Even in my shattered state I trembled, for here the full appetite of the fire was evident. It seemed that half of Antioch must be ablaze. Fat gouts of smoke rose over the flames, lifting the cries of men and beasts to the heavens. If this continued, Kerbogha could watch our destruction from the citadel on the summit, then ride down to pick over the ashes of our army in triumph.

Half-blinded by the flames and deafened by the noise, I reached the rampart. It was broad enough that in normal times four men could easily have marched abreast, yet now the space between the towers was choked with humanity. Still they surged forward, pushing into the teeth of the battlements where ropes dropped into the darkness on the far side of the wall. Some were the stout hawsers that we used for the siege engines; others were more rudimentary, bridles and tunics and cloth torn from tents hurriedly knotted together. The pilgrims clambered over each other, vying to snatch the hastily devised ropes and slide down out of the city. Such was the unrelenting pressure of crowding bodies that many were tipped from their perches before they had a hold.

I turned away. That was not the path for me. Along the walls to my right the crowds thinned, and though at first I had to batter my way across their flow my route gradually eased as I moved further from the gate. A few hundred yards away, indeed, the rampart was almost deserted: I passed through deserted watchtowers and met not a single challenge. So it was that when I did hear voices, from beyond a door ahead of me, I was well warned.

I no longer believed that I had any ally in that city save the Varangians, and I was half a mile or more from their camp. I slowed my pace and edged my way towards the guardroom door.

'You must sail as soon as you reach the harbour,' I heard from the other side. 'Allow no delay. It will not be long before Kerbogha strikes at Saint Simeon to bar us from the sea, and you must be away before that.'

A second man mumbled a reply, but I did not heed it. From the moment I had heard the first voice, an icy fear had frozen me still. I knew it, its commanding tones and brusque arrogance. He had set the city alight to roust out the feeble and fearful because he had no men; now it seemed that he was sending his followers away. What was Bohemond doing?

'Order the vessel's master to make for Tarsus – you have enough gold to persuade him?' I heard the chink of coin. 'Good. Cross through the Cilician Gates, and seek out the Greek king Alexios in Anatolia. My last report was that he was campaigning at the lakes, near Philomelium, though he may have moved since. He should not be hard to find.'

'They will call me a coward.' I realised that the second voice was also familiar to me, though I could not name its owner.

'You will say that you had no choice. You will tell the king that you left Antioch only so that the Lord might preserve your sword arm to kill the Ishmaelites. That Kerbogha stood in the gates when you left, and that you heard the doom of our army as you fled. Make sure that the Greek understands there is no merit in coming to our aid – that the only course open to him is to retreat to his palaces.'

'I will tell him,' said the second man doubtfully. 'It will be all too easy to persuade him, for our doom is nearer than you admit. The city burns, the army flees – and you would have me delay the only man who could rescue us? I will do as you ask, but it is madness.'

'A man may risk all on the throw of a single die. If he loses, they call it madness. But if he wins, William, suddenly it is greatness. When my father challenged the decadent might of the Greeks, when he landed his army on the shores of Illyria, he burned his baggage and scuttled his fleet so that not one man could succumb to cowardice. It is the same now. I will win this city myself, or not at all. Twice I have been denied the kingdoms which were mine by right – it will not happen a third time.'

There was a pause; perhaps they whispered, or embraced,

or stood in silence. At length Bohemond said: 'God go with you, William.'

'Better He stays here. You have more need of Him.'

I heard the clinking of armour and the scrape of boots on stone, followed by the creak of a rope stretching taut. Then nothing. And then, quite suddenly, the sharp rap of footsteps approaching the door. It swung in so quickly that the hinges did not even squeak, and I barely had time to leap back into the shadow behind it. I crouched low, hoping that Bohemond had not heard me.

I need not have worried. He stepped straight past my hiding place, and a few of his long strides carried him away. He disappeared into the next tower and was gone.

I waited a few minutes for him to be well away, listening for any other companions he might have left behind. But there were none. I eased out onto the rampart, into the blue twilight. A thick rope was secured onto the battlements, dropping down to the dry meadow in front of the walls, but I did not examine it. I had eavesdropped enough to know who had descended it: William of Grantmesnil, Bohemond's piggish brother-in-law. Doubtless others would discover it soon. I could scarcely comprehend the treacherous ambition of Bohemond's plot, but this was not the time to wonder at it. I hurried away.

I knew that I had reached the right tower when I found the door barred. I hammered on it with my fist, though there was little enough strength left in that, and shouted in Greek for them to let me in.

They must have been on their guard, for they challenged me almost immediately. 'Who are you?'

'Demetrios.'

I heard the heavy clatter of beams being thrown aside. The door swung open, though its frame was filled almost immediately by the huge bulk of the man standing within.

Behind him I could see a cluster of Varangians staring in amazement, the turbaned head of Mushid the swordsmith, and Anna, her arms crossed and her eyes crimson.

'Fool,' said Sigurd. 'We thought you had died thrice over.'

I stumbled forward and slumped against his chest, oblivious to the rough touch of the iron mail. His bear arms closed around me, swaddling me in darkness.

They let me sleep for an hour – they could not have stopped me, for the moment Sigurd let me go I sprawled exhausted onto the stone floor. Then they roused me to demand answers. We made a fire on the top of the tower, for after so long in dark caves I craved light and air, and Sigurd roasted a small cube of meat on the end of a spear.

'Horseflesh,' he explained. 'I found a Norman who had slaughtered his mount and was selling it, a bezant a portion.'

'He will regret that when Kerbogha comes.'

'He has probably already fled – or died. Have you seen what Bohemond did to the city?'

Sigurd waved an arm to the south-east. From our height, the devastation of that quarter of Antioch was easily visible. The blaze no longer raged, for the wind had turned the flames back towards the mountain where they had already devoured all there was to consume. Yet its embers still glowed red, winking in the night like a carpet of light, as though a bucket of live coals had been tipped out across the city.

'I have seen what Bohemond did,' I said wearily. 'I was there.'

'So was I.'

'Why?'

'I was looking for you.' Sigurd pulled the spear from

the fire and held it towards me. I scorched my fingers as I slid off the dripping meat, and shook it in the air to cool a little.

'Sigurd has spent two days searching the city for you,' Anna explained. She was sitting against the parapet at a little distance, unwilling to come too close to me.

'I gave up when I saw the madness Bohemond had unleashed. I would not have found my own brother in that rout. And now, perhaps, you can tell me where you have been.'

The meat had cooled in my hand; I popped it in my mouth, desperate to savour it after my long, unwanted fast. Too quickly, it was gone – and though I knew what it had cost Sigurd, and loved him for it, it only sparked a more ravenous hunger.

'I went in search of Odard. I wanted to know . . .' I paused. What had I wanted to know? 'I wanted to know if he had killed the boy – Simon, his servant.'

'Had he?'

'I don't know. I think so.' I could barely remember. 'His wits had deserted him – he gibbered without meaning. I – I killed him.'

Anna leaned forward sharply. 'What?'

Without meeting her gaze I told how the Tafurs had made me fight Odard, how the dagger had plunged itself into his heart, how I had run until I could run no further, then been struck down by the robbers. 'When I awoke, I was in a cave. I did not know it at first, but it was a lair of heretics.'

'What heretics?' Sigurd asked.

'The heretics who carve their backs with crosses. Sarah, the woman who visited Drogo in his tent, she is their priestess.' I shuddered, remembering the dark hours in their cave. 'I saw their rituals; I heard their secrets – terrible lies which should not be repeated. They fed me artemisia to ease my pain, and bound me.'

'Artemisia would have numbed your senses as much as your pain.' The physician in Anna was quick to speak. 'Doubtless they hoped to stupefy you.'

Perhaps they had. Even to think on what Sarah had told me was like touching a scar. Was it the pain of error, though, or the stabbing fear of truth?

'When the fires started they fled their cave. I escaped, found my way to the walls and came here.'

There was silence.

'What will you do about the heretics?' Sigurd asked.

'What can I do? I did not see their faces, save one. If I report them to the Frankish priests they will be burned alive.'

'If you do not, their impiety may infest the whole army. God may abandon us.' Sigurd had a soldier's fear of affronting the deities, and an exhaustive knowledge of the ways in which they might take offence.

Anna had less care for divine sensibilities. 'God may abandon us?' she echoed. 'Look around you. He *has* abandoned us. The city burns, the army flees, and Kerbogha is at hand to deliver the killing blow. What does it matter if a rabble of Franks want to dispute the nature of the substance of the Trinity?'

'This was not that sort of heresy,' I said. 'It was deeper. Darker.'

Anna banged her fist on the stone beside her. 'It does not matter, Demetrios! The ship founders, and all you care about is the set of the sail.'

'If we are bound to die, it is important to die piously,' I insisted.

'Are we bound to die?'

I looked out across the ravaged city again. It was not a quiet night: screaming and crashing and shouting still resounded in the darkness, punctuated by the occasional clash of steel. Who could guess the calamities they signalled, the battles raging unseen around the fragment of wall we sat on? For all I knew, we could be the last Christians left in the city.

'I do not know if we are doomed. All we can do is stay here as long as our defences stand, and see who comes to find us.'

'Nonsense,' Sigurd growled. 'Feeble nonsense. If we are to die, we should die like men, taking our fight to the enemy. When I come to see my ancestors, I will not have them scorn me as a coward.'

'And what will you do if they condemn you for rushing too fast to meet them?' Anna demanded. 'You will not be able to come back.'

'You fear to die too soon. I only fear to die badly.'

'Enough!' I lifted my hand to still them, and in the pause I heard shouts from below. I scrambled to my feet and looked down through one of the embrasures. Two horses stood patiently in front of the tower door; I could not identify their riders, for both wore cloaks even though the night was hot. One leaned forward to speak with our guard, and whatever he said must have satisfied the Varangian for he took the horses' bridles and tethered them to a ring in the wall, then ushered the men into the tower. The slap of footsteps rose from the stairwell behind me, sounding ever louder, until a cowled head popped up through the opening. It looked around, blinking in the firelight, then fixed on me.

'Demetrios. I hoped to find you here.'

The man's hands came up and pulled the hood back from his face. He wore neither hat nor helmet beneath it: his grey hair was matted and tousled. At his neck, behind the beard, I saw the gleam of mail. Clearly he had not changed his clothing since we had met by the palace.

'Are there not more important matters in Antioch to attend, your Grace?'

Adhemar climbed out of the stairwell and, glancing at me for permission, seated himself against the wall between me and Sigurd. His companion sat beside him. He did not pull back his hood, and Adhemar did not name him.

'What news of the city?' Anna's impatience swept her manners aside. 'Has it fallen?'

Adhemar shook his head slowly. The flames reflected on his face dug out every crevice and wrinkle, the deep pits around his eyes: he seemed immeasurably old.

'We hold it, praise God. We have tried Him sorely.'

'Bohemond tries God like none save the Devil,' added Adhemar's companion, with a rasping anger that I recognised immediately as Count Raymond's. 'And for now it earns him the Devil's luck.'

'How many men were lost tonight?' I asked.

'Who knows? Those who burned to death in the flames will never be found; those who escaped will never be numbered, unless Kerbogha finds them and sends trophies of their bodies. But I fear that Bohemond has lost more through the fire than he has gained.'

'And those who do remain have lost what hope they had,' said Raymond savagely. His hood had slipped back a little, and I could see the glint of his single eye staring at me. 'They had little enough before; now there is nothing. In a rout, men become like cattle and even the bravest falters. If their miseries are inflicted by their own captain, what confidence can they have?'

'Bishop Adhemar, Count Raymond – you have not come here, so late on this night of fire and death, to seek commiseration in our shared peril. Why have you come?'

My blunt speaking silenced them for a moment. Raymond hunched his legs to his chest and fiddled with the straps of his boots, while Adhemar stroked a finger over his cheek and stared at the fire. At length, speaking carefully, he said, 'It concerns a pilgrim, a Provençal named Peter Bartholomew.'

There was a speculative note in his voice which implied that we had entered a negotiation, that he sought to barter for information. I tried to hide my surprise. Bartholomew had turned up so often: in the cathedral, in the heretics' cave, in the tumult by the palace – why not also in the Bishop's cares?

'I know Peter Bartholomew. He came to Anna for relief from a boil. I saw him again as I left you in the square by the palace this evening.'

'Is that all you know?'

'Should I know more?'

Adhemar sighed. 'As you saw, he threw himself at me in the square by the palace. He was greatly agitated. Much of it seemed to come from you, from a fear of what you might have told me.'

'I told you nothing,' I said evenly.

'I know that – but he did not. And I wonder how much it affected the fabulous story he insisted that I hear.'

'What story was that?'

I was giving Adhemar no help, but there was nothing he could do. Reluctantly, he unclasped his cloak – it must have been stifling in the June heat, even at night – and began.

'He told me he had seen a vision. More accurately, he told me that the Lord had sent him a vision. Now, many men see visions, the poor and simple more than most. Certainly, some are divinely inspired, others the product of credulous enthusiasm or wishful thinking. And sometimes, I fear, of calculated interest.' He spoke these last words with special emphasis. 'As a bishop, a shepherd of souls, my duty is to establish the truth of such visions.'

'Christ manifests himself in many ways,' I said solemnly. Count Raymond scowled at me.

'I need not trouble you with the details of his vision,' Adhemar continued. 'Enough to say that Saint Andrew had visited him in a dream and had spoken of a holy relic, a glorious artefact of our Saviour's life. The saint told him this thing was concealed within Antioch itself, and gave Peter instructions on how it might be found. No fewer than four times, apparently.'

'He is nothing if not persistent,' muttered Raymond.

'So?' I asked. 'Follow the saint's commandments. You will know soon enough if the vision came from Christ.'

Adhemar pressed his fingers together. 'It is not so easy. If we seek it in secrecy, and only reveal it when it is found, who will believe that it is the relic we claim? If we seek it openly, and do not find it, we shall be scorned and reviled. You have seen the sentiment of the army, Demetrios. The panic is calmed, but their courage balances on a single straw. If they lose faith in their leaders, or believe that God has deserted them, the straw will break and we shall be plunged into a pit from which we will not rise. That is why I must know what I can of Peter's motives.'

He fixed his gaze on me, demanding an answer. Still I prevaricated.

'This relic might be valuable.'

'*In*valuable,' said Adhemar. 'As a sign of God's continuing favour, a symbol that He is with us still, it would be beyond measure. It would lift the hearts of the army, restore their trust. And as a standard in battle it would surely bring us victory.'

'And great honour to the men who found it,' I observed. 'A Provençal pilgrim's vision, received by a Provençal count and his bishop. The men who say that Bohemond should lead would be silenced; Count Raymond's prestige would be unchallenged.'

'If you say we do this only for gain, you are a fool,' spat Raymond.

'If you say you have no thought for gain, you take me for a fool.'

'No,' said Adhemar. 'Of course we will gain. But that is not our motive. What benefits us benefits the army.'

'Now you sound like Bohemond,' Sigurd said.

Raymond rose in anger. 'Perhaps we do. Who better than a mercenary to understand his wiles? But we are not so alike as you think. What serves Bohemond well serves your Emperor ill. What serves us serves Alexios better.'

I thought of Bohemond's instructions to his brother-in-law on the wall, the treacherous gamble he had devised. Bohemond's star would only rise at the Emperor's expense. And if his fixation was such that he would cut himself off from all hope of relief, he would not hesitate to be rid of the only Byzantines remaining with his army.

Yet still I waited. Peter Bartholomew was no friend of mine: he was a heretic, and he had conspired with heretics to keep me captive. But could I condemn him to be burned alive for that? I had been the instrument of so much death already.

I looked up. In the surrounding silence, all gazes had come to rest on me: Sigurd's, Anna's, Raymond's and Adhemar's. All I desired was to be free, to be away from Antioch and safe with my family. It seemed that even so simple a prayer could not be answered without more killing.

'Only God can judge the truth of Peter Bartholomew's vision.' I saw Count Raymond about to speak again, thinking that I spoke platitudes to delay him, and hurried on. 'But as to why he might fear me, I will tell you this. It will not please you to hear it. Heresy has infested your flock. For two days the heretics held me in a cave under the city. I saw their rites, and heard their lies.'

Adhemar had gone very still and his skin was pale as the moon. 'What manner of lies?'

'That the world was made not by God but by the Devil. That every fleshly thing is evil. That we are children of Satan.' I struggled against my revulsion to remember more, but every word of it was like chewing mud. It was enough.

'That is a wicked heresy indeed,' whispered Adhemar. 'How could the Army of God . . . ?'

Under his hood, Count Raymond's reaction was better hidden. 'That is bad. But what does it have to do with Peter Bartholomew's tale?'

Through his horror, Adhemar had guessed. 'He was one of the heretics. He saw you talking to me and feared that you had betrayed his secret. He invented the vision to impress me with his piety, to stall his punishment. Well? Was it so?'

His question hung unanswered. Sigurd lifted the spear he had used to roast my meat and thrust it into the flames like a blacksmith, stoking the embers. They chattered and crackled, spitting sparks into the air above. I shivered.

'If I tell you that he was a heretic, you will burn him alive.'

'If he believes what you say he believes and has taught its corruption to others, he deserves it,' said Raymond.

'What can I do?' Adhemar spoke as much to himself as to any of us. 'If I try him for his crimes, if I roust out this nest of heretics, there will be more hatred and more killing among us when unity is our greatest need. If enough schismatics adhere to their foul church, there might even be war between us. We would gift Antioch to Kerbogha.'

Anna looked at him without pity. 'Enough Christians have died in flames already. If Peter Bartholomew reports this vision, perhaps it is a sign of his repentance.'

'Or of his fear of execution,' said Sigurd.

Adhemar stood. 'I will think on what you have told me and make my decision in the morning.' He looked up at the sky, though a pall of smoke still hid the stars. 'I fear it is already not far off.'

'I have told you nothing,' I warned him. 'I have not accused Peter Bartholomew of anything.'

'I know. Be assured I will not treat him as if you had. Not yet.'

The bishop began to make his way down the stairs. He stooped terribly, I noticed, as if under an enormous burden.

'A dishonest man may still be granted a true vision,' I called, on impulse.

Adhemar did not answer.

'I thought you were dead.'

It was too hot to sleep. Anna and I lay naked on the tower, alone. We did not touch, but faced each other resting on our sides. The gully of air between us seemed charged with heat, and my chest ran with sweat.

'Perhaps I should have died.' So many others had, by my hand or my acts.

Before I could move, Anna had lifted her arm and slapped me hard on my cheek. 'Never say that. Never.' Her voice trembled. 'It is awful enough being in this cursed city. Without you . . .'

'You do not know what I have done.'

'I don't care.'

'I have killed men, and I have let them die. I have consorted with heretics. I have heard things—'

Anna raised her hand again, and I did not try to avoid the blow. 'Be quiet. If you must give in to despair, do not try and draw me into it.' She rolled over, setting her back to me. Now there was only silence between us.

A yearning to confess my part in the downfall of the city, a guilt such as I had not felt since I was a boy, overwhelmed me. In my mind, I formed the words a hundred times over; sometimes I opened my mouth to speak them, but each time fear choked them back. Even as she loved me – because she loved me – Anna hated me for the pain that my absence had inflicted on her. It would be many days, I feared, before she could forgive me, and the vice of Antioch was not a place for loosing emotions.

'What shall we do?'

'Await our fate. Face it when it comes. I have overheard Bohemond conspiring with his brother-in-law. He will go to the Emperor, and he will announce that we are slaughtered. The Emperor will not come.'

Anna turned back to me. 'How can he do that? We are already drowning – must he pile on more stones to speed us down?'

'He would rather die than give up Antioch.' I remembered the promise that he had made to the princes. 'If the Emperor comes, Bohemond's title will be snatched away.'

I sensed Anna shivering in the darkness – was it fear or rage? At last, in a faint voice, she asked again: 'What shall we do? How can we await our fate if there is no hope?'

'How can we do otherwise?'

'You sound like Sigurd – obsessed with dying.'

'It is hard not to think of it.'

'Think of life – think of your children, your new grandchild. Surely you cling to the hope of seeing them again?'

'No.' I shook my head, though she could not see it. 'That would make it unbearable.'

'For me, it is all that I can bear.'

κ θ

Dawn came quickly. In the south-east, smoke still rose from the ashes of the city, and the morning air was bitter. Soon it would boil, for midsummer was ten days hence, and there was no canopy of cloud that day to shield us. It was not a happy thought as I pulled on my heavy quilted tunic, and my chain mail over it. I soaked a rag in water and tied it around my neck so that I would not burn my skin on the iron. I tied my helmet by its chin-strap onto my belt. Whatever enemies the day might bring, I would be ready for them.

I did not have to wait long. As I stepped out of the tower, I saw a Norman standing facing Sigurd in the street below the wall. They seemed to be arguing furiously, but by the time I had descended from the rampart the knight was gone.

'Who was that?'

Sigurd spat on the ground. 'One of Bohemond's lieu-tenants.'

'What did he want?'

'He wanted nothing. He *demanded* that my company go to reinforce the Normans on the mountain and help them defend the city against the Turks in the citadel.'

My pulse quickened. 'You can't go.'

'So I told him. But you know that the Normans are not easily denied. He swore that if we did not come Bohemond would burn us out of our towers and slaughter us for cowards.'

'Either way we die.' I felt sick. Bohemond had sent his brother-in-law to cut us loose from the Emperor's aid; now he would rid himself of the last Byzantine checks on his ambition. Either he would murder us as deserters, or put us in the forefront of the battle, like David with Uriah, and let the Turks achieve his purpose.

Nor could I doubt that Bohemond would make good his threat if we did not go. He had burned down half the city, Franks and his own kinsmen alike, to bolster his army; he would happily add a handful of Varangians to the pyre.

'At least on the mountain we can die well.' Sigurd folded his arms. His shield and axe leaned against the wall behind him, and he had a pair of small throwing axes tucked in his belt. 'I will take a dozen men and do as Bohemond demands. The rest will stay here and defend our camp, and you and Anna.'

'Not me.' My stomach churned as I spoke, but I hurried on. 'I will come with you.'

Sigurd snorted. 'How long since you left the legions, Demetrios Askiates?'

'Nineteen years.'

'And you will march up that mountain, to a battle you have no part in, because a bastard Norman orders it? You will be dead in the first minute.'

'I will go,' I insisted.

'This is my calling, not yours. What would Anna think of you for doing this?'

I scowled. 'If Anna asked *you* not to go, would you obey?'

'This is different.' A troubled look passed over Sigurd's face. Both of us, I think, felt things we wished to say but could not.

He kicked his foot in the dust, and turned to pick up his axe. 'We should go, before Bohemond murders us from impatience. If you want to march into death, that is your concern.'

It made no difference. Wherever we went in the city, we walked in death, and if it came I felt a strange certainty that Sigurd would guide me to it bravely. Anna would have condemned such a thought, but to me it was reassuring.

The path up the mountain began in the south-eastern quarter. The main avenue, with its long colonnades and broad paving, had served as a noose on the fire: when we crossed it, we stepped into a burnt realm of ash and charcoal. Twisted buildings hung bent and shrivelled like balled-up paper, and smoke belched up as from naphtha pits.

'This is the kingdom that Bohemond makes for himself,' Sigurd muttered, awestruck. 'The cost of his ambition.'

How much else would be felled by his pride, I wondered? I did not speak it aloud, for I had not mentioned Bohemond's latest treachery to Sigurd. There seemed scant purpose in destroying the last vestiges of his hope. Instead, I grunted my agreement and tried not to breathe the morbid fumes.

It took little time to cross the city. The labyrinth of alleys, which two days earlier had snared me in its endless tangle, had been razed to the ground. As long as we took care to avoid the places where embers burned, or where pieces of iron still nursed the fire's heat, we could walk the roads we chose.

Too quickly, we arrived at the foot of the path, where the gentle rise of the river valley met the steep slope of Mount Silpius. At first the way was easy, a broad scar rising across the face of the mountain past terraced olive groves and high villas perched on the rock. The pine trees which crowded between them still shaded us from the climbing sun, and it was as well they did, for my armour weighed on me terribly and the shield on my back constantly tugged me backwards. Sigurd had been right: nineteen years out of the legions was too long.

Even at that hour we were not the only ones climbing the road. Ahead of us I could see cohorts of knights marching in loose order, shouting and laughing, perhaps to disguise their fear. I had expected to see them, and was content to keep a safe distance lest they chose to whet their scorn on us. What I had not expected were the women: scores of them, from barefoot girls in torn smocks to wizened grandmothers wrapped in black shawls. Every one of them carried a vessel filled with water – buckets, jars, urns, barrels. The smallest children carried cups, holding them out in rapt concentration like chalices, while some of the stronger adult women had casks yoked over their shoulders in pairs. They stretched as far ahead as I could see, and as far back, a river flowing miraculously up the mountain.

Sigurd pointed to the summit, his arm raised almost vertical. 'A bad place for hot work.'

'No easier for Kerbogha, at least.'

Whether it was the rising heat of the day, or the sight of so much water around me, I was suddenly consumed by thirst. A scrawny girl, no more than seven or eight years old, was passing; I knelt, stretched out cupped hands, and as clearly as I could said: 'Water?'

She did not stop.

'Water,' I repeated. 'Please.'

She shook her head. It was stained black with soot, everywhere save on her forehead, where a finger had marked a crude cross in the grime.

'For the fighters,' she said, staring at her cup. 'Not Greeks.'

After that, the way only seemed hotter. After a time,

the path switched back sharply, and took us south-east, straight into the sun. My armour began to burn where it rubbed against me, and whether I screwed my eyes shut or kept them open I was blinded. The path narrowed; it was too high for villas here, and too steep for trees. Our pace slowed as our fellow travellers were squeezed closer together onto the constricted road. It reminded me of crossing the Black Mountains into the plain of Antioch, when treacherous paths through steep gorges had proved almost impassable. Men had pulled off their armour and flung it into the ravines; they had sold their horses rather than have the effort of leading them. Even the sure-footed could not hold the path: whole trains of mules had been lost over the precipices. *A hard journey and a sweet arrival*, we had consoled ourselves at the time.

Now the corpses began to appear. Casualties of the fighting on the mountain, men had tried to return to the succour of the city and had failed. At first scattered, then ever more numerous, they lay sprawled where they had fallen. Some bore few wounds, so peaceful-looking that you might have thought they were merely dozing to break the long climb. Others were so badly injured that it seemed a miracle they had managed to stagger so far to die. All were naked, stripped bare by looting and now become the habitation of flies.

'Are you sure you want to go on?' asked Sigurd.

I could not speak, for searing nausea had joined the thirst in my throat. All I could manage was a limp wave forward.

At the next corner the road began to level. It was little consolation, for by now we were high up, only slightly below the height of the middle summit. The sounds of the armies drifted down to us – though not, as yet, the sounds of war. At the roadside two stakes had been driven into the ground like gateposts. One had a crossbar nailed to it, so that it took the form of a crucifix; the other tapered to a spike on which a Turk's head was impaled. I shivered as we passed them.

Ahead of us, the path continued across the neck of the mountain into a small dip between the middle and northern summits. Atop the latter, on a high rocky promontory thrusting out to the west, I could see the unbroken walls of the citadel. The purple banner of Kerbogha hung from its tower.

'This is as far as we go on this road.' Sigurd pointed to our right, over the hump of the middle summit. 'Bohemond's camp is over there.'

We picked our way up the hill, through the outlying positions of the Frankish army. It was like no battlefield I had ever seen – a victory, a rout, a battle and a siege all heaped over each other. Groups of men squatted in the scrub, sharpening blades and saying nothing. Archers crouched behind boulders and watched for a Turkish sortie. There were no cavalry. Scattered among the living lay the dead, dozens of them – though nothing compared with the number in the killing ground of the valley between the two summits. Within bowshot of both camps, those corpses could not safely be retrieved by either side, and so they rotted. The stink was merciless. Only the crows moved with impunity, for none could waste the arrows to fell them.

'Some of them have been there for a week,' said Sigurd.

I stared at him, amazed, as I counted back on my fingers. A week and a day – that was all the time we had been in the city. As many days as we had spent months outside the walls, yet it felt a hundred years longer.

And on every one of those days Bohemond had fought to win the one fragment of the city that he did not hold, while the Turks sought to overthrow him. I could see why neither had prevailed, for it was obvious even to me that this battlefield was no place for tactics or ingenuity. It was a shallow valley between the two opposing summits, bounded on one side by the wall along the ridge, and on the other by a cliff edge. Between those limits, all the armies could do was push against each other, face to face in an endless trial of strength. It was almost as if the Lord had made it to this purpose, for the bare earth was red as blood and the broken rocks as sharp as spears. At the very centre, in the belly of the valley, a jagged hole yawned open like the gates of Hell. All was black within.

'The cistern,' said Sigurd. 'Bohemond smashed it open to parch the garrison in the citadel. Now it is fouled with the bodies of the fallen.'

We carried on up the hill. The high battlements of a square tower rose in front of us, and as we crested the summit we could see the full expanse of the walls spreading out from it. The main force of Bohemond's army was concentrated here, and I saw immediately why he had risked firing the city in his hunt for more men. They were in a perilous condition. They sat on the ground in the noon heat, swatting flies and praying, waiting for the next onslaught. Few were not wounded.

I looked to the foot of the tower. Clearly, we were not the only men to have climbed the mountain that morning. Gathered in a circle, apparently heedless of the dying army about them, the princes held council. I could recognise Adhemar's domed cap, Count Raymond's stiff bearing, the various figures of Count Hugh, Duke Robert and Tancred. Of the first rank, only Duke Godfrey was missing. Towering over them all, his chin raised in pride or defiance, was Bohemond. We made towards them. I longed to confront Bohemond in front of the others, to make them know that he had cut us off from all hope of rescue, but I did not dare. He would deny it outright – the word of a prince against the word of a Greek spy – and afterwards he would ensure that I never spoke again.

Before we even reached the princes, one of the Norman captains stepped into our path. I did not recognise him, though with a week's blood and dust and beard on his face he might have been my own brother and I would not have known it. He looked at us and at the file of Varangians behind us.

'Are these all your men?'

'All that can fight for you,' said Sigurd. 'Where shall we go?'

The Norman pointed down the slope, along the wall which stretched like a ribbon to the citadel. 'The last tower.' He drew his sword and swung it through the air to loosen his arm. From the far side of the wall, and within the citadel, I could hear the battle-cry rising. 'You must hold it – and attack the Turks from their flank when they come.'

I looked to the nearest stairs, thinking that we would approach the tower along the top of the wall. But the Norman shook his head.

'The tower doors are barricaded, so that the Turks cannot advance along the walls. The tower is cut off.'

'How . . . ?'

'There is a ladder. Go to the foot of the tower and call up to them. Tell Quino that I have sent you.'

The thought of the coming battle had already begun to numb me, but the name he spoke cut through all my defences. 'Quino?'

'Quino of Melfi. He commands the tower.' The Norman must have seen the turmoil on my face. 'Why? Do you know him?'

$$\lambda$$

Perhaps the ancients were right, and we mortals are merely playthings of a capricious fate. Certainly the gods of old would have laughed at this latest turn, that Sigurd and I should be thrown together with our enemy to fight for our lives. Even I had to acknowledge the grim irony of it. And, after a flash of confusion, I accepted it. This was destiny; I could not fight it.

I looked along the wall. Our tower must have been about a hundred and fifty paces away, close enough to be within bowshot of the citadel.

'Pray the Turks don't choose this moment for their attack,' said Sigurd.

With our backs to the wall, our shields on our right arms, we edged down the slope. Sigurd led the way. Even pressed against the stones there was no shade, no shadow, for the sun was at its zenith and spared nothing. Sweat poured down my face, so much of it that I thought my armour might rust from my body. A sudden terror assailed me: that I would tug my sword from its sheath and find my palm too slippery to grasp it. I wiped my hand on the hem of my tunic, then touched it to where the silver cross hung under my armour.

Stepping sideways like crabs, crouching beneath the rims of our shields, our progress was faltering. On these heights the wall was the only path, and the broken ground reached right to its foot. Spiked plants scratched welts of blood across my bare hands, and several times I was tipped back against the wall when the ground at my feet gave way. I gripped my shield tighter and tried to ignore the thoughts of Quino that raged in my head.

We skirted the first tower and continued down. Here the wall followed the line of the ridge exactly, so that the slope fell away steeply beside us. At the bottom, the black mouth of the broken cistern yawned open, ready to swallow us if we lost our footing.

Sigurd pointed to the line in the valley where the corpses began. We were now almost level with it.

'From here, the Turks can kill us with their arrows. Be careful.'

But the Turks – assuming that they were watching us from the round towers of the citadel – chose not to spend arrows on a forlorn column skirting the fringe of the wasteland. Perhaps we were not worth the effort. Perhaps they reasoned that we were bent on our own doom, approaching it with every step, and needed no dispatch.

The last twenty paces were the hardest, in full view of two armies and the heavens, too far from one and too near the others. The cloying smell of the yellow flowers on the hillside swam in my senses; now the bushes that brushed me seemed like soft grass. If I lifted my gaze to the mountains far across the Orontes I could almost imagine I was back at the monastery of my youth in Isauria, seeking beeswax and honeycomb with the other novices on a June day.

The rap on my helmet was so unexpected that I almost fell down the slope in fright. Had the Turks chanced a shot while I dreamed? Ahead of me Sigurd was crouched behind his shield and staring angrily back.

'Keep down,' he hissed. '*I* know that you could not kill so much as a beetle with your sword; *they* do not.'

Chastened, I squatted low, and though my thighs begged

me to relent I managed to keep my eye below the rim of my shield until we had crossed the last stretch and had come to the foot of the tower. The shade was as elusive as ever, but at least in the corner where the tower met the wall we were hidden from the Turks. I rested my shield gratefully on the ground, straightened, and looked up.

Quino's men must have watched us coming, doubtless wondering whether our few men were all the relief they would get. A mailed head peered over the edge of the wall, so low that he must have lain on his belly, and stared down. Against the searing sky, I could not make out his features.

'We were promised more,' he complained. 'Are there others?'

'Only us.'

A rope ladder, crudely made, rattled down the wall. Slinging my shield over my back, I held the ladder taut for Sigurd, then climbed after him. It swayed under me, and with so much weight to carry I had to be dragged over the lip of the rampart onto the broad walkway at the top. The rest of the Varangians were coming up behind me. On a sign from the guard, I lay flat behind the parapet. I had forgotten that Kerbogha's army waited on the far side.

'How do we get inside?' I asked, looking at the barred door.

As if in answer, I heard a clattering from above and saw another ladder dropping down from a window in the tower. The window must have been several yards higher up the wall, far above the protection of the battlements. I wondered how I could reach it without becoming a target for the archers beyond.

'Climb swiftly,' the Norman said, tugging on the ladder to make sure that it was fast.

I moved my shield back to my right arm. It would make

for a harder climb, but at least it would be some protection against arrows in my side. Though what hid me from the Turks equally hid them from me: I had made a corner for myself, and had to mount the twisting ladder blind to everything beyond the walls. There might have been a company of archers nocking their arrows, or a ballista being pulled taut, or a spear-thrower, and I would know nothing until the missile slammed into my shield.

Nothing was fired, and nothing struck me. I could see the windowsill approaching, a black arch in the stone. Then I was level with it, struggling to keep hold of the ladder while I slipped my shield from my arm and pushed it through ahead of me. A new horizon opened in the corner of my vision, a dappled landscape of green and brown, but I did not examine it. I reached through the window. There were no hands to help me, but I fastened my fingers onto the ledge and heaved. Then, with a clatter of weapons and armour and stone, I was inside.

Brushing dust from my face, I moved clear of the window. Outside, I could hear Sigurd starting to climb the ladder; inside, nothing moved. There was another arched window facing the one I had entered by, boarded over with planks, and rows of narrow slits along the other walls. Somehow they did not seem to admit as much light as they should have.

'Who are you?' asked a voice from the gloom.

I stepped back, surprised. As my gaze took in the darkness, I saw where the voice had come from. A pale face, its owner squatting below the line of the windows. There were others beside him, I saw – half a dozen or more, all hunched over, forlorn and abandoned.

'I have come for Quino. Quino of Melfi.' Doom surrounded us, and the deaths of Drogo and Rainauld, even Simon, were drops in the ocean of blood which had been spilled. But if God had ordered it that Quino and

I should be thrown together at the last, perhaps it was to a purpose.

'Quino keeps the watch upstairs.'

'Then he will know that I have come.'

I doubted he would welcome me; indeed, I half expected a shower of stones tipped down as I climbed the final ladder. This one was solid at least, though withered and aged so that the knots bulged out like bones. Above me a square of light showed the way. I could feel its warmth on my face, a single beam plucking me out in the darkness.

Then I had emerged into the open air, and was face to face with Quino.

It took a moment to see Quino clearly as my sight struggled with the renewed brightness. Even then, it was hard to lock my gaze on him, for there was so little to see. He had always been wiry; now he was emaciated. I could see where the hunger had devoured him, eating out his cheeks and pulling away his hair until he looked to be nothing more than a skeleton in armour, like a relic of some long-forgotten battle found in the desert. He sat alone against the battlements, his sword propped between his legs, and stared with blank eyes. All around him were scattered the tools of archery: bows and bowstrings, arrows in quivers and in criss-crossed heaps, as if a storm had swept through a bowyer's workshop. There were even a few of the barbarian *tzangras*, crossbows that could fire short bolts clear through steel. I had witnessed their effects in Constantinople. I picked one up, remembering an afternoon once spent learning its ways, and heaved on it until the bowstring was latched into its hook. The bone arms which sprouted from the stock tensed into a perfect arc. Rummaging through the arrows on the floor, I at last found one of the right length, and slotted it into the wooden groove. When it was done, I pointed the bow at Quino, who had watched me all the while, neither speaking nor moving.

'Have you come to kill me, Greek?' What strength remained in him must have retreated inwards, for his voice still held its familiar bite.

'The Turks will do that soon enough.' To my left, Sigurd hauled himself through the hole and sat against the wall. Below, I could hear the Varangians investigating the tower's defences. 'I have come to hear your confession.'

Quino scowled, though it seemed a great effort for him. 'You are no priest. You are not even a true Christian.'

'Truer than you.'

Quino suddenly seemed to forget our conversation. He twisted around and stared through the embrasure. 'They are massing again. Soon, when the day is hottest, they will come. We will not withstand them here.'

'All the better, then, to ease your soul. Before you go to join Drogo and Rainauld – and Odard.'

His eyes flickered up. 'Odard? Odard is dead?'

'Three days ago. He died fighting.'

'Then I am the last to live. It will not be long. Soon the curse we drew down on ourselves will run its course. And you, Greek, the scorpion who comes to prick my conscience, you will be ruined with us.'

'The curse you drew down?' I repeated. 'The curse you drew down when you allied yourselves with a sect of heretics?'

Quino coughed – or perhaps he laughed, a dry sound, as though the skin had been stripped from his throat and only the bones rattled. 'You have been busy. Are the Pure Ones dead also? I saw a column of smoke rising from the city yesterday.'

'Some of them have died. But enough live to betray you.'

294

Again that terrible laugh. 'And what of it? Will the bishop come here, scuttling along that wall to put me on my pyre? He will have to hurry.' A bent arm clawed at me to come nearer. 'Come. Come and see.'

All this while, Sigurd had sat in silence, ordering the scattered arrows into piles by the embrasures. Reluctantly, I passed him the crossbow and crawled across the floor to the far wall.

'Look out there.'

Keeping an arm's distance from Quino, I lifted my head to the battlements and looked out. The tower faced east, away from Antioch and into the mountains behind. A high, broad valley stretched out before us, a cradle between Mount Silpius and the peaks beyond. I had seen it before, on a foraging expedition the previous autumn, when small fields still sprouted the stalks of the harvest and the land was green. The farms, the fields, the crops and the trees were long gone, wasted by the siege: now, in their place, an army had grown. They spread out over the rolling plateau in their thousands, some in makeshift camps, others marching in columns of ominous purpose.

'You see the pavilion with the purple banner? That is Kerbogha.'

I looked where Quino pointed, filled with a thrilling dread to see our terrible enemy, but amid so many men and arms I could not make out the tent.

Despite that, it seemed clear that the army was moving, that its shimmering legions were swarming towards the citadel. I turned back to Quino with new urgency.

'Did you kill Simon?'

'Ask him yourself. You will see him soon enough.'

'And you will not, if you take your sins to the grave.'

Quino bared his teeth. Possibly it was a smile. 'We have been living in the tomb for months – I do not fear death.

And I have followed enough gods in this life that surely one will take pity on me in the next.'

'I can see movement in the citadel,' Sigurd interrupted. 'There are banners waving behind the walls.'

'I was at Amalfi with Bohemond when the news came.' From the distance in his voice, I thought Quino might be there in Amalfi again, though I did not know where it was. 'The city was in rebellion, and we besieged it. High summer. A Frankish army passed nearby – bound for Jerusalem, they said. They sent envoys to us, proclaiming their pilgrimage. That very afternoon Bohemond declared he would follow them. He unclasped his cloak and tore it into pieces; the women sewed them into crosses. Red, like his banner. He gave them to his captains and swore that all who followed him to the Holy Land would win honour, riches, blessings. Had there been a ship in the harbour, I think we would have sailed it to Tyre that very day. Imagine it, Greek. The promise of salvation, of casting off our sins and starting anew on holy ground. A second baptism.' He broke off, choking as if his lungs were seized with dust. 'It has not happened as I thought.'

There was a long pause. Sigurd was peering out at the citadel, looking anxious, and I felt the weight of every passing second.

'Did you kill Simon?'

'Yes.'

His voice was so hoarse that I thought for a moment it was merely his armour scraping over the stone.

'Because you thought he had betrayed your heresy to me?'

'Yes.' If this was a confession, there was no taint of remorse in it.

'You followed the priestess Sarah in her false religion. You received her baptism and knew their mysteries.'

'Yes.'

There was a ritual in his answers like the rhythm of a prayer. I looked to see if he even heard my questions but his eyes were shut, his head bowed.

'The gates are opening,' Sigurd warned.

'Did you kill Drogo and Rainauld as well? Because they threatened to confess? What was the mark you put on Drogo's forehead?'

'No.' His voice had been ground down to a whisper.

'Was Drogo unwilling to follow you in your blasphemy?'

'Hah.' Quino looked up, a terrible smirk contorting his skull. 'In pursuit of secret truths, Drogo followed none save the priest. It was Drogo whom Sarah first converted, and Drogo who tired of her religion soonest.' He grimaced. 'After we had scarred ourselves with their cross.'

'And afterwards you turned to the pagan gods – at the cave in Daphne?'

Quino nodded, like a condemned man offering his neck to the executioner.

'You did not take the bullock to eat. You sacrificed him to Mithra, according to some ancient evil rite.'

'Mithra?' Quino's voice was parched of all emotion, yet he seemed confused. 'He said we sacrificed to Ahriman.'

'Who said this? Drogo?'

'The priest. The priest who led us there.'

A strange reticence, almost like fear, seemed to have come over Quino. My whole mind was stretched taut, screaming to hear who this priest had been, but a sharp crack from the far side of the tower broke my train of thought. Sigurd was crouching by the battlements, struggling to reload the crossbow.

'They're coming.'

I took another bow from the floor and braced my feet against its horns, then tugged back like a rower on the galleys. The string snapped into its lock, and I slipped the bolt into the groove. From within the tower, I could hear feet hurrying up the ladder.

'Look to the east,' croaked Quino. He still sat slumped against the walls; I doubted there was enough strength in his arms even to nock an arrow. 'They will try and gain the walls.'

I glanced down. As he had said, there were companies of Turks running towards us in loose order, ladders held between them. Archers followed behind them, loosing arrows into the sky to keep us pinned down. One arced into the nest of the turret, though it struck no one.

'More over here,' shouted Sigurd. I crawled across to join him. Inside the walls, in the valley between the summits, Turks were pouring out of the citadel. There seemed no end to them: they covered the land in a wave of steel and iron. There was no tactic or strategy, for the ground did not allow it – they simply surged forward, borne on their own momentum.

Yet even within a wave there are eddies and currents. The cistern in the middle of the valley which Bohemond had smashed open served as a breakwater, and the Turkish advance slowed as they split around it, squeezed against the walls on one side and the precipice on the other. Many were caught at the foot of our tower.

'Fire,' I shouted, though I doubt whether anyone heeded me. We were no longer Byzantines and Normans, merely desperate men trapped in an ocean of our enemies. What the Emperor's diplomacy and Adhemar's prayers had failed to achieve, battle now wrought. Quino had called me a scorpion, and a scorpion I had become, trapped in a corner and stabbing my sting at all who approached. I had never been an archer, but the crossbow is an easy weapon with which to kill. Stretch, lock, load; kneel by the battlements, thrust the bow between them, and fire. Aim a little above the target, to correct for the angle of flight – though with so many Turks bunched below our walls, a blind man could hardly have missed. That was my rhythm, my whole life reduced to half a dozen movements in endless repetition, and the single remnant of my humanity was the terror I felt each time I revealed myself at the embrasures, that an enemy arrow might fly through and strike me down. It was not an idle fear: the Norman garrison and Sigurd's Varangians were all around me now, firing with whichever bows and crossbows came to hand, and already two were sprawled out dead or injured.

Afterwards, I realised how tangential we must have seemed to the generals watching from their hilltops: Bohemond to the south, and Kerbogha in the citadel to the north. The real battle was down in the valley, though I saw it only in brief flashes framed by the battlements, and then only as a background to the men I aimed for. First the Turks were pressed back behind the cistern, struggling to squeeze their numbers past it; then, when I next looked, they were far beyond, charging up the opposite slope against the Norman defences. Such was the power of their charge that I almost expected to see them cresting the mountain on my next glance. But instead they seemed to have faltered. Their front rank was in ragged disarray, and eroding ever further as the Norman archers above poured arrows into them. Bohemond must have built a wall or a barricade, I realised, hidden among the low scrub just high enough to hold the attackers beyond the Norman line.

I had watched too long. In battle, the only spectators are the dead. I ducked back, pressing myself against the wall, and felt a breeze stroke my cheek as a Turkish arrow whistled through the battlements beside me. It flew across the tower and struck deep into the back of one of the Normans. He slumped over the parapet.

There was no time for relief or guilt. I was already bent

forward trying to stretch the bowstring back. Load. Kneel.
Now the Turks had passed Bohemond's obstacle, and were
face to face with the Normans. I could not even see where
the armies joined: they were a seamless expanse of shields,
helmets, flashing blades and death, while the white serpent
writhed on its crimson banner above.

'Look to the walls!'

On my right, a wide-eyed Norman with a patchwork
tabard was pointing down to the wall which led to the
citadel. I crawled over and looked out. A company of
Turks was running along the rampart, a ladder carried
between them. I snatched up my bow and fired at them,
but against moving targets my aim was poor.

The rest of our men crowded against the wall and loosed
their arrows down on the Turks, desperate to escape this
new threat. Some of the attackers fell, dark shadows on
the pale stone of the rampart, but most did not. Now
they were at the door where the tower met the wall, and
they could lift their shields over their heads to ward off
our stream of arrows. In vain we tried to dislodge them
by casting down rocks which had been gathered onto the
turret. With one we unbalanced a Turk's shield, opening
his defence to the fatal arrow that followed, but otherwise they clung on. I could hear them battering on the
wooden door, though it was barricaded with stone and
would not yield.

'Ladder coming up,' shouted one of the Normans.

There were no more rocks to throw, and the Turks were
so close to the tower that we could not fire down on
them. I looked around. Quino was on his feet, sword in
hand, his bones animated by new life.

'You, you, you.' He pointed at three of the Normans.
'Come down to the next level. They will try and climb
in through the window. You—' His claw-arm swept over
the rest of us. 'Keep their reinforcements at bay.'

'I will go with him,' said Sigurd. He was beside me, though I had not noticed him there.

'Make sure you come back.' I felt a stab of self-pity at losing him, as if my shield had been cut away, but I did not try to stop him. As a soldier, Sigurd valued archery as a tool of victory. As a warrior, he despised it for a coward's trick.

The five men disappeared into the gloom below, and for a moment afterwards there was peace in the tower. Four men lay where they had been struck by Turkish arrows, two dead and two dying. I would have given them water, but there was none to give; I tore strips of cloth from the dead men's tunics and tied them about the wounds of the living to staunch the flow of blood. Then I peered out the other side of the tower. The battle still raged on the slopes of Bohemond's mountain, though its clamour seemed curiously remote. The Turks were still checked; perhaps they had been pushed back a little, though it was hard to tell. But more companies were issuing forth from the citadel to join them, while Bohemond had no reserves.

There was a crash from below, and I glanced down through the opening in the floor. The planks over the window had been splintered away, and a shaft of light poured into the guardroom. By it, I could see a dead Turk hanging over the sill. Sigurd stood with his back to the wall and his axe raised, ready to strike down any who came through the window. Opposite, a Norman waited in the shadows with a loaded crossbow. Our besiegers would need more than a high window and a ladder to take this tower from us, few though we were.

I looked again to the rampart between us and the citadel. There were no more Turks coming to our corner of the battlefield. Kerbogha was concentrating all his might on Bohemond's standard. I stared at the fortress, the round buttresses rising out of the rock of the mountain and the square towers above. Tatikios once told me that it had been built by the great Justinian five centuries earlier: it seemed strange that a Turkish warlord and his Frankish enemies should now contest it.

There was another commotion in the guardroom. I heard the crack of a crossbow, and then a scream as an arrow struck flesh. The Norman opposite the window had been pitched forward onto his knees, and had his hands pressed to some wound I could not see. The dead Turk on the windowsill had been pulled away, clearing the opening, and as I looked at it a volley of arrows – four or five at least – swept through. I heard them clatter against the walls. A Turk hurled himself in after them; Sigurd's blade swept down and he was dead. But there must have been another Turk crouched on the ladder behind, for before Sigurd could pull his axe free the man had vaulted into the room. For a second there was no one to oppose him, and it was all the time he needed to bring his sword up. Sigurd's axe was loose again; he lunged at the Turk, but he had hurried his blow and it was easily dodged.

Another Turk was at the window. They had their bridge-head, and they would not lightly let it go. I tried to fire my crossbow, but Sigurd was too close and my aim not so true. Then the Turk had leaped down into the fray, and was lost in the confusion of clashing swords and shouts.

'Up the ladder!' Above all the noise, Sigurd's voice rang out. If he called the retreat, their situation must be grave. I saw a Varangian mount the ladder, with others climbing after him. I knelt by the opening, crossbow in hand, and tried to make out my enemies. Almost all our men had gained the top of the tower now: below, there was a hand on the ladder, but I could not see the arm, let alone the face. It climbed two rungs, paused, and was dragged down again. Then it reappeared, and this time it came high enough that I could see tufts of an orange beard under the helmet. Still someone tried to pull him back. With a blow that might have cracked the ladder in two, he stamped down and was free. He flew up the ladder one-handed and bounded onto the turret top.

'Close up that hole,' he shouted.

I looked around the tower, which was strewn with spent arrows and bodies. Several shields, too cumbersome for the archers, lay abandoned amid the debris. I hauled them across the floor. Sigurd was crouched by the ladder, axe in hand, and as a Turkish head appeared he brought the weapon down so hard that it cleaved both helmet and skull in two. The man fell back into the hole.

'Quick.'

Sigurd and I dragged the shields into place over the opening. Almost immediately, one was thrust aside by the next attacker on the ladder. Without thinking, I picked up my crossbow and fired it into his chest. The effect of the bolt at close range was terrible: it drove through the scales of his armour and exploded into his flesh with a spray of blood. The last I saw was an anguished face falling away.

'More weight.' Quite callously, Sigurd had lifted one of the corpses by its feet and was pulling it over the shields. Numbed, I did likewise, and was startled when the body let out a scream of pain. I had forgotten that some still lived.

'How many crossbows?' Sigurd asked. It was a needless question, for he could see as well as I that there were three, in addition to the one I held. He threw one towards the Varangians who had taken up longbows by the parapet, where they could still fire on Kerbogha's army below.

'Load that.'

'What will we do?' I asked. The fighting in the guard-room must have been terrible, for of the dozen Varangians we had brought only five still stood, together with two Normans. I could already hear the thud of a spear or axe hammering on the shield barricade, and most of our arrows were spent.

'We fill this tower with their dead.' Sigurd wiped his axe clean on the skirt of his tunic. The battle-craze that possessed him was beginning to relax its hold, but only a little. 'We kill them until we have made a stair of their corpses, or until they set the whole tower alight as our pyre.'

There was a blast of trumpets. A great shout interrupted Sigurd's doom-saying. I looked out over the parapet to the south, and my heart almost died with hope. Battles, like fires, must move to endure; they abhor stasis. It had been clear that the Turks and Normans could not remain locked in combat, that eventually one or other must force themselves forward. I had expected it to be Bohemond's forces who broke first, but instead they seemed to have prevailed. The Turks were streaming back to the citadel in disarray, their courage gone, while exultant Normans chased close on their heels.

'Bohemond is making a mistake,' said Sigurd, resigned. 'It is a feint. The Turks will draw his men from their positions, then turn and slaughter them.'

But for once his gloom was misplaced – or Bohemond's luck too strong. The Turkish army was routed; I could see them vying with each other to press through the citadel's gate to safety.

'Listen.'

The pounding on our makeshift barrier had stopped. I crossed to the northern battlements and saw Turks running back along the wall. When none followed, Sigurd and I pulled the bodies and the shields aside, while the Varangians kept crossbows ready against any enemies who remained.

The room below was empty, at least of the living.

'We had better be swift,' I said. My voice rang hollow in my ears, as if my soul were watching my body from a great distance. I remembered what the priestess had said of the angelic spark captive within our clay, and shook my head. This was not the time for such thoughts.

As gently as we could, though not nearly so gently as to stop them weeping with pain, we manhandled the wounded down the ladder, then repositioned it against the outer window. Those who were not hurt lowered the injured onto the walls, while Sigurd and I examined the fallen in the guardroom, seeking the living.

There was only one: Quino. We found him slumped in a corner, his tabard soaked in blood where a Turkish sword had pierced his belly. At first I thought he was dead, but some movement of my shadow must have stirred his senses for I heard a gurgling moan. It seemed incredible that there had been anything in him to bleed, so skeletal had he appeared at the top of the tower. Then, he had looked almost eager for death, yet now that it had come for him some stubborn remnant of his soul clung to life. We bound his wound with the clothes of the dead, passed him down through the window, and began our long trudge back across the valley.

λ α

Sigurd carried Quino in his arms – he was so frail that he could have weighed little more than a child – while the rest of us bore the other wounded between us. It was a hard journey over the broken landscape, and we jolted them terribly as we picked our way over hummocks of the dead. Once a Varangian's bandage caught on a briar and was torn from his side, spilling yet more blood into the red earth. Mercifully, no one attacked us. Only scavengers and devourers of carrion shared the field with us: crows and flies and lean-faced women stripping the fallen of their possessions.

Even the Norman lines were deserted. With Kerbogha's army forced back into its citadel, the Normans had retreated onto the mountain top. We passed in silence through their defences, makeshift barricades of heaped stone and masonry. They would not have served to pen a flock of sheep, but they had been enough to break the Turks, whose corpses in some places were piled higher than the walls themselves.

Pausing for a moment, I looked ahead. The Normans seemed to have gathered in a great crowd on the crest of the mountain, hundreds of them ranged in a circle around a figure I could not see. Were they celebrating the victory? They were remarkably muted – almost solemn.

We laid the wounded in the shade of a boulder, where the women could bring water, and hurried up the slope.

The crowd was thick; the blood and sweat that stained their armour almost steamed off them in the heat. Nonetheless, Sigurd and I managed to push through until we found a small rise from where we could see the centre of the circle.

All the princes I had seen earlier were there: Raymond and Bohemond, Hugh, Robert and Tancred – and Adhemar, seated on a rock between them. Beside him stood a priest in white robes, a slight man with a mop of dark hair. Like all of us in those days, his cheeks were sunken and his eyes dull, but there was a twitch in his shoulders that bespoke nervousness, the anticipation of some spectacle to perform. I knew him: he was the priest Stephen, one of Adhemar's chaplains. I had seen him often in the bishop's tent.

Adhemar was speaking. 'Christ has granted you this victory. But like all the works of man, it will soon become dust. Kerbogha's forces are so legion that he may fling them at us as often as he likes, heedless of loss. We cannot match him man for man. For the eternal victory, we must implore God's aid.'

A fit of coughing overwhelmed the bishop. At his side, I could see Bohemond with an ill-tempered scowl on his face, despite the battle he had won. Raymond, by contrast, wore a strange smirk.

'Truly, we have tried God's indulgence. Some have hidden themselves away, deserting the just battle from craven fear. They tremble to become martyrs to Christ. Some – many – have worked evil pleasures with the pagan women of Antioch, and the stink of it has reached even into Heaven. A few have forsaken God in their hearts. He has made our camp a barren wilderness; He has filled it with scorpions and serpents, and left us to be preyed on by wolves.'

Some of the men around me looked sullen – they could

not have expected such a harangue in victory – but many more seemed abashed and afraid. Doubt had fallen over them, and there was a desperation in their gaze which hungered for solace.

'Yet do not fear.' Adhemar's voice rose, carried on a new strength. 'Our Lord is a merciful god, and He listens to the saints who intercede for us. He has sent a token that He keeps faith with His pilgrims.'

A murmur of wonder rippled through the crowd, and they pressed in closer.

'Last night, this priest was granted a vision.'

The priest, Stephen, stepped forward. His arms were rigid by his sides, though his left hand flapped involuntarily against his thigh; he looked like a mouse before a flock of hawks. He looked at the ground, and spoke so softly that Adhemar had to urge him several times to raise his voice.

'It came to me last night. In the fire and the panic, I took refuge in the church of Saint Mary. Many terrors assailed me and I prayed to Christ, imploring His mercy. When I raised my eyes, three figures were before me.'

'Describe them,' Adhemar ordered.

'Two men and a woman.'

'Did you know them?'

'Your Grace, I did. But they were not of this Earth.' He hesitated, as though even he faltered before the wonder of his vision. 'They were wreathed in a cloud of gold, which shimmered behind them so that they stood out from the darkness. They had the form of humans – but no substance. To the right stood a man, very old. His beard was white. In one hand he carried a staff mounted with a cross, while in the other he bore a ring of keys that jangled as he moved. He was Saint Peter, the prince of the apostles and guardian of Antioch.'

At a little distance from the priest, Bohemond stood

fidgeting with the hem of his tunic. One of his red eyebrows seemed inclined upwards.

'To the left was a woman. Her robe was blue, trimmed with gold, and her face looked as serene as the stars. In her arm she cradled a child, whose countenance radiated the light of heaven—'

'The mother of God,' Adhemar interrupted. 'And the third?'

'He stood in front of his companions and his face was solemn, though beautiful beyond all men. He clutched a Bible to his heart, and when he spoke it was with the sound of many waters. He asked if I knew him, and I answered no, for I feared to lift my thoughts to such presumption. But even as I denied it, a radiant cross appeared above his head. Again he asked if I knew him.'

There was something pedestrian, almost rote in the way Stephen recited the words, but his speech had drawn in every man among the Normans. They were held rapt by his performance; Count Raymond, standing before us, looked as though he himself could see the vision at that very moment.

'I replied: "I do not know you, but I see a cross like our Saviour's."

'"I am He," He answered.

'My Lords, I fell at His feet and beseeched His mercy, and the loving Virgin and the blessed Peter fell at His feet also, praying Him to aid us in our distress.'

'What did He say?'

The memory of the miracle, or the attention of the crowd, had filled the priest with confidence. He crossed himself, turned his face to the heavens and closed his eyes.

'He said, "All along the length of your journey, through every toil and peril, I have walked beside you. I broke open the walls of Nicaea, and I held your lance at Dorylaeum. When you suffered torments before Antioch

I grieved, and when you strayed like lost sheep I lamented your wickedness. It was I who brought you safe into Antioch, rejoicing as you drove the pagan host from my house. At that hour, the angels sang in Heaven, and my holy father was well pleased."

'Then he opened his book, and it seemed it was written in letters of fire so that I could not read its words. "Tell my people," He said, "that if they are with me, I am with them. They will fast, and offer penance, and in five days I will grant a miracle that all will see. I am with you, and none in Earth or Heaven shall stand before me."'

Stephen's head slumped forward. 'He closed his book, yet the light did not dim. Indeed, it grew brighter, and brighter still. I lowered my eyes; I closed them, and covered them with my hands, but still I could not shut out His divine light. When I looked again, He was gone, and I was alone in the church.'

The priest stepped away, shrinking back into himself, and the spirit which had animated him departed. It was as if the sun had retreated behind a cloud, though the sky was immaculately clear. A wondrous silence gripped the mountain top.

Adhemar sat still on his rock, his back straight and his hands folded together. 'Amen.'

His word was like a pebble cast into the middle of a pond, rippling out through the crowd. *Amen. Amen. Amen.*

'And you will swear that all you have said is true?' Adhemar asked the priest.

'Before God and all His saints.'

Adhemar waved his hand, and two more priests emerged into the centre of the circle. One held a book bound with silver; the other an ornately jewelled golden crucifix. Adhemar stood, took them, and passed them to Stephen. His hands, I noticed, were shaking again.

Stephen lifted the book.

'This is the gospel of Christ,' said Adhemar. 'Do you swear by its truth the truth of your vision?'

'I swear it.'

'This is the cross of Christ. Do you swear on the pain of our Saviour the truth of your vision?'

'I swear it.'

Adhemar turned to take back his holy artefacts. But the priest was not yet finished.

'I will swear by whatever oath will satisfy you. If there is any man here who doubts me, I will climb to the top of that tower' – he pointed to the tower in the wall, where Bohemond's banner flew – 'and throw myself down. If I speak truly, surely I will be borne up on the hands of angels, so that not one toe touches the ground. Or, if you prefer, I will suffer the ordeal of fire. The truth of God's righteousness will guard me from the flames. Does any man ask it?'

He spoke with fervour, though there was a nervous reticence in his eyes which was at odds with his words. I saw Bohemond open his mouth as if to speak, but he closed it again as Adhemar calmly answered: 'You have sworn on the gospels. That is enough.'

A murmur of assent rumbled through the crowd.

'We will—'

Adhemar was silenced as a man broke free of the crowd and ran towards him. He fell to his knees at the bishop's feet and – in a braying voice which Kerbogha himself must have heard in the citadel – declared: 'Mercy, your Grace: I too have received a vision of the Lord.'

Confusion and consternation erupted from the massed Franks, but if Adhemar felt any surprise he mastered it quickly. He stooped down and raised the man to his feet, then turned him to face the crowd.

I had thought that I recognised the voice, the self-righteousness and wheedling. The face I certainly knew.

His hair had been combed since the night before, and a new tunic put on him, but the crooked nose and sneering lip were the same. Truly, it seemed there was nowhere that Peter Bartholomew might not appear.

'I have beheld His glory too.' He thrust out his chest like a cockerel readying its crow. 'In dreams and in visions, Saint Andrew the apostle has visited me.'

I sensed a certain hostility among the throng. Perhaps they did not like Bartholomew's sudden arrival, or were unimpressed by the lesser saint he had seen. Perhaps they knew him as I did.

Adhemar, though, was indulgent. 'How often?'

'Four times.'

The crowd stirred. This was better.

'Did he speak to you?'

Peter nodded greedily, then remembered his humility and bowed his head. 'He did. With words so wondrous that I scarcely dared believe them.'

'What did he say?' called a soldier from the crowd.

'He said: "Know my words and obey them. When you have entered Antioch, go to the cathedral of Saint Peter. There, hidden, you will find the spear of the centurion Longinus, the holy lance which pierced the side of our Saviour as he hung on the cross at Calvary.'

I felt warm breath against my ear as Sigurd leaned close. 'I have seen the lance of Longinus. It is in Constantinople, in the Chapel of the Virgin at the palace.'

'I know.'

Peter Bartholomew did not think so. 'Suddenly, it seemed that the saint led me through the city and into the church of the apostle Peter. He reached his hand into the ground – stone and earth were like water to him – and drew forth the lance and gave it into my hands.'

Reliving his vision, Peter had stabbed a fist down and

then raised it above his head, brandishing his invisible relic to the crowd. All stares were fixed on it.

'The saint told me: "Behold the lance which opened Christ's side, whence has come the whole world's salvation."

'I held it in my hands and wept. I asked to take it to the Count of Saint-Gilles, for at this time we were still hard pressed outside the city walls, but the saint said, "Wait until the city is taken, for then your need will be greatest. At the hour I appoint, bring twelve men to this place and find it where I have hidden it."

'He plunged his hand back into the ground, before the steps which lead to the altar, and the lance was gone.'

I looked around. Whatever his failings, Peter Bartholomew was a convincing preacher. His vision seemed to have surpassed even the priest's in the crowd's estimation.

'You said this happened while we were still camped before the walls,' Adhemar probed.

Peter tilted his head defiantly. 'It did.'

'Why, then, do you only tell us now?'

'Because I was afraid. Because I was poor and you were mighty. "Counts and bishops will not listen to a humble pilgrim," I told myself. "They will think I tell lies to win favour, or food." But the saint persisted. Twice more he visited me, commanding me to reveal this miracle, and each time, after he had gone, fear restrained me. Then, yesterday, he appeared again. His eyes flashed, and his red hair burned like fire. "Why do you contemn the Lord your God?" he demanded. "Why, when Christians suffer, do you hold back the words of salvation?"'

Peter's head was bowed in shame, his hands clasped penitentially before him. 'As soon as I could, I came to you, my lords, and confessed all. And I will swear it,' he added, 'by any holy relic or ordeal you demand.'

313

If Adhemar was tempted to demand such proof, he did not show it. 'It is not necessary,' he declared. 'Yesterday, in the depths of our distress, as the city burned' – he glanced significantly at Bohemond – 'and the Turks assailed us, our Lord granted two visions to the faithful. Hearing them together, we cannot doubt His divine purpose. To this pilgrim He promised the great gift of the holy lance, and to Stephen relief four days hence. This is how it will come to pass. We will wait three days in fasting and prayer. On the fourth day, in accordance with Peter's vision, we will take twelve men to the cathedral and open the ground where the saint prophesied. There, if we are true, the Lord will fulfil His promise and grant us His miracle.'

'What if they find nothing but earth and stone?' Sigurd whispered in my ear.

'But first,' Adhemar continued, 'this holy revelation should rekindle the flame of God's purpose in our hearts. Who can doubt that the Lord is with us? Though we are bloody and embattled, besieged by enemies and beset by suffering, He shares our torments and sustains us. We are His people, the sheep of His pasture, and He does not forget us. Therefore let every prince and noble, and every knight, pilgrim and servant, reconsecrate himself to our holy cause. Swear by the sacrament of Christ that you will not leave Antioch until we all leave Antioch together, in triumph or defeat as Christ wills it.'

Bohemond stepped forward, drew his sword, and held it before him with the hilt upright like a cross. 'I swear by the cross, by the sacraments and by the saints, that I will remain in Antioch until death takes me or victory is assured.'

Count Raymond, eager to match this piety, knelt behind his own sword. 'We are the fellowship of Christ. By one bread and one blood, we are made one with Him. I will not forsake Him.' He rose and put his arm around Peter

Bartholomew's misshapen shoulders. 'As for the herald of the Lord, I will take him into my camp and honour him.'

One by one, the other princes sank to their knees and made similar vows. Then Adhemar turned to the massed army and had them do likewise.

'Our three days of fasting and penance have begun,' he said. In the middle of the kneeling hordes, he alone remained standing. 'Confess your sins, make clean your hearts, and prepare your souls for the eternal victory.'

A chant rose from one of the priests behind him. *'Tradiderunt me in manus impiorum, et inter iniquos proiecerunt me . . .'*

'Congregati sunt adversum me fortes et sicut gigantes steterunt contra me . . .' the army answered.

Sigurd and I slipped away, back down the mountain.

λ β

For three days we suffered fasting and penance as Adhemar had ordered. It needed little effort, for there was not a crumb of food to be had in Antioch. And although it was a time of prayer there was no respite from fighting. Each day Kerbogha attacked the Frankish defences, and each day Bohemond repelled him. At night I could see the watchfires burning on the mountain, and during the day the plumes of smoke where they cremated the dead. I did not return to the battle but spent my days pacing my short stretch of wall, looking out over the plain and the river, though I knew that no help would come.

On the third night Sigurd and I sat with Mushid on the top of our tower. The swordsmith was a curious presence who came and went to his own inscrutable schedule, but he had become a frequent guest during our time in the city. It was one of the few places where he could be safe, and I enjoyed his company. Though Anna thought him unsettling, I found that his talk diverted me from the evils which surrounded us. And I valued the morsels of information his travels occasionally unearthed.

'All is not well with Kerbogha's army,' he was saying. 'For almost a week, he has poured out his troops against Bohemond. Many Normans have died, but even more Turks have perished and the city has not been taken.'

'It can only be a matter of days.' Sigurd was in a foul humour, as he had been since we had returned from the mountain. 'Our army is besieged by Turks on one side, and famine on the other. They cannot fight two enemies for long.'

Mushid nodded. 'But Kerbogha has his enemies too. Thirst, for one. He has ten thousand men camped on that mountain, where there are no springs or streams to feed them. It is a week until midsummer, and every day they fight another battle. Each day they lose diminishes their strength.'

'Each day we win diminishes ours.'

'But Kerbogha's army is a fragile creation. The Emir of Aleppo will not fight with the Emir of Damascus, because they have had their own war too recently. The Emir of Damascus looks over his shoulder, because in the south his lands are under attack from the Fatimids of Egypt. The Emir of Homs and the Emir of Menbij have a blood-feud, so they do not speak. The Saracens despise the Turks: they ask why they should fight so far from home when it is the Turks who will claim the spoils. And Kerbogha, whose rank is not so great as his reputation, must yoke these unruly beasts together to pull his chariot. If they continue to bite each other and pull apart, soon the axle will snap and the charioteer will be left helpless.'

'That is not the Ishmaelites you have described,' I said. 'It is the Franks. Bickering princes jealous of each other's glory; different races divided against themselves. If Kerbogha's army thirsts, it can retreat to the Orontes to drink. In our hunger, we can do nothing but starve.'

'And why does an Ishmaelite care so little for the fate of his brethren?' Sigurd asked. He did not dislike Mushid, but he did not trust him. He preferred the lines of battle to be clearly drawn; the presence of an Ishmaelite who was not an enemy unsettled him. 'Whose side do you take?'

'The side of war.' Anna had climbed the stair below and

317

emerged onto the tower, her pale dress stained with blood. 'As long as nobody wins, his swords will keep gobbling up lives.'

'How is the patient?' I tried to deflect the conversation from the awkward direction she had sent it. 'Has Quino spoken yet?'

Anna sat beside me. 'Nothing has passed his lips save air – and little enough of that. He is dying quickly.'

'He would be dead already if you didn't waste your time on him,' Sigurd complained. 'Why should a murderer and a heretic live when worthier men die?'

Anna did not answer but looked at me for justification.

'Because every life is precious to God.' I glared at the others, trying to mask my discomfort. The truth, as they perhaps suspected, was that everything which mattered was beyond my grasp. My life was balanced on a sword-edge, whose hilt was in the hands of Franks who cared nothing for me. I would survive or fall as an unthought consequence of their destiny. Only in pursuing the truth of Drogo's death did I have any mastery of my fate. Or perhaps I deceived myself.

'Look there.' Mushid had leaped to his feet and was pointing at the stars like some magus of old. 'There – in the north.'

I stood. For a moment I saw nothing but the constellations, as fixed and immutable as ever; then, following Mushid's outstretched arm, I saw a new star imposed on the heavens. In brightness it dimmed all the others, and its light seemed to grow broader and brighter as I watched.

'It's falling over Kerbogha's camp,' said Sigurd.

It fell from the sky, passing across the canvas of stars behind and growing ever larger in our sight. Falling from heaven like Lucifer, I thought.

'Look.'

Through some divine magic, the star was no longer

whole. It had split into three, branching out like the prongs of a trident as it plummeted to the ground. Each fragment still glowed with the residue of its starlight and behind them I saw little tails, like cloaks billowing in the wind.

'*The third angel sounded his trumpet, and a great star fell from heaven, blazing like a torch,*' murmured Anna.

'The Triune God descends on Kerbogha's camp,' said Mushid. 'There is hope for you yet, it seems.'

'Or else the star of Bohemond falls from its firmament,' Sigurd countered. 'Its ruin comes from the north.'

Mushid smiled. 'What was it that the angel said at the birth of the prophet Jesus? "Be of good cheer." Your god has spoken to your peasants, to your priests, and now He gives a sign to every man in this city that He is with you. The time of dreams and miracles is upon you.'

I stared at him. In those last words his mild voice had strengthened, deepened, as if resonating to some deeper truth. He sounded almost like a prophet, or an oracle.

'Little less than a miracle will save us,' said Sigurd.

Anna looked at him, her gaze impenetrable. 'You had better pray, then, that God does not disappoint when they excavate the church tomorrow.'

Later, while the others slept, I descended the tower and crossed the road behind the wall. We had commandeered one of the houses here: a low, square building set around a courtyard. Under the Varangians' hammers, the doorway had been enlarged to admit a horse and the courtyard turned into a makeshift stable. Only three of the animals survived, gaunt and weak, but their warm scent on the night air comforted me. As I passed, I heard one of them huffing in his byre.

Beyond the horses, in a long room whose furniture had long since become firewood, Anna had set up her infirmary.

I spoke a few quiet words with the Varangian who guarded it and let myself in through the open door. I walked hesitantly, afraid lest I should step on the wounded who lay on the floor, but my eyes were well used to the dark and I disturbed no one.

At the far end, a little removed from the others, I found Quino. He lay wrapped in a white blanket, an indistinct bundle like a butterfly in its cocoon. His head was raised on a balled-up tunic, and he breathed in short, ragged bursts. I feared that Anna was right, that it would not be long before even that was too much effort.

'What do you know?' I asked softly. 'Who led you into your impiety? Was it Drogo?'

Quino did not answer, and without another miracle I feared he might never speak again. Anna had said he had a fever; the bandages around his belly were soaked with the blood and bile which oozed from his wound, and there was no food to feed his strength.

The guard had come over, and joined me looking down on Quino.

'Has he said anything?' I asked. 'In his dreams, perhaps?'

'No.' The guard poked Quino with the toe of his boot. 'Nor will he. He'll die tomorrow, I think.'

I remembered Mushid's words. *The time of dreams and miracles is upon you.*

'Perhaps his life will return.'

But even in the realm of miracles that had only happened once.

λ γ

Certainly no miracles happened overnight. Next morning Quino was still in the grip of his wound, silent as ever. After a few minutes watching him I left Anna and her patients and made my way towards the church of Saint Peter.

Long before I reached the church, I felt the change that had come over Antioch. A day earlier, it had been a city choked in the last throes of a siege, squeezed in Kerbogha's fist. The strain had told on every face – human, animal – even the walls had seemed about to crumble to powder. Now it had the air of a holiday. Men walked with a surer purpose, neither crawling in despair nor running in terror. Women braided bright cloths into their hair – all the flowers had long since been eaten – and did not pull their children back when they tousled in the street. The sun, which yesterday had scorched us with unyielding fire, now seemed to bless us with its warmth, and the blue sky offered unblemished promise.

At the main avenue, between the colonnades, I found crowds gathered in anticipation. They lined the road as if for a saint's day, and for a moment I was transported to the *Mesi* in Constantinople, waiting for the Emperor and five hundred burnished Varangians to parade by. It was strange to think that my road to Antioch had begun with just such a procession.

We did not have long to wait. After about quarter of

an hour I heard trumpets sound near the palace, and shouts rise down the road to my right. They rippled nearer like gusts of wind, though no breeze disturbed the heat of the morning, and burst out all around as the column came into view.

Four Provençal knights came first, pushing back the crowds to clear a way. They wore clean white tabards emblazoned with crosses, though when the cloth billowed out I saw dried blood on the armour beneath. Next came Bishop Adhemar on a white horse. Doubtless he intended it to be a magnificent steed, its coat as bright and soft as wool, but in truth it was a mangy beast, half-lame. In those days, any horse that walked was miraculous enough. Adhemar sat erect in the saddle, though he grimaced with the effort; he seemed weighed down by the enormous cope, stitched in gold with images of the saints and prophets and the resurrection, that he wore. There was a sword at his side and a cross in his hand, and a horn bow slung from his shoulder.

Behind him, on a pair of emaciated mules, were the blessed visionaries, Stephen the priest and Peter Bartholomew. Each bore an icon of the apostle who had blessed him: Saint Peter and Saint Andrew. Stephen did not look to be enjoying the attention of the crowds: his head was hunched down into his cassock, and his lips seemed to move with the words of some silent prayer. Peter Bartholomew had no such humility. His chin was as high as Stephen's was low; he faced the sun and mirrored its beam onto the surrounding pilgrims, serene in its countenance. In emulation of his namesake, Little Peter, he had even put on a hermit's short cloak over his tunic.

In two lines, the dozen men who were to dig the hole came next. They were humbly dressed, though in an artful, deliberate way different to the mass of pilgrims around them. Certainly there was nothing lowly in their station.

Count Raymond himself led the near column, and a bishop the other; priests and knights filed behind them. After them came more priests, seven of them, chanting the liturgy with their eyes closed. *Lord hear my prayer, and let my cry come unto thee.* It had resounded through the city so often in the past three days that I had learned the unfamiliar Latin.

The crowd surged after the priests, flowing in the wake of the procession as it marched on to the church. I stepped out from the shadow of the colonnade to join them, and was carried along the road in a tumult of hymns and prayers. From deep within their parched bodies the pilgrims discovered new wells of strength to which they gave voice with an almost desperate frenzy. They had found hope, and the agony of its frailty only made them sing harder.

With every yard we travelled, the pace of the procession slowed, and by the time we reached the square in front of the church it was barely moving. There was no hope of entering the sanctuary itself, for those who had gone before were crammed between its pillars and spilling out down the steps, but that did not deter the crowd. They stood in vigil, waiting for the miracle. When Adhemar began to pray at the altar all fell silent, though none could hear him.

The prayer finished. Somewhere, far beyond my sight, Count Raymond lifted his pick to break open the foundation of the church. At that moment, I doubt there was a single soul in Antioch who did not believe the lance was there, where he struck. There was little alternative.

The blow rang out, faint and feeble at that distance. A pause, and then another. Then others joined in, hammering at the stone. The noise was curiously muted, like a child banging a pot with a spoon, but it held us absolutely in its thrall.

A whisper came back through the crowd. 'They have cracked open the paving.'

I sighed. Even with twelve men digging, I feared it would be a long wait.

The sun climbed higher. The shadows slipped away, and with them, little by little, the expectant audience. Hope waned in the faces around me; prayers turned to gossip, and then to a despairing silence. The chime of hammers and picks gave way to the muffled sliding of spades in earth. The heat in the square was savage, unbearable, and even in the church it must have sapped the will of the diggers. I wondered if Count Raymond and his priests were regretting their great show of piety.

I lingered for an hour, stifling my rising doubts with protestations of faith. Then I succumbed and returned to the house by the tower. Anna was there, wiping Quino's forehead with a damp cloth. There seemed little else she could do: his bandages had been changed recently, but already blood had fouled them again.

'Has he spoken?' How many times had I asked that in the last three days?

'He can barely open his mouth to drink. Have they found the lance?'

'No. It seems that Saint Andrew did not specify how deep it might be buried.'

I paused, interrupted by a fit of choking by my feet. Quino's hand shot out from his side and scrabbled on the floor; his eyes opened, and he seemed to be staring on me with horror. I bent low and inclined my ear, but there were no words, only the hiss and gurgle of air. His eyes closed, and he lapsed back into whatever dreams possessed him.

Afternoon came, and with it a stillness that settled over the city like dust. The festive atmosphere of the morning had gone; when I drifted back to the church of Saint Peter, there were no crowds to keep me from its door. A cluster of watchful pilgrims stood in a circle before the altar, but it took little effort to push through them and look down into the pit which the diggers had excavated for themselves. A rampart of earth and broken stones surrounded the hole, and I thought I could see a stump of bone among the rubble. Had they disturbed the grave of some early saint or martyr? It would be an unfortunate beginning.

On the opposite side of the hole, I saw Count Raymond stand back from his labour and mop his face. The cloth must have been stained with the red soil they had excavated, for it left a weal of earth across his grizzled cheek. His tunic was likewise smeared with sweat and mud. He pushed out his chest and tipped back his head, and I could see the weariness in his aged limbs. It was in his face, though, that he seemed oldest.

'I must go,' he said.

'My *lord*!' said Peter Bartholomew indignantly. 'We do Christ's work here, as commanded by His most holy saints. You cannot leave it unfinished.'

Tired and worn he might have been, but there was strength enough in Raymond's eye that even a man as shameless as Peter stepped back under its glare. 'I am called to defend this city – and you – from the Turks. That too is Christ's work.'

'It is right to do so.' Adhemar sat in front of the altar on his episcopal chair, staring down on the diggers like a stone saint. 'Count Raymond should relieve Bohemond's watch on the citadel.'

'But in my dream the saint commanded twelve men to accompany me.'

There was a spade in Raymond's hands and for the briefest instant I thought he might swing it, mace-like, into Peter's self-righteous face. Or perhaps that was my hope.

The count pulled himself out of the pit and wiped the earth from his hands. He pushed through the onlookers, followed by a gaggle of his knights and attendants. As he passed me I saw bitterness in his features, disappointment that he had sought but had not found.

Another knight was found to take Count Raymond's place and the digging went on. The heat under the silver dome grew and the watching crowd thinned. From out in the city, I heard the terrible squeals of a mule or donkey being slaughtered, and wondered if it was the one that Peter Bartholomew had ridden that morning. It would have been no use for war, and there now seemed little hope that we would need a baggage train again.

The hole deepened. The men who dug were in it up to their waists now, and still they turned up nothing but potsherds and gravel. They stabbed at the earth; had they actually found the lance, they would probably have struck sparks from it. Anger and defeat and misery filled the pit, and spilled out to infect the few pilgrims who remained to watch.

I left, and for an hour I wandered without purpose through the streets. I walked in the shadow of the walls, hearing snatches of conversation from the guards above. I found a small church tucked behind an abandoned bakery and entered its stifling gloom to offer a few private prayers. After a time, I found myself near the quarter which Bohemond had burned down two days earlier, and I marvelled that already shoots of life were growing back from the ashes. Tents had been pitched on clear ground, and awnings stretched from the walls and timbers which still stood. Mothers sat on scorched rocks feeding their babies, and children black as Nubians chased each other through the ruins. Their shouts seemed uncommonly loud in the open, silent space.

As the shadows began to creep back over the city, I retraced my aimless steps to the church of Saint Peter. A single glance confirmed that no miracle had occurred in my absence. The knot of watchers around the hole was thinner than before, and even from the door I could see Adhemar's impassive figure beyond them. He and Raymond had gambled on a charlatan, and their last effort to thwart Bohemond and the Turks had failed. No wonder the bishop seemed so forlorn, alone on his chair above the low business of digging.

I walked back to the house by the walls, feeling the copper gaze of the setting sun on my face. I did not need Sigurd's knowledge of portents to ascribe it a meaning.

As soon as I came within sight of the door, the guard hailed me. 'Demetrios. Anna has been seeking you. The Norman has woken.'

In an instant, the lethargy of a hot afternoon was washed from my mind. 'How long since?'

The Varangian shrugged. 'Not long. But it will not last long, either. She said it was the last coil of his strength unravelling.'

I ran through the gate and across the courtyard, under the plane tree into the infirmary. In my haste, I may have kicked against some of the other patients on the floor, but I was heedless of their cries. I came to the end of the room, where Quino lay, and knelt beside him. His black eyes were open and the dullness that had glazed them was wiped away. He tried to raise himself on his elbow as he saw me, but the effort was too much.

'Quino.' I spoke gently, as to a child, though desperation consumed me.

'I am dying.'

'Yes.' Sometimes it is a mercy to deceive the dying, but I sensed that Quino craved only honesty.

'You are the scorpion, Greek. Now you have stung me to my grave.'

I did not argue. 'Will you give me your confession?'

A gurgling, choking sound rose from Quino's throat, and he screwed up his face in agony. Wishing Anna were there, I put my arm about his shoulders and lifted him upright. The coughing subsided.

'I do not think . . . I do not think God will grant me life enough to confess my sins.'

'Then tell me what you can. Tell me who killed Drogo.'

Quino's eyes rolled back in his skull, and I tightened my grip on him. Every fibre of my being implored Christ to save him long enough to answer me.

'Who killed Drogo?'

Though I had him cradled in my arm, the strength to keep upright was still beyond Quino. As tenderly as I could, I laid him back on the ground.

'Do you repent it? Your heresy?' I remembered him on the tower, even before the Turkish arrow had pierced him. A man broken by his conscience.

'I am beyond . . . repentance.' His life was measured in words now, each one bringing him nearer death. 'Soon . . . I will know.'

'Who killed Drogo?'

'He took us to the cave. In the valley. He knew the ancient magic. The old gods.'

'Who? Drogo?'

'He offered truth.' Impossible though it seemed, I thought I saw a smile touch Quino's fractured lips. 'But I will find it first.'

'Who offered truth? Did he kill Rainauld also?'

'He killed the bull. He took us to the cave. He—'

Another spasm racked him. I looked around, hoping desperately that Anna would return to minister to him, but there was no sight of her. There was only the guard,

328

standing by the door and watching uncomprehendingly.

But the coughing seemed to have dislodged some canker on Quino's soul, for when he spoke again it was with a firmer voice. 'He knew our sins. He swore that if we betrayed him we would burn in flames. But already I am falling into the fire. His hold is broken.' Again, the ghostly smile. 'It is funny, is it not, Greek? I came so many miles, through desert and starvation and war, to follow the cross. And here, in this godless waste, I lost my soul to an Ishmaelite.'

'An Ishmaelite?'

'The swordsmith.'

Afterwards, I despised myself for leaving a broken man to die alone. At the time, I had no other thought. Without even pausing to tell the bewildered Varangian what had happened, I ran out of the building and up the stairs to the walls. An absent guard had left a spear leaning against the battlements, and I had the presence of mind to seize it before I stepped through the door.

After so many months of searching and ignorance, I found my quarry with disarming ease. Mushid was sitting on a stool in the guardroom, his face fixed in concentration as he rasped a whetstone along the edge of his sword-blade. He looked up in surprise as I burst in.

'What is it? Has Kerbogha entered the city?' He saw the spear in my hand. 'Is this the holy lance which pierced the side of the prophet Jesus? Have you stolen it?'

I levelled the spear at him. 'Put down your sword.'

His smooth features creased with concern. 'What has come over you, Demetrios? Are you unwell?'

I jabbed the spearhead at his belly, and he jumped back in alarm. Fixing his stare on mine, he laid the sword on the ground with great deliberation. As he straightened, his face was clear and guileless as the sky.

'Have you joined the Franks in their hatred of my race and my faith? Will you kill me in the name of your god?'

'If I kill you, it will be your own doing.'

He held out his arms, like a priest administering a blessing. 'I will not provoke you.'

'You killed Drogo.' The spear twitched in my hand as I said it.

'I was Drogo's friend.'

'Then you betrayed his friendship.'

Mushid shook his head in slow sadness. 'I honoured it to the end. I grieved for his death. Why do you accuse me, Demetrios?'

'Quino. He has few breaths left in him, but there were enough for him to name you as the one who led them into sin and idolatry.'

Everything in the room seemed suddenly very still: Mushid, my spear, the light which pierced the slit window. When the swordsmith spoke again, his words were sharp and finely crafted. 'You believe the single, dying word of a heretic Norman? A man from a race so full of hate for my own? The thought of an Ishmaelite left alive in Antioch must have tormented his soul, and so he has sent you, his willing accomplice, to finish the murder his countrymen have committed. Nor can I answer his charge, for doubtless if we go down he will be dead.'

'He has not seen you, Mushid. He did not know you were here, or even alive. What would it profit him to name you?'

'He knew I was Drogo's friend. He hated me as an infidel. I am easy to blame – especially if he wished to hide his own guilt.'

'He was about to die. There was no gain in deception.'

Mushid allowed a smile to break the tense set of his face. 'There is much difference between dying and death.'

'Not for Quino. You may say what you will, but you

will not keep me from believing him. You befriended Drogo when his soul was troubled, and you offered him secret knowledge of ancient evils. You led him to the cave at Daphne, and you introduced him to the rites of Mithra.'

'Mithra?' Impatience began to rise in Mushid's voice. 'I have never heard of this Mithra.'

I remembered Quino's words on the mountain. 'You named him Ahriman.'

'Ahriman, Mithra – I am a Muslim. It is forbidden to worship any god but Allah.'

'As you yourself once told me, your faith permits things in war which are not otherwise allowed. Passing as a Christian among your enemies, for example.'

'Only to a purpose. How would I gain if I introduced Drogo and Quino and their companions to the worship of false gods?'

Mushid was mocking me – I could hear it in his voice, see it in his sneering eyes.

'How would you gain?' I wondered. 'You found them wandering in the wilds of heresy and doubt. Their friends and brothers had died; disease and famine ravaged their camp. The army faltered before Antioch, and so – it seemed – did their God. You came among them as a wolf among sheep; you preyed on their thirst for salvation. They were lost, and you promised them a way home. Instead, you took them over the precipice, into the abyss of apostasy whence they could not return. Once they had bowed down before Mithra, or Ahriman or whatever evil name you worshipped him by, they were beyond all hope of redemption. They were chained into sin, and you held the key.'

The sneer was gone from Mushid's face. His gaze flickered past me, as if looking at something over my shoulder, but I did not turn to follow it. The door was shut behind me and I had not heard it open: there was no one there. Nor did I doubt that Mushid, the maker and wielder of swords, would be past my guard in an instant if I ever relaxed it.

'Why did I do that?' he asked. It was not a taunt this time. Perhaps he was curious to hear his deeds recounted to him, or to test my skill at guessing.

'I do not know. I do not know who you serve. You are an Ishmaelite, yet you worked to betray the Ishmaelites who held Antioch, to their ruin. You are a Saracen, yet you mingle freely with Franks and Romans. Whose side do you take, Mushid?'

He laughed softly. 'You see much, Demetrios – but only with the eyes of the *Rum*. When you look west, you see Franks and Normans, Provençals, Lotharingians, Bulgarians, Serbians and English. A man drops one word from your creed, or bakes his bread differently, and he is of a different church. Not one detail is missed. But when you look east, you and all your people, you see only dark faces and turbans. Turks, Arabs, Egyptians, Persians, Berbers – you do not care which we are when we cross your path. You do not care whether we are of the *Ahl al-Sunna* or the *Shi'at 'Ali*, whether we obey the Caliph in Baghdad or in Al-Qahira, because you do not understand why it should matter.'

'What is your faith?' I asked.

'It does not matter. I am of the minority – indeed, even in the minority I am of the minority. We are the few in the midst of the many. We walk in shadows and meet in secret and whisper in men's ears. Yet our faith is pure.'

'You oppose the Christians?'

Mushid rolled his eyes. 'I am like you: I oppose whoever does not believe. I told you once that when you came into Asia Minor you blundered into an ancient game. Did it not occur to you that I too was part of that game?'

'And Drogo and his companions? Were they part of it too?' There was so much that I did not know, so many tangled questions, but at last my mind began to cleave a path through them. 'Did you hope that by leading them into this unspeakable sin you would gain a hold by which you could govern them? That they would be your spies and agents in the Christian army? Did you kill Drogo and Rainauld when they refused you?'

'Drogo was a willing adept. He refused me nothing.'

We were skirting the truth, I was sure of it. Mushid's words had the manner of practised evasions, careful twists of fact, riddles. Even now, confronted with his deceit at the point of my spear, he played with me.

'If Drogo did not refuse you—'

How to tell what happened next? From the wall behind me, I heard running footsteps approach. Before I could think, the door was flung open and Anna's voice was shouting at me that Quino was dead. But I could not listen, for the arc of the opening door had caught the butt of my spear and wrenched it away, throwing me off balance. It was all the opportunity that Mushid needed. His blade was in his hand and he was past the tip of my spear, lithe as a tiger beneath his white robe. A stinging pain exploded in my head as the fist which grasped his sword thumped into my face, and as I reeled backwards I saw the blade driving for Anna. I was powerless to prevent it; she fell beneath his charge and did not move.

I scrambled to my feet and ran to the doorway. Mushid had not paused to savour his victory, had not even looked back on his handiwork: already he was in the far tower and descending the stairwell. There was a Varangian at its foot; I shouted to him to stop the Saracen, but even as he looked up to see who hailed him Mushid pushed past and sprinted into the alley beyond.

Fearful of what I might see, of finding something from

which there would be no release, I lowered my gaze to where Anna lay at my feet. She was on her back, eyes closed; I could not see any blood, but I knew that meant little.

Her eyes blinked open.

'Are you hurt?' I could hardly bear to ask it, for fear of the answer.

'His blade passed by me. Why—'

I left her question unanswered. As much as I knew, I could explain later. For now, a single purpose drove me, hopeless though it was. Mushid had already vanished into the alley when I reached the door; by the time I was at the foot of the wall, he would have had enough time to be halfway up the mountain. Nonetheless, I chased him. With every pounding stride I offered prayers to God: that I would find Mushid, that I would avenge the evils he had worked, that I would strike him down for assaulting Anna. After a time I began to see the futility of my head-long search; my malnourished legs began to falter, my lungs to ache. I remembered the grace which had spared Anna from harm, and offered belated thanks for that, but still I stumbled on.

I came into the square in front of the cathedral and halted – not from pain or reason, but because a sudden crowd blocked my path. The great throng of the morning had returned, and though the light was fading, all stared at the figure standing on the steps before the portico. The cone of his bishop's mitre was silhouetted against the light of the candles which his acolytes held behind him and his hand was raised aloft, clasping a bundle of purple cloth. It was barely larger than the fist which held it: if it was the spear, it was no great portion of it.

The crowd fell silent as Adhemar spoke.

'The lance is found.'

All around me, men and women fell to their knees in

wonder. Some beat their brows on the ground; others lifted their arms to Heaven and sang hymns of praise and thanksgiving. Even in the twilight, every face radiated exultant joy. Sounds of ecstasy and weeping filled the air. 'Salvation has come.'

λ δ

*A*nd *God came down, and dwelt among us, and we beheld his glory*, the evangelist says. I wonder. Was it so simple? If I had lived a thousand years earlier, would I have known Christ as the Messiah, or would I have joined the crowds who jeered him on the cross for an impostor and a fraud? Until Antioch, I imagined myself with the apostles; now, I am not so sure. Did I witness a miracle? From what I have been taught of the ways of God, there is no question: a poor man, despised by his people but beloved of Christ, dreamed a vision; the saint's message was obeyed, and the promised relic was found in the appointed place. What could be more obvious?

Yet knowing the ways of man, doubts remain. A heretic had this dream months earlier, he said, yet he did not reveal it until his crimes were known and his punishment was at hand. It saved him from death in flames. Those princes in the army most likely to benefit seized on his prophecy, and presided over its fulfilment. And when even they had lost hope – I later heard – when the diggers cast down their picks and spades in despair, it was Peter Bartholomew who leaped into the pit and scrabbled on his knees until he unearthed the precious fragment. Some said that it looked more like a roofer's nail than the tip of a lance; others swore that they had seen the sacred blood still crusted on its point. It seems to me now that

336

they believed, and then saw as they believed. For my part, I did not know what to believe.

One day during the fortnight after the discovery of the lance, I put my thoughts to Adhemar. I doubt that I was the first to ask him, for his answer was practised.

'Saint Augustine writes that there is only one miracle, the miracle of miracles, the creation of this world. All that is in this world proceeds from that, and is thereby miraculous. The signs and portents that we ascribe to God's wondrous acts do not occur contrary to nature, but *by* it. If it seems to us that the Lord has gone against the natural order of things, it is merely our understanding of the natural order which is imperfect.'

It did not seem to me that he had answered my question, but I dared not challenge him further. Too many of my doubts about the miracle's provenance attached to his role in it.

Curiously, it was Anna who defended Adhemar best. I had expected that she, so sceptical of mystics and soothsayers, would dismiss the lance as a ruse and a sham. Instead, she seemed happy to accept it.

'Of course it is ambiguous,' she said. 'Of course it is open to every suspicion and doubt. How else could the Lord test our faith?'

'The conjurors in the market seek my faith. I do not oblige them simply because they ask.'

'Because your reason tells you that they are bent on fraud. But how would you have answered if a humble carpenter had proclaimed himself the Son of God, the Saviour of the world, and called you to cast off all possessions and follow him?'

'That was different. He performed miracles by which he might be known.'

Anna folded her arms. 'Exactly.'

And though I prayed every night, imploring Christ to

strengthen my faith beyond the weakness of doubt, the truth remained veiled.

Certainly, for those who did believe, the miraculous beneficence of the lance was plain. On the very day when it was found, Kerbogha's army came down off the mountain, leaving only a passive garrison to guard the citadel. Some said it was because they were exhausted, parched of water and broken by too many days of defeat. But Bohemond himself declared that a single further assault would have shattered his ranks, and so this respite was ascribed to the lance. Indeed, its power seemed to have robbed Kerbogha of all stomach for battle: not only did he withdraw from the mountain, but he did not seek to break down our defences elsewhere either. He disposed his army around Antioch's walls, besieging the gates and bridges, and waited for us to starve.

And there, even the most fervent advocates of the lance began to lose faith. Kerbogha's new strategy saved us from the press of battle, but nothing could cure the misery of our condition. Famine consumed us. Each day it seemed there was nothing to eat, yet each day after there was less. Limbs shrank into themselves until skin and bone fused together, while bellies – by some cruel junction of humours – swelled as if we had gorged ourselves. Men pulled apart dung with their bare hands, seeking even a single grain which might remain undigested. We stripped the trees of their leaves and ate those, boiling them into green soups to stretch them further. Afterwards it looked as though winter had come to the orchards. The few who still had horses cut open the beasts' veins, draining their blood into cups and drinking it. One day I saw a Lotharingian knight lead his horse through the streets, shouting that for a bezant any man could buy the cup of salvation. Later, I saw a mob chase him away, hurling abuse and stones and beating on his heels with sticks. I could not tell if it was the greed or the blasphemy which had offended them.

Such was our hunger that time itself seemed to contract. Counting now, it seems impossible that a mere twelve days passed from taking the city to finding the lance but that we endured a full two weeks of starvation afterwards. With no battles, and no strength, the period passed like a dream. My sight grew hazy, as if I was fading from the world, and my mouth was filled with a sweetness like ripe fruit, though I had eaten none in months. Every day I sat on my tower, half-asleep, staring out on the vastness of Kerbogha's camp, the opulence of his tents and the brilliance of the horsemen who rode between them. At night, I lay half-awake on my stony bed, listening to the bleating of the herds that Kerbogha's army had brought to feed themselves. I remembered the pagan legend of King Tantalus, neck-high in water but ravaged by an unquenchable thirst, and wondered if the lance had brought us not to Heaven but to Hell.

One evening, while Anna and I lay sleepless in the tower, I confessed the secret of my part in the city's downfall, my guilt for the slaughter that followed. It had weighed so heavy on my soul that I feared it might be too enormous to reveal, but now I did not have the strength to withhold it. It poured out, almost unbidden, and Anna listened in silence. When I was done, I could hardly bear to hear her response.

Again she surprised me. Her words were neither harsh nor angry, but gentle. 'It was not your doing. If we had not come into the city, Kerbogha would have crushed us in our camp. What happened afterwards, the slaughter of the Ishmaelites – that is for the Normans to repent, if God will forgive them. You cannot take the burden of their sins upon yourself. There was only ever one man who did that, and he died a thousand years ago.'

339

Reason told me that she spoke truly, but reason alone could not wash my conscience clean. Yet her words proved to be a balm: at first they made little difference, but over time, working their way into the wound, they began to knit together the lacerations in my soul, to heal me. Even so, the scar would remain.

The Army of God was dying. Day by day, life by life, we withered on the famished vine of Antioch. If the miracle had come, it had not been enough. So, thirteen days after the finding of the lance, two days before the high feast of Saints Peter and Paul, Adhemar summoned every man in the army to the square in front of the church. The casket which held the holy relic of the lance was placed on a table before him, open to view. The princes, Bohemond and Tancred, Hugh, Godfrey, and the two Roberts lined up behind him. Only Raymond was absent. Whatever miraculous powers the lance held, they had not helped him. Nor, if he had hoped to use it to prick Bohemond's swelling ambition, had it served his purpose. All his might and riches could not ward off the wasting disease that ravaged the hungry in their weakness. He had kept to his bed for a week, and there had been no others with the power or the inclination to check Bohemond. He was undisputed master of the army; Raymond, it was rumoured, was close to death.

Adhemar fared little better. His health had been failing for months, and though he could still walk and ride, the pain of the effort was clear each time I saw him. Only the need to keep his flock together, the knowledge that his presence alone could unite the princes and reassure the pilgrims, gave him strength to continue. Looking up at him now, I could see little remnant of the kindness and patience which had once animated him. He had given his soul to nourish the army, and there was nothing left of him.

'Brothers in Christ,' he began. 'Pilgrims on the holy road to Jerusalem. Truly it is written, "The Lord scourges with whips every child whom he loves."'

A thousand skeletal faces stared lifelessly back at him.

'But it is also written, "There is a time for peace, and a time for war." Look around you. If the time for war is not now, it will never be. Our strength fades, our hopes die. In another month, Kerbogha will march into Antioch and find only the dust of our bones. Have we come so far, for that? Has the Lord brought us into this wilderness to kill us with hunger?'

Adhemar lifted his gaze above the crowd, stretched out his staff and spoke to the heavens. 'Lord, why should your wrath burn so hot against your chosen people? By your mighty hand were we led from the lands of our birth: will Kerbogha the Terrible now boast that you brought us here only to kill us in the shadow of the mountain, to tear us from the face of the Earth? Avert your wrath. Do not wreak disaster on us in the sight of our enemies.'

A strange energy seemed to course through Adhemar; his whole body shook with reverence. He turned his gaze back to the masses in front of him. 'What fools are we who question God's divine purpose? How far beyond our mortal sight are His plans? If He has brought us here to die, then it is to die in His name, to His glory, the beautiful deaths of the martyrs. How can we fear so holy and wondrous a fate? If we strike forth from this city, this holy city where the saints Peter and Paul first preached the true gospel, and die in battle, how great will be our reward in Heaven? Merely to think on it would make one long for death. Fight the Turks in the name of Christ, and however the battle falls, our sins will be washed clean in blood.'

He dropped his voice. 'But if we win — if we drive Kerbogha from the field and trample the ruins of his godless army under our feet — our glory will echo down

341

the ages with the greatest heroes of old. Think of it. The Lord has blessed us with this holy relic, the very lance with which Christ's blood was shed. If we turn it against our enemies, feeble and hungry though we are, how will they stand against it?

'God's promise is plain. If we stay, if we hide behind these walls of despair until famine takes us, we shall die the deaths of sinners. But if we take up our crosses, if we march onto the plain and fight, then whether we live or die the victory shall be ours. We cannot rest but we will lose. We cannot fight but we will win.'

Like a storm gathering its winds, Adhemar's voice had risen to a thunderous roar far beyond the frailty of his body. Now, suddenly, his strength departed and he slumped forward on his staff. A chaplain rushed to his side and took his arm, trying to steer him back into the shelter of the church. But the bishop had not finished.

'We are the Army of God, and the people of God. We have journeyed together, we have suffered together, and if God wills it so we shall die together. No prince or bishop will force you into this battle: we must decide together. What do you say?'

For long moments, an utter silence gripped the square. Then, starting from the back and sweeping forward, like a squall over water, a single phrase. *Deus vult.* God wills it. The shout rose; men who a moment earlier had barely had the strength to breathe now bellowed it forth. God wills it. God wills it. The princes on the portico took up the cry, the priests prayed it like a hymn, until even Adhemar's lips moved to its simple rhythm. God wills it.

I did not like their chant: as far as I could see, nothing had come of it save ambition and murder. I turned to leave. I did not think that there was any part for me in the coming battle.

A hand touched my elbow and I looked back. A priest,

a short man with a balding head and a harelip, was staring at me. He seemed familiar – one of Adhemar's chaplains, perhaps.

'Demetrios Askiates?' The name was unfamiliar to him, and his cracked voice struggled to pronounce its foreign sounds.

'Yes.'

'My lord the bishop Adhemar asks that you join him tomorrow. The fighting will be fierce, and your company of axemen will be much sought after.'

'Tell him . . .' I paused, not knowing what to say. To the depths of my soul, I had seen enough of slaughter and the Franks' battles. Whatever Adhemar might say, I was not of their race, and I would not choose to share their fate. But nor could I deny the simple truth of his proposition: if we did not fight, we would die in the city.

'I know what Sigurd would choose,' I muttered, to the confusion of the priest.

'Shall I tell him that you will come?'

'Yes.'

'Good.' His deformed lip stretched into a mulish smile. 'God wills it so.'

'We will find out tomorrow.'

λ ε

We mustered at first light, a wraithlike army gliding through the grey streets of Antioch to the appointed places. Count Hugh, who had surprised all by volunteering to lead the vanguard, assembled his troops at the bridge gate; Duke Godfrey, with the greater force, came behind him, while Adhemar waited in the square by the palace. He must have been awake for hours, perhaps all night, but he gave no sign of it. Mounted on his white charger, he rode along the ranks, reassuring the waverers and blessing the penitent; he received messengers from the other princes and answered them; he conferred with his knights and agreed their strategies. I remembered the last surge of Quino's strength before he died, and wondered if it was the same spark of a fading light that now animated Adhemar.

'To think this rabble once threatened an empire.' Sigurd rubbed his axe for the dozenth time that morning, and stared unhappily at the men around us. 'Now half a legion of Patzinaks could sweep them away in an hour.'

'Let us hope that sixty thousand Turks cannot.' It was hard to deny Sigurd's judgement. Among the hundreds gathered in the square, there could not have been two who bore the same arms. More than half wore Turkish armour, or carried the round Turkish shields that we had captured with the city. Some – the unhorsed knights – had swords, and many carried spears, but there were still too many more with nothing but billhooks and sickles. They might have been going to harvest rather than a battle.

Almost alone in this multitude, the Varangians kept their discipline and their pride. We had spent the night hammering dents out of our helmets, repainting the golden eagle of Byzantium on our shields, and polishing every speck of rust from our armour. When the trumpets summoned us, we had marched down in a double column, thirty of us, with a measured tread which would not have sounded amiss in the halls of the Emperor's palace. I had walked beside Sigurd at the head of the column, though I did not deserve the place. Above us we carried not the standard of the cross but that of the eagle. Sigurd had insisted on it.

'The body of Christ.'

I looked down. Priests were moving along the line, offering us consecrated bread from small silver caskets. I had taken it in my mouth and swallowed it before I even realised it was unleavened, after the Latin usage. At that moment it did not matter. I wondered where they had found the grain to bake it.

'Brothers in Christ.' Adhemar reined in his horse in front of us and looked out over the ranks. A helmet had replaced his mitre, though he still wore his cope over his armour. Beside him, also mounted, the harelipped priest carried the holy lance in its reliquary.

Adhemar opened a book. 'Remember the words of the angel to the meek, and do not be afraid. We do not struggle against enemies of blood and flesh, but against the powers and dominions of darkness in this world. If you would stand fast against them, take up the armour of God: gird on the belt of truth and the mail of righteousness. Lift the shield of faith, which quenches every burning arrow that Satan may throw at you. Put on the helmet of

345

salvation and draw the sword of the spirit, for that is the word of God.'

From the road behind him, towards the gate, the sound of a great shout and a blast of trumpets echoed back to us. Murmurs of apprehension ran through the crowd, but Adhemar lifted a hand to stay them.

'The gates have been opened, and the battle is nigh. Hold fast to all that is true, look to your swords, and by God's grace, by God's will, we will prevail. Every death that we die echoes into Heaven, the perfect sacrifice of the martyrs. Every drop of Turkish blood we spill makes atonement for our sins. For long months we have been chained in hunger, suffering and siege. Today we break free.'

An uneven cheer rose from the army, but it soon faded away. The most they could expect from the day was a swift death; words merited little now.

Sigurd pointed to the mountain behind us. 'I hope Bohemond did not depend on surprise.'

Stretched out between two spears, a black banner had been mounted on the citadel. The garrison must have looked down on our preparations with all-seeing eyes, missing nothing; doubtless the flag now signalled our advance to Kerbogha in his camp on the plain.

As I remembered from my years in the legions, the longest minutes in any war are those before battle. I said so to Sigurd.

He answered curtly. 'The longest minutes are those when you count the dead.'

After that, I did not speak. The few men who were mounted patted their horses and whispered in their ears; some of the rest sang psalms or prayers, but most stood in silence and waited, listening for the call.

A messenger came running back from the gate. 'Count Hugh has driven back the Turkish bowmen, and Duke Godfrey is on the plain. It is time.'

Without prompting, the herald who rode beside Adhemar put his trumpet to his lips, then waved the blue banner of the Virgin forward. Line by line, rank by rank, we filed out of the square and down the road to the bridge. Women lined the route, and some threw olive branches or garlands at our feet. But there were no leaves on the boughs, and the garlands were only thistles and weeds. There were no cheers or singing.

We came to the gate. The great doors stood open, mighty columns of oak flanking our path, while on the ramparts above and to the side stood a line of priests, crucifixes held aloft. With their arms outstretched, silhouetted against the sky, they took on the form of crosses themselves, or scarecrows. I heard them casting prayers and blessings down on us as we passed, but I was not comforted. And then we were under the arch, past the threshold, and on the white stones of the fortified bridge. Locked in my phalanx and between the high balustrades, I could not see the river; even the sound of its flow was drowned out under the tramp of our boots.

We came between the two turrets that guarded the far bank, and for the first time in almost a month I trod the earth outside the city. I could not savour it, for now we were on the killing ground. The men who had gone before us had met the Turks here: the human evidence was all around our feet. Most seemed to be Franks.

'Fan out, make the line.'

The deceits of a battlefield are infinite, and seldom kind. As our column began to unfold, the ranks of men ahead of me evaporated: suddenly I was no longer safe in their midst but thrust to the forefront of our advancing line. The landscape opened in front of me: now I could see the plain rising up from the river, the forking road to Saint Simeon, the charred mound where I had quarried gravestones for a watchtower all those months ago. Hard

347

on my right, the battle had already been joined. Duke Godfrey's men were locked in combat with a company of Turks barely a hundred paces away, shielding our advance.

'Forward,' came Adhemar's order.

Though it was an early hour, I realised that my face was soaked with sweat. Was I so terrified? No – it was not sweat which glistened on my cheek but a fine mist falling from the grey sky. I had barely noticed it in my concentration.

Sigurd wiped the dew from the nose of his helmet. 'Someone in the heavens watches over us. The Turkish arrows will not fly so far from wet bowstrings.'

'Nor will swords and axes be so easy to hold.'

'Look to your right!'

Our line shuddered as every man in it craned his head about. Adhemar had led us beyond Duke Godfrey's company, hoping to cross the plain and position us on the flank. But our enemies had advanced too quickly, and now our own flank was exposed to the reinforcements who had splashed across the river from their siege encampments.

'Wheel right, wheel right!'

Adhemar's aides were galloping their mounts furiously along the line, repeating the order, though there was little need. Barbarians the Franks might be, but they had campaigned for a year in hostile lands, and those who survived had learned a discipline which the ancient Praetorians themselves would have envied. The men on the right, nearest the Turks, halted immediately and turned to face their foes, while those at the far end ran in a wide arc to re-form the line against the enemy. As I turned, I felt the clench of fear in my stomach, the terror that I would move and the man beside me would not, that I would be left exposed. Certainly it was a desperate effort to re-order ourselves so quickly, and I could still hear the thud of shields locking together as the first wave broke over us.

I looked ahead to the line of Turks who rushed towards us. For a moment I saw them clearly: the swords rising and falling like reaping hooks as they ran; the red skirts swirling around their legs; the dirt that their boots kicked up. Then the battle closed in around me, drawing me into its fold, and I knew nothing of its course save what happened in the few square feet in front of me. My sword was my light, and beyond its radius was only a throbbing, heaving darkness. Shields clashed; swords and spears stabbed between the openings, and men fell. Sigurd's axe swung with a keen joy: I saw men reel away with their helmets split open, or their arms severed from their shoulders. Sometimes it seemed we moved forward, and sometimes back, the sinews of our army tugging and flexing. We never broke.

At length – no one measured the minutes and hours of battle – the space ahead of us widened. The Turks were falling back. I heard horses cantering behind me, and their riders shouting at us to hold fast. At our feet the ground was stained red, a ragged line painted across the earth.

'Are they defeated?' I asked, dazed.

Sigurd poked a toe out from beneath his shield, and kicked at one of the bodies lying in front of him. 'This one is. For the rest, this was simply their vanguard.'

Even as he spoke, the truth of his words was made evident as a new host of spears appeared, marching towards us. Against every expectation, I was struck by how few they seemed. Why was an army of tens of thousands attacking us in hundreds? Where were their horsemen against our ragged infantry?

The distance between us closed, and thought gave way to instinct. I fought.

★　　★　　★

For a time, the fine rain kept the dust matted to the ground, so that the battle retained a strange, savage clarity such as I had not known before. Then shrouds of smoke began to billow across from behind us. Glancing back for the briefest second, I saw a line of Normans with their backs to us, hacking and lunging at a curtain of fire. The Turks who had besieged the southern gate must have come around to attack our rear. Naphtha throwers were in their ranks, and their fiery missiles kindled flames in the tangled grass and thorns that the feeble rain could not quench. The Army of God now held only a narrow finger of ground reaching out from the bridge, with enemies on both sides. I could not see to count our men, but surely the greater part of our force must have been committed. If Kerbogha launched his cavalry at us now, we would be swept away.

Yet still the Turkish horsemen did not come. The battle raged as fiercely as ever – and hot, too, with the fires behind. Now it really was sweat which coursed down my face, and the air was rank with smoke and boiling steam. The press of bodies and armies against each other was unrelenting, unyielding. Lift the shield to parry a sword thrust; bring it down on a spear striking low. Stab where the enemy laid himself open; retreat before his counter-blow could shiver your steel. The souls of the living departed, and we became mere creatures of war.

If we had wavered, if we had ever taken more than a single step back, then I believe we would have broken and been slaughtered. But we did not. Desperation, hunger, faith – whatever drove us, it set foundations of stone under our feet and kept a lethal wall of iron and steel before us. And all the while a distant part of my being insisted that despite our efforts, despite the fact that I could barely duck my head behind my shield any longer, let alone lift it, this was not the true test. I have been in battles which hung on a knife-edge and were lost, and in those which were won, but in each there came moments of panic where it seemed all order was shattered, when we truly believed ourselves beaten. In the battle of Antioch, that moment never came. The men who stood beside me never faltered, and the killing blow was not struck.

And then the face of the battle began to change. There were fewer enemies ahead of us, and more allies behind. They surged on and we were driven forward, yet every pace we advanced seemed to place our enemies further away, not closer. The line that had held like rock now cracked; gaps appeared, but no one called for them to be closed. And still we drove on.

'What is this?' I shouted in Sigurd's ear. 'Kerbogha's cavalry will cut us down like wheat.'

He shook his head. Soon he began to outstrip me, and though at first I tried to keep pace, after a few strides I could see that I would not catch him. I slowed; then, hardly thinking, I stopped dead. The hordes of our army, the Normans who had sallied forth to reinforce us, swept around me, and I was little more than a twig in their stream. They charged past and vanished into the haze, and I was left alone.

Was this a victory? It did not feel like one – but nor did it seem like a defeat. The smoke was all around me, blocking out the sun; Kerbogha himself could have ridden by with all his train and I would not have seen him. I stumbled around the abandoned field, trying to find a path back towards the city, and let the number of the fallen be my guide. At the high-water mark, where our line had stood, they were almost like a carpet on the earth. Just beyond, I found the Emperor's banner, the golden eagle, still in the ground where Sigurd had planted it. I leaned on its staff, exhausted, and rubbed the tears from my stinging eyes.

Though the army had moved on, dim figures still moved

through the fog – the wounded, the compassionate, the corpse-robbers – so I did not see his approach until he was almost upon me. The snap of an arrow-shaft under-foot lifted my head, and something familiar in his gait held my gaze just long enough to take in his smooth face, his close-trimmed beard, and his black eyes. I could not guess what part he had played in the battle, for he carried a round shield and a straight sword. With no turban wound around his helmet, he could have passed for any Frank who had looted his arms from the dead. Only his armour looked foreign: flat, serpentine scales sewn over each other, rattling and shaking as he moved. I did not suppose it was a coincidence that he had found me there.

'What do you want?' There was no hiding the desolate weariness in my voice. The very thought of fighting now turned my limbs to lead. 'The battle is over. You have lost.'

Even among so much death, Mushid could laugh. 'I have lost nothing. And you, Demetrios, you will not touch the victory.'

I stepped away from the standard and lifted my sword. Even that took all the remnant of my strength. Mushid was fresh, and a more practised swordsman than any I knew. It would be a short fight.

'Killing me will not bury your secret. Others know it.'

He pulled off his helmet and threw it aside. 'Who? Your barbarian giant? Your physician whore? I will find them in time. Then I will find other Franj to aid me. Now that they hold Antioch, it is more important than before that I have eyes among them.'

'You could have saved yourself much effort if you had not killed Drogo.' I could not parry his sword; my only thought was to engage him with words, and hope that Sigurd might return.

Irritation flashed in the eyes beneath his tousled hair.

352

'I told you: I did not kill Drogo. He was an obedient adept.'

I stepped back two paces, circling to my left. The killing blood was in Mushid's veins, and words would not deter him long. 'Adept at what? The mysteries of some forgotten pagan? Sacrificing bulls in lost caves?'

'You have a keen mind, Demetrios, but you should listen more. My god is Allah, the one true deity. The matter in the cave, it was . . . a device. One step on the journey.' Pride entered his voice. 'What do I know of the worship of pagan idols? I invented the ritual, to feed those hungry for belief. There are many stairs on the path to knowledge, and sometimes it is necessary to come through error into truth. In the cave, Drogo and his friends abandoned the false god of the Christians. They crossed a chasm which could not be bridged, dividing them from their past. This was the first step.'

His words had bewitched me, as he knew they would, and I had allowed him too close. His sword hissed through the air, so sharp that it glided through my skin unchecked. A gash opened on my right forearm, and more blood spilled onto the ground.

Mushid was moving faster now, almost like a dancer. The tip of his sword darted like a dragonfly, probing my guard, though it was more an exercise than a necessity. 'On the second rung, it is annihilation. The soul must be wiped clean, ignorant even of its ignorance. All error and false belief must be purged. And so this is what I told Drogo: that there is no God.'

The blade flashed. I stumbled to avoid its arc and as I flung out an arm for balance I felt a hot iron bite the palm of my hand. Mushid was not trying to kill me, or not yet – rather, he seemed to be working to the rules of some cruel, self-imposed game.

Hardly less agonising were the words he had spoken. I

ached to answer them, to rebut the terrible lie he had told, but all I could manage through my pain was a mangled cry. 'Lies. Lies.'

'Of course.' Mushid stepped carefully over a body and continued circling me. 'But again, a necessary lie. Drogo needed to renounce all gods before he could acclaim the true God. How could he accept truth, if he had not known falsehood? And he believed me. He proved it.'

This time I had learned to shut my ears to his words. When the blow came, I just managed to lift my sword to meet it. The toll of clashing steel rang between us.

'Do you know how he proved it, Demetrios the unveiler of mysteries? How in one act he obliterated the power of God and cast himself free of his people? He summoned Rainauld to a lonely dell, and he plunged a dagger into his friend's heart. For if there is no God, as he believed, if no one will punish evil, who can do wrong?'

I was so dazed that I barely knew myself any longer. A part of me tried to wield my sword against my enemy, a part dismissed his tale as a feint, and a part wept that the answers I had sought so long were now becoming manifest, but too late. As for which part mastered the others, I had not the strength to decide.

'But it was a lie,' I whispered. 'Drogo's evil *was* punished.'

Mushid scowled. 'I took Rainauld's body and hid it in the culvert. When I returned to the dell, Drogo was dead.' He raised his sword over his shoulder, hefting it for the killing blow. 'A waste. He would have been a true disciple. Through him I could have reached deep within your army and guided it to my purpose, to destroy the godless Sunni who blaspheme the name of the prophet, and make my own faith master.'

He swung his sword like an axe at my neck; I parried with an upright blade and felt the impact shiver through my wounded arm. My sword dropped from my hand

and I fell back. Mushid stood over me, wreathed in smoke.

'Farewell, Demetrios. You will—'

Lying on my back, I felt the ground beneath me shudder. Was it an earthquake? They had happened here before, dreadful portents from the depths of the Earth. But this did not feel like a tremor to shake down houses and trees. There was a rhythm in it, a pounding like a drum, yet faster than any man's hands could beat.

A line of horsemen thundered out of the smoke, lances couched beneath their arms. Their shields were painted with the red bear, and I saw Tancred's stallion galloping at their head. I doubt whether they knew Mushid, whether they even knew his race. They were in battle, and he was in front of them. He did not have time to move, or even to face his doom. The spear tore apart the plates of his armour, plunged through his chest, and emerged on the other side. For the merest second, I saw his eyes widen and his face begin to contort into a scream. Then he was gone, lifted off the ground and swept on by the relentless drive of the knights. He must have been dragged fifty yards before the Norman pulled free his lance.

I sank back. Blood had turned the earth to a crimson mud; I was mired in it, and did not have the strength to escape. I leaned my head on the corpse behind me, and shut my eyes.

Afterwards, many men tried to explain how our feeble, tiny army had defeated a force ten times its strength. Many invoked Christ: had He not sent us His lance, they asked? Some who had fought on the western extremity of the battle swore that at its height three white riders had appeared in the hills and charged home against the Turks, and it was commonly agreed that these three had been the warrior saints: George, Mercurios, and Demetrios my

355

namesake. Others heard reports from captured Ishmaelites that it was Kerbogha's faithless allies, resenting his power and remembering past injuries, who had abandoned the field and left him helpless. This too was much credited to Christ's intervention. Some suggested that the routed infantry of Kerbogha's vanguard had panicked the ranks behind and turned them from battle, but who could tell? The truth was that none could explain it, not even Kerbogha himself.

Tancred's horsemen pursued Kerbogha and the remnants of his army far beyond the plain of Antioch, all the way to the Euphrates. There, Kerbogha took a boat across the river and passed beyond knowledge.

Antioch was freed.

After Peter and the angel had passed unnoticed among the guards, they came before the iron gate which led out of the city. Unseen hands opened it for them. They walked outside, and along a lane, when suddenly the angel departed. Then Peter said: 'Now I know that the Lord has sent his angel and rescued me from the hands of Herod, and from death.'

The priest at the front of the church looked up from his book, and scanned the watching faces of his congregation lest any miss the miraculous symbolism. He spoke in Latin, but I knew the story well enough: how when Saint Peter had been cast into prison and condemned to death, the chains had fallen from his wrists and an angel had brought him to safety.

I slipped out through the great doors at the back. On this, the feast of that miracle, I needed no Frankish priest to explain the analogy. Nor did I care to hear the Latin rite in a Byzantine church. Besides, I had an appointment to keep.

I stepped into the square, flinching as the sun struck my face. It was the first day of August, and the afternoon heat seemed to burn the very air itself. All was still. The stone fragments of the Ishmaelite tower lay where they had been pulled down, waiting to be broken up and to become new walls and homes and churches. In the far corner of the square I could see a group of Genoese merchants clustered in a circle, haggling over some argument or other.

Like crows, they had arrived almost before the battle had finished, looking to feast on the trade which our victory had opened. Bohemond had granted them a market and houses: doubtless their caravans were already pushing out along the roads to the east. They would bring back spices, and news and gold, and Bohemond would take the choicest portions to fill the treasury of his new realm.

I looked up at the mountain looming over us. In the glare of the sun, its colour seemed to fade and every line and wrinkle of its ancient face was made plain. There must have been a breeze at the summit, for I could see the crimson banners streaming out from the citadel in proud dominion. With Kerbogha vanquished and all hope of relief gone, the garrison had surrendered it to the princes, and they in turn to Bohemond. Now the banner of Provence flew only over the bridge gate and the palace, where Count Raymond isolated himself with his jealousies and regrets.

I saw two figures walking towards me across the square and I hurried to meet them. Seeing them from a distance, Sigurd so vast and Anna so slight beside him, I was struck anew by how much a month of rest had restored us all. The lands around Antioch might still be a wilderness, but in the rest of the world summer still brought the usual crops. With the siege broken and the roads open, the markets in the city had flourished again. Our cheeks and bellies had filled, not with bloated bile but with nourishment, and strength had returned to our arms. A month, I marvelled: a month and more since we had met Kerbogha on the plain, yet it seemed a single day. At first I had kept to my bed, too exhausted to stand, while Anna nursed me; then, when I could walk, I had wandered through the city in a daze, astonished that I could pass in and out of the gates as I pleased. For nine months those walls had been our cage, first on the one side and then the other:

it seemed almost impossible that I could go through them at will.

'How are your bandages?' Anna took my hands and twisted them round, peering at them back and front. The cloths were clean. Her salves had served their purpose, and though Mushid had cut deep the wounds were beginning to heal. She still took every opportunity to examine them – probably to be thorough, but perhaps also as a reminder, a soft rebuke for the risks I had taken.

'They seem healthy.'

'Good,' said Sigurd. 'Then we will soon be able to make the journey to Constantinople.' Even more than I, he longed to be in the queen of cities, to be away from the Normans and out of this desert, to be back in the palace serving the Emperor.

'Soon,' I agreed. 'When we are strong enough, and the summer heat abates. After so much struggle, it would be unfortunate to die of thirst on the road home.'

Sigurd scowled. 'The weakness of the Franks has seeped through those bandages and into your blood, I think.'

Perhaps it had. None of the Franks, certainly not their princes, had showed any eagerness to continue on their road. The men who had marched across Anatolia in the height of summer would not do the same in Syria. When we arrived, Antioch had been merely a barrier on the greater path to Jerusalem; now, for many, it seemed to have become the object. What did it matter? For me, Antioch would be the limit of my journey, and that was enough.

I squeezed Anna's arm. 'I will come back to you in an hour,' I promised. 'I have been summoned up the mountain.'

I left them in the square and hurried through the city to the road which twisted up Mount Silpius. The southeastern quarter, where once Sarah's heretics had held me captive, had changed again: the ruins had been razed and

359

the ashes ploughed into new fields. As I walked across them, I wondered what had become of the priestess. She had vanished in the fire, and I had heard no word of her since. Perhaps I could have asked Peter Bartholomew, but since the vindication of his vision he had become revered among the pilgrims and his lapse into heresy was doubtless washed from his memory. Would his flock care if they knew? Or would they look into their hearts, and see how sorely their own faiths had been tested during the darkness of the siege? Drogo had not been the only one whose suffering had driven him to error.

I reached the path and began climbing. The last time I had come this way, burdened by armour and the prospect of battle, it had seemed like the way of the damned. Now, with wild flowers growing at its edge and the pines rustling above, it was a bucolic idyll, perfect on a summer's day. Only the occasional flash of bone in the grass, where the burial parties had missed the remains of a forgotten corpse, gave testament to its past. My feet crunched on the dry stones and earth; the heat held me in its stillness, and when I closed my eyes the sun was like a shining white veil before me. As I swung my legs, I could feel every sinew in my body as if it were newly born, as Lazarus must have felt when Christ awoke him.

At a bend in the road, where it turned back across the face of the mountain, I forked away onto a small path. For a few minutes I walked alone in the pine forest, my footsteps muted on the fallen needles; then I came onto the open hillside and the view spread out before me. I could see the Orontes, much diminished by the summer drought yet still gleaming as it curled to the sea. On its banks, on the plain, teams of men and oxen were cutting furrows and pruning back the trees in the orchards. It was strange to see the ground without the tents which had sat there for so many months. From that height, the fragment of land between the walls and the river seemed so thin, so tenuous. Had it really been our world for eight months?

The path ended at the gate of a low villa, built out on terraces on the southern arm of the mountain. The blue banner of the Virgin hung from a spear by the doorpost, and a pair of Provençal knights guarded it. I told them my name and they admitted me, first to a garden, then to a blue courtyard tiled to resemble the sea. Looking down was like peering into clear water: small fish and great leviathans swam side by side, while silver waves rippled through the design where an imaginary sun caught the waves.

The guard led me down a stone corridor, its alcoves populated with marble figures, and through a door to a chamber at the end. It must have been built on the very edge of the terracing, for the arched windows gazed out on a precipitous drop, with the mountainside below and the southern hills beyond. Sunlight slanted through the openings and picked out the sweet threads of incense that hung in the air. Below the windows stood a bed, pushed into the corner and covered with thick blankets despite the heat. Its occupant was propped up on cushions, his eyes closed to the sun, and in the gilded light the lines and harrows of his face were cleansed away. A priest knelt beside him, whispering prayers.

I bowed awkwardly. 'Your Grace?'

The hooded eyes eased open, wincing at the light. 'Demetrios?'

'I am here.'

A hand lifted from among the blankets and waved the priest away. 'Leave us.'

The priest frowned to have his supplications interrupted, but made no complaint. He backed away, bowed, and left the room.

'Is the door closed?' Adhemar asked.

I looked. Whether from curiosity or carelessness, the priest had left it slightly ajar. I fastened it shut, then took a stool from the corner and set it beside Adhemar's bed. There was a smell about him that no amount of incense and unguents could quench, the dank smell of a room long unopened. I had found it before among the old and the sick, though seldom for long.

'Come closer, Demetrios.'

I leaned nearer.

'The day is beautiful?'

'Hot, my Lord.'

'Better the heat of the sun than winter's frozen grip. It is good that I have lived to see Antioch in this light.'

'It is your prize. Your victory. You have brought us through the siege.'

'Christ has brought us through the siege,' he reproved me. The stern set of his face relaxed; he chuckled, though it swiftly became a rattling cough. 'Christ, and Bohemond's ambition.'

'His ambition would have sundered the army apart if you had not tempered it.'

'But it was not enough. *I* was not enough.' Adhemar clutched my arm. 'This was to be a new path, a new way. A great enterprise to bind all Christians together, not under the princes of the Earth but under the guidance of Heaven. We built this road, Pope Urban and I – we preached its foundations and we set a great multitude upon it, in the hope that it would bear us to the peace of Jerusalem. Instead, it has led us into the wilderness of sin. Though I think now that even if it had brought us to the gates of Heaven itself, still Bohemond and his rivals would have quarrelled over the division.'

The effort of his speech had been great; he sank back in his cushions and closed his eyes again.

362

'When we set out, Pope Urban told me that faith was a bloom which flowered in the desert. It is not. Hate and doubt are all that flourish here. What we tried to uproot we have instead only nourished and watered. The princes will kill. They will kill and plunder as they did before, only now they will do it in the name of Christ. They will kill in His name, because I have preached it, and He will weep in Heaven.'

'You did what was necessary,' I said, remembering Anna's words. 'You cannot blame yourself for what became of it.'

'No!' There was rare strength in Adhemar's voice. He fumbled within his nightshirt and pulled forth a jewelled cross. 'This was once the symbol of passion, of humility, of mercy.' He twisted it on its chain so that he held it upside down. 'I have made it a sword.'

I did not speak. There were no words of comfort that I could say. I looked down on Adhemar, at the muscles twitching in his face where life and death vied for mastery. The breath seemed to be faltering in his throat; his heart was faint.

The struggle in his body eased, and for a moment I thought that life had left him. Then, in a dull voice as if speaking through a veil, he whispered, 'Did you ever discover the killer of Drogo?'

It was the last question I had expected of him. Perhaps it was the cords of his mind unwinding which had recalled that distant memory.

'There was a Saracen. For a time, Drogo had lapsed into heresy. This Ishmaelite preyed on Drogo's doubts and seduced him into worse error. First idolatry, then apostasy. He wished to make Drogo his creature, his spy. He had Drogo lure Rainauld to the dell and kill him, to test his loyalty.' It was a bitter truth that the man I had sought to avenge had himself been a murderer.

Deep in his pillows, Adhemar nodded. He shuffled

deeper under his blankets, turning this way and that in search of comfort. Even when he lay still he looked in pain, though it would not be for long. The breaths that hissed through his dry lips grew ever more faint.

'I was walking in the fields,' he whispered. His thoughts were dissolving; I could not tell if it was a month earlier or a lifetime he remembered. 'Walking, and praying. I found them in the dell, alone.'

Seated low on my stool, I stiffened. What memory was this?

'They embraced as brothers. As he stepped away, he kissed Rainauld on the cheek. Then he stabbed the knife in his heart. He fell without a word.'

Now there was no sound in the room. Even the murmur of the guards outside had ceased, though they could not have heard Adhemar's frail words. The sound barely reached my own ears.

'I saw the Saracen.' Adhemar's eyes were open again, but staring away into time. 'He hid behind a boulder. When it was done, he took Rainauld away and left Drogo.'

'You saw Drogo murder Rainauld?' I breathed.

Adhemar's gaze came back to focus on me. 'Demetrios. Bring me my cope. In the chest.'

Fighting back the questions which demanded to be asked, I opened the iron-bound chest he indicated and dragged out the great crimson cope. Images of Christ and the apostles and prophets were stitched into it in gold, and its weight was immense, heavier than armour. As best I could, I wrapped it around Adhemar's shoulders.

'Now lift me in my bed.'

I crooked my arm about him and raised him so that his head came above the ledge of the window. His eyes were in shadow, but he slowly turned his face until it gazed onto the hills beyond.

'That way lies the promised land, the land of Israel. I

364

will not cross over there, but the Lord has granted me to see it.'

Unsure what he wanted, I continued to hold him up. 'I went to him,' Adhemar whispered. 'Perhaps I should have stayed hidden, but I could not. I could not . . .' The faint voice tailed away, and I almost shook him in desperation. 'I could not comprehend why he should kill without mercy. Without passion.'

He leaned back in my arms, and I lowered him to the cushions. His neck had become so thin that I feared I might snap it in my impatience. I heard a gurgling in his throat and feared the end had come; I prayed God to spare him, not from mercy but from a compulsion to hear his secret, to know.

'Do you know what he told me?' Adhemar's face had slackened. The wrinkles unwound themselves, and he looked almost like a child.

'That there is no God?' I guessed reluctantly.

Adhemar's eyes widened with surprise. 'Yes. That there was no God. That priests were liars, and the faithful fools. That it was no evil to kill, because none would punish it. He laughed in my face and called me a charlatan.'

'And you slew him.' There were tears on my cheek, though I did not notice them.

'I slew him. I slew him, because it was too terrible to hear his words. Because he was a murderer. Because after all the agonies and battles we had suffered in Christ's name, Drogo forsook Him. He stood there, smiling and bloodied and unrepentant, and I knew evil.'

More coughing racked Adhemar's body. 'He denied God, and declared himself almighty. He killed, because there was none to judge him. But I was there. I judged him. In the flower of my anger, I became the angel of vengeance and struck him down. I put the mark of Cain on his brow, so that men might know him as a murderer, and left his body to be devoured by carrion-eaters. Then I fled from that awful place.'

'Where I found him.'

Adhemar nodded, and seemed to drift into sleep for a while. I put my hand on his throat, but the life still beat in him, however faint. I looked around the room and out of the windows, trying to numb my troubled soul. For a year my faith had endured famine and slaughter, pain and despair. Now, I did not know what to believe.

I felt a hand on my wrist and looked down. Adhemar was trying to speak, though he could barely form words. 'Water?'

I stood, glad of any movement, and crossed to a table in the far corner which held a stone jug and a cup. The water splashed my fingers as I poured it, warm and brackish, but it seemed to suffice for Adhemar. I held the cup to his lips and let him drink, then wiped his mouth on the hem of my sleeve.

'I repent it, Demetrios.' His hand still gripped mine, with all the strength within him. 'I killed Drogo because he offended God, yet in my rage I committed the same offence. Worse. He killed denying God; I killed in His name. I saw evil and I tried to destroy it. Instead, I let it consume me. He will judge me harshly when I come before His throne, and I will deserve it.'

I tipped the cup to his mouth again, unable to speak. Outside the window a flock of birds wheeled in the sky, while from the courtyard I could smell the smoke of a fire being kindled. Dusk was coming on.

'What?'

I thought I had heard a whisper from the bed, and looked down to see what Adhemar had to say. But my ears had deceived me: he had not spoken, and he would not speak again. His unseeing eyes were open, and his head was crooked to one side, as if at the last he had recognised some long-forgotten face. With trembling hands, I pulled the cope around him, then took the silver cross from my neck and laid it on his chest. Perhaps he would find some use for it where he had gone.

Outside the room, a cluster of priests and knights were waiting in the corridor. Suspicious stares fixed themselves on me as I passed.

'He is asleep,' I told them. 'He desired half an hour in peace.'

More crowds had gathered in the courtyard beyond, pacing fretfully over the sea-blue tiles. News of Adhemar's condition must have spread through the city, for there were many nobles, as well as priests and pilgrims. I saw Bohemond standing among a knot of his retainers, a head above them all, and Duke Godfrey whispering with Robert of Normandy in a corner. Even Count Raymond had come, ashen-faced and sour. I ignored them all, and pushed through the gate to the hillside beyond.

The path to the city lay before me, but I was not ready to go back. Instead, I climbed a little way up the hill, picking my way between thorns and rocks. On a small outcrop on the shoulder of the mountain I found a boulder and seated myself against it, looking out over the hills. The land below was in shadow, though the tips of the hills and the mountain above were still tinged with gold.

For a long time – an hour, perhaps, though I did not count – I sat in silence. Sometimes my eyes gazed on the landscape, sometimes to the far horizon where thought and memory and sight converged. There were questions in my soul which would not soon be answered, but what solace I could find I found in their contemplation. How much suffering and death had been worked in this place in the name of God, of gods, of all gods and none? Had it redeemed our souls, as Christ's suffering had redeemed

367

His? I did not think so. We had built our own cross and nailed ourselves to it, exulting in our piety even as we bled, then wondered why our god had forsaken us. We had set ourselves tests of faith, and failed them. Adhemar, at his end, had seen clearly: God would judge us harshly, and we would deserve it.

The last light had sunk behind the western hills, and a grey haze embraced the air. I rose. I had abandoned Anna and Sigurd long enough. I should go down.

As I turned to go back, I glanced over my shoulder. The mountains were little more than purple shadows against the deepening sky, and the valleys between had vanished. The course of the Orontes was hidden, and darkness covered the road beside it.

The road we had fought so long to clear.

The road to Jerusalem.

Τελος

Historical Note

The battle for Antioch is perhaps best understood as the Stalingrad of the First Crusade. In both cases, invading armies made rapid progress across enemy territory before becoming mired for months outside cities too large and tenaciously defended to be taken. In both cases, the besiegers were then themselves surrounded, with the crucial difference that the crusaders were eventually able to break out and raise the siege. Had they failed, Pope Urban's vision of conquest would have foundered as surely as did Hitler's in 1942. It is hardly surprising, then, to discover the catalogue of greed, intrigue, treachery and extraordinary violence that attended the siege. In general facts and chronology, as well as in the characters of the leaders, I have tried to be as faithful as possible to the (often contradictory) sources. The privations that the army suffered, the sudden taking of the city two days before Kerbogha arrived, the finding of the Holy Lance, and the extraordinary victory against overwhelming odds in the final battle, all happened much as I have described. Contemporary chroniclers could find no explanation other than the miraculous, and modern historians offer few more solid answers.

The one area where I have taken substantial liberties with history is in the matter of the heretics. The sources make no reference to the appearance of heresy among the crusaders – as you would expect from a group of clerical chroniclers glorifying the papacy's great achievement – but we know that the crusaders did encounter local heretics en route. There was a strong puritanical element among the mass of non-combatants, and it frequently voiced itself in opposition to the decadence of their leaders. Given how disastrously awry those leaders seemed to have led the crusade during the terrible winter of 1097–98, and how impossible it was to disentangle the spiritual and political spheres in the medieval mind, it seems entirely plausible that social protest would naturally have led some pilgrims to more radical theologies. In a group of exceptional piety, enduring extraordinary suffering and finding themselves beyond all bounds of their known world, it seems reasonable to suppose that some would have looked beyond the confines of ortho-doxy for relief – particularly in the spawning ground of faiths that was and is the Middle East. The heterodox beliefs I describe are based on ideas that were both contem-porary and enduring, but are not meant to reflect the precise tenets of any particular sects.

Acknowledgements

In trying to make sense of the tangled history of the First Crusade, I have relied principally on the judgements of two clear-thinking historians: Steven Runciman's *A History of the Crusades* (Penguin) and John France's *Victory in the East* (Cambridge University Press). Elsewhere, the heretical ritual and creation myth in chapter 26 are adapted from translations in Walter Wakefield and Austin Evans' *Heresies of the High Middle Ages* (Columbia University Press); the passage from Tertullian in chapter 12 is adapted from a translation in the Christian Classics Ethereal Library (www.ccel.org); and the visions of Peter Bartholomew and Stephen in chapter 31 are adapted from translations by August Krey in *The First Crusade* (Princeton). Most of all, I am indebted to Dr Susan Edgington, who very generously gave me access to the draft typescript of her translation of Albert of Aachen's narrative. When it is eventually published by Oxford University Press, it will fill one of the great remaining gaps in the historiography of the First Crusade. I have used the work of all these historians and many others; sometimes I have probably confused their scholarship, and sometimes I have deliberately abused it for my own purposes. Any errors or distortions in this book are of course my own.

I am particularly grateful to all those who helped me on my research trip across Turkey, especially Ohrlan Pammukale, who taught me the true meaning of Turkish hospitality. My wife Marianna stoically shared the heat, the driving, the dodgy kebabs and the language barrier; then came home and offered me her usual unstinting support. Helen, George, Iona and my mother read the first draft: their enthusiasm and criticism was a great help. As ever, my agent Jane Conway-Gordon moved in mysterious ways and performed wonders.

At Random House, I owe a great many thanks to my wise and patient editor Oliver Johnson, his assistant Emily Sweet, my publicist Emily Cullum, Richard Ogle and the long-suffering design department, Chris Moore for the artwork and Rodney Paull for the wonderful maps - as well as all those whom I never see working behind the scenes.